First came
FROM THE BITTER LAND.
Then
SCATTERED SEED.
Now, the third generation:
GLITTERING HARVEST,
Maisie Mosco's magnificent chronicle
of a family in love and crisis,
struggling to preserve its faith.

GLITTERING HARVEST

Maisie Mosco

BANTAM BOOKS
TORONTO · NEW YORK · LONDON · SYDNEY

The characters in this book are entirely imaginary and bear no relation to any real person, living or dead.

GLITTERING HARVEST
A Bantam Book / June 1982

PRINTING HISTORY
First published in Great Britain by
New English Library Limited,
Barnard's Inn, Holborn,
London EC1N 2JR in 1981
under the title of *Children's Children*.

ISBN 0-553-20664-8

Published simultaneously in the United States and Canada

Bantam Books are published by Bantam Books, Inc. Its trade-
mark, consisting of the words "Bantam Books" and the por-
trayal of a rooster, is Registered in U.S. Patent and Trademark
Office and in other countries. Marca Registrada. Bantam
Books, Inc., 666 Fifth Avenue, New York, New York 10103.

PRINTED IN THE UNITED STATES OF AMERICA

0 9 8 7 6 5 4 3 2 1

A good man leaveth an inheritance to his children's children.

Proverbs

PART ONE

Chapter One

The steady thrum of the aircraft's engines was lulling Sarah to sleep. "Such a long journey," she muttered, jerking herself to wakefulness when her head nodded forward. She straightened the white lace jabot that relieved the severity of her high-necked gray dress and patted her black felt hat which she had refused to take off, though David, with whom she was traveling, had advised her to do so.

"You'd be more comfortable if you unfastened your seat belt," he told her.

"Comfortable I don't expect to be."

David smiled at her stoic expression. This was his mother's first flight, the BOAC *Stratocruiser* had been airborne for three hours, a meal had been served and cleared away and the passengers had settled down to read or snooze. But Sarah would not allow herself to relax.

He peered along the aisle to where a blond stewardess, who reminded him of Betty Grable, was leaning on the liquor trolley, chatting to a man in a pin-striped suit. "Let me get you a drink, Mother."

Sarah treated him to a withering glance. "*Shikker*, my eldest son would like me to be."

"Perhaps you should have taken the sedative your youngest one offered you," he teased.

"Let Nat keep his pills for his patients," Sarah retorted. "If I took notice of the two of you, they'd have to carry me off the airplane when we get to New York."

"A drop of brandy won't make you drunk and it'll steady your nerves," David said placatingly.

Sarah cast a censorious look at the two miniature bottles on his table, the contents of which he had already imbibed. "In that case, it's no wonder yours are so steady."

She took a mint imperial from the paper bag on her own table, popped it into her mouth and put the bag into her

3

cardigan pocket. "Fix my table back in place for me, David. Even on an airplane, a person doesn't have to be untidy," she declared while he was doing so. "Or turn into a drunkard and a drug-taker, when they're not one on the ground."

She averted her gaze from the window, through which the rosy-hued heavens were all too visible. "Me, I'm trying to forget I'm not on the ground! When we came to England from Russia, I thought I'd never pluck up the courage to ride on a tram. If anyone had told me that one day I'd travel in one of these things, I'd have said they were *meshugah*."

"That was fifty years ago," David said.

"Fifty-one," Sarah corrected him.

David had not flown the Atlantic before, but had made several business trips to the Continent by plane, and air travel had begun to seem commonplace to him. "In those days, flying was only for birds," he shrugged.

"And maybe it still should be," Sarah countered. "For one thing, if airplanes hadn't been invented, nobody would have been bombed in the war. And for another, if God had intended people to fly, wouldn't He have given them wings?"

David could think of no suitable reply. Sarah's side of a discussion was often a mixture of logic and godliness, skillfully blended to allow no argument, he thought dryly.

"Only to see Sammy and Miriam again would I be where I am now," she said fervently.

"I offered to take you to America on the *Queen Mary*, didn't I?"

"Being seasick like I was on the herring boat, I can do without."

Sarah had never forgotten her one and only sea voyage which over the years had assumed legendary proportions, the creaking timbers of the vessel and the reek of its cargo dramatically embellished when she recounted the tale to her great-grandchildren.

David's recollections of that journey were less detailed. He had been only eight years old when the Sandbergs fled from the Russian pogroms to put down roots in a free land. "All I remember about the herring boat is Moishe Lipkin nearly falling overboard," he said with a grin.

"Such a mischievous child Moishe was," Sarah reminisced. "Who would have thought he would grow into a sensible man and end up working for you in your business?"

"Who would have thought I'd ever have a business?"

"Nothing you've achieved is any surprise to me," Sarah said, surveying him. The double chin he had acquired in recent years, along with a paunch, did not detract from the strength of his countenance, or the confident air that had always been his. "Successful is what I expected you to be."

David thought of his struggle to raise himself and his family from Manchester's old Strangeways ghetto, where they had settled as poor Jewish immigrants. Now, he owned a substantial home in a leafy suburb, and a fashion-rainwear factory whose products were becoming internationally known. He had recently bought a Bentley and could afford to take his mother on a trip to New York. But his was no overnight rags-to-riches story.

"When a person looks back, it's all like a dream," Sarah said reflectively.

David took a cigarette from a slender gold case and lit it with a matching lighter. "Not to me."

They fell silent and he picked up a fashion magazine he had brought to show to his brother Sammy. On the cover was a Sanderstyle raincoat from the range David's daughter had designed for the winter collection. It was not the coat Shirley would have chosen for the purpose, but David had not allowed her to decide. She had a good business brain, in addition to being a talented designer, but there were times when he and she clashed and he had to remind her who was the boss.

"What are you thinking about?" Sarah asked, eyeing his tight-lipped expression.

"An argument I had with Shirley, yesterday," David replied crisply. He still had a tight feeling in his chest from the aggravation. "She wants me to pension off Eli," he told his mother.

Sarah looked shocked.

"And Peter thinks the same," David went on. "The only time Shirley and her husband seem able to agree about anything is at the factory when they're ganging up against me!"

"You're going to give in to them about this? I hope not," Sarah said hotly. "What has poor Eli done to deserve it, except to grow old?"

"My common sense tells me it's time he went," David

answered. "But my heart won't let me do it to him. He must be left to retire when he feels the time has come, the way Father did."

David had not taken that attitude regarding his father at the time, Sarah remembered. She had had to battle with him about it and had eventually won. Her husband had remained in charge of the factory pressing-room until shortly before his death. But David's desire to retire Abraham long before then had sprung from anxiety about his failing health, she thought in mitigation. He had been unable to see that an aging person's self-respect must be considered, too.

"I'm glad you see it that way, now," she said quietly.

"Well, I'm starting to get on a bit myself, aren't I?" he grinned.

"Fifty-nine is still young."

David supposed it was, to someone approaching their seventy-sixth birthday. He patted his mother's hand. "But the way the years rush by, my daughter and son-in-law will soon be wanting to put me out to grass! As for Eli, he'll go on being nominally Sanderstyle's head cutter. Even though all he does, nowadays, is get in the way of the men at the cutting bench. How can I tell someone who taught me the trade, when I was a lad, that his services are no longer required? Eli used to comfort Father and me when Isaac Salaman ticked us off. When none of us dreamed I'd marry Salaman's daughter and finish up owning the factory."

"In those days, you couldn't call it a factory," Sarah said with a shudder. "It was a sweatshop. Where people like you and your father worked for a pittance, to make men like Salaman rich."

"But it gave me a starting point," David answered. Marrying Bessie Salaman had changed his life. A half-share in her father's business was the dowry she had brought him and, when Salaman died, she had inherited the other half, together with his accumulated capital and the property he had owned.

"I feel bad about you leaving Bessie behind," Sarah said.

"As you won't sail and she won't fly, and the reason we're going is to reunite you with Sammy and Miriam, I had no option."

Which hadn't stopped Bessie from sulking about it, David recalled sourly. And right until the very last moment. He had escorted his mother into the airport departure lounge with his wife's stare of baleful recrimination burning his receding back. It had taken two whiskies to make him forget it!

"I'm very grateful to you for bringing me, David," Sarah added.

And it's as well Bessie isn't with us, he thought, surveying his mother's pensive expression. She hadn't seen Sammy and Miriam since they emigrated in 1947 and it was now 1956—a long time for an old lady to be separated from people she loved. And Bessie's ill-feeling toward Miriam, to whom David had once been engaged, might have surfaced and marred the reunion for Sarah. For him, too.

"You must take Bessie an extra-nice present from New York," Sarah counseled him.

"Yes, Mother," David smiled. Pulling strings to keep the family peace had always been Sarah Sandberg's chief occupation and even in an airplane, thousands of feet above the Atlantic, her matriarchal instincts remained in full play.

Chapter Two

After Nathan had finished his morning surgery, he went to the kitchen at the back of the house and plugged in the electric kettle. The resident caretaker usually made coffee before the doctors set off on their rounds, but she had slipped out to do her shopping.

There were still some patients in the waiting room. Nathan could hear their voices drifting along the corridor and his partners had not yet emerged from their consulting rooms.

Once, he and Lou Benjamin could almost have set their watches by what time surgery would end, he recalled while spooning Nescafé into three blue beakers. Well, give or take the seasonal flu epidemics and the odd emergency. But those days were over and had been since doctors became paid servants of the Welfare State. The citizens who footed the bill made sure they got their money's worth. Even a common cold would bring them running to the surgery. Only a handful of the patients Nathan had just seen required medical attention and it was the same every day.

His nephew entered as the kettle reached boiling point.

"My stack of mail was a mile high this morning, Uncle Nat," he said, pouring water into two of the beakers. "But I've stopped having nightmares about being buried alive beneath a ton of forms, now we've got clerical help," he grinned.

"Me too," Nathan said gratefully. The escalating paperwork created by the National Health Scheme had made it necessary to employ a secretary. But she could not cope with all of it and there were still times when he felt more like an administrator than a doctor.

Ronald was leaning against the sink, drinking his coffee, his long-legged, broad-shouldered frame dwarfing his uncle's short, slight one.

His figure is like David's was at his age, Nathan thought. But that was the only trait Ronald shared with his father. Had he taken after David in nature, the rapport that existed between Nathan and him would not have been possible. For the same reasons that prohibited friendship between Nathan and David. They maintained a superficial, brotherly relationship for their mother's sake, but were poles apart in every respect and had never got on.

Nathan watched Ronald set his beaker on the draining board and run a hand through his blue-black mane. His own hair had once been that color, but was now entirely silver—though he wasn't yet forty-six. In keeping with the premature lines on my face, he reflected wryly.

Ronald cut into his introspection. "We must get someone in to paint this room," he said, glancing at the jaded blue walls and taking a notebook and pencil from his jacket pocket, to scribble a reminder.

"You're a paragon of efficiency," Nathan smiled.

"And I often wonder how you and Uncle Lou managed before I qualified and joined you!"

Lou Benjamin was not a blood relative, but had always been an honorary uncle to Nathan's nephews and nieces.

"So do we," Nathan replied. If he had had a son, he would have wanted him to be just like Ronald. Cheerful and practical, with the kind of mind that pounced upon the crux of a matter immediately. In the latter respect, Ronald would have made a fine lawyer, Nathan reflected. But he had chosen medicine and it was Nathan's daughter, Leona, who had elected to study law.

"Me, I don't have time to stand around daydreaming!" Ronald grinned noting his contemplative expression.

What doctor does? Nathan thought, watching Ronald stride briskly from the room. Before Ronald joined the practice, Nathan and Lou had not paused for a morning break. But he had told them this was carrying professional dedication too far and had gone out, there and then, to buy the electric kettle, so their coffee could be made in double-quick time.

Last week Ronald had mentioned the possibility of instituting an appointments system for the patients, to allow the doctors to schedule their working day, and Nathan had no doubt that his nephew would soon put his idea into operation.

Lou had said, privately, that he wished he had thought of it. But practicing medicine in a businesslike way would not have occurred to their generation of practitioners, Nathan reflected now. Would the time ever come when the whole profession functioned on those lines? he wondered. When the British Medical Association would be the equivalent of a trade union protecting its members' interests? Nathan doubted it. Those who dealt in life and death could not expect the ordered routine others enjoyed.

Lou entered, polishing his spectacles. "We need a forty-eight-hour day to get through all our work," he grumbled, echoing Nathan's thoughts. "What the hell did we want to be doctors for, Nat?" he demanded, plonking the glasses on his beaky nose.

Talk of this kind was commonplace between them but, this morning, for Nathan it rang a distant bell. "You seem to have forgotten that I didn't," he replied. "That I have my eldest brother to thank for my lot!"

In truth, it had been his mother's decision, when he was still a child, that medicine would be his profession. Having a doctor in the family lent prestige which couldn't be easily acquired any other way, he thought with the acrimony these recollections invariably aroused in him. But it had been David who had made sure Nathan wasn't allowed to forget how his kith and kin had sacrificed to educate him—made him toe the line so Sarah would get her wish.

"And a lot of good it's done you to go on harping about it," Lou declaimed censoriously.

Nathan left him making his coffee and went to collect his bag and list of house calls. Lou was his closest friend, but there were and always had been levels on which they were unable to commune. Lou hadn't hoped to be a classics scholar, so he ended up taking people's blood pressure;

medicine was what he had wanted. And nobody had shaped his life in other respects. They hadn't needed to. Lou had never been a dreamer. His feet were planted firmly upon the ground.

Nathan quelled the sense of injustice his partner's words had engendered. He hadn't bothered telling Lou that these days he did not harp on the past. As you grew older, you learned the futility of brooding about things you could do nothing about.

He had left the surgery and was getting into his car when Lou rushed to his side.

"Thank goodness I caught you, Nat! Bridie just phoned, in a panic."

"What has she done? Set fire to the chip pan?" Nathan snapped, though he could not imagine his capable Irish housemaid doing any such thing.

"I'm coming home with you and we can talk on the way," Lou answered. "Let's get a move on," he added brusquely.

Bridie sat by the bedside, gazing at her mistress's face. So lovely and peaceful she looked. As if sleep had drawn a curtain to shut out the bitterness that curled her lips in her waking hours.

Before Mrs. Sandberg began taking the little pink pills she kept in the bathroom cabinet, Bridie had often heard her walking the floor at night and had wondered if he could hear it, too. How could he not, when his room was next door to his wife's? But Bridie had never known him get up and go to her. An' why wud he? she thought now. A man had his pride an' oh what a pretty pass things had cum to between them!

After Doctor had returned from the war, but not to his marriage bed, Bridie had been terribly distressed. A body couldn't live under their roof without knowing they didn't get on, but she hadn't let herself think it was that bad.

They'd been newlyweds when she came to be their maid—and her heart had been warmed by their love and laughter, she remembered. But something, Bridie knew not what, had happened to spoil everything, like an overnight blight destroying the bloom on a beautiful young tree. 'Tis the rot that set in then that's led to this, Bridie thought, surveying Rebecca with sorrow. An' a wunder it's taken this long, if the truth be told!

She rose from her chair and went to look out of the window, to see if Dr. Benjamin's car was approaching. It seemed like an hour since she telephoned the surgery, but the bedside clock told her it wasn't more than a few minutes.

Her mistress was still breathing, she noted thankfully. And with not a tangle in her lovely black hair, as though she had not stirred since closing her eyes. But the breathing was shallow; her chest, beneath one of the creamy satin nightdresses she always wore, scarcely rising and falling.

Bridie took one of Rebecca's smooth, slim hands in her own large, work-roughened paws. Dear sweet Jesu, please don't let her die. P'rhaps it was wrong to pray to the Savior for a Jewess, who had no faith in Him. But He'd been Jewish, too. And had many times answered Bridie's call.

Nathan and Lou were traveling up Bury New Road, as fast as the traffic would allow.

"Rebecca must've been hit by a virus," Nathan said.

Lou gave him a sidelong glance. He had shown no emotion, as if they were *en route* to a patient's bedside, not his wife's, and Lou, though he knew there was no love lost between Nathan and Rebecca, was shocked.

"I can think of a more likely reason why Bridie can't waken her," Lou answered tersely. "Those damned sleeping pills." He observed Nathan's change of expression. "And why you're surprised to hear me say so, I can't imagine. For someone whose sideline is psychoanalysis, you'd make a good mechanic when it comes to understanding your wife! You've never been able to cope with her problems the way you do so successfully with your patients."

"Possibly because, in her eyes, I'm responsible for them," Nathan retorted.

"That I can't argue with. But she's my patient, not yours. And it wasn't with my approval that you let her have the pills."

Nathan bristled. "What would you do if your wife became a chronic insomniac?"

"With Cora there's no danger. It's a wonder I'm not one, from the way she snores!"

"So it's fine for you to be smug about my setup."

"Your setup was on the cards before you even entered into it," Lou snorted. "Which doesn't mean I'm not sorry for you.

But I'm sorry for Rebecca, too. From the moment your mother showed you the *shadchan's* photograph of her you resented her," Lou declared, harking back to their student days.

"Unlike you, when the matchmaker approached your parents about Cora," Nathan countered cynically.

Lou shrugged. "So the first time I met Cora I gazed into her eyes and saw the practice her bank balance was going to buy me," he admitted. "Afterward, I loved her for herself."

"You weren't burdened with my handicaps, Lou. The idea of marrying for material reasons wasn't anathema to you. Nor were you already involved with someone else."

"But if I had been, she'd have been Jewish. I'd have had more sense than to get mixed up with a *shiksah*. Like you did, Nat."

Nathan had not thought of Mary Dennis for years and did not allow his mind to dwell upon her now. He turned the car into the leafy avenue in which he lived and paled when he saw an ambulance parked outside his house.

"I took the precaution of calling the emergency service," Lou said as they walked up the garden path.

Nathan fumbled in his pocket for his latchkey. "You're convinced Rebecca's tried to end it all, aren't you, Lou?" he said savagely. "And you blame me."

Lou took the key from his trembling fingers and inserted it in the lock. "I'm not in the business of blame, Nat. That's your speciality. And Rebecca's. At the moment I'm keeping my fingers crossed that she'll be all right and that you'll come to your senses and make something of your marriage."

"What makes you think I haven't tried?"

Chapter Three

"I hope everything is fine at home," Sarah said to Miriam while they strolled along West 179th Street.

"You've only been gone a couple of days, Ma."

Sarah watched a small black girl dart into the path of a yellow cab and heaved a sigh of relief when the child's mother hauled her to safety. "In a family, plenty can happen in a couple of minutes."

"Watch out for that dog-dirt on the sidewalk," Miriam warned. "And enjoy your vacation, will you! Stop worrying about the family."

"Just because I'm now in a place where holidays are called vacations and pavements are sidewalks, she expects me to change the habit of a lifetime!"

Miriam linked Sarah's arm affectionately. "I wouldn't want to change a thing about you, Ma. You don't know how good it is to have you here."

"David, too, I hope."

"Provided he doesn't try to get up to his old tricks again."

Sarah stifled a sigh. David was generosity personified and there was nothing he wouldn't do for his kith and kin. He had put Nat through medical school and lent his sister and brother-in-law the money to open their shop. Esther and Ben had repaid that loan long ago, but wasn't the thriving business they owned today built upon it? And where would Miriam and Sammy have been without him? Not many men would have employed someone as incompetent as Sammy— even a brother—but David had done so until Sammy emigrated to the States. In every way possible he had made sure his brother was not disadvantaged because he was lame. Yet Miriam saw fit to make disparaging remarks about him! Sarah thought hotly.

"You're a wise woman, Ma. But you've always been blind where David's concerned," Miriam said, noting Sarah's expression. "You don't have the slightest idea what I meant about him getting up to his old tricks, do you?"

"So why don't you tell me?"

"I'd be wasting my time. You wouldn't understand. It was the reason we came to live in the States and I've never regretted coming."

"The family have talked a lot about why you and Sammy emigrated. As you gave us no explanation," Sarah said after a silence. "We thought perhaps you wanted a new start to help you get over losing Martin—and that you couldn't bear to talk about it. Not even to us."

Miriam's emerald eyes darkened with pain, but her voice remained steady. "I'll never get over losing Martin."

Sarah had plenty of grandchildren and, in her old age, had been blessed with great-grandchildren also. There was now another Martin in the family—his cousin Marianne had named her child after him. But each of the brood had his own special place in Sarah's heart and the one Miriam and Sammy's boy had occupied would never be filled.

"But I don't pine for him anymore," Miriam added quietly. "Where would it get me?"

Sarah stole a surreptitious glance at her. Beautiful she'd always been and still was. Tall and striking-looking. But it was hard to relate this composed woman with the Miriam to whom she had said farewell at Liverpool Docks, eight years ago. Who had boarded the ocean liner tight-lipped with bitterness, after delivering a parting insult to David, Sarah recalled.

Miriam changed the subject. "Washington Heights isn't short of synagogues, but there's going to be a new one on this street."

This was the first time Sarah had ventured out of the apartment since arriving in New York and she hadn't expected it to turn into an excursion down memory lane. She tried to give her attention to something Miriam was saying about Fort Tryon Park, but her mind continued its journey backward and paused at a wartime afternoon she would prefer to forget.

"Turn up your coat collar. You're shivering, Ma," Miriam said.

Sarah did as she was bid, though the shiver had been a shudder of recollection. Why didn't people pause to consider the consequences before they said things that could never be unsaid and did what could never be undone? She could still see her grandson Arnold Klein standing in her parlor, where the family were having *Shabbos* tea, his fingers fidgeting with one of the gilt buttons on his naval officer's uniform while he announced his intention to marry a Gentile. For a Jewish clan there could be no greater tragedy, Sarah had thought. Until Miriam went to answer the telephone and learned that her son was dead.

"Why did you turn against David that day?" Sarah asked her.

"Which day?"

"You know which day. You behaved as if David was responsible for Martin's death."

Miriam stared thoughtfully down at the pavement. "I guess I just had to loose my grief, Ma," she said slowly. "Hit out at somebody for the way I felt."

But Sarah was not satisfied with that explanation. Miriam had attacked David physically and the incident had marked the beginning of her open hostility toward him. At present, while he was a guest in her home, she was being pleasant to him, but Sarah, always sensitive to undercurrents, was not fooled. The hostility was still there.

"By the way, you're now on Broadway, Ma," Miriam conveyed as they reached the street corner.

Sarah stopped in her tracks. "This is Broadway? It can't be!"

Miriam watched her craning her neck to look up at the street signs. "That's what Sammy and I thought the first time we stood on this corner."

"Where is the Great White Way?" Sarah demanded, sounding cheated. "Which Mr. Crosby croons about on my kitchen wireless set? And all the theaters with the famous names written in lights?" She surveyed the surroundings, which reminded her of Manchester's Cheetham Hill Road, except that the street and the pavements were very much wider. Even the October morning sunlight could not disguise the drab urban grayness.

"Broadway's always a shock to foreigners," Miriam told her.

Sarah could not contain her disappointment. "A shock is right!"

"They expect the whole of it to be glamorous, but the only part that is, is the section around Times Square. Which I'll take you to see," Miriam consoled her. "The rest is just an ordinary main road running through the center of Manhattan. Split into neighborhoods where people live."

Miriam took Sarah's arm and steered her to a block of shops, where they paused outside a greengrocery to examine the tempting display of fruit and vegetables.

"Nobody at home will believe me when I tell them I went shopping for lemons on Broadway," Sarah said prodding a couple to test their freshness. She handed them to Miriam. "Here. In case you've forgotten, I like lemon tea after a meat supper. Ones that size, I never saw in England."

Miriam smiled. "You know what they say about America, Ma. Everything here is bigger and better."

"So long as you're happy here," Sarah answered. To have everything bigger and better had never been Miriam's aim in life. Her lack of interest in material things had clashed with David's ambitious nature, Sarah recalled, and had resulted in their broken engagement.

"What's happy?" Miriam countered. "I've yet to meet the person who is."

*   *   *

David had asked Sammy to show him the garment district.

"Look out, David!" Sammy shouted when they alighted from a taxi on Seventh Avenue.

David dodged out of the way as a beak-nosed lad with a *yamulke* on his head sped by pushing a loaded clothes rack. Another was advancing at breakneck speed from the opposite direction and he had to leap aside again.

"I'd heard it was like this around here," he said to his brother. "But I didn't believe it."

"This is just a part of it, David. The garment district starts at Forty-second Street and goes right on down to Thirty-fourth," Sammy informed him. "They call the lads who push the rails stockboys," he added as a swaying consignment of dresses rushed past.

A few yards away, a lad was negotiating his rail between the traffic, to the other side of the street.

"They need traffic cops, specially to direct them," Sammy grinned.

"You're not kidding," David said.

To an Englishman, even a garment manufacturer, this had to be seen to be believed. Heard, too! he thought listening to the earsplitting clatter around him. Added to it was the impatient honking of vehicle horns and the holler of many voices trying to make themselves heard above the clamor. The garment district in Manchester, thriving though it was, was quiet as a graveyard by comparison.

He leaned against a grimy wall, gazing across the street at the gloomy buildings opposite, which shut out the sky. A pall of exhaust-smoke hung in the air, with accompanying fumes. No doubt the factories were pleasant enough inside, even air-conditioned, David had heard. But the district was like a madhouse, with everyone competing in a race against time.

He watched the worried-looking men, dark-suited and white-collared, scurrying in and out of doorways. My American counterparts, he thought with a smile. If Abraham and Sarah Sandberg had settled in New York instead of Manchester, David would probably have been one of them. He could feel their anxiety pressing down upon him, just from standing briefly in their midst.

Which garment manufacturer wasn't under pressure? he asked himself with a sigh. But it seemed to be much worse

over here. The faces were all Jewish, he noted, but that he had
expected. It was the same in England. A Jewish trade. These
men were the sons of immigrants, just as David was, whose
forebears had arrived penniless in a new land. Yet they had
made the garment trade their own.

"Had enough?" Sammy smiled.

"I wouldn't mind seeing inside one of the raincoat factories."

"You're supposed to be here on vacation."

"You know me. And I haven't changed," David replied.

"I'll get one of my neighbors who's a cutter to fix it with his
boss for you to visit their place one day," Sammy promised.

Sammy had not changed, either, David reflected wryly.
Knowing his brother, the "one day" he had vaguely mentioned,
would never come. It was as well Sammy hadn't gone into the
garment trade when he came to live in New York. Without
David to look out for him, he wouldn't have survived. But
Sammy had found work in a furniture factory and, David had
noted, seemed content with his lot.

"How's Harold Bronley treating you?" David asked him
while they ate pastrami sandwiches in a lunchroom on Forty-
seventh Street, cheek by jowl with the jewelers who peopled
that area—some of whom looked, to David, more like Jewish
scholars than traders.

"How d'you mean?" Sammy said uncertainly.

Sammy's employer was related to Chaim and Malka
Berkowitz, with whom the Sandbergs had lived during their
first few weeks in England, and had been there when they
arrived—a small boy, with his parents and baby brother, on
their way to the States, David recalled.

"Does Harold ever invite you and Miriam to his home?" he
asked Sammy through a mouthful of dill pickle.

Sammy took another bite of his succulent sandwich. "I'm
just one of his workers, David. Why would he ask me to his
house? And Miriam wouldn't want to go if he did."

"Why not?"

"He lives on Long Island, at Great Neck. With the other
millionaires."

And mixing with millionaires wouldn't suit Miriam, David
thought; his sister-in-law's contempt for the moneyed knew
no bounds. "Harold and his brother have done very well for
themselves," he remarked.

Sammy grinned. "Whenever I see Ivor Bronley's name on
the movie screen, I can't believe a big Hollywood producer

like him once sat on the Berkowitzes' kitchen floor, with you and me, guzzling down borscht."

"We were guzzling it, too," David reminded him with a smile. "We hadn't had a good meal since we left Russia."

They fell silent, remembering those long-ago days. The humble little house, with its cluttered sideboard and ever-present smell of cooking. Their father's search for work in the warren of sweatshops Strangeways then was, and the quarrels between their parents as time went by without Abraham finding it. The dankness of the parlor in which the Sandbergs had slept, curled up in *perinehs* on the floor, with the nighttime sounds of mice scuttling around them.

"So," David said, collecting himself, "how've you been since you moved to this side of the Atlantic, Sammy?" Today was his first opportunity to talk privately with his brother.

"Fine. If you don't count the aches and pains I get from my arthritis. But I had those in England, didn't I?"

David glanced at Sammy's lame leg, stretched stiffly beside the table. Like a dead thing, he thought with a pang, averting his eyes from it. "Nat said there's a new drug they prescribe for arthritis now."

"Cortisone," Sammy supplied. "But I wouldn't take it. I've heard it has terrible side effects if you're on it regularly, which I'd have to be. I'd rather be a cripple."

"Don't call yourself that!"

Sammy reached for a paper napkin and wiped his mouth. "Why not? It's what I am."

"But you weren't born one. You became one because of me."

Sammy had resumed eating and paused in mid-bite. "What are you talking about, David? I was lamed when a Cossack cantered his horse over my leg."

"But I was responsible for you being in the place where it happened. Mother warned me it wasn't safe for Jewish children to play on the riverbanks, but I paid no heed."

The events of that summer morning beside the River Dvina had changed Sammy's life, made it impossible for him to be as others were. The family had blamed the cruel Cossack, but David, though he'd been only five at the time, had blamed himself and still did.

"Don't be a *shlemiel*," Sammy said to him inadequately.

David surveyed his unhealthy pallor and thinning gray hair, which had once been red. Sammy was still a handsome man, but there were dark shadows under his eyes and a fragility about him which had not been there when he left England.

"While I'm in New York, we'll find out who's the best orthopedic specialist here and I'll take you to see him, Sam."

"Medical treatment here is expensive."

"So what?" If David could do something to help Sammy, he wouldn't care if it took every penny he'd got.

Chapter Four

Marianne sat at the kitchen table, sipping her tea and perusing the *Times* book reviews. When a review was bad, her heart ached for the author and if it was good, she was happy for him or her. You had to be a writer yourself to know that a novel, or a play, was part of whoever had penned it. Not just a piece of work, but a precious offspring.

Her flesh-and-blood offspring had his gaze glued to the copy of *Treasure Island* he had propped up against the marmalade jar. "Hurry up and finish your breakfast, Martin!" she scolded him. "You'll be late for school. And you shouldn't read while you're eating."

"Your mother told me you always did," he replied, shoveling cornflakes into his mouth.

Marianne checked her exasperation. When you were in your thirties, with a cheeky kid of your own, it was hard to bear in mind that you too had once been a troublesome eight-year-old. "My mother was much stricter with me and my brothers than I am with you," she told Martin.

"She lets me do anything I like, when we go to Manchester to stay with her," he replied perkily.

Marianne took the book away from him. "Because she doesn't have to put up with you all the time. And if you don't get a move on, I'll smack your bottom."

"You can't. I'm sitting on it."

She gave up the battle and went to fetch the mail, which had just thudded through the letterbox. Had they spoiled Martin? They had tried not to, but perhaps it was inevitable with an only child. Maybe she should see another gynecologist, make a further attempt to give her son a brother or sister? But what was the point, when the two operations she underwent to help her conceive, had proved futile? And she didn't want her life to be disrupted by a baby now, when her career was at last beginning.

Her husband emerged from their bedroom, stifling a yawn. "Any mail for me?"

Marianne shook her head. "Just a letter for us all, from my grandmother," she said, smiling at Sarah's spidery handwriting on the airmail envelope.

Ralph followed her into the kitchen, poured himself some tea and buttered a slice of burnt toast. "I'm still waiting for the art gallery to send me a check for that seascape of mine they sold," he complained.

"With slow payers like them, we wouldn't eat very often if you'd given up your job, to paint full-time."

"A fat chance there is of me ever doing that."

"Why not, Dad?" Martin asked.

"An artist has to be well-known before he can rely on his work to provide an income, son."

"One day you will be," the boy assured him. "Mum thought she'd never get a play on the stage, didn't she? Or a book published."

The novel Marianne had written about her wartime experiences in the women's services, had finally found a publisher and would be out in the spring. And last week she had learned that a West End producer had taken an option on one of her plays. This change in her fortunes had been brought about by the literary agent to whom, after amassing a drawerful of rejection slips, she had eventually sent some manuscripts.

"You'll just have to be patient, Dad," Martin said comfortingly.

Marianne ruffled his unruly black curls. His precocity was sometimes endearing. Especially when he talked to his parents like a Dutch uncle, she thought wryly.

Ralph had taken his pipe from his jacket pocket and was sucking it pensively. Was he contrasting her progress with his own lack of it? She wound her arms around his neck and kissed his cheek. "Taking an option on a play doesn't mean it's definitely going to be produced," she said to minimize her achievements. "And if you and Martin don't get out of here, I'll never get my new book finished! I can't put my typewriter on the table until the breakfast things are cleared."

Ralph smiled. "You have been known to."

After her husband and son had left to fight their way

through London's morning rush hour, Marianne sat down to drink another cup of tea, instead of rushing to leap into a bath, throw on a jersey and slacks and begin her day's work stint, as was her habit.

Self-discipline, she had discovered, was essential to a writer. When nobody was breathing down your neck urging you to work, it was easy to do nothing. Usually, the thought of her good fortune in having her days free to write, while her husband had to spend his in an ad agency studio, drove her to the typewriter and, once there, creative impetus kept her chained. But for once she wouldn't rush, she thought, opening her grandmother's letter.

Her gaze went no further than the first line. "My dear children," Sarah had written, and Marianne's eyes brimmed with tears. What are you blubbering about? she asked herself, fumbling in her housecoat pocket for her handkerchief. Because Sarah had addressed them that way, and there'd been a time when Marianne wouldn't have expected her to. When she hadn't dared hope that Ralph, who wasn't Jewish, would ever be accepted by the family. How could I have hoped for it? she thought reminiscently. After my brother was exiled by our parents for marrying outside the faith?

But Marianne's dilemma had been resolved happily. Somehow, her Uncle Nat, who in his youth had loved a Christian girl, had made the family see reason. Marianne had never learned the details of his confrontation with them, but it had taken place in her grandmother's house and she had a feeling that Sarah had supported him.

Though the old lady adhered to the letter of the Jewish law herself, and, in some respects, Marianne's parents did not, her attitudes in general were more flexible than theirs. More sensible, too, Marianne reflected. Perhaps, when you'd lived as long as Sarah had, you came to realize that if you didn't bend with the wind of change, you'd break. She had probably pointed out to Esther and Ben Klein the folly of cutting themselves off from another of their three children. Only Marianne's eldest brother, Harry, had married-in, done what was expected of him.

The telephone rang and Marianne stretched out her hand to lift the receiver from the wall. One advantage of a tiny kitchen was that everything was at arm's length, she thought while the operator was putting through a long-distance call. The disadvantage—some would say, she thought dryly—was that it wouldn't house a washing machine, and there wasn't room on the meager work-surface for an electric mixer. Marianne wouldn't want either. The former would tempt her to throw in mounds of laundry, which would result in lots of ironing. The latter would prey on her conscience each time her eye fell upon it, because writing was more important to her than giving her husband and child homemade cakes. The only modern gadget she owned was a pressure cooker, to enable her to cook the evening meal in twenty minutes flat.

Her sister-in-law's bright and breezy voice crackled in her ear. "Sorry to interrupt you if you're in the throes of creation, Marianne."

"On the contrary, I'm being lazy this morning."

"You should be lazy more often. I never knew anyone who drives herself like you do."

"That isn't my mother's opinion of me. She accused me of being bone idle last time we stayed with her and she noticed the holes in Ralph's socks."

"I wasn't referring to your domestic sphere."

"I know that, Lyn. But being a housewife and mum is supposed to come first," Marianne sighed. "And I have to admit that I suffer from an inner conflict about it."

"That's why there's a preponderance of male authors. And everything else, too," Lyn replied. "Because women have always let their conditioning win."

"Whether you do or not, depends on the kind of husband you've got," Marianne said, comparing Ralph's attitude with that of most men of her acquaintance. He had always encouraged her to pursue her career. To him, a woman was as entitled to self-fulfillment as a man and he had never once complained about her work impinging upon his creature comforts.

"I'm sure it does," Lyn replied. "But, as I have no career aspirations, or talents, with my husband it doesn't arise. We heard from your grandmother this morning, Marianne. I thought I'd let you know, in case you haven't heard yet."

"How thoughtful of you." But Lyn was that kind of person. "I was just reading a letter from her, when you called."

"She seems to be having a lovely time. Probably holding up the traffic on Broadway, while she crosses the road!" Lyn chuckled.

"It wouldn't surprise me." Anyone who knew Sarah Sandberg could envisage her doing just that, Marianne thought with a smile. Yet Lyn had never met her. She was Arnold's wife, the cause of his rift with the family. And, though many attempts had been made to return him to the fold, he was still turning a deaf ear.

"You and Uncle Nat have given me a colorful impression of your grandmother," Lyn conveyed.

Marianne and her uncle were the only members of the clan with whom Arnold had maintained contact. "One day, my brother will come to his senses and take you and your children to meet all the family," she said with feeling.

"I doubt it," Lyn answered crisply. "He prefers to pursue his vendetta. The fact that I have no family for our kids to be part of, that Matthew and Margaret are being deprived of something important, doesn't seem to matter to him."

After Lyn had rung off, Marianne bathed and dressed and converted the kitchen table to its other function as her desk. But she was unable to chase Lyn's words from her mind.

Would Arnold's children feel deprived when they grew up? As if they were part of nothing? Matthew was now eleven and Margaret seven. The quarrel between their father and his family was no secret to them and Marianne had seen them look envious when her son mentioned his grandparents, who were theirs, too. Probably some emotional damage had already been done.

And not just on that account, she reflected. Arnold attended synagogue and observed the Jewish festivals. Lyn was not a churchgoer, but at Christmas she decorated a tree for her home—just as her husband lit candles at *Chanukah*. When Passover coincided with Easter, which it did often, Matthew and Margaret ate *matzo* with their father and received Easter eggs from their mother. And, because *Chanukah* fell in December, the tree and the *menorah* stood in their living room side by side.

There's no reason why Judaism and Christianity shouldn't be honored under the same roof, Marianne thought—but how confusing it must be for those kids. Her brother and his wife had elected to let them choose which creed they wished to espouse, when they were old enough to decide. Meanwhile, Matthew and Margaret remained on the fringes of both, were being raised as neither.

Because Jewish law deems a child to be of the religion of its mother, no such uncertainty existed for Martin. Ralph, though he believed in God, was not a practicing Christian and had accepted without demur his son's ancient birthright.

Marianne inserted a sheet of paper into the typewriter—
maybe its blank stare would impel her to start work!—and
cast her mind back to the time when she had equated her
religion with the wearing of shackles. To the dos and don'ts of
orthodoxy that had dogged her youth, and the guilt and pain
which had ensued from rebelling against them. In order not
to rebel, you had to be blessed with the blind faith Sarah
Sandberg had—with which Marianne had very definitely not
been blessed.

When had she begun questioning the relevance of Laws
made in the wilderness to the life Jews, like everyone else,
lived today? From the time she was old enough to think. It
had led her, eventually, to Reform Judaism, and the discovery
that large numbers of her brethren whose intellectual eschewal
of the Orthodox way might otherwise have made them religious
dropouts, had taken the same path as herself.

Of Marianne's family, only her Uncle Nathan's branch had
done so. The others, including her parents, had declared
they would never set foot in a Reform synagogue, Marianne
recalled with a smile. The smile was because they would one
day have no choice but to enter one—unless they intended
missing Martin's *Bar Mitzvah*, which Marianne knew would
be unthinkable for them.

She picked up her grandmother's letter, to finish reading
it, and had a sudden vision of Sarah leading the Orthodox
Manchester contingent into a Reform *shul*, to hear Martin say
his Portion of the Law, five years hence.

Sarah would be the only one of them who wouldn't be
there under sufferance, Marianne thought warmly. Once she
had accepted a situation, she approached it with no half-
measures, and a good heart.

Chapter Five

"It's ridiculous, us coming here for tea as usual while Ma's
away in the States," Bessie declared edgily to those assem-
bled in her mother-in-law's parlor.

Sigmund Moritz helped himself to a second slice of the

strudel she had contributed to the repast. "So go home, Bessie. But don't take your cake with you."

Bessie gave him a vinegary glance, then cast a surreptitious one at the beautiful brunet her son Ronald had married three years ago, with whom she still did not feel at ease. "I bet Diane thinks our family's crackers, opening up an empty house just to have tea in it."

"It does seem a little odd," Diane said.

Ronald fondled her olive cheek. "No more so than your family's antics—and customs—seem to me."

Diane was a *Sephardi*, one of South Manchester's community of Jews of Spanish and Portuguese extraction, whose ethnic culture was vastly different from that of the *Ashkenazi* community on the north side of the city, of which the Sandberg-Moritz clan was part. As elsewhere in the country, the *Sephardis* worshiped in their own synagogues where, Ronald and his relatives had been surprised to discover, the pronunciation of Hebrew was unlike that to which they were accustomed. In Manchester, the *Sephardis* had their own club. There was little social contact between the two communities and marital unions were rare.

"At my in-laws', they don't know from strudel," Ronald grinned, watching Sigmund wolf down yet another slice.

"No, they only know from sesame seeds," Bessie said unkindly, though she enjoyed sampling the traditional *Sephardi* delicacies Diane prepared, including the little seed-coated cookies at which she had just poked fun. What Bessie did not enjoy was the feeling that the *Sephardis* were, somehow, a cut above her own kind. There was a refined elegance about the women which made her feel overdressed, a certain something which, try though she might, and despite her expensive wardrobe, she could not achieve. Nor could she get close to her daughter-in-law, who was presently surveying her through lowered eyelids.

Only for Ronald would I have broken with tradition, Diane, who still felt like an outsider at these family gatherings, was thinking. And landed myself with such a mother-in-law! she added.

But who could get close to people who say *Mabruk*, instead of *Mazeltov*? Bessie thought, casting her mind back to her son's wedding, at which she had felt like a guest on foreign territory. To *Ashkenazis*, the *Sephardi* ways were foreign—which more or less summed it up.

Esther Klein, whose daughter-in-law, though *Ashkenazi*, was a thorn in Esther's side in other ways, exchanged a meaningful glance with Bessie.

"It isn't fair that my husband has to work on Saturdays," that young woman had, as was her habit, just declaimed.

Esther eyed the sapphire eternity ring her son had given his wife on their last wedding anniversary—to wear beside the diamonds she already had. There'd been a time when Esther had worked in the Kleins' store and hadn't arrived at the *Shabbos* gathering until it was almost over, she thought, recalling how her feet had ached from standing behind the counter in those days. But her daughter-in-law, whose father was a wealthy doctor, had been bred in the lap of luxury, never done a day's work in her life.

"Tell Harry not to work on Saturdays, Ann, if you don't mind cutting down on the luxuries his earnings buy for you," Esther told her with asperity.

Bessie returned to her initial grumble. "If we hadn't agreed to Ma's ridiculous request, we needn't have set foot outside our own homes in this weather," she said, glancing through the window at the rain-lashed laburnum by Sarah's garden gate.

Sigmund stopped fiddling with his watch-chain and sighed. "A harper you always were and a harper you will always be, Bessie." But he too was wishing he had stayed by his own fireside. Without Sarah's presence, this didn't feel like *Shabbos* afternoon. And the bickering was liable to get out of hand.

"Well!" Bessie gasped when she had recovered from the insult.

"Zaidie Sigmund is right, Mam," her daughter Shirley endorsed. "I mean, as you are here, why not settle down and enjoy your tea?"

"Mam won't settle down to anything until Dad gets back from New York," Ronald said with a smile.

Bessie hid her discomfiture behind her teacup. What Ronald had just said was true and everyone probably knew it. "All the same, I wish I hadn't humored your grandmother's whim," she replied to Ronald.

"Sarah Sandberg doesn't indulge in whims," Hannah Moritz, who had been thoughtfully silent throughout the afternoon, declared.

"Well, what would you call it?" Bessie flashed.

Hannah got up to take a piece of the Sachertorte her sister-in-law Helga had brought. "I think Sarah wanted the comfort of knowing her absence wouldn't spoil *Shabbos* for us. To her, these tea parties at her house epitomize *Shabbos* for the family; I can't recall a single Saturday afternoon when there hasn't been a gathering here, in all the years I've been a member of this clan. Even when your mother-in-law takes her summer break in Southport, Bessie, she only stays there from Sunday till Friday."

"I don't think even Bessie needs to be told that Sarah's *Shabbos* tea parties are by now an institution," Sigmund said brusquely. The brusqueness did not disguise the tremor in his voice as his gaze rested upon an empty chair by the window, in which his late son had always liked to sit. "How many times did I warn Carl that one day he would be run over by a bus, if he didn't stop crossing the road with his eyes glued to a newspaper?"

Carl, whose absentmindedness was legendary, had, two years ago, met his death in approximately that fashion. The vehicle had been a lorry, not a bus and he had, according to witnesses, stepped from the pavement into its path while folding a newspaper he had been standing reading—which fitted the family's image of him.

Sigmund emitted a long sigh and everyone fell momentarily silent. Carl's death had been a crushing blow to him and some had feared he would not survive it, that it would be the final and finishing blow in the series of them he had managed to survive. The loss of his beloved first wife, whose suffering he had witnessed for years. A disastrous second marriage, from which he had fled to his children, scarred but wiser. And the untimely death of his eldest grandson Martin, during the war.

Hannah stroked his wrinkled hand. The old man was now in his eighties and very dear to her. Carl had been her husband, the one love of her life, and she and Sigmund had grieved for him together. But she had been blessed with twin sons and through them still had much to live for, she thought, glancing at them gratefully.

Sigmund's gaze too roved in their direction. "What are you boys reading today?" he inquired, eyeing the books on their laps and pulling himself together.

"*Dialectical Materialism*," Henry replied for himself, with a toss of his straw-colored mane.

"Surprise, surprise!" Leona Sandberg, who, today, had been uncharacteristically silent, exclaimed sarcastically.

Henry was a student at the London School of Economics and had begun to display left-wing tendencies while still a schoolboy.

His brother was studying law at Manchester University along with Leona, and held up a legal tome in reply to Sigmund's question. "I sometimes think I'll never absorb all I have to," he said with the appealing smile that made people forget how plain he was.

"You will," Hannah declared confidently. Frank was like her. A plodder, but what he set out to do, he did. He resembled his dead father in looks only. Henry, whom everyone said was the image of her, was the one who had inherited Carl's brilliant intellect. And also, she reflected with chagrin, his feckless nature.

"The stuff you read will get you nowhere, Henry," Leona said with a derisive smile.

"I haven't decided yet where I want to get," he retorted.

"And you probably never will."

"Pack it in, you two," Frank said, thankful that, these days, he only had to intervene in their squabbles during college vacations. When he and Leona were together without Henry, her red-haired temperament was less evident.

"Why aren't your parents here?" Ronald asked Leona. "Uncle Nat didn't tell me he wouldn't be coming."

Leona avoided his eye and hoped her father would remember the story he had told her to tell. "I explained to the others before you got here, Ronald." Did her smile look as stiff as it felt? "Mummy isn't feeling well. Dad's put her on a course of tablets—she has a high temperature and he's staying with her to see how it goes."

"Your dad didn't mention a temperature, when I rang up to speak to your mother this morning," Bessie said. "He gave me the impression she was just a bit off color."

Leona now found it difficult to meet her aunt's gaze. What a mess! she fumed inwardly. Mummy would probably tell Auntie Bessie the truth, eventually—they were close friends, as well as sister-in-law. Make Leona look like a bare-faced liar. Which, in this case, she undoubtedly was. But a liar under duress. Why had she let Daddy persuade her to turn up here and do what he called "putting up a front"? Her parents' traumatic relationship had never been easy for her to live with. When she was younger, they had tried to pretend in her presence that all was well between them, but they couldn't hope to fool a young woman as they had a little girl. Leona had known by the time she was twelve that they hated each other. And now they no longer bothered to hide it. Things had reached such a pitch lately, that she had begun making excuses to avoid eating with them and in term time often ate supper, as well as lunch, at college.

"Tell your mother I'll pop round to see her tomorrow," Bessie said.

"No!" Leona exclaimed. "Mummy might be infectious," she added feebly, breaking the surprised silence her sharpness had engendered.

Ronald came to her rescue. "It's best to wait until Uncle Nat says you can visit Auntie Rebecca," he told his mother.

"I'll ask Daddy to give you a ring," Leona promised her. Let him tell his own lies to the family! If he had any sense, he'd know it wasn't possible to keep anything from them.

Her Aunt Hannah gave her an encouraging smile, as if she knew Leona was, somehow, in need of support. Leona got up and went to sit beside her. Hannah was her favorite female relative—perhaps because we're not real kin, she thought wryly. There was no blood tie between the Sandbergs and Moritzes and only one marriage tie. Yet we think of ourselves as one big clan, Leona ruminated. And, family history had it, the welding had begun in 1905, in the old Strangeways ghetto, long before Sammy Sandberg had married Miriam Moritz.

"Come and have supper with us tonight, Leona," Hannah invited.

"Thank you," Leona said, grateful for a reason to delay going home.

"Oh dear. I was looking forward to a peaceful evening," Henry grinned.

"Too bad!" Leona flashed.

"If Henry's company gets too much for you, I'll take you to the pictures," Frank promised.

Leona gave him a warm smile. Frank was so nice and Henry so beastly, she thought as she had since their childhood. But there was an exciting crackle in the air when Henry was around. Frank, bless his heart, was incredibly dull.

Bessie's maid, Lizzie Wilson, brought the youngest generation into the parlor, after giving them tea in the kitchen.

"Don't you think I'm old enough, now, to have my tea with the grown-ups on *Shabbos*?" Shirley's ten-year-old daughter asked her father indignantly.

"Certainly, Laura darling," Peter Kohn replied with the continental charm he had never lost, though he had left his native Vienna to seek refuge in England before the war. "But your mummy doesn't agree."

"If you had your way, she'd be a spoiled brat," Shirley said, giving him a sour glance.

"Like you were, my dearest," he answered.

The rest of the family were unperturbed by the exchange—public bickering was not unusual between Shirley and Peter—but Leona noted Laura's tense expression and drew the child toward her. *The poor kid probably feels like I did at her age,* Leona thought, stroking Laura's ginger curls. *Like a bone between two dogs.* But Laura wasn't a lonely, only child as Leona had been. She had her little brother, Mark, for company.

Mark and his cousin, Howard Klein, were squatting on the hearthrug, building a tower of toy bricks for Ronald's toddler, Alan. Beside them, Howard's little sister Kate waited, big-eyed, for the tower to topple.

Laura broke away from Leona and helped it on its way with a temperamental prod of her red-slippered foot, and pandemonium was let loose. Alan began screaming and was retrieved from the floor by his father. Kate wept bitterly, with him, and had to be comforted by her mother. Mark and Howard set about Laura and were dragged away from her by Shirley and Esther.

"If my husband had to spend every Saturday afternoon with his family, as I do, and put up with what goes on, he'd know what it's like for me!" Ann Klein exclaimed while soiling her dainty handkerchief with her small daughter's tears. "Harry's better off working! And for a girl of six, Kate, you behave like a baby!"

Laura and Mark were, simultaneously, receiving an up-braiding from Shirley.

"Oi," Sigmund sighed listening to the clamor. "It takes me back."

"Me too," Esther agreed.

The first children to create pandemonium in this room were now parents themselves. *And seemed less able to cope with it than we were,* Esther reflected. *Perhaps because the* parents of today were a different breed. More self-interested. Ann was holding little Kate at arm's length, making sure the child's sniffly nose didn't brush against her own garments. Instead of cuddling her close, as Esther would. And who, years ago, would have thought of dispatching their kids to the kitchen to eat *Shabbos* tea, so they themselves could enjoy it in peace and quiet?

Bessie, who had detached herself from the hubbub and was gazing through the window, cut into Esther's thoughts. "All we need now is visitors!" she exclaimed.

A tall, dark-haired young woman was walking up the garden path, clutching the hands of two reluctant-looking children.

"Who are they? I don't recognize them," Esther said, peering over Bessie's shoulder.

"Of course you don't," Leona said as the threesome disappeared from view into the front porch. "I didn't know they were coming, or I'd have prepared you for it. They're Arnold's wife and children."

Esther, who had risen from her chair, lowered herself back into it. Then the doorbell rang and Leona went to let them in.

Leona had often visited Arnold's home with her father and liked and respected his wife. It was hard to feel sorry for Auntie Esther, whose refusal to accept Lyn had resulted in Arnold's exile. But nobody could remain unmoved by the expression of pure joy on Esther Klein's face, Leona thought as she ushered the visitors into the parlor. Or by the tears now gushing in rivulets down her rouged cheeks. The grandchildren she had never expected to see had come to her and her emotion was uncontainable.

The suddenly charged atmosphere reduced even the little ones to silence.

"Two new cousins and another auntie have come to join us," Leona told them.

"You're Matthew and Margaret, aren't you?" Howard Klein said to the two children. "Their father is our dad's brother," he enlightened Kate. "Auntie Marianne told me all about them."

"You've certainly given us all a lovely surprise," Leona smiled to Lyn.

"That's an understatement, if ever I heard one!" Ronald

declared. "Personally, I think it's bloody wonderful." He took
Lyn's coat and Leona removed Margaret's plaid cape and
tam-o'-shanter.

"Margaret looks a bit like Marianne did when she was
little," Bessie remarked. "And Matthew's got Harry's nose."

"And Arnold's red hair, bless him," Esther added dabbing
her eyes.

Matthew, who was unused to the ways of Jewish matrons,
cast an agonized glance at his mother, then stood fiddling
self-consciously with the buckle of his gabardine belt.

"You don't look old enough to go to Manchester Grammar
School," Howard said, eyeing his cap. "I mean you're not as
tall as Mark and me, are you?"

"But I'll be twelve in December," Matthew replied stiffly.

"We'll be eleven in July," Howard said, putting his arm
around Mark's shoulder.

"They were born on the same day," Shirley told Lyn.

"And behave like Siamese twins," Ann put in with a smile.
"Take off your cap and coat, love," she said to Matthew.

"I expected to have to leave my cap on," he remarked
while removing it, "as this is a very Jewish house."

His elders smiled at the superlative, but could not help
feeling somewhat uncomfortable. It was understandable that
the boy had anticipated rigid orthodoxy within this family.
Hadn't they rejected his parents because of it?

"I'm afraid we're guilty of breaking a few rules," Ronald
said to him dryly.

Matthew eyed his uncovered head. "So I see."

"What kind of house do you live in?" Kate asked Margaret.

"A Christian-Jewish one," she replied.

Lyn laughed off a moment of awkwardness. "Actually, it's
semidetached." Like its occupants, she thought. But, hopefully, they would not, now, remain that way. "You haven't
kissed your granny," she said prodding her children in Esther's
direction.

Matthew gave Esther a wary peck. Margaret clung to
her mother.

"She'll kiss me when we get to know each other," Esther
said, trying not to sound hurt. Did these kids think her an
ogress? Who could blame them if they did? an inner voice
chided her. She had shown her son the door in a fury of
righteousness and his innocent children had suffered for it.
The warm family feeling their cousins had known from birth

had not been there for them. But it was now. Her heart was full of love for them and she would make sure they knew it, now she'd been given the chance.

"I'm so happy you came," she said simply to Lyn after Matthew and Margaret had gone with the other children for a tour of their great-grandmother's house.

"I've been thinking about it for some time," Lyn told her. "And a chat I had on the phone with Marianne made up my mind. But I was lucky to find you all here today, wasn't I?" she added with a smile. "I was so busy plucking up courage to come, I quite forgot Bobbie was still in America!" She noted that the family looked surprised to hear her use the Yiddish word for Grandma. "Arnold talks about her a lot," she informed them.

"And the rest of us?" Sigmund inquired. "You don't have to be scared of us, my dear," he added before she had time to reply.

Lyn laughed. "I don't scare easily!"

The family appraised her. Although she was exceedingly slender and her features delicate, there was something about her that told them this was so.

"What I had to find courage for was to defy my husband," she declared. "And what he'll do when he finds out I've been here—"

"He doesn't know?" Esther seemed unable to take this in. "I thought he'd be along later. That maybe he had to work this afternoon, like his father and brother."

"I shall telephone Arnold and give him a piece of my mind," Hannah declared in the crisp tone the family called her "schoolmarm voice," which she always employed when she meant business. "If he wishes to maintain his masochistic policy, that's his privilege. But no man has the right to inflict the consequences of his own foolishness upon his wife and children."

"Good for you, Aunt Hannah!" Leona applauded and received a derisive smile from Henry and a surprised glance from Frank.

"I'd be grateful for your support," Lyn told Hannah.

"Rest assured. You have it." There was nothing Hannah admired more than a woman of independent spirit and, in her view, there were too few around. Only Sarah, Marianne and herself among the womenfolk of the clan, though Leona was shaping up very nicely, she reflected approvingly. "But I shall intervene only on your behalf," she told Lyn. "It's useless trying to talk Arnold into a reconciliation. He'll come around to it in his own time."

"When will that be?" Esther muttered unhappily.

Lyn went to sit beside her on the sofa and took her hand. "Who can say? He's your son and my husband and we both know him only too well. But I've taken a step in the right direction and that's something."

Esther compared this warm and friendly young woman with Harry's cold fish wife and swallowed down her mixed emotions. "With all the excitement, we forgot to offer you some tea. Ask Lizzie to make a fresh pot for your sister-in-law, Ann," she said, putting the official seal on Lyn's place in the family.

Chapter Six

Sarah surveyed the imposing apartment building on West Eighty-sixth Street, in which her old acquaintance from Dvinsk now lived. "Chavah Bronsky has certainly gone up in the world!" she remarked to Sammy and Miriam, while they waited for David to pay the cabdriver for the journey from Washington Heights.

"Her name is Bronley nowadays, like her sons'," Sammy corrected Sarah. "And she's had time to better herself, I guess. Since you last saw her, Mother."

Half a century ago, though it seemed like yesterday, Sarah reflected, recalling the comely young matron who had sat in the Berkowitzes' Strangeways house nervously contemplating the next stage of her travels to a new life.

"My Ezra thinks the streets of New York are paved with gold, that's why we're going there instead of staying put like you, in England," Sarah remembered Chavah saying—or words to that effect. Her husband had found his gold in the furniture trade, with the small factory his eldest son had later turned into a million-dollar concern. And had himself gone to an early grave.

"A lot of well-off Jews live here," Sammy informed his

mother and brother when David joined them by the porter's lodge.

Miriam cast a dismissive glance around her. "Who needs it?"

But a person has to admire what Chavah's family has achieved, Sarah thought, though she agreed.

"And why we have to go everywhere by cab, just because Ma and David are visiting us—" Miriam went on, to Sammy. "When we usually travel by subway or bus."

"Cabs are more comfortable for Mother," David said.

"That I'm prepared to concede. But why do you and Sammy use them to get around when Ma and I aren't with you?" Miriam persisted. "Sammy told me you always do."

"I suppose because I'm accustomed to the convenience of my own car. To not having to rely on public transport," David answered lightly.

"And money is no object," Miriam countered, removing the smile from his face.

The end of his New York vacation was drawing near, and perhaps it was as well, David thought as they crossed a courtyard to the section of the building where Chavah's apartment was situated. Miriam was displaying more prickliness toward him every day.

"It was nice of Chavah to give this party for us before we go home, David," Sarah said, diplomatically changing the subject.

"She wants to show off her home to you, Ma," Miriam said with a sardonic smile.

"Maybe she would also like to see me again, for old times' sake," Sarah replied as they stepped into the discreet red-carpeted lift.

David managed not to glare at Miriam. Why must she always attribute insincere motives to everything affluent people did, as if having money automatically removed any genuine feelings they had ever had? Because she had no respect for achievement, or for the rewards it could bring. And had never bothered to draw more than a thin veil across her contempt for those who enjoyed material success. Which included himself.

Her own simple life-style had not been changed by coming to New York. Though the apartment block in which she and Sammy lived was not a smart one, those of their neighbors David had visited had well-furnished homes. Miriam's was

almost a replica of her home in Manchester. Clean and tidy,
but lacking any vestige of luxury. She was the kind who
would not discard a carpet, or sofa, until it grew irreparably
shabby. And not because she was mean; she was anything
but, David ruminated. She simply had no interest in appearances, in having people know her husband could afford a
home as good as his neighbors'; Sammy worked in Harold
Bronley's antique-reproduction department and, though he
did not earn a fortune, was quite well paid.

Miriam was pulling her gloves onto her long graceful
fingers. How many times did I watch her do that when we
were a boy and girl? David thought, with an ache in his
throat because she was still breathtakingly beautiful. But he'd
finally accepted that she wasn't for him and he'd been right. A
man with ambition needed an acquisitive woman like Bessie
to spur him on. Not one like Miriam, who had ridiculed
David's hopes and efforts, done her best to undermine him.

But oh, her beauty! he thought again. Enhanced, tonight,
by a simple black dress and jacket, which a local dressmaker
had run up for her, David had heard her tell his mother.
With it, she had on a long emerald-green scarf that matched
her eyes. She had wound it casually around her graceful,
white neck and on her graying hair was a little black hat—
homemade, probably, David guessed, recalling how Miriam
had made similar fetching concoctions for herself in her
youth, when she'd worked in a millinery shop.

Bessie, he thought with tolerant amusement, would have
rushed to Fifth Avenue to buy half a dozen outfits at Saks, had
she accompanied him to New York. Like she made straight
for Harrods the moment they arrived in London and returned
to their hotel with a cabful of dress boxes and cartons of
china. But Miriam had told him she never went to Saks, even
to look around. Or to Lord and Taylor's either. David had
bought her and Sammy a new dinner service from Lord and
Taylor's, which Miriam had said was the first thing they had
ever had from there.

Miriam met David's gaze in the lift's ornate mirror. "A
penny for your thoughts," she said mockingly.

David remained silent.

"Being your thoughts, they'd have to be worth much more
than that," she said with barbed sweetness as the lift halted at
the fifth floor.

David saw Sammy's expression cloud and bit back a sharp

retort. He wouldn't let her provoke him into a verbal exchange that would upset his brother.

"Stop kidding David along," Sammy laughed to Miriam, but the laugh sounded forced.

Having me around is a strain for him, David thought with regret. Thanks to Miriam. The pleasant veneer she had worn at the beginning of his visit had soon worn thin. The last few evenings, she had gone to bed immediately after Sarah had retired to the guest room, leaving David, who was making do on the living room studio couch, alone with Sammy.

Sammy had delayed his annual holiday, in order to spend time with his mother and brother. But all he and I ever talk about is old times, David reflected as they entered Chavah's apartment. He saw Miriam eyeing him while handing her jacket to the maid and wondered, as he had when she emigrated, what had impelled her to put the Atlantic Ocean between herself and the family. Her expression, when he met her gaze, was sphinxlike, telling him nothing.

"These surroundings you won't have any complaints about," she said to him, patting her chignon while checking her appearance in the foyer mirror.

Damn her! David thought, aware of the tightness he had felt in his chest during the flight returning to plague him. His mother and brother were out of earshot, following Chavah through the wide archway that opened onto the living room. "I don't recall having complained about anything," he replied shortly.

"Complain was the wrong word—I should have said despise."

"What the hell are you talking about?"

"Every time you've walked into my apartment, I've seen what you think of it written in your eyes."

Miriam kept her tone even, but David could feel her hostility bristling in the air, so strongly that he was momentarily shocked into silence.

"If you came to live in New York, you'd have us out of our modest home in no time, wouldn't you?" Miriam declared. "Transplant us, like you did when we lived in Manchester, to where you think it's fitting for a brother and sister-in-law of David Sanderton to live," she said emphasizing the surname to show her contempt for David's having rejected the one to which he was born. "And you'd have Sammy out of the job he loves doing—just because doing it will never make him rich."

David found his tongue. "What's wrong with wanting the

best for your family? And doing what you can to make sure they get it?" he demanded.

"Has it never occurred to you that your idea of what's best for them might not be theirs? That people must be allowed to live their own life in their own way? You laid down the law to Sammy from the time he was a child until we left England."

"Is that how you see it?" David said bitterly. Why was it that everything he did for others was, sooner or later, flung back into his face? He'd received the same treatment from Nat. And, in many respects, from his son Ronald.

"You've come here to have a tête-à-tête?" Chavah called from the living room and came to fetch them, monstrously overdressed in flowing purple georgette, through which the corset confining her ample girth bulged at front and rear.

"All the *hors d'oeuvres* will be eaten up if you don't take your share quickly," she smiled, escorting them to where the others were being served by her maid.

Sufficient delicacies to feed the guests at a fair-sized Jewish wedding were temptingly displayed on a huge buffet.

"What is that black stuff in the dish with the ice?" Sarah inquired suspiciously.

"You've never seen caviar before?" Chavah exclaimed, sounding astonished. "Give the lady a nice big portion, Pearl," she instructed the maid.

"A dime a dollar you ain't gonna like it, Ma'am," Pearl declared, ladling some onto Sarah's plate.

"So I don't have expensive tastes," Sarah shrugged, after eating a little had proved Pearl right.

"For caviar, you have to acquire a taste." Chavah's son Ivor, who had flown in from Los Angeles that day, clamped his cigar between yellowed teeth and helped himself to some.

Miriam smiled sweetly. "All a person needs is the money to acquire it."

She's going to spoil Mother's evening, David thought angrily and was relieved when Ivor—who must be thick-skinned! —laughed, as if Miriam had cracked a joke.

Sarah too felt strained. Who wouldn't, with Miriam in this mood? "Such a wonderful spread; you must have been busy in the kitchen for a week," she complimented their hostess politely.

"In New York, you don't have to slave to give a party," Chavah informed her. "A seven-course meal, even, a person can get sent in."

"If they have the wherewithal," Miriam added.

"That, I wouldn't dispute."

"Miriam enjoys cooking," Sarah intervened hastily.

"There are still a few old-fashioned women left, I guess," Chavah said with a smile and a shrug.

Miriam put down her fork and looked about to choke. "In my neighborhood, most women are what you call old-fashioned, Mrs. Bronley. I don't doubt that plenty of them would like to live like you do, but they have no choice."

Chavah glanced complacently around her lavishly appointed home. "So what can you do?" she smiled. "A person makes the best of what they have." She blew some nonexistent dust from an ormolu-embellished table and gave her maid a reproachful glance, before turning her attention to Sarah. "So how do you like my new decor? I just had the apartment done over by a designer everyone is raving about," she went on as if Sarah's admiration could be taken for granted. "My last designer I wouldn't use again after what he talked me into. Louis Quinze he made me live with. For eighteen months."

"Who is this Louis Quinze?" Sarah inquired with interest.

Chavah exchanged an amused glance with her sons. The furniture manufacturer had just arrived and was lowering his bulk into one of his firm's baroque-reproduction chairs.

"What are you? Greeners, in England?" Chavah smiled to Sarah while replacing a wispy lock that had somehow eluded the lacquer securing her blue-rinsed bird's-nest.

"Louis Quinze is foiniture," Sammy's boss supplied.

"Oh," Miriam said. "I always thought he was a king of France."

Harold Bronley said nothing, but David could tell he did not appreciate being taken down and that he did not like Miriam. Sammy might find himself out of a job if she didn't watch it.

"Right now, we call this the blue room," Chavah informed her guests.

Sarah was not surprised to hear this, as the carpet, drapes, upholstery and walls were all of varying shades of blue.

"In my Louis period, we called it the pink and gold room," Chavah went on with a reminiscent shudder.

"Why don't you just call it the living room?" Miriam asked. "Or the rainbow room; then you wouldn't need to keep changing the color when you refer to it," she added snidely.

Chavah seemed unable to think of a reply.

David thought it time to change the subject and went to sit beside Ivor. "So what kind of film are you making just now," he said, managing to smile. "Tell me all about it. It isn't every day I'm in the company of a famous producer."

"For a busman's vacation, my son hasn't come to New York," Chavah interceded before Ivor had time to utter. She planted a kiss on his gleaming bald pate. "To see his mom, he's come. Isn't that so?"

Ivor brushed some caviar off his gray mohair jacket, swallowed down the contents of his mouth and lit a cigarette. "As she won't come to Los Angeles to visit me."

"Because every time I've been there, my Ivor has there a new wife," Chavah informed Sarah, tight-lipped.

"It's an occupational hazard, Mom," Ivor quipped.

Chavah shook her head, sorrowfully. "Never fool around with the hired help, I've told him. Starlets, I warned him, are not for you. But does he listen to me? His first few weddings I went to—even though the girls were *shiksahs*," Chavah told Sarah. "A mother has to stand by her children. But at my age, who can go on flying back and forth, coast to coast, like a shuttlecock? The traveling is getting too much for me."

"How many wives has he had?" Sarah inquired, sounding shocked.

"Five—I think," Ivor said furrowing his brow. "But who's counting?"

"Your mother is counting," Sarah scolded him.

"His children I'm counting, also—some of whom have been turned against me by their mothers," Chavah sighed.

"Ivor's a pushover for wedding bells," Sammy's boss put in. "He oughta have stayed a bachelor, like me."

"Don't let my brother fool you. A paragon of virtue he isn't," Ivor conveyed. "Whenever I drop by to see him, his place is crawling with dolls."

Sarah was glad the Sandbergs had not moved on to America, which, in their early-immigrant days, her husband had once suggested. She shuddered inwardly at the immorality that might have ruined her children and grandchildren if they had grown up here.

"In England, what we've just been talking about couldn't happen," she declaimed to Chavah. "Especially not among Jews."

"It doesn't happen to everyone in the States," Sammy said, putting his arm around his wife. "Not by a long chalk."

This was the first time he had spoken since his employer arrived and Harold glanced at him as though he had forgotten he was there.

David noted the glance. That's how it's always been with Sammy, he reflected with a pang. His brother was content to be swallowed up by personalities stronger than his own.

"I hear you've arranged for Sammy to see a consultant," Harold said to David.

"What!" Miriam rasped. "You've been busy behind my back, have you?" she said turning a glance of hatred upon David.

Sammy gripped her shoulder, to calm her. "Don't blame David. I didn't want to build up your hopes, in case nothing can be done for me."

"That doesn't mean I don't have a thing or two to say about it to your meddling brother."

The atmosphere was now rippling with embarrassment. Chavah turned to the buffet and began rearranging some slices of tomato around a depleted mound of paté. Ivor ran his finger around the inside of his shirt collar. Harold had paused with an unlit cigarette *en route* to his lips and was watching Miriam and David with interest.

To Sarah, the way they were staring at each other was frightening. As if they had reached a point in time to which they had been leading up all their lives.

"You'll talk to David later," she said quietly to Miriam. "Chavah's apartment is not the place."

"Don't be upset on my account, Sarah," Chavah said. "We all know how it can be with families."

"In ours, we have a self-appointed fixer," Miriam declared in a voice thick with animosity. "But I won't have him interfering in my life again."

Sarah saw David wince. "What is it?" she asked him anxiously. Beads of perspiration had broken out on his forehead and his complexion looked suddenly tinged with gray.

"Nothing. Just a bit of indigestion," he managed to reply before he slumped to the floor.

Chapter Seven

Shirley and Peter were together in David's office when Sammy telephoned with the news that David had collapsed.

"Uncle Sammy said he'd rung the surgery, but Uncle Nat and Ronald weren't there," Shirley, who had taken the call, told her husband. "He thought it best for one of us to tell my mother."

"Yes, dear," Peter said, patting her shoulder comfortingly.

Shirley gave him a cool glance. "Is this what it takes for you to be nice to me?"

Peter sighed and resumed signing the day's mail, which Sammy's call had interrupted.

"How can you sit there doing that, when my poor father's had a heart attack?" Shirley shrilled at him. "Get out of his chair. I don't want you sitting in it. He isn't dead yet."

Rita Sternshein entered from her adjoining office. "What's going on in here?" she demanded.

Rita had joined the firm when she left school and stayed on as David's indispensable secretary. Initially, she had been his sole clerical employee and had also modeled garments for visiting buyers. Nowadays the buying was done in an elegant showroom on the ground floor, where a couple of trained models showed off the sample coats.

Rita glanced briefly through the glass partition that divided the office accommodation, to check that the typists, whom she ruled with an iron hand, still had their heads bent industriously over their machines. "What's the matter with you two?" she asked, returning her attention to Shirley and Peter, whom she did not view as her superiors, despite them being who they were. "This is a business, not a fish market," she informed them cuttingly. "And please hurry up with those letters," she added to Peter. "They'd have been signed and in their envelopes by now, if your father-in-law were here."

Shirley told her the news from New York and saw Rita's pockmarked complexion pale. It had often crossed Shirley's mind that her father, as well as Sanderstyle, was Rita's *raison d'être*, and did so again now. Rita, whose face was as ugly as her figure was perfect, had never married, or even had a boyfriend in her youth. She was now middle-aged. With nothing to keep her warm but a secret passion for her boss, Shirley guessed, pitying her.

Rita pulled herself together. "He'll have another heart attack when he finds out what his daughter and son-in-law have been hatching in his absence," she said, pulling down the jacket of her clinging jersey suit and marching from the room.

"We shall have to forget that idea, now," Peter said when he and his wife were alone.

"Will we?" Shirley replied crisply.

"In my opinion, yes."

"Who gives a damn about your opinion?" Shirley surveyed Peter's handsome countenance; the finely chiseled profile, deep blue eyes and fair hair which had captivated her when they were teenagers. He'd been every young girl's ideal. The romantic lover whom Fate, via Hitler, had sent to be Shirley Sanderton's soulmate—or so it had seemed to her then, she remembered sourly. If Peter hadn't been Sigmund Moritz's great-nephew, orphaned before the Holocaust even got under way, he wouldn't have come to Manchester and been taken in by her parents, become her husband and the father of her children. But the Peter to whom she had given her heart had disappeared along the way.

"You'd be nothing without me and my dad," she said to him coldly.

"Thank you for telling me, my darling."

Shirley threw an ashtray at him and watched it bounce off his shoulder onto the carpet. "You'd be laboring on a kibbutz in Israel, like that girl Hildegard who came over from Vienna with you ended up doing, if you hadn't married me!"

"But I did marry you, my dear. And I try to make the best of it."

Shirley flounced to the window, with an angry toss of her auburn locks. The way Peter maintained his habitual charm when they quarreled served only to fire her own rage.

She stared unhappily down into the parking lot, at the empty space her father's car usually occupied, thinking of him lying in a sickbed all those miles away. Her instinct was to fly to his side. But he wouldn't want that. He'd want her to hold the fort, here. Some bales of pastel-colored gabardine were being unloaded from a lorry by the warehouse entrance, reminding her that she had not yet completed her designs for the spring range. She hadn't been able to spend much time in her studio during Dad's absence; Rita was an efficient secretary, but had had to call on Shirley to make decisions. She would have to make up for lost time by working on her designs at home, in the evenings. While Peter watched television! she thought, casting a smoldering glance at him. His nine-till-six attitude toward the family business was incomprehensible to her.

"In some ways, you're like Uncle Sammy," she told him, returning to the desk to get a cigarette.

Peter picked up an onyx lighter and flicked a tongue of flame into life.

"What you do here is only a job to you, like it was to my uncle before he emigrated. But he wasn't a director," Shirley pointed out. "What you are, Peter, is a director with a worker's attitudes."

He applied the light to her cigarette and fanned away the smoke she blew into his face. "Call me what you wish, my darling. But nobody can say I don't do my work well."

This, Shirley could not deny. He had applied his clever mind to sales management with great success. What riled her was his lack of enthusiasm for Sanderstyle. His heart was not in it.

Her father's old friend, Moishe Lipkin, was now exports manager and, though he was not a relative, was more wrapped up in the business than Peter had ever been. But Dad and Moishe were getting old and less able to cope with strains and stresses. Increasingly the load would have to be carried by Shirley, whose husband refused to share it.

"I don't see Dad's illness as a reason to forget we've received a takeover bid while he's been away," she declared, stubbing out her cigarette.

"So that's what you've been sitting thinking about, is it?" Peter eyed his wife's curvaceous body, accentuated today by a green knitted dress. "If only your nature were as appetizing as your appearance, dearest. But it was foolish of me to suppose your thoughts were solely concentrated on your father's ill-health."

Shirley, who had perched on a corner of the desk, removed her gaze from her long legs and treated Peter to an icy stare. "It's precisely because of Dad's sudden ill-health that I'm sure it'd be right to accept the offer."

Peter smiled. "Do you really expect me to believe self-interest doesn't enter into it? You were ready to accept the offer before we received the call from New York."

"Of course I bloody was!" Shirley flared. "Because selling out would be a great relief to me, too."

"Even though the bid stipulates that you and I must remain to run the business?"

"But we wouldn't be carrying the can, would we?" Shirley said shrewdly. "But we'd be well paid, nevertheless. And running a business for strangers I wouldn't lose as much sleep over."

"As usual, you have everything beautifully worked out."

Shirley ignored the interruption. "And I'd be my own boss in the studio, which, up to now, I've never been." Included in the takeover bid was the promise of a free hand for Sanderstyle's present designer. It did not surprise Shirley. Even David Sanderton would have to admit that it was his daughter's fashion sense that had put their garments on the map.

"Your self-centeredness in this particular matter shocks even me, darling," Peter said, "well though I know you." Shirley being her own boss in the studio implied the removal of David, which the takeover would accomplish. There was no place for him in the new setup.

"I've thought for some time that your dad should be taking things easier, enjoying the fruits of his labors," Peter said. "That's why I agreed with you that he ought to accept the offer. But I didn't have much hope of him doing so. There would simply have been an almighty row between you and him, Shirley. If that were to happen now, it could do him great harm."

"And carrying on as he has been doing couldn't? In my view, having a heart attack will have brought him up short and it won't be too difficult to make him see sense."

"I wish you luck, my darling," Peter said with a rueful smile. If that was how Shirley saw it, she didn't know her father.

Chapter Eight

Sarah stopped pacing the corridor and sat down on a chair outside David's room, still unable to quite believe that this had happened. That David, the strong one of the family, was lying gray-faced and limp in a bed at the Washington Heights Jewish Memorial Hospital.

Since her eldest son was *Bar Mitzvah* he had been like her right arm, sharing with her the burdens and decisions her husband's nature had not equipped him to share. And in her widowhood, David's concern for her had been twofold. Her other children cared, too, but she had never had the special relationship with them she had with David.

Sarah's hand fluttered nervously to her brooch as a nurse stepped out of David's room.

"Why not go home and get some shut-eye, Mrs. Sandberg?" the pleasant-faced woman suggested kindly. "I guess you'd feel better if you got out of those clothes," she added.

Sarah was still wearing the garments she had worn last night. "Only my shoes feel a little tight," she murmured absently.

The nurse knelt down to unlace them for her.

Nurses are a special breed, Sarah thought while she was doing so. Here, they wore white dresses, instead of the starched aprons worn in England, but behind the uniform they were all the same. Kindness personified. "Thank you," she said gratefully, easing her swollen feet out of the restricting leather. "What is your name?" This nice lady was a person, not just an anonymous ministering angel.

"Kowalski, ma'am."

"You're Jewish?"

"No, ma'am. Polish Catholic."

"In the Jewish Hospital in Manchester, England—where I come from—some of the nurses are nuns," Sarah told her. "My friend Mrs. Lipkin, who had there an emergency operation, came round from the anesthetic and thought she was dead, and had gone by mistake to the Christian heaven, when she saw a nun dressed in white bending over her."

46

They shared a laugh, then Sarah's gaze strayed anxiously to the door of David's room.

"He'll pull through," Nurse Kowalski assured her. "I'll make it my personal business to see that he does."

Sarah managed to smile. "All right. I trust you."

"But no sneaking in there when my back is turned," the nurse requested. "One visitor at a time, his physician instructed, and you don't wanna land me in trouble, do you, ma'am?"

"I wouldn't dream of it," Sarah said.

But why doesn't Miriam come out of the room and let me sit with my son for a while? she thought, watching the nurse's solid figure recede along the corridor. Sammy had not yet returned from making the telephone call to England. He had said something about phoning the airline office, also, to defer Sarah and David's return flight, and that this would probably take longer than getting through to Manchester because the lines were always busy.

For how long would their return home be postponed, Sarah wondered? The doctor had said David's heart attack was only a mild one. But the first forty-eight hours were, nevertheless, critical, he had added, and Sarah had never known time pass so slowly as it had since she heard him say it.

David emerged from a deep sleep and saw Miriam sitting beside his bed. When he had dozed off, his mother had been there. And before that, though he couldn't remember quite when, Sammy. He had been remotely aware of daylight darkening to night and then, though it seemed but a moment later, the grayness of dawn. Now it was dark again, with only a night-light casting a pale glow upon the quiet room.

"Is that your perfume I can smell?" he asked Miriam. The air was heavy with a sweet fragrance. "Or have they been spraying something in here?"

"Neither," Miriam smiled. "It's the flowers Chavah sent you. And, by the look of them, she must have called up the best florist in town!"

David turned his head and saw a lavish floral arrangement on a table by the window. "That must have set her back a few dollars."

"Now I know you're getting better," Miriam said.

But she had said it without sarcasm, David noted. "How long have I been here?" he inquired. "I've lost track of time."

"Because you've spent most of it sleeping. They've been giving you shots," Miriam told him.

"Those, I remember."

"Well, they had to do something to make sure you don't leap out of bed and rush back to England to see what's going on at your factory," she joked.

"There's no danger of that," David answered. An all-pervading lethargy had him in its grip.

"This is your third day here," Miriam informed him.

"So I've missed my flight home, what can you do?" he said with a shrug.

"I didn't expect you to be so philosophical about it."

"When you think you're going to die, you get that way."

Miriam smiled. "With you it won't last. And you're out of danger now." She smoothed a wrinkle in the counterpane. "Ma wouldn't leave the hospital until you were. Sammy's taken her home."

"You look as if you need some sleep, too," David said, surveying her weary appearance. "Why didn't you go with them?"

"I wanted to stay until you woke up."

"Being the dutiful sister-in-law, are you?" David said brusquely.

"When did I ever do anything out of a sense of duty, David? I'm not like you."

Again, her voice was devoid of the cutting edge with which she customarily addressed such remarks to him. They fell into an awkward silence, heightened by the ticking of David's watch on the bed table and the squeak of a trolley being trundled along outside the door.

Was that guilt in Miriam's expression? David wondered, studying her surreptitiously. Something was gluing her to his side. "If you've got it into your mind that the words we had at Chavah's put me where I am, forget it," he told her. "I'd been heading this way for a long time."

"Then why didn't you pull yourself up?" she demanded fiercely. "Instead of bulldozing on, like you've always done?" Miriam averted her eyes to the basket of flowers. "You're your own worst enemy, David," she said with a catch in her voice.

"I had the impression you thought I was yours."

Miriam stared down at the wedding ring his brother had put on her finger, after David married Bessie. The gold band had had time to grow thin, but what had once been between Miriam and David was hovering in the room.

"I've spent the last two days analyzing my feelings," Miriam said.

"And what conclusion did you come to?"

"That I'm a foolish woman."

"I've always considered you a highly intelligent one."

"Not intelligent enough to have known what I've been doing."

"What have you been doing?" David asked, feeling as if he was leading her across a dangerous stream via stepping stones.

"Punishing you—and myself—because we weren't right for each other," Miriam said quietly. "Because I've always known in my heart that, in the only way that matters, we were."

Miriam had not used the word "love," but that was what she meant and, remembering, David's whole being was suffused with regret. But regret was an eroding emotion and he brushed it aside. Miriam had allowed hers to sour her life.

"I'm glad we've had this chat," he told her gruffly. Then he felt her lips brush his brow, and the gentle touch of her hand on his.

Miriam got up from her chair by the bed and put on the warm coat Sammy had fetched for her from home. She had not left the hospital since David was brought here from Chavah's apartment, but her exhaustion was leavened by a new sense of peace.

"I'll see you tomorrow, David," she smiled. "And I hope we can be friends, from now on."

David gazed for a moment into her brilliant green eyes, that were still the loveliest he had ever seen. "There's nothing I want more."

"There's never an ill wind, as your grandmother is fond of saying," Nathan said to his daughter.

They had been watching the news on television, and Leona rose to switch off the set. "I presume you're referring to the situation in the Middle East?"

The news was currently dominated by the Suez Crisis. Anglo-French reaction to Nasser nationalizing the Canal in July had, this week, culminated in the Sinai Campaign.

"Only to protect their own interests would Britain and France offer arms to Israel," Nathan voiced his opinion on the two countries having done so. "And it's given the Israelis an opportunity to protect theirs."

"I read that the Israelis don't mind the Canal being nationalized," Leona said. "That they've joined in the assault only because Egypt's been getting arms from Russia, and has signed a pact with Syria to unite their military strength. But the whole of politics is opportunism," Leona added disdainfully. "Everyone masking their real selves behind whatever veneer they choose to present to the world," she declared, thinking of Henry Moritz, who would probably spend his life dabbling in politics. It was never possible to fathom what Henry was thinking behind his charming smile.

"The Israelis have to play the same tactical game as everyone else. They'd be stupid not to grasp this chance of sending troops into the Sinai Peninsula and the Gaza Strip," Nathan summed up. "And stupid they're not! But how did we get onto this subject?"

Leona took a russet apple from a bowl of fruit on the coffee table and polished it on her tartan skirt. "You said there was never an ill wind."

"I was thinking about your mother."

"Oh," Leona said guardedly.

Nathan watched her sink her teeth into the apple. How could the peaky-faced kid she'd been, have grown into such a beauty? Her once fiery hair had darkened to a coppery tone that enhanced the healthy glow in her cheeks. She had inherited her mother's tawny eyes. And her shape was the kind that made young men turn to look at her in the street. Sooner or later, she would meet one who'd want to make her his own, Nathan thought with a jealous pang. Steal her from her father.

"Is there a smut on my nose?" Leona inquired, aware of him studying her.

"If there was, it wouldn't be noticeable among all those freckles," he smiled.

"So what's with the ill wind?" Leona felt constrained to ask. "Personally, I fail to see any good coming out of Mummy's attempt to end her life." The aftermath of her mother's act had hung in the air ever since, though she and her father had, as if by tacit consent, not discussed it. Leona had no desire to do so now, but perhaps it was time the air was cleared.

"Your mother insists that she wasn't trying to do any such thing," Nathan told her. "She said she woke in the night and couldn't remember taking her pills, so she swallowed some down. That kind of thing does happen, Leona. And I want to believe her."

"Of course you do, Daddy. Because the other alternative would make you feel responsible, wouldn't it?" There. It's out at last, Leona thought. If we're going to clear the air, let's do it properly. "If you had done what Mummy did, I'd have said the same to her," she added.

"I see."

"Of course you bloody see!"

"Is that the kind of language students use to their parents these days?"

Leona ignored the rebuke. "You and Mummy are miserable together. So far as my mind will carry me back, and that's quite a long way, you always have been."

"Can we get back to the ill wind?" Nathan said stiffly. "I was referring to Uncle David's illness—"

"You said you were thinking of Mummy," Leona cut in.

"About the way she's shaken herself out of the doldrums and gone to look after Auntie Bessie."

Nobody had been surprised that Bessie was inconsolable when she learned David was gravely ill. Only her fear of flying had stopped her from rushing to his side, and added to her fears for him was guilt because she had not done so. When told he was out of danger she had refused to believe it, though David had spoken to her on the telephone. Rebecca had moved in with her and had promised to stay until David returned home.

"I wouldn't have thought your mother capable of putting someone else's troubles before her own," Nathan told Leona. "But I'm sure it's good for her."

"So speaks the part-time psychoanalyst!" Leona exclaimed, leaping up from her chair and tossing her apple core onto the fire.

"I had no idea you were so contemptuous of my sideline," Nathan said shortly.

"I'm not. You do a lot of good work."

"And the private part of it pays your mother's expensive dress bills. Yours too, so don't be so damned condescending, my girl!"

"I'm sorry, Daddy," Leona said after a silence. "But when you spoke about Mummy, you sounded so clinical."

"I'm a doctor, aren't I?"

"You're also her husband—or would you rather I didn't remind you?"

"Who could blame me if I needed reminding," Nathan said bitterly. Leona was a grown woman and knew that her parents had not shared a bedroom for years.

"You have my sympathy," she said. "But so does Mummy." She stared into the leaping flames in the grate, a faraway look in her eyes. "When I was a child, I was terrified that you'd get a divorce," she said quietly. "But I was only thinking of myself, the way kids do. Afraid of what it would do to my life. But now, I wish you had." She raised her eyes to look at Nathan. "When I look back on my childhood, what I remember most vividly is mealtimes. You and Mummy talking about nothing but me. As if I was all you had in common."

"I wish you had happier memories," Nathan sighed.

"I used to wish Uncle Lou and Auntie Cora were my parents," Leona revealed. "Lila Benjamin was always saying she wished her legs were long, like mine, instead of dumpy—but I'd have swopped them with her gladly—what I mean is I wanted to be her, instead of me, because she had such a happy home."

Nathan got up to poke the fire, though it did not require poking. Leona's revelation of her childhood longing had had a profound effect upon him.

"And like I said, I wish, now, that you and Mummy had split up. If their marriage is a mess, a couple ought not to stay together for their children's sake—they're not doing the kids any favors. In addition to what the children have to live with while they're growing up, they're landed with the responsibility for two unhappy parents, years later."

"So you feel responsible for your mother and me, do you?" Nathan smiled, trying to make light of it. "But I think it will be some time before you'll need to help your aging mum and dad to cross the road."

"What I feel responsible for—and you know it—is your present plight," Leona declared. "You'd have ended your marriage years ago, if it hadn't been for me."

Would we? Nathan wondered.

"When you were still young enough to find happiness elsewhere," his daughter said.

To a twenty-year-old, someone my age must seem past it! Nathan thought wryly. As if the capacity for romantic love was the prerogative of the young. Which Nathan had still been when a second chance was presented to him. During the war, he had found himself briefly serving in the same military hospital as his boyhood sweetheart, Mary Dennis. But he had let Mary walk out of his life again. And not just for Leona's sake; because the sanctity of marriage and home was the core of Jewish life.

Though Rabbinic Law provided for divorce, few availed themselves of it. Those who did created a nine-day wonder in their local community and, even had Mary been a Jewess, Nathan could not have brought himself to subject the Sandberg family to the inevitable gossip.

The latter consideration would not influence him now. He had rid himself of that inhibition for good and all. But he remained the root cause of his wife's unhappiness and, though he fluctuated between hating and pitying her, if their marriage was ever to end, it must be Rebecca who cut the knot. He would never abandon her.

Chapter Nine

Before Sarah left New York, Sammy took her to see the Cloisters in Fort Tryon Park, so she could describe those ancient monuments to her Christian neighbors when she went home.

Who would have believed it? she cogitated while they strolled along a carpet of rain-soaked leaves. She had been dreading David's discharge from the hospital, afraid that Miriam would revert to the sharp-tongued manner with which she had treated him before his collapse. But during his convalescence, the opposite had been the case, as though David's illness had caused Miriam to suddenly value him as the rest of the family had always done. Miriam could not do enough for him and, Sarah reflected, in many respects seemed as lighthearted as she had been as a girl. Sarah and Sammy had left her and David chatting companionably together—a sight Sarah had never expected to see.

It was now the end of November. An abortive campaign had been fought about the Suez Canal, on the other side of the world, and a rumpus raised about it at the UN, here in New York, under Sarah's nose. But the whole affair which, had she been at home, would have worried her, had washed over her as if it had not happened. Instead, she had existed in a kind of trance, which she attributed to her unfamiliar surroundings.

A pang of homesickness assailed her as she took Sammy's arm, so she would not slip on the soggy mound they were traversing. "My front garden path will be even worse than this, with nobody there the whole autumn, to sweep up the leaves," she said. "And I hope Mrs. Evans has taken good care of my cat."

Sammy smiled and surveyed her frail figure, huddled in a heavy black coat. Her shoulders had a slight hunch to them that hadn't been there when she arrived, as if the weight of anxiety about David had left its mark. "Now it's almost time for you to leave; you've begun worrying about what's going on at home!" he teased her. "You're a born worrier, Mother."

"Lately, I haven't been able to think of anyone or anything but David," Sarah answered. "Like your father once said to me, even I am not capable of worrying about my children more than one at a time!"

"And which of us will you give your sole attention to next?" Sammy chuckled.

Sarah turned to look at him. He still walked with a limp, as he had since the age of two; even the built-up shoe he wore could not prevent that. And the lines beside his mouth had deepened since he left England. But they were from physical pain, not the evidence of discontentment which marred Nathan's handsome features, or the fruits of business anxiety that had prematurely aged David. Life had dealt Sammy some cruel blows, Sarah reflected with sadness, but despite this, he was and always had been the happiest of her four children.

"Your leg I hope will never get any worse, Sammy," she said. "And in other respects, you I don't need to worry about." She paused by a bench, brushed some leaves off it and sat down. "Let's take a rest."

"But not for long. There's a damp mist in the air and I don't want you to catch cold, Mother."

"The mist I prefer to the hurricane, that day I went to Fifth Avenue with Miriam," Sarah exaggerated.

Sammy laughed. Miriam's description of his mother battling to hold down her skirts had amused everyone but Sarah. "With the Hudson on one side and the East River on the other, New Yorkers are used to being blown about. Manhattan is an island, Mother."

"So is England. But in Manchester, the River Irwell doesn't do that to you," Sarah declaimed. "Nor did the Dvina, in Dvinsk," she recalled.

A bulbous-nosed senior citizen eavesdropping from the other end of the bench lowered his *Herald Tribune*. "Did I hear you mention Dvinsk—excuse me for interrupting?"

Sarah nodded. "I came from there. But I'm English, now."

"No kidding. American I can tell you're not. Me, I'm from Bialystok," he said, folding his arms and resting them on his sizable paunch. "But a friend of mine—he's moved to the Bronx to live with his married daughter—comes from Dvinsk."

"For Jews, it's a small world," Sarah smiled.

Sammy was studying the old gentleman's face. "Haven't I see you at *shul*?"

"Which *shul* is that?"

"The *Beth Hamidrash Hagodol*, on West One hundred seventy-fifth."

"My own synagogue he's telling me the address of! But I thought I knew all my fellow-congregants."

"I guess I don't put in an appearance too often," Sammy said, sounding ashamed. "Only on *Rosh Hashanah* and *Yom Kippur*, I'm afraid."

The old man shook his head sorrowfully and exchanged a glance with Sarah.

"Our children are not like us," she shrugged.

"That you can say again! And with their children, it's even worse. Already three of my seven grandchildren, they've married-out."

Sarah was about to admit that two of hers had done likewise, but was not given time to open her mouth.

"But so long as they don't marry *schwartzers*, today we gotta be thankful."

"A fine thing for a Jew to say!" Sarah exclaimed rebukingly.

"In your country, you don't got no color problem," the old

man retorted. "Only a sprinkling, who came since the war, I heard you got there."

"It's people like you who make such problems." Sarah rose from the bench and bade him the customary farewell she had heard on all sides during her stay in New York. "Have a good day." But she did not sound as if she meant it.

"I guess you put that guy in his place, Mother," Sammy smiled when he caught up with her. She had turned on her heel and marched away before he had time to get to his feet.

Sarah was seething, but her anger was tinged with distress. "A racist Jew I never expected to meet."

"Jews can be as prejudiced as anyone else, Mother."

"But it's wrong that they should be, when we've suffered so much from prejudice ourselves. I can remember you and David and Esther getting jeered at by Christian children every day, on your way home from school."

"If I had a dollar for all the times I got spat at and called a dirty Yid, I'd be a wealthy guy," Sammy reminisced.

"By the time our Nat was old enough to start school, it wasn't that bad," Sarah recalled. "Jews are still looked on as different—even in England—but sooner or later people begin to accept you."

"I doubt if that's ever gonna happen with the blacks."

"Why shouldn't it?" Sarah demanded.

"Because the Jews have never been a social problem. Like the blacks, unfortunately, are here."

"What is a social problem?" Sarah inquired as Sammy had known she would. With his mother, one explanation always led to another.

"Don't expect me to explain in detail, Mother. You know I don't have the head for it," Sammy smiled. "All I can say is if you lived here, you'd understand."

"Nothing would make me understand how a Jew could think like that man does," Sarah declared adamantly.

"Look—the Cloisters," Sammy said, thankful for an excuse to change the subject. When something lodged in his mother's mind, there was no getting it out! Long before most people had even heard of Hitler, she had warned the family about the creeping danger of Fascism. When the persecution of Jews began in Europe, she'd been incensed that Oswald Mosley was still allowed to preach the evil in England—and had taken her grandchildren to hear him speak, to drive home the danger to them, Sammy recalled. If she lived in

New York, he would not put it past her to march down Park Avenue waving a banner supporting the black cause.

Sarah had halted to survey the Cloisters. "Wait until I tell Mrs. Evans and Mrs. Watson what you have in your local park, Sammy," she said, studying the imposing edifice. It was difficult to believe that parts of medieval monasteries and chapels had been brought from Europe and rebuilt here, stone by stone. "You have to hand it to the Yanks, the things they do," she said with admiration.

"You haven't stopped saying that since you got here," Sammy smiled.

"It's true." Each time Sarah saw the New York skyline and the feat of engineering that was the George Washington Bridge, linking the city with the State of New Jersey, she marveled anew.

"It's a pity you won't be able to tell people back home that you rode to the top of the Empire State Building," Sammy teased her.

"My life he would like me to risk!"

During the bus ride back to 179th Street, Sarah was unusually quiet.

"You're looking very thoughtful," Sammy said.

"Who wouldn't? In two days' time, I'll be back in England. But America I'll never forget."

Chapter Ten

On the first Friday in December, Ralph arrived home from work and found Marianne in their bedroom, packing a suitcase.

"Leaving me, eh?" he joked. "You might at least wait until your book's published and let me enjoy some reflected glory!"

Marianne flung a slipper at him, then went to kiss his cheek, which it had narrowly missed.

"I'd cut my throat if you ever did leave me," he said, giving her a bear hug.

"Don't bother sharpening your razor. It won't be necessary."

"Where are we going to?" he inquired, removing his tie and dropping it on the bed, where a couple of his shirts and sweaters were waiting to be packed.

"Manchester."

"Surprise, surprise! You and your blinking family."

"It's your family, too, love. And has been for some time."

"I'm joking, sweetheart."

"You'd better be."

Their lighthearted banter continued while Marianne finished packing and Ralph changed into the old sports jacket and flannels he always wore to drive up north. But Marianne's thoughts remained on his jest about reflected glory. He made that kind of crack too often these days, she thought unhappily. Her career was important to her, but she didn't want it to affect her relationship with Ralph.

"What's the reason for the pilgrimage this time?" he grinned.

"My grandmother and Uncle David got back yesterday. Bobbie rang me this morning and said it would be nice if all her family were with her at tomorrow's *Shabbos* tea party."

"And that's as good as a summons," Ralph said.

"To everyone except my brother Arnold."

Their son appeared in the doorway wearing his best coat and clutching the small *tallith* bag his Grandpa Ben had bought for him, without which he never went to Manchester. Ben Klein never lost the opportunity to take him to an Orthodox *shul* and, when Martin was in town, took the morning off in order to do so, instead of working on the Sabbath as usual. Marianne found this paradoxical, to say the least, but to her the way of the so-called Orthodox was one big paradox.

"Hurry up, you two!" Martin said. "Mum's made some sandwiches and tea for us to have in the car," he told his father.

"What, no chicken soup?" Ralph smiled.

"What's that?" Martin answered. "I can't remember when I last had a real Jewish Friday-night dinner."

"You'll get a real *Shabbos* lunch at Grandma Esther's, tomorrow," Marianne said, hoping she did not sound as guilty as she felt. "I don't have time to make chopped-liver and *tsimmes*. But neither of you looks exactly starved."

"But I shouldn't be surprised if Lancashire hotpot began coming out of our ears," Ralph warned.

"I wrote a poem about Lancashire, at school today," Martin said. "About the factory chimneys. And got ten out of ten for it."

"Good on you!" Ralph said in his native Australian vernacular.

Marianne smiled. "Maybe Martin's going to take after his namesake."

Ralph had heard so much about Martin Sandberg, he felt as though he had known him. A large framed photograph of Marianne's dead cousin in RAF uniform lived on their sitting room bookcase. And sometimes she would get some of the poems he had written out of the big box in which she kept her treasures, and read them aloud. Much of the poetry was melancholy and the rest macabre, from which Ralph had formed a picture of an unhappy young man, the kind who was lonely even in a crowd.

"Writing poems is easy," Martin said, to his parents' amusement. "But I don't want to be a poet. I'm going to be an author, like my mum, when I grow up."

"Talking of which, how's the novel of the century going?" Ralph said to Marianne as they left the bedroom.

Marianne managed to smile, but did not reply.

Martin could not wait to get to Manchester. Nothing excited him more than the prospect of a weekend with the family. His great-grandmother's house had an attic full of interesting lumber, which the children were allowed to play with on Saturday afternoons. There was a huge wicker skip there, in which was an assortment of articles so well preserved with mothballs the smell caught your throat when you lifted the lid. Grandma Esther's wedding dress was inside it, but Martin could not imagine it fitting even half of her, now. There was a rusty-looking black skirt Sarah Sandberg had worn long ago, which she said was made of something called bombazine. And two coarse woolen caps with shiny peaks, that Martin's great-uncles, David and Sammy, had had on their heads throughout their long journey to England, in the old days when no Jewish male had ever uncovered his head. Several old velvet *tallith* bags were in the skip, too, their burst seams past repair; as if they had done long service carrying Abraham Sandberg's prayer shawl and *siddur* to *shul*, Martin thought. And a collection of musty black *yamulkes*, one of which had a few ginger hairs on the lining. Perhaps Abraham had worn that one before his hair turned gray?

"People must have been very religious in the olden days," Martin said contemplatively from the back seat of the car, when the Deans were on their way.

"What on earth put that into your head?" Marianne asked.

"I was thinking about the attic."

Marianne smiled reminiscently. As a child, she too had spent many fascinating hours there and there must be a good deal more family history closeted in that dusty room by now.

Ralph was chewing on the tongue sandwich she had just handed him. "They had more time to be religious," he replied to Martin's observation. "Life wasn't lived against the clock, like it is today."

"But people like my grandparents, and their Christian equivalent, would still find time," Marianne declared with conviction. "And there's still a minority whose lives revolve around religion, Ralph."

"Don't just tell me. Write a book about it."

Martin stopped peeling a banana. "Why are you always so frivolous about Mum's work, Dad?" he asked hoping the word "frivolous" meant what he thought it did. "Mum doesn't make jokes about your work, does she?"

"I'd have a job to," Marianne could not stop herself from saying. "It's so long since he's done any."

Ralph's hand tightened on the steering wheel, but he kept his tone light. "And what would you call how I spend my days, sweetheart? My evenings and weekends, as well, as I usually bring overtime home?"

"Mum wasn't talking about your advertising layouts," Martin said.

"Why should she even bother to think about them?" Ralph answered. "They're only our living."

Marianne was eating a sandwich and had trouble in swallowing it down. What she had feared, and tried not to believe, was now staring her in the face. Ralph, the least selfish of men, had begun comparing her lot with his own. Resenting her freedom to pursue her art, while the need to support his family prohibited him from pursuing his. Marianne could not blame him. Had the situation been reversed, the iron would have entered her soul long ago.

"I wonder how much I could earn as a typist?" she said casually.

"I beg your pardon?" Ralph said.

"If I contributed to our income, by taking a part-time job, you wouldn't have to work at the agency full-time, Ralph. You'd only have to do a little free-lance work for us to get by, and spend the rest of your time doing what you really want to do."

"Forget it, sweetheart."

"Don't you want to paint pictures anymore, Dad?" Martin asked, sounding upset.

"Not at the expense of your mother's career, when it's just getting off the ground," Ralph answered.

There was no doubt in Marianne's mind that he meant this. Which did not make her feel any better.

"And for a youngster," he said to Martin, "you have altogether too much to say."

"Usually, I'd agree with that," Marianne said. "But not on this occasion. Your career is as important to this family as mine, Ralph."

Ralph touched her cheek affectionately, without taking his eyes off the road. "It would be if I had one, sweetheart. You'd better settle for being married to a sparetime painter, who's never likely to be anything more."

Marianne's heart sank. Had he settled for that? Come to terms with the trap marriage and fatherhood was? If so, the resentment he was increasingly unable to hide would surely worsen, and erode their happiness.

She eyed his craggy profile, which was undeniably strong. Yet he lacked the ruthlessness necessary to succeed as an artist, in any field, which Marianne had long since discovered was in her own nature. It had enabled her to break free of her conventional upbringing, eschew the family ethos to live in London, which few Jewish girls had dared do in those days. There she had reencountered Ralph, whom she had met briefly during the war.

Martin leaned forward to drop his banana skin into the paper bag on her lap and gave her a sticky kiss, before curling up to the back seat again. She could sense his sympathy for her. For his father, too. Young though he was, he had perceived that his parents were troubled by an insoluble problem, the intricacies of which were beyond him. What would he say if he knew he was the sole reason for their marriage? Marianne wondered wryly. When he grew up, perhaps she would tell him the whole story. How she and Ralph had lived together because she'd promised her mother and father she would never marry out of the faith. "It isn't like you to break a promise, Mum," Martin would say to her. And she would have to explain that only getting pregnant had caused her to do so. And that, in the end, her parents had forgiven her for everything.

Martin returned her briefly to the mundane. "Anything else to eat, Mum?"

Marianne handed him a pear. He would never be faced with the painful dilemmas of her youth. There was nothing he could do that she wouldn't try to understand. Her forgiveness would never be necessary.

As for her husband, she must put on her thinking cap. Marriage was like a plant that had to be nurtured, her grandmother had once told her. And was just as liable to wither, if you let it, Marianne thought, once a canker began eating away its roots. She would get a part-time job, whether Ralph liked it or not. Present him with a *fait accompli*. Make it possible for him to cut down his work at the agency. The rest would be up to him.

"You're too quiet. What are you plotting?" Ralph smiled.

"Who, me?" How well he knew her!

Chapter Eleven

Sarah was ensconced behind her two outsize teapots, happily surveying the familiar Sabbath afternoon scene. Her parlor was a spacious room but today did not seem large enough.

The ravenheads and redheads who were Sarah and Abraham's descendants were cheek by jowl with Sigmund and Rachel Moritz's smaller brood who, except for the absent Miriam, all had fair or mousy coloring. Present, too, were those who had become part of the clan by marriage. Two of whom were Gentiles, Sarah reflected, glancing at Lyn and Ralph—something she could not have imagined herself accepting. But the pain incurred by not doing so was worse, she had learned.

Her gaze roved to Matthew and Margaret, who were helping themselves to sandwiches at the octagonal tea table. How good it was to have Arnold's wife and children within the fold at last. David's recovery was not the only answered prayer for which Sarah had fervently thanked God in *shul* this morning. And if Arnold would one day turn up here with them, her cup of joy would be full to overflowing.

"Why aren't you eating?" she asked Martin. She had insisted that the children be allowed by their parents to have tea in the parlor, as this was her first *Shabbos* home from America. If Sarah had her way, they would never be relegated to the kitchen.

Martin patted his stomach. "Who could eat tea after a lunch at Grandma Esther's?" He eyed the table. "Just my luck I'm not hungry when I could have smoked salmon!"

"Auntie Bessie brought it for the sandwiches, so today would be a real party," Sarah told him. The expensive delicacy was not usually part of her *Shabbos* afternoon repast.

"In the States, they eat it for breakfast," David conveyed. "Only they call it lox."

"I don't even get it for supper," Martin told everyone.

Marianne laughed. "What he means is we can't afford it."

Shirley smiled complacently. "I suppose a person has to live within their means." She eyed Marianne's gray tweed skirt, yellow sweater and sensible shoes. You could put together a smart outfit even if your budget only ran to Marks and Spencer, but Shirley's writer-cousin had never been interested in clothes. Only Marianne would turn up at their grandmother's *Shabbos* gathering dressed for a country hike!

Peter was studying his wife, comparing her careful elegance with Marianne's casual appearance. Shirley had on a brown wool crepe dress she had bought from Kendal Milne's model gown department that morning, and the string of cultured pearls her father had given her when her son was born. She was chicness personified, from her bouffant coiffeur to her tan alligator court shoes. But the joy of living that had once softened her artifice was no longer there.

"A person can live without luxuries," Sarah smiled to Marianne. "So long as you're happy, what does it matter?"

"It doesn't," Peter said.

Rebecca got up from the sofa. "I can't remember a single *Shabbos* afternoon when Ma didn't say, 'So long as you're happy.'" She handed her teacup to Sarah to be refilled. "As if happiness were dependent upon this, that, or the other! Happiness is different things to different people," she informed her mother-in-law. "There's no universal recipe for it."

She returned to her seat to drink her tea, but slopped some of it onto the carpet and the others noted that her hands were trembling.

This was the first family gathering Rebecca had attended since taking the overdose and everyone had studiously ignored her strung-up demeanor. They were well practiced in doing so. She had shown signs of her private trauma for years, though never so markedly as now.

"Stop pretending there's nothing the matter with me, when you all know I'm shot to pieces!" she exclaimed. "You think I'm a nutcase, don't you?" she said stridently.

Sarah was thankful that the children had just left the room, to play in the attic. "Nobody thinks anything of the kind," she said to Rebecca.

"Why don't you and I go and have a nice quiet chat in the dining room, Rebecca?" Bessie suggested soothingly.

"You're my pal, Bessie. Don't you start humoring me, too."

"If you don't feel well, I'll take you home, Rebecca," Nathan said quietly.

"What for? I don't get treated any differently there than I do here. Everyone, including you, seems to think they have to be careful with me—just because I woke up in the night with a muzzy head and took some more pills to make me fall asleep again!"

Leona got up and left the room. Frank Moritz put down the book he had been pretending to read and followed her. A moment later, Henry left, too.

"What am I? A leper or something?" Rebecca said with a wry break in her husky voice.

Nathan exchanged a glance with Ronald.

Rebecca noted the glance and laughed. "Don't bother putting your medical hats on, you two! I'm not ill. Just bloody miserable. But my husband will probably diagnose me as paranoiac, after the things I've just said."

Lyn Klein, for whom this was the first full family gathering she had attended, stared into the fire to hide her embarrassment. Arnold had told her that the atmosphere at Sarah's tea parties sometimes rippled with undercurrents, but she had thought he was exaggerating. She could feel the animosity between Rebecca and Nathan. Sigmund and David looked as if they were forcibly restraining themselves from speaking. Shirley and Anne were carefully devoting their attention to playing with the cat, which was sprawled on its back at their feet. Marianne was examining her fingernails and Ronald studying the carved cornice as if he had never seen it before.

"You'll get used to it," Ralph whispered in Lyn's ear. "It took me quite a time to."

"A fine homecoming for Mother and me this is!" David boomed, unable to contain himself any longer.

His daughter-in-law went to sit beside him. "Don't get upset, Pop, it's bad for you," she said. Initially, she had not liked David, but time had revealed to her the soft center beneath his habitual ebullience.

David patted her cheek. "You're a good girl, Diane." And a more affectionate one than my daughter, he thought, glancing at Shirley, who had seemed cool—or was it strained? —with him since his return home.

"Tell us some more about New York," Esther requested.

Sarah heaved a sigh of relief. The conversation was back on an even keel.

"David's told us hardly anything," Bessie said, giving him a sidelong glance.

"Dad isn't himself yet." Ronald eyed his father's weary posture and pale countenance.

"Who isn't?" David said.

"It will take you some time to recover your full strength," his son answered professionally.

"Nonsense. I'll be back at the factory next week."

"Isn't that a bit soon, Dad?" Shirley said.

"For what?" David asked edgily.

Sarah prepared herself for the next bout of conflict. She could feel it coming.

Laura Kohn, who had entered and seated herself on her grandfather's lap, wound her arms around David's neck. "Don't worry about Grandpa, Mummy," she smiled to Shirley. "He won't have to work at the factory for much longer, will he?"

Shirley and Peter glanced at each other surreptitiously.

"Little piggies have big ears," Peter declared ruefully.

David set Laura on her feet and rose ominously from his armchair. "Would you like to tell me what my granddaughter knows, that I don't?"

His daughter and son-in-law remained silent.

"What's been going on at Sanderstyle while I've been away?" he asked Bessie.

"Would I know?" she shrugged. "I'm only Shirley's mother and your wife. When it comes to the business, the two of you tell me nothing."

Two angry patches of color appeared on David's high cheekbones.

"Don't get worked up, it isn't good for you," Nathan warned him.

"All of a sudden our Nat is showing concern for me!" David said, venting his feelings upon him.

Nathan turned on his heel and left the room.

"If we go on like this, the parlor will soon be empty," Lyn whispered to Ralph.

"It wouldn't be the first time," he told her in an undertone. "At first, it's a shock to us untemperamental *goyim*. So is how quickly they get over it."

Over the outburst—but not the grievance, Lyn thought. It seemed to her that her husband's family was caught in a web of long-standing grievances. But Arnold had carried his too far.

"I'm waiting for you to explain," David said to Shirley and Peter.

"We'll go into it another time," Shirley replied.

"We'll go into it now! What have you got planned for me? An early retirement?"

"Not in the way you mean," Shirley said.

David gave her a look that caused her to quail. "How many ways are there?" He sat down in his chair, as if the surge of strength that had enabled him to rise in anger had ebbed away.

"How dare you do this to your father, Shirley?" Sarah demanded imperiously. "What kind of daughter are you?"

"A better one than he gives me credit for. But Dad isn't going to believe it." Her father was looking so agitated, she had no option but to tell him what she must here and now. With her interfering relations present to take his side. And before she had forewarned her mother and brother.

Marianne, whom Shirley have never considered a friend, let alone an ally, came to her rescue. "Why don't the rest of us clear out of here for a few minutes?" she said tactfully. "Let Shirley and Peter talk to Uncle David privately?"

Hannah Moritz, who remained her usual calm self whatever the circumstances, agreed. "I was about to suggest it."

Shirley gave Marianne and Hannah a grateful smile. "I'd appreciate it, if nobody minds. But I'd like Mam and Ronald, and Bobbie to stay."

"I wouldn't dream of leaving," Sarah said. There was nothing affecting any branch of her family that she did not make her personal concern.

"Get on with it," David said to Shirley when their relatives had departed to the dining room. He listened without interrupting, while she outlined "the golden opportunity" that had come his way.

"Is that what you call it?" he said when she had finished speaking. "Maybe it is. For you and Peter to get rid of me."

"There's rarely a sole reason for anything," Peter said. "To be entirely honest, which I'm afraid my dear wife is not being, I wouldn't mind if Sanderstyle no longer belonged to the family. It's no secret that I personally have no emotional involvement with the firm."

"Too true!" Shirley cut in nastily.

"It might remove some of the strain from our relationship if you hadn't," Peter told her. "But my main reason for hoping you'll accept the offer is that you've worked too hard for too long," he said to David.

David did not doubt his son-in-law's sincerity, though he had begun to doubt his daughter's. "I appreciate your consideration for me, Peter. But I'm not an old man, even though I probably seem one to you. And next to my family, my business is my life."

"We don't need telling that," Shirley said.

David gave her an icy glance. "Which makes what you're suggesting all the more distasteful to me. The pattern of your life wouldn't be changed by the takeover, I gather from what you've told me. But you don't seem to have given a thought to what your father would do with his days."

"Get under his wife's feet," Bessie said. "And I don't think I'd like it."

David permitted himself a weary smile. He ought to have expected his wife to see things from her own point of view.

"Dad isn't the kind to retire," Ronald said to his sister. "If you'd mentioned this to me in advance, I'd have told you to forget it."

"No doubt, as you don't have to work with Dad," Shirley retorted. "He's a very difficult man."

Sarah could remain silent no longer. "As he has you to deal with, I'm not surprised. What you deserve, Shirley, is that one day your children should be this way with you."

"They wouldn't need to be. Not about the business. What Peter calls my emotional involvement with it isn't that at all. It's just my sense of family responsibility. I'm not sentimental about Sanderstyle, like Dad is. If it was mine, I'd sell it without a second thought."

Mark had come quietly into the room to fetch his sweater—the attic was a draughty place—and paused by the door, arrested by what Shirley had just said. "You wouldn't really sell Sanderstyle, would you, Mum?" he asked her accusingly.

"We seem to have another big-ears in our family, Peter!" Shirley exclaimed impatiently. "If Laura hadn't heard what wasn't intended for her, this matter could have been dealt with in a businesslike way, at the office."

"You won't let Mum sell Sanderstyle, will you, Grandpa?" young Mark appealed to David. "Because I want to work there, with you, when I grow up."

David gazed into the little boy's earnest dark eyes. "So that's your ambition, is it?" he inquired thoughtfully.

"I just said so, didn't I?"

"And I'm happy to hear it. Now run along and play, Mark."

David waited for Mark to leave, then turned his attention to Shirley. "The discussion is over," he declared shortly. "And don't ever bother reopening it."

"So one day you'll drop dead at the factory," Shirley shrugged.

And your son, not you, will inherit the business, David decided. Ronald had not wanted to come into it and to Shirley, he had distressingly learned, it meant nothing more than pounds, shillings and pence. But she would never have the power to sell her father's life's work to strangers.

Chapter Twelve

After walking out of Sarah's parlor, Leona had grabbed her coat from the hallstand and left the house. Frank had put on his and followed her and they were now tramping along Cheetham Hill Road in the chilly evening air.

"It's going to rain," Frank said.

"Who cares?"

"You will, if you get soaking wet. We haven't got an umbrella."

"Why must you be so damned practical, Frank?"

"A person can't change their nature."

More's the pity, Leona thought. "I feel like doing something utterly shocking!" she exclaimed mutinously. "To let off steam."

"Don't be daft, Leona."

She eyed his unremarkable profile and sighed. Henry wouldn't have told her not to be daft; he'd have suggested something shocking to do. Leona would then have capped his suggestion with a more outrageous one of her own and so it would go on. There had been a running battle for supremacy between her and Henry all their lives.

"Let's jump on a bus," Frank said as they reached a bus stop and saw a number sixty-two approaching.

Jumping on a bus was as exciting a suggestion as Frank was ever likely to make!

"The rain's started," he said, holding out his hand to catch a drop.

And even that suggestion was made for a practical reason.

"I'd rather jump on one that's going the other way," Leona said, to be difficult, and darted recklessly between the traffic to the opposite side of the road.

"Be careful!" Frank shouted from the curb.

Frank's trouble was that he was too careful!

"At this time on a Saturday, the buses to town are full up, with people going out for the evening," he said when he joined her and the bus soared past, its passengers crammed together like winter-coated sardines. "Why wait to get on one, which we probably won't, when we have no particular reason to go to town?"

"Having no particular reason to do something can be a reason in itself to do it," Leona said loftily.

"In one of those moods, are you?" Frank turned up her coat collar, to protect her neck from the downpour. "Green suits you," he remarked.

Henry would have added that it went with her mentality.

"Your hands must be freezing, Leona. Where are your gloves?"

"In my bloody pocket," she said irritably.

Frank fished them out and put them on for her, as if she were a child. "What would happen to you without me to look after you?" he chided with a smile.

Leona returned the smile. But if she let him go on looking after her, she would never find out. She had not really been aware that he did, until they began going to the same college. Then it struck her that he always had. She could remember

Frank drying her tears when they were small children. And
Henry scoffing at her for crying. And once, when Henry had
snipped the end off one of her pigtails, Frank had socked him
on the nose.

"We may as well walk to town," she said striding off
abruptly.

"What will we do when we get there?" Frank inquired
when he caught up with her.

"Does it matter? With you, the means always has to be
justified by the end!" And why did he never argue with her?
Insist on doing something his way, instead of always allowing
Leona to have hers? Even the preferences and protests he
occasionally voiced were geared to her welfare.

I'm an ungrateful bitch, she thought contritely, glancing at
his dripping wet hair. And Frank is a darling, for putting up
with me. How many men would subject themselves to an
unnecessary drenching, to satisfy the whim of a bloody-
minded girl? Certainly not Henry. But Frank was the very
opposite to him. Kind and considerate. A wonderful person.

So why have I begun seeing his virtues as faults? Leona
asked herself as he steered her around a puddle. I didn't
before Henry went away to college in London. In the days
when we were a threesome—with Frank's role that of the
referee! Only since she and Frank became a twosome had
Leona found herself comparing him with Henry. Seeing him
as a person, instead of just the pleasant half of the Moritz
twins.

A black limousine, with white ribbons strung festively
across the bonnet, flashed past and Leona caught a glimpse of
a bride and groom, seated with their arms around each other.
They must have been married at St. Luke's, or one of the
other churches higher up the main road, she guessed, and
were now on the way to their wedding reception. And to a
thrilling new life.

The sense of romance which always affected Leona when
she saw a bride, took her momentarily in its grip. Then the
thought of her parents' marriage swiftly dispelled it. Her
mother had once told her that she'd been madly in love with
her father when she married him. This rare confidence had
been followed by a stern warning that marrying a man you
were sure you could trust was more important than whether
or not he excited you.

The rain had turned to sleet, but Leona barely noticed it. Was it seeing the bride that had returned her mother's words to her mind? Not that alone. It had something to do with what she'd been thinking about Frank and Henry, who were not her blood relatives, though she'd always considered them cousins. They were just two boys with whom she happened to have been raised in the Sandberg-Moritz family circle. And Frank was in love with her. She couldn't go on refusing to recognize it.

He had not said so in words, but had no need to, Leona thought when, a little while later, they were seated opposite each other in the aromatic warmth of a Kardomah Café on Market Street, sipping the hot, milky beverage known in that establishment as a coffee-dash.

Frank watched her take off her beret, which was wet enough to require wringing out. "You look like a half-drowned marmalade cat," he smiled, leaning over to mop her hair with his handkerchief. "A very beautiful one," he added in his matter-of-fact way.

Only Frank could tell a girl she was beautiful without it sounding remotely romantic, Leona thought wryly. His gentle brown eyes were surveying her quizzically through the horn-rimmed spectacles he had worn from such an early age, they were part of his personality. Like the snub nose that lent a misleading perkiness to his pale features, and the slightly lumbering gait that went with his stocky build. Sometimes he irritated Leona, but he was cuddly and comforting like the teddy bear she used to take to bed when she was small. A safe and reassuring presence. She would trust Frank Moritz with her life. And, according to her mother, nothing was more important than that.

"My mother was very young when she married my father," Leona said thoughtfully. "She was only eighteen."

"And?" Frank said helpfully. Being a good listener was another of his virtues.

"Perhaps it was because she was so young, and Dad was the only chap she ever dated, that she made a mistake."

"Possibly," Frank answered. "Though I don't think age or experience necessarily comes into it." He stirred his coffee-dash carefully. "I've known you were the right girl for me since I was five."

Leona avoided his eye.

"Or that's how it seems to me now," he added quietly. "There's never been any other girl but you, Leona. And there never will be."

"I can think of one or two at college who would be disappointed to hear it," Leona said lightly, and saw Frank's expression cloud.

The brown-uniformed waitress was depositing a plate of pastries on the next table, where a dark-haired girl with oversized breasts was exchanging a lingering glance with the pimply youth holding her hand. Young couples at other tables were similarly engaged and Leona visualized the same scene being enacted, right now, in tea shops up and down the country. The Saturday-night atmosphere was in the air, heady as the girls' scents mingling with the aroma of coffee drifting from the urns on the service counter. Heavy with the promise of exciting hours to come, redolent of romance with a capital R.

"Fancy seeing a film?" Frank asked.

Leona shook her head. How could he be so matter-of-fact, when he had just expressed his feelings for her?

"If you like, we can go to the college dance?"

"No thanks."

"What would you like to do, then?"

Be with someone who sets me alight, Leona thought. "Let's have another coffee-dash," she said.

"Henry's thinking of staying on in London during the Christmas vacation," Frank told her while trying to attract the waitress's attention.

"I don't suppose he'd ever come home if his socks didn't need darning occasionally."

"Would it bother you if he didn't?"

"What sort of question is that?"

"A very pertinent one, I think."

"Pertinent to what?"

"You and me. But one of these days you'll come to your senses, Leona."

"Would you mind telling me what you're talking about?"

"The way you're wasting your love on Henry."

When Nathan and Rebecca arrived home from the tea party, Rebecca went upstairs to soothe her nerves with a warm bath. Bridie was spending the evening with a friend and silence hung heavy as a pall in the house, accentuating Nathan's loneliness.

He tried to settle down in the living room and read but even the poems of Catullus, which carried him back to the hopeful years of his youth, provided no solace tonight. And the ache in his loins, which he usually managed to ignore, was giving him no peace. How long was it since he had had a woman?

The last time had been in Switzerland, when he went to a medical convention and accepted the invitation of an attractive French doctor to share her bed. And the encounter with Henriette, whose surname he could not remember, had been like partaking of a good meal after a long fast.

Sometimes he lay awake at night remembering it. The casual way in which Henriette had removed her clothes, as if there were nothing untoward about stripping before a casual male acquaintance. About sexual pleasure between a man and a woman. The very opposite of Rebecca, for whom sex was, and always had been, the root cause of her anti-Nathan phobia. She had built a wall around her natural feelings after discovering Nathan had still been in love with Mary when he bedded his bride. And had penalized him with deprivation, Nathan thought bitterly. Driven him into the kind of occasional encounter he had enjoyed with Henriette.

"Oh, you're skulking in here, are you?" Rebecca said from the doorway.

His wife was still a luscious-looking woman, Nathan noted, allowing his gaze to rove from her shapely hips to the billowing cleavage visible at the neckline of her beige satin wrapper.

"Would it worry you if I had an affair?" he asked her.

"Why should it?" she replied brusquely. "You're nothing to me."

But a flicker of apprehension had shadowed her lovely eyes, Nathan noticed. Was it possible that she still loved him? If so, she was even more of a masochist than he'd taken her for. "In that case, maybe I will," he said.

"Who with?"

"There are plenty of willing women around. They're not all cold fish, like you."

Rebecca's lower lip trembled.

"I seem to have touched a raw nerve," Nathan said unkindly.

"Who made me become one?" she asked accusingly.

"Yourself. And until you realize it, you'll continue to be one," he informed her. Before the trouble between them began, she had been the opposite of cold. They had made love with joyous abandon. A distant remembrance of Rebecca lying naked on their bed, her body gleaming silkily in the lamplight with her raven hair spread upon the pillow in a glorious tangle, caused Nathan's pulse to throb.

"What are you thinking about?" Rebecca asked him.

"The way we were," he said thickly and was unable to stop himself from touching her.

"What're you doing?" she said nervously.

"What I ought to have done long ago," he answered in a voice which did not sound like his own. "Taking what's mine." He forced her down onto the sofa and crushed her mouth with his. But why wasn't she trying to push him away? Instead, her soft arms were around his neck as he undid her wrapper. She wanted this as much as he did. And soon, her sweetness was all around him.

Happiness such as he had never expected to experience again soared within Nathan, and sensual delight came second to the balm refreshing his soul. The lonely years were over. His marriage would be a real one, from now on.

David was seated in his wing chair, contemplating the artificial coals enlivening the electric fire in the living room hearth. He would have preferred a real fire, but such homely comforts had been banished from his life. Bessie was afraid of soot soiling her wallpaper and upholstery and was currently campaigning for central heating to be installed.

"You'd be more comfortable lying on the sofa," she said to him solicitously.

"I'm fine here, thanks."

"I'll get you a footstool, then."

"Don't bother!" he flashed. "How many times must I tell you I'm not an invalid? I did my recuperating in New York."

"With your sister-in-law fussing over you, instead of me."

Miriam had not fussed, but David thought it best not to say so. "I'm sorry you were deprived of the privilege, love," he said in a light tone. This was the first time since his return that Bessie had mentioned Miriam. The omission had been more telling than anything she might have said and David did not want the conversation to develop along acrimonious lines.

Bessie was hovering beside him, with her mink coat draped over her arm.

"You'll be late for your night out, if you don't leave soon," David said glancing at his watch.

"It isn't a night out, David," Bessie answered reproachfully. She smoothed down the skirt of her black cocktail gown. "And if you'd rather I didn't go, I won't. The girls will understand."

The branch of WIZO of which Bessie was an active member, had arranged a fund-raising dance for that evening.

"Someone else can take charge of the tambala, it doesn't have to be me," she added, fiddling with her pearls.

David rose from his chair, took her coat and helped her on with it. "I want you to carry on exactly as you did before I went to the States, Bessie."

"When you were well, you used to come with me to the social functions."

"I am well," David said. "And I'll come with you to the next one, love. I'm still a little tired from the flight home, or I'd come with you tonight."

Bessie eyed him anxiously. "You will tell Lizzie, if you suddenly feel faint, or anything?"

David curbed a sharp reply and ushered her out of the room.

The maid popped her head out of the kitchen doorway. "T'master'll be all right, Mrs. Sandberg. Ah'll tek good care of 'im."

David lost his temper. "If the two of you don't stop this, I'll get on the next plane back to New York! And what's with the Mrs. Sandberg, Lizzie? When our name has been Sanderton for umpteen years!"

"Ah mun be gettin' absen'-minded in me old age," Lizzie apologized.

"I'll forgive you," David smiled.

Lizzie returned the smile. She and her employer had long ago established a perfect understanding. And after thirty years under his roof she felt entitled to speak her mind. "But Ah don't think t'rest o't'family's ever forgiven you."

David was the only Sandberg who had Anglicized his name.

Bessie was fiddling with her hair in front of the hall mirror. "I still feel guilty about leaving you to spend the evening alone," she said to David.

David took her arm, opened the front door and bundled her out of the house.

"Ah'll never get over t'missis learnin' to drive," Lizzie said.

David shut the door, after watching Bessie back her car gingerly down the drive. "And I'll never recover from what it cost me in driving lessons. If you'd like to watch TV I'll go and sit in the dining room, Lizzie."

"Turn yer out o't' lounge, Mr. Sanderton?" she replied as if he had made an outrageous suggestion. "Ah wouldn't dream of it. Besides, Ah'd rather listen to *Sat'day Night Theatre* on't'wireless."

"I was thinking of getting a TV set for the kitchen," David told her.

Lizzie straightened her flowered pinafore and went to remove some dead leaves from the ivy that lived in a dark corner of the oak-paneled hall. "Save yer brass fer summat more useful," she said in her no-nonsense manner. "Just because yer brother's bought one fer Bridie, yer don't 'ave ter do t'same fer me."

David watched her angular back recede toward her own domain—she had fought Bessie's attempts to modernize the kitchen which, to David, was the comfiest room in the house.

"As yer don't want fussin' over, Ah shan't mek yer a cup o' cocoa 'til yer asks fer it," she called over her shoulder.

A surge of affection for her welled up in David. Good old Lizzie. What would they do without her? She had stood fast with his family through thick and thin. And had put her oar in when she felt it necessary! David thought with a smile. Especially when, in her view, those around her needed bringing down to earth. She'd been only a gangling girl when she came to work for him, but even in those days she had shown her mettle. And would doubtless give Shirley a piece of her mind if she knew what his daughter had planned for him.

David returned to the living room and his solitary armchair, more weary than he would be prepared to admit. The confrontation with Shirley at his mother's, that afternoon, had come as an immense shock.

Was there no end to the disappointments life had in store for him? But perhaps it was to be expected that his daughter, whom he had ensured would never have to struggle for a livelihood, would not place the same value on the fruits of his toil as David himself did. The thought was cold comfort, for at the back of David's mind was a word he had never before had to apply to Shirley. Disloyalty.

Would he one day suffer the same disappointment from Shirley's son? David thought not. There was about Mark a quality of sincerity his mother had never displayed. David had seen it shining from his eyes, that afternoon.

The doorbell chimed its repetitive tune and David heard Lizzie go to open the door.

"What brings you out on a nasty night like this?" he heard her say in the warm voice in which she addressed her favorite members of the clan. "It's Mr. Ben, ter see yer," she called to David.

"Don't get up, I'm only your brother-in-law!" Ben Klein said when he entered the room. "And in your house, I can help myself to a drink." He went directly to the cocktail cabinet and poured himself a stiff Scotch. "A nice bit of furniture, this," he remarked, eyeing the carved walnut piece. "I've always thought so."

David could see a muscle twitching in his cheek and knew he was just making conversation, that his mind was churning with whatever was worrying him.

"I'll tell you why I need a drink when I've had it," Ben said sipping the liquor. "Not that I couldn't have had one in my own house, of course," he added with the twisted smile that lent charm to his somewhat saturnine face.

He tossed down the rest of the whiskey and David was surprised to see him pour himself another. Ben wasn't a drinker. What the hell was wrong? They were more like brothers than brothers-in-law. Before Ben married Esther, he had been the Sandbergs' lodger in their little house in Strangeways and David had taken to him the moment they met. He had recognized in Ben the same stamina and will to succeed that was in himself. And the same selfless protectiveness toward kith and kin. When one of them had a problem, he invariably turned to the other.

"I heard you had a barney with your daughter before I arrived at Ma's this evening," Ben said. He sat down in the red leather club chair on the other side of the hearth. "You can fill me in on the details later. First, I have to get off my chest the latest aggravation I've got with my son. As usual, Harry thinks he knows better than I do!"

"I've had to put up with that from Shirley for years," David sighed. "So what's Henry on about now?"

"He wants me to open another store. And in town, no less! There's a small shop to let, near Market Street—I was so worked up, the name of the street it's on didn't register with me—which he says will do to begin with!"

"Hm," David said thoughtfully.

"Hm, is right!"

"Have you discussed this with Esther, Ben?"

"If I hadn't, I wouldn't have needed a drink. Your sister agrees with her son, that it's time we expanded." Ben sprang up from his chair and paced the room. "For her, that boy can do no wrong! She thinks everything Harry says is a pearl of wisdom. Being cut off from her other son has biased her. It's affected her judgment."

"Come off it, Ben," David said. "When it comes to business, nothing has ever affected my sister's judgment. Esther is as shrewd as you or me and always has been."

"She says it's me who's biased. That I won't entertain the idea just because it's come from Harry," Ben said with asperity.

"She could be right."

"Whose side are you on, David?"

"You came here for my advice, I presume? Not just for sympathy?"

"Sure."

"Then forget about taking sides."

Ben sat down in the chair again and David paused to survey him. There was about him the hurt weariness that comes from a contretemps with someone you love who is also a thorn in your side. Which just about sums up Ben's relationship with Harry and mine with Shirley, David thought wryly. We look on their business ideas as lacking in caution, likely to land us in Queer Street, and are inclined to forget that they've helped us to build the business up. David and Ben had done the back-breaking spade work unaided, but plenty had been added since and credit must be given where it was due.

"The trouble with Harry is he wants to run before he can walk!" Ben burst forth.

"Cool down," David said, noting that the eczema that always broke out on Ben's hands in times of stress was well in evidence.

"A chain store tycoon my son wants me to be—overnight!"

"Who'd manage the new shop?"

"What new shop?"

"I agree with Harry and Esther. It's time you spread your wings. And I have no ax to grind."

"I thought you'd agree with me," Ben said uncertainly. "I mean I want to expand, but I wasn't thinking of doing so yet."

"Now's the time, Ben, while trade is on the up. That's a very important factor."

"Another important factor is it would be a way of getting Harry from under my feet! The answer to who'd run the new shop is him, of course. Me, he considers too old-fashioned to manage the kind of store he has in mind, he had the *chutzpah* to tell me! What kind of store that is, I didn't bother to ask him."

"And that's what you'll doubtless have your next barney about," David smiled.

"Too true!"

"Meanwhile, I suggest you sleep on it."

"The last time we expanded the business, I didn't have time to," Ben reminisced.

They sat in companionable silence, remembering the wartime blitz which had wiped out both their premises. Ben's alternative to going out of business had been to rent the only vacant property in the locality, which had, by chance, been sufficiently large to house a walk-around store. David had initially had to make do with a disused church, but had eventually acquired another factory, in a building much more spacious than his original one.

"In those days, a person didn't have to make such decisions; it was in God's hands," Ben smiled as they emerged from their private thoughts and surveyed each other—two aging men, yet each could still see the one-time young man in the other.

"The first time I saw you, you'd just come home from work at your not-yet-father-in-law's sweatshop," Ben recalled.

David was engaged to Miriam then—and Esther to Carl Moritz, he remembered. "And, if my memory serves me correctly, you ate two helpings of my mother's potato *latkes*, when we sat down to supper, but found time to make eyes at my sister," David laughed.

"How was I to know she had a fiancé?"

"Carl couldn't afford to buy her a ring. I didn't buy Miriam one, either. And Bessie's—she, of course, had to have one," David smiled, "was bought with her father's money."

"Who could afford engagement rings in those days?" Ben grinned. "In Strangeways? Esther didn't get one from me until we'd been married a few years. But in some ways people were happier then, David." Ben's expression clouded. "Kids didn't do to their parents what Arnold and Marianne did to their mother and me. I like Ralph, needless to say, and I wouldn't be without my grandson Martin for the world. The same goes for Lyn—I haven't known her for long, but I can tell already she's worth a dozen of my Jewish daughter-in-law. And Arnold's children, I adore them both. But, when I think of what we've been through because of it all—"

Ben took out his handkerchief and blew his nose emotionally.

"If your kids don't put you through the mill one way, they'll do it another," David said after a silence.

Ben rose to leave. "That, I've had time to find out. Esther and me, we couldn't have had a happier marriage. I was thinking about it on the way here tonight. Every row we've ever had has been because of our children."

In that case you're fortunate, David thought as he saw Ben to the door. David wouldn't describe his own marriage as unhappy, but it wasn't happiness either. And there were times when it could only be termed an uneasy peace.

Marianne and Ralph were spending the evening at Arnold's home.

"A fine thing, us having to come here without Mam and Dad," Marianne said to her brother scathingly. "As we're only in Manchester for the weekend, it would be nice if all of us could spend the time together."

"I agree," Lyn said.

Arnold, who was seated by the fire, said nothing.

"Isn't it time you made *sholom* with the family?" Ralph asked him.

"My husband is a prize *shlemiel*," Lyn declared.

Arnold smiled.

"You find this amusing, do you?" Marianne demanded.

"The way my wife and your husband come out with Yiddish and Hebrew words certainly is. If I were them, I'd turn up my nose at anything Jewish."

"Typical!" Lyn snorted.

"Don't be so bloody stupid, Arnold!" Marianne exclaimed. "They're married to Jews."

"But they weren't wanted, were they? By our precious family. And, if I were them, I couldn't forgive that."

Marianne got up to help herself to one of the marshmallows Lyn was toasting over the hot coals. "Well, you're not the forgiving kind, are you, my dear. As everyone knows."

They lapsed into silence and Marianne's gaze roved restlessly around the room. Her brother had done all right for himself. Arnold was now a partner in the law firm to which he had been articled. And was obviously not short of money these days, Marianne thought, noting the new leather Chesterfield and armchair. The carpets and hangings were new, also, and of a good quality. Lyn had excellent taste and had chosen for them a muted shade of gold.

The room, like Marianne's own living room, was a cross between a library and a lounge. The walls were lined with books—unlike Harry's living room, Marianne reflected with a smile, which had an ornate bar, though Harry wasn't a drinker, and—which reflected Ann Klein's tastes—a flock-patterned wallpaper, unhidden by books. Harry had never been a reader.

Marianne's gaze came to rest on the mantelpiece, where photographs of Lyn's dead parents stood side by side with the *Chanukah menorah*. But nowhere in the house was there a picture of Esther and Ben Klein who, to Arnold, might just as well be dead. He never talked about them and kept his lips firmly sealed when others did, Marianne reflected, glancing at her brother and seeing that, in repose, his face was sad. What a fool Arnold was! He had a wife who loved him, whom he adored, two children, and was not short of material comforts. Yet his unforgiving nature barred him from being a happy man.

"If you think it's odd that Ralph and Lyn don't hate everything Jewish, how come you don't feel that way yourself?" Marianne asked him with her eyes still on the *menorah*.

"Don't think I haven't asked myself that," Arnold answered brusquely. "My mind tells me I'm behaving illogically. But my heart propels me to *shul* every *Shabbos*."

"I don't recall your heart doing that before you married Lyn," Marianne said.

"It didn't."

"Then what propels you probably isn't your heart. It's your conscience, Arnold. Guilt."

"Oh yes?" he flashed.

Marianne held her brother's gaze steadily. She was aware of her husband and sister-in-law carefully avoiding looking at them, but Ralph and Lyn's withdrawal was understandable. They were wary of treading the dangerous ground all four in this room knew too well and, as a rule, instinctively skirted, as was sometimes necessary in even the happiest of inter-marriages.

"Guilty I'm not," Arnold declared, "because I don't reckon I've done anything wrong."

"How can you possibly say that? When, like me, you committed the unforgivable sin?"

"Don't be so melodramatic!"

"In our religion, that's what marrying-out is," Marianne reminded him. "And though not many of our brethren live entirely by the book nowadays, the sin we're discussing still remains, for most, a grave one. And I maintain, Arnold, what I said that started all this off—that you know you're guilty of it, whether you admit it to yourself or not. So you've become more formally religious in every way open to you, to compensate."

"Stuff and nonsense! Don't you agree with me, Lyn?"

"As you're asking my opinion," Lyn said, poking the fire carefully, "I think Marianne's theory is very interesting."

"So do I," Ralph put in.

Arnold glanced at his wife, then watched Ralph painstakingly light his pipe. "What the hell do you two know about it?"

Lyn exchanged a glance with Ralph.

"We might be *goyim,* but we nevertheless are capable of observation," Ralph said electing himself the spokesman. "There's a Jewish account executive at our agency, Len Richards. I think you met him once, Marianne—"

"And I didn't like him," Marianne cut in. "Too smooth."

"But he'll go far—"

"What has this to do with anything?" Arnold interrupted. "I had the feeling you were about to compare this chap my sister doesn't like with me," he glared at Ralph.

"But only in one respect, Arnold. Like you, he's married to a *shiksah,* and he too seems to be a fervent *shul*-goer."

"So is Marianne, nowadays," Arnold said. "I wonder if she's applied her guilt-theory to herself?"

"As I've always accepted my guilt, it wasn't necessary," Marianne informed him. "I've begun going to *shul* regularly because I happen to enjoy—and really understand—the Re-

form services. But I don't live according to the letter of the
Jewish Law, like you do, Arnold."

"And like Len Richards does," Ralph supplied. "His wife
buys the meat from a *kosher* butcher."

"So do I, because of Arnold," Lyn said.

"Well, I don't," Marianne confessed. "But then, unlike Len
Richards and my brother, I'm not busy compensating for my
sin."

"Why do you always make trouble?" Arnold accused her.
"Except when you visit us, Lyn and I never talk about
religion."

"The rest of the time you just think about it," Marianne
answered dryly. "And don't tell me that isn't so."

"Of course it is," Lyn declared vehemently. "With Arnold a
repentant Jew, me an unrepentant nonchurchgoing Christian
and the kids nothing? If we were childless, it wouldn't matter,
and I don't think it would if Arnold weren't so pointedly
devout. But, as things are—I've suggested, more than once,
that the kids and I convert to Judaism, but my husband won't
hear of it."

"Under any other circumstances, would you choose to be
Jewish?" Arnold asked his wife.

"I doubt it."

"Exactly," Arnold said. "As for Matthew and Margaret, in
my view they're lucky."

"How do you make that out?" Lyn inquired, exchanging a
glance with Marianne. Was Arnold really unaware of the
confusion he had created for his children?

"They'll have something I didn't have. Religious choice,"
he said, proving that he was.

"That was the idea, and initially I agreed," Lyn persisted.
"But now, I'm far from sure."

"And, as you've seen fit to entrench them in the bosom of
my family, they'll probably choose to be Jewish—God help
'em!" Arnold said bitterly. "If I had my way, I'd abolish
religion."

"Me too," Marianne endorsed. "But, as it still exists, I've
come to terms with it."

Ralph eyed her fondly. "You look like a kid of ten, in that
dress, Marianne."

"It shrank in the wash," she said ruefully, pulling the red
knitted garment down over her skinny knees.

"My wife wouldn't really like to abolish religion," Ralph

grinned to Arnold and Lyn. "For her, it's all bound up with family life, Sarah Sandberg-style."

"So I enjoy being part of a clan," Marianne shrugged, flicking her thick black fringe away from her eyes.

"I'm sure I shall, too. When I get used to the dramatics," Lyn smiled.

Ralph laughed. "Having had time to get used to them, I agree." He observed Arnold's stiff expression. "So would you, Arnold. If you'd stop being so bloody stubborn and give it a try."

"I don't have time for hobnobbing with relations these days, Ralph," Arnold answered brusquely. "I've committed myself to politics."

"And with your stiff upper lip there's no need to tell us to which party," Marianne said.

"That's right. And, sooner or later, I shall be a Tory MP."

"I was hoping he wouldn't mention it," Lyn, who shared Marianne's Liberal views, said.

Marianne returned to the main topic of the evening: what else but getting her brother back within the family fold had all that talk been about? "Even the prime minister has time for his family," she said pointedly.

Arnold made no reply.

"What can you do with a man like him?" Lyn sighed.

"Let him stew in his own juice," Marianne said crisply. She disliked clichés, but that one summed up her sentiments regarding her brother. The trouble was that her parents, who weren't getting any younger, must continue to suffer in consequence. And for what? Nothing more than Arnold's stupid pride.

Chapter Thirteen

A few days after Ben had visited David at home, Harry called to see him at the factory.

"Sit down, lad," David invited the anxious-faced man his eldest nephew had become. Harry had always been the image of Ben, but in his youth there had been a sparkle to him. As there probably was about me in my youth, David reflected. But oh, how fleeting that sparkle was! There was nothing like responsibility for knocking it out of you.

"No thanks," he smiled when Harry offered him a cigarette. The worried businessman's palliative was now forbidden to David. "The doctor in New York ordered me to kick the habit—his words. Tell me how? I said. Try eating candy when you feel like a smoke, he answered. He'd like me to suffer from obesity, instead!"

"Nice flowers," Harry remarked, admiring the vase of bronze chrysanthemums on David's desk.

"From the staff," David told him with a pleased smile. The welcome he had received from his employees had touched him. But he hadn't taken kindly to their reminding him that he had made himself ill from overwork, or to their warnings that he must take things easier. Moishe Lipkin had given him a bunch of black grapes and this, too, had upset David. Black grapes were for invalids and David did not see himself in that light.

Harry's cigarette smoke drifted tantalizingly to his nostrils. "So say whatever is on your chest, Harry—and stop puffing smoke onto mine," he said edgily.

"My dad must have told you what I have in mind for the business?"

"Yes."

"So what do you think, Uncle?"

David got up and glanced out of the window. Some floral print was being carried into the warehouse loading bay. Floral-patterned raincoats? What was Shirley thinking of? Not thinking of—doing! She must have ordered the stuff behind David's back, while he was away; it had to be for some potty idea she'd dreamed up for next summer's range—and before she'd even finished designing the spring one!

"You really want to know what I think?" he said, turning to face Harry and giving him the kind of look he would shortly give Shirley. "Your father hasn't said yes to you yet, has he?"

"If he had, would I be here?"

"Then give him time to consider it."

"What is there to consider? Either we open another shop, or we don't."

"But our generation—your father's and mine—doesn't like to be bludgeoned into things, Harry."

"You don't want to see reason, either. At least, my father doesn't!"

"Whose idea of reason?" David demanded. "About expansion, I happen to agree with you. But what makes you think you always have to be right?"

"I'm a good businessman, Uncle. And you know it. But Dad's scared to let me take chances."

"And that's his privilege," David declared. "He's still the boss, isn't he?"

"That's the trouble."

"I beg your pardon?" David treated his nephew to an icy stare.

"What have I said?" Harry asked uncomfortably.

"It's what you've inferred that's turned my stomach. Now do me a favor and get out of here, Harry." What is it with the children of men like Ben and me? David asked himself. That they can't wait to get us from under their feet.

Harry shrugged his shoulders, got his coat and left. He had not picked up his cigarettes from the desk and David took one and lit it, to soothe his ruffled feelings.

"Three days back at the office and he's already breaking doctor's orders!" Rita Sternshein exclaimed from the doorway of her sanctum. She strode to David and snatched the comforting weed from his hand. "I'll put up a No Smoking sign in here," she declared as she marched out again. "So your callers won't tempt you."

Shirley entered carrying a sheaf of fashion sketches. "Do you feel up to glancing at these, Dad? Old Eli's been breathing down my neck for them; they're the final drawings for the spring range."

"I'm surprised you're bothering to show them to me," David snapped.

"I can't give the go-ahead until I get your say-so, can I?" she answered with a humoring smile.

"Unfortunately," David said in an accusing voice.

Shirley sighed and glanced at her wristwatch. "Let's leave it until tomorrow, Dad. It's four-thirty and you look as if you've had enough for today. Go home and rest."

David bit back a sharp retort.

"You can't expect to get back into your normal routine immediately. And I don't want you to overtax your strength." Shirley's voice was kind and considerate. She's trying to handle me carefully, David thought with a pang. The way I once had to deal with my father.

"I promised Mam I'd look after you," Shirley said.

And if he let them, between them they'd make him into a useless old man!

"But it shouldn't be necessary," Shirley added. "Why don't you do yourself a favor and accept the takeover bid?"

"I told you the subject is closed," David thundered, feeling his heart palpitate wildly. Did Shirley imagine that, little by little, she could wear down his resistance?

Shirley shrugged her slim shoulders. "I'd tentatively arranged a meeting with them for after Christmas."

"Well you can bleddywell unarrange it! Sanderstyle will never go out of the family."

"Why do you say bleddy? Instead of bloody?" Shirley asked with calculated irrelevance.

"Because I was raised in the Strangeways ghetto! And no matter how high I climb up in the world, traces of my roots will always remain."

Shirley walked to a scratched cheval mirror David kept in a corner of his office and fussed with the bow at the neck of her lemon silk blouse. "You and your roots, Dad!" she smiled. "And the way you hang onto things that remind you of them—like this mirror, that was fit only for the junk shop years ago, but you keep it because it was in your first little factory and came out of the blitz intact. And that battered old orange box that was your very first bookcase, when you were a kid—you've still got that, too, haven't you?"

"Why shouldn't I hang onto things that mean something to me?" David demanded.

"Have I said you shouldn't?"

"Then what are you saying?"

"That it's part of the ridiculous sentimentality that's stopping you from selling out." Shirley turned from the mirror to look at her father. "In some ways, you're hard as nails, Dad, but in others—" She shook her head eloquently. She returned to the desk and kissed David's cheek. "What am I going to do with you?" she sighed.

"Get it into your head, here and now, that it isn't your place to do anything with me," David said stiffly.

Shirley gave him a hurt look and left the office.

David almost called her back to quiz her about the floral-patterned cloth he had seen being delivered, but felt too exhausted to face the argument which would doubtless ensue. During his prolonged absence, his daughter had taken the reins into her hands. But she would have to be made to loose her hold on them. Accept that nothing had changed. That David was still the boss.

He would have to find a way of handling her, as she was carefully handling him. Try not to antagonize her. A great designer she indubitably was, he had to concede as he studied the sketches she had left with him. Better than some who had been trained at art school. Two of Shirley's drawings were of casual coats with zipped fronts and pockets, the kind of smart-yet-easy garments David had seen in the factory he visited in New York—but when had his daughter's ideas not been up-to-the-minute?

David's surge of pride was short-lived, stamped out by remembrance of Shirley's ominous words. "If Sanderstyle were mine, I'd sell it without a second thought," she had said. His daughter had cooked her own goose—though she wouldn't know it until after David's death.

He reached for the telephone to call the firm's lawyer, then changed his mind. Aaron was a family friend and would be horrified by David's intention to sidestep Shirley in his will. "You're setting up trouble between Shirley and her son, when you're gone," Aaron would caution anxiously. As most Jewish lawyers would, David reflected dryly. Who could know better than them the hysterics they might have to deal with when the will was read!

David flicked the intercom switch, to speak to Rita. "I have a small legal matter to attend to and it isn't suitable to use our usual lawyer. Fix me an appointment with someone. And it might be best if he isn't Jewish."

"Are you bringing a case against the community?" she joked.

"I'm not in a laughing mood, Rita."

"You're telling me. And you've set me a poser, haven't you, Mr. Sanderton? The phone directory doesn't have a page headed 'Christian lawyers'! How about the one you once told me you went to high school with? Only I can't remember his name."

"Jim Forrest?" Why not? David thought. It would be interesting to reencounter his boyhood friend. "I'll make the call to him myself," he told Rita.

David had had no contact with Jim since leaving school, but had not forgotten him, or the gracious life-style of the Forrest family. David's one visit to their home in Alderley Edge had seemed, to a lad from grimy Strangeways, like excursion to another world, he recalled. And had been his incentive to rise above his circumstances.

Rise? David thought, casting his mind back to his early struggles. Claw was a better way to describe it. But he'd got where he'd set out to get, hadn't he? No, not quite. His detached house in Prestwich was fine for the moment, but not until he owned a mansion in Cheshire, like "Forrest Dene," would he really have arrived.

Chapter Fourteen

Nathan's newly kindled hopes for marital happiness were swiftly extinguished. After their brief sexual reunion, his wife had risen from the sofa, pulled her wrapper around her and without a word gone to the cabinet to pour herself a drink, which she had taken upstairs to her room. And Nathan had read in her expression disgust for herself, as well as for him.

Since then, she had not eaten a single meal with Nathan and sometimes did not bother to come to the table when Leona ate at home.

"This household is enough to put any girl off getting married!" Leona exclaimed to Nathan one evening when they were dining alone.

"There are plenty of happy couples."

"Really?" Leona made no pretense of eating the fried plaice Bridie had put before them. "When I think of most of the couples in our family, I'm far from sure."

Nathan, who had finished eating his fish, helped himself to some Dutch cheese.

Leona was absently contemplating the tart that her mother, who occasionally emerged from her apathy to cook, had baked that morning. What was that old saying? "Apple pie without cheese is like a kiss without a squeeze." Which summed up her feelings for Frank, she thought gloomily, cutting a slice of the pie for her father, who enjoyed the Lancashire custom of eating it with cheese.

"Frank's asked me to marry him, Daddy."

"Oh?" Nathan said carefully. But he was not surprised. Frank Moritz was the kind to choose a girl he had known all his life. The salt of the earth, who would make an impeccable husband.

"You don't seem very thrilled to hear it," Leona said.

"It's you who has to be thrilled, Leona. Not me."

"I told him I'd think about it. We wouldn't get married before we've both got our law degrees. So there's no hurry to make a decision, is there?" Leona said.

Nathan eyed her for a moment. Not a flicker of excitement had shown in her expression or voice. It was as though they were discussing an outfit she had seen in a shop window and was considering buying. "You don't love Frank, do you?"

Leona continued peeling the tangerine she had just taken from the fruit bowl. "Not in the romantic sense of the word. But that could be a good reason to say yes. Loving someone the way my mother once loved you can be, in the end, disastrous. With me and Frank, there'd be no room for disillusion. He would never do anything to hurt me. I know him through and through. I can trust him."

Was his daughter eyeing him accusingly? Nathan wondered. On her mother's behalf? Leona's long lashes were veiling her glance and he could not be sure. She had told him she did not blame either of her parents for their sorry plight. But, instinctively, she was bound to have allied herself with the female side. "Perhaps if you knew the whole story about why things went wrong between Mummy and me, it would help you to understand—"

"I don't want to know it," Leona cut in vehemently. "Understanding can't erase my memories, or make it less unpleasant for me to live with you both in this house. And as getting married is a convenient escape from it, I shall probably accept Frank's proposal."

Nathan was shocked by the depth of her bitterness, and appalled that she would consider marrying Frank for such a reason. "Hang on, Leona. Until you really fall in love," he advised her gently.

"Haven't you heard a word I've said, Daddy? That kind of love frightens me. It only brings pain. People end up tied to someone they hate, because of it. Like you and Mummy. And Peter and Shirley."

"Nevertheless, you should take the chance that it won't happen to you."

Leona played with the tangerine peel on her plate. "As I've

fallen in love with a rotter, I know in advance that it would. But there's no danger. Henry isn't in love with me."

Nathan was stunned. "Henry Moritz?"

Leona smiled miserably. "That's right." She noted her father's anxious expression. "Don't worry, Daddy. In the unlikely event of Henry ever proposing to me, I'd run a mile in the opposite direction."

"I'm glad to hear it." Nathan would not, as Leona had done, term Henry a "rotter." But he was self-engrossed and unreliable, and lacked the backbone Nathan considered essential in a man. "Does Frank know about this?" he asked.

"He knew before I did. It was Frank who made me finally admit it to myself." Leona poured herself some water and set down the crystal jug firmly. "Now I've told you, let's forget it, Daddy. Be thankful you have such a sensible daughter."

But Nathan was assailed by an uneasy sense of déjà vu. Give or take the details of personality, this was the Miriam and David and Sammy situation, all over again. When a woman married one brother though her heart yearned for the other, the shadow of the past walked with her all her life.

"Take my advice. Say no to Frank," he urged Leona.

"You're hardly the person to be giving advice on this subject," she replied.

Chapter Fifteen

The family had clubbed together to buy Sarah a washing machine for her birthday.

"I don't want one," she declared when Esther telephoned to tell her. "What would I put in it? My woolen underwear I wouldn't trust not to shrink. And the linens I've preserved for years, I wouldn't want it to ruin, either."

"My machine doesn't ruin anything," Esther said exasperatedly.

"So you've been lucky. But buy me something else."

"A television you've already got."

"Which I don't watch. It gives me sore eyes."

"How can it, if you don't watch it? And jewelery, you're not interested in," Esther went on. "How many more cardigans can we give you?"

Last year, the family had given Sarah individual gifts, which she preferred. A joint birthday present was always preceded by this kind of heated debate between Sarah and whoever the others had appointed their spokesman.

"A washing machine it is, Mother," Esther declared firmly. "But we want you to choose it."

"How many kinds are there?" Sarah asked resignedly.

"You'll see for yourself, when you go to the showroom, in town."

"Now she wants me to go to town!"

"It will be a nice outing for you. Shirley will take you in her car. This afternoon."

"That's very good of her," Sarah said grudgingly. Sometimes, like now, she wished her children and grandchildren were a little less good to her.

"Only for you would Dad give me time off to go shopping," Shirley smiled when she arrived. "But you're not going to town wearing that old thing are you, Bobbie?" she said, surveying Sarah's ancient black coat.

"It's nice and comfortable. And it was good enough when I went to Fifth Avenue with Miriam," Sarah answered huffily.

"Nobody knew you, there, did they? And even so, you wouldn't have worn it in New York if you'd been with me. Really, Bobbie! Anyone would think we were a poor family, that you couldn't afford anything better. You've got at least three coats with fur collars in your wardrobe, which you never bother to wear!"

Shirley left Sarah standing in the hall and rushed upstairs. She returned with a brown swagger, trimmed with beaver and reeking of mothballs. "It's time this one had an airing," she grimaced. "We'll have to keep the car windows open, or we'll both asphyxiate."

Sarah reluctantly took off her old favorite and allowed Shirley to help her on with the garment Bessie had brought back for her from a shopping spree in London, and which Sarah did not like. Mrs. Evans next door complained that her daughters-in-law were mean to her, but Sarah's were too generous. They bought things for Sarah according to their own taste—of which she was again reminded when Shirley handed her the model hat Rebecca had purchased to match the brown coat.

"That's better," Shirley pronounced after Sarah had removed her old black felt and donned the swirl of velvet.

"Better for you, maybe," Sarah grumbled. "But not for me. The wiring in this hat pinches my head and the eye veil tickles my nose."

"I'll go and get you another hat, then. A straw would look more right, anyway, as it's a sunny spring day."

Shirley put a foot on the stairs, but Sarah pulled her back.

"If I have to have a washing machine taking up space in my back kitchen, what can I do? But a fashion parade this isn't."

Shirley laughed and kissed her cheek. "You look very smart, Bobbie. As a lady in your position should."

Sarah followed her outside to the car. "And what position is that, Shirley?"

"There you go again, Bobbie! You're the mother of a well-off garment manufacturer, aren't you? And we've got two doctors in our family, also a couple of budding lawyers," Shirley lectured her as they drove along Heywood Street. "People of standing have to keep up appearances. How does it look for you to be seen looking as if you buy your clothes at a jumble sale?"

"Stop the car! I want to go home!"

"Now, now," Shirley said soothingly. "I wasn't insulting you."

"No?"

"I just want to be proud of my grandmother."

Sarah controlled her anger, but an icy calm replaced it. "And without fine feathers you can't be proud of me?"

"Aren't fine feathers and what goes with them what you wanted for your family when you used to live in Strangeways?" Shirley said.

The question brought Sarah up short. The days when life had seemed an endless struggle were far behind her and she rarely thought of them. But her granddaughter's words had returned them to her memory, full force.

They were driving past the Jewish Home for the Aged on Cheetham Hill Road, where some of those who had shared that struggle were now eking out their last weary years. Yossel Lensky was a resident there, Gittel Lipkin also, and a long-ago scene from their past and hers flashed before Sarah's eyes. What would Shirley have said about how Sarah had looked then? One of a cluster of travel-stained immigrants waiting outside Exchange Station.

A girl like Shirley would turn up her nose at the sight of that poverty-stricken group, Sarah thought. And would probably refuse to cross the threshold of the dank little house in which the Sandbergs had begun their new life. For Shirley, it would not be good enough, but for Sarah it had been heaven just to have her own roof over her head, free of the oppressive fear that was the Jews' constant companion in Russia. But soon Sarah had, as Shirley had reminded her, begun hoping for something better than Strangeways for her family. And striving to achieve it. Freedom alone had not been enough.

Materially, her dreams had come true. The Sandbergs had done very well for themselves, Sarah reflected. But she could not have envisaged the distasteful effects affluence would have upon some of her own flesh and blood. How their attitudes and values would change along the way. It was as if they wore money like blinkers over their eyes and were unable to see what really mattered, she thought, glancing at Shirley.

"Every five minutes you change your hairstyle," she remarked to her.

"André, my hairdresser, doesn't approve of a woman keeping the same style too long."

Sarah compared her with Marianne, who cut her own hair and still wore it as she had as a child. Marianne had no pretensions to grandeur but was a source of distress to Sarah in other ways, putting her work before her domestic responsibilities. Leona, too, seemed to have what Sarah considered masculine ideas, she thought with a sigh. But what else could result from women having careers? Becoming writers and lawyers?

"There've been too many changes in my lifetime," Sarah pronounced to Shirley, who was edging the car into a vacant space in Albert Square.

"And there'll soon be another. You're getting a washing machine. Whether you like it or not!"

Sarah was bemused by the display of labor-saving equipment in the electricity showroom. Food mixers and vegetable peelers. Ironing machines, even! Next, they'd invent cookers that switched themselves on and off, so a woman would hardly need to be in her kitchen at all! It was no wonder that those who could afford to buy such things had little else to do but think about their appearance. Or turn their attention to business, as Shirley had done so successfully and still look as if she had just stepped out of a bandbox. But what did her friends who stayed at home do with their time?

Shirley wanted Sarah to have a Bendix automatic washer, like her own. Sarah chose a simple, twin-tub machine, just to be perverse. Also it was cheaper. "What does it matter which I have, when I won't use it?" she said to her exasperated granddaughter as they left the showroom.

Shirley took her arm and steered her toward St. Anne's Square. "Let's have some tea, Bobbie. Though what a person needs is a stiff whiskey, after shopping for something with you!"

What Shirley's housewife friends did with their spare time became clear to Sarah when they entered Sisson's Café and made their way to a table. Elegant young matrons were greeting Shirley on all sides.

"Now you know why I wanted you to dress up, Bobbie," Shirley whispered as a tall blonde in a well-cut tweed suit came over to speak to her.

"How goes it, Shirl? All of a sudden you're a lady of leisure?"

"I've been buying my grandmother a birthday present. This is Shelley Finklestein, Bobbie."

"Pleased to meet you, Mrs. Sandberg," Shelley smiled.

"I remember your grandparents," Sarah told her. "They lived in the next street to us, in Strangeways. Your Zaidie, God rest his soul, was our rag-and-bone man."

The smile disappeared from Shelley's face. "Really?" she managed to say.

"How else did he turn himself into a wealthy scrap-merchant? Everyone had to start somewhere."

"Have you noticed how many colored faces there are in Manchester, these days?" Shirley said hastily changing the subject and fixing her embarrassed gaze on a West Indian woman who was mopping up some spillage by a table near the door.

Shelley latched onto the new topic gratefully. "The last time I went to London, I noticed at Euston Station there was a whole gang of them cleaning out the trains."

"Who else you get to do the dirty jobs, nowadays?" Shirley said.

Sarah put down the teatime menu she had been clutching tightly in her hand. The conversation reminded her of her encounter with the old man in Fort Tryon Park, and she found it equally distressing. "Once, it was the Jews nobody had respect for," she said with asperity.

"Lower your voice, Bobbie!" Shirley hissed. The ladies at the next table were not Jewish.

"But it's true," Sarah retorted. "And we shouldn't forget it."

"My grandma's a bit of a character," Shirley sighed to her friend.

Shelley eyed Sarah warily and took her leave.

A bit of a character indeed! Sarah thought hotly. Things had come to a pretty pass when your grandchildren felt they must apologize for your honesty. When reminding young people of their families' beginnings made them squirm with shame.

Shirley ordered their tea. "Peter and I are having an *en suite* bathroom put in," she said, to take her grandmother's mind off whatever bee was buzzing around in it now.

"A what?" Sarah played edgily with a cake fork, while Shirley explained. "Your rich grandfather, Isaac Salaman, was the only person I know who had a bathroom, in the old days. But he smelled as if he never took a bath."

Shirley was glad Shelley was no longer within earshot. "And what's the moral of that story, Bobbie? With you, there always has to be one!"

"That money and possessions, like fine feathers, don't make the person," Sarah told her scathingly.

Chapter Sixteen

Marianne's first novel received lukewarm reviews.

"I'd rather have had bad ones than be damned with faint praise!" she exclaimed, throwing the offending newspapers down on her agent's desk. She flung herself gloomily down on the big leather sofa. "What the critics have written is so bloody condescending, Charlie!"

The tall balding man patted her shoulder comfortingly. As her dad would have done, Marianne thought, and wondered if all authors' agents were like Charlie. Businessman, literary adviser, calmer-of-nerves and father-figure, all rolled into one. They needed to be if all authors were like Marianne.

"You're lucky it was reviewed at all," Charlie told her. "Plenty of good books never get a line written about them. How's the play coming along?"

"I've lost interest in it, Charlie."

"You feel bruised, I suppose?"

"Yes."

"Well wait until you've been battered, pet, before you let what the critics write affect your work. And even then, don't let it."

Marianne gazed at the copy of her novel on Charlie's desk, then averted her eyes.

"In the end, it's the reading public who decide on a book's success. And I have a hunch that *On Parade, Girls* is going to make you a lot of money," Charlie said.

"To hell with money! Four years of my life is in that novel—which I spent writing it."

"Tell me something I don't know," Charlie said, inserting a Turkish cigarette into a silver holder.

"I'll leave, if I'm boring you."

"You're not boring me, you're breaking my heart, Marianne. And I shan't have time to put it together again before another client does the same. What you're pouring in my ear is every writer's story, give or take the details."

"Tell that to Arthur Miller and Somerset Maugham."

"I should only have them for clients!" Charlie said, borrowing the jargon of his Jewish friends. "Do you really think, Marianne, that those two distinguished gentlemen got where they are overnight?"

Charlie paused to light his cigarette when his secretary entered with coffee, and waited for her to leave before resuming his lecture. "I've never encountered a writer who hasn't had his ups and downs. And if you're going to be put off finishing your play, because your novel hasn't been greeted like *Gone With The Wind*, you're not the girl I take you for, Marianne."

Marianne added "psychologist" to his rolled-into-one attributes.

After leaving Charlie's office, Marianne called at the advertising agency for which she was doing some free-lance copywriting, to deliver the work she had completed and collect some more.

She had not approached Ralph's agency, though, years ago, she had been employed by them. Doing so would have made it impossible to present Ralph with her *fait accompli*. When presented with it, his response had not been the one Marianne desired. "If you want to earn some extra cash for yourself, fine," he had said. And was still refusing to use her earnings for the purpose for which she had intended them. As he would, no doubt, refuse to allow her royalties from *On Parade, Girls* help to free him to pursue his art. Her husband's ideas were as old-fashioned as Marianne's were modern. Nothing could persuade him it wasn't his place to be his family's sole provider. But Marianne retained the hope that one day he would see sense, and meanwhile was salting away in the bank every penny she earned.

But, just for once, she would be extravagant! she thought and splurged a ten-shilling note on some tulips and daffodils from a barrow near Covent Garden. It wasn't every day she had a book published, faintly praised or not.

When she arrived home, the telephone was ringing.

"Where have you been on such a day?" her mother's reproachful voice inquired before Marianne even had time to say "hallo." "Your father ran out first thing this morning to buy all the newspapers, but when we rang up—over and over again—you weren't there." Esther paused only for breath. "The whole family's been trying to phone you."

"I went to see my agent."

"He must be a happy man, the money he's going to make from you. Leona rang up to tell me your book is all over town. What's that banging I can hear? Chopping fish I know you're not."

"I'm trying to thump the lattice window open, it seems to be stuck."

"With dirt probably, since the last time you cleaned it," Esther rebuked her. "Such a bohemian my daughter is! But Dad and I are proud of you, Marianne."

Tears stung Marianne's eyelids. She had never expected to hear those words from her mother.

"Of course, we haven't had time to read your book yet," Esther said before she rang off.

Marianne smiled and got up from the kitchen stool to put the flowers in water. The day her advance copies of the novel arrived from her publisher, she had mailed one home—why did she still think of Manchester as home? It was some weeks since she sent the book, but her parents would probably never find time to read it, she thought with tolerant amusement, and a feeling for which she could not find the right word, though it was tugging at her heartstrings. Perhaps it was nostalgia for the homely background from which she had sprung, which she had put behind her and returned to only as a visitor.

Marianne's telephone rang repeatedly throughout that afternoon. Every single member of the family called to offer congratulations but, of the elders, only Sigmund, Hannah and Nathan had read her novel.

"I borrowed it from your parents," Sigmund said. "Though I had a job to persuade them to part with it."

"And?" Marianne held her breath. His opinion mattered.

"It shows promise."

"Thank you." That, from Sigmund Moritz to whom books were meat and drink, was enough.

The final telephone call was from Shirley.

"Is that Jane Austen speaking?" she joked.

"No. It's the ghost of Emily Brontë. Who's that? Coco Chanel?"

They shared a laugh which, for once, was devoid of the thinly veiled hostility that had always existed between them.

"I'm glad you made it, Marianne," Shirley said with uncharacteristic warmth. "I always knew I'd end up a fashion designer, but I didn't think you'd ever be an author."

Ah! Back in character, Marianne thought.

"Remember when we were youngsters, evacuated to Wales together during the war?" Shirley reminisced.

"How could I ever forget it?" Marianne answered dryly. They had got on each others' nerves to the point of screaming pitch. "You nearly drove me mad."

"Ditto. But we always had respect for each other's work, didn't we? You used to sit scribbling and I sat sketching. Sometimes, you even said my drawings were good."

Marianne laughed. "I wouldn't have dared to say they were bad! Not that they were, by the way."

"You never allowed me to read anything you wrote," Shirley reminded her. "But I always admired the way you stuck at it."

"Yet you didn't think I'd make it?"

"How many do?" Shirley said with the practicality she had shown even as a child. "Talent and application aren't enough,

Marianne. A person needs *mazel,* too. Who knows if I'd have
become a designer if I hadn't been lucky enough to be the
daughter of a garment manufacturer?"

Was her cousin actually displaying a trace of humility?
Marianne wondered.

"But, knowing me, I probably would."

Not at all! Shirley didn't know the meaning of the word
humility. And was, as ever, obsessed by material things,
Marianne thought, listening to her eulogize about her new *en
suite* bathroom—price and all. Nevertheless, Marianne was
moved by Shirley's call.

As Charlie had said, her career would have its up and
downs. Book reviewers and theater critics might love her
today and loathe her tomorrow, or remain forever condescending. But there was something infinitely reassuring in
still being "our Marianne" to her relatives. In the certainty
that she for them, and they for her, would never change.

Chapter Seventeen

David rose from an uncomfortable armchair in Forrest, Sharpe
and Hollis's waiting room and went to gaze edgily out of the
window at the quiet courtyard below.

"Solicitors always keep you hanging around!" the portly
gentleman in rimless spectacles and a pin-striped suit, who
was his companion in impatience, complained. "If I did this
to my customers, they'd go elsewhere to buy their goods."

"Mine, too," David agreed.

The man picked up a three-week-old copy of *Punch,* from
the circular oak table dominating the room, and left David to
his thoughts.

Why had he put off making his will? And, now he was
about to do so, why did he feel so jumpy? Because it
somehow brought you that much nearer to death's door?
Possibly. But in David's case there was also the distressing
reason for him having decided to leave Sanderstyle to his
grandson, instead of to his daughter.

Jim Forrest had been out of town when David initially
called him for an appointment, and his secretary had not

known exactly when he was due back. It had then been December 1956, and was now summer, 1957. In the meantime, Shirley had not been too troublesome and David had pushed the matter of his will to the back of his mind. But yesterday his daughter had returned it to the forefront, he thought with feeling. David had complained of indigestion after eating too much trifle at Mark's tenth birthday party, but Shirley had insisted that it was heartstrain, from overwork—and had revealed that she was still in touch with the consortium who wanted to buy him out.

If it had not been Sunday, David would have telephoned Jim Forrest there and then. Instead, he had lain awake all night, unwilling to close his eyes, lest he die in his sleep before willing the business to Mark. If he died intestate, Sanderstyle would be split in whatever proportions the law decreed, between Bessie, Ronald and Shirley. Then Shirley would buy her brother out and, with her father gone, her mother would be putty in her hands. Oh no! David had thought. He had phoned Jim's office at nine sharp this morning and been told that Mr. Forrest had no free time until next week. But his desperation must have shown in his voice—the secretary had eventually said she would manage to fit him in.

"Mr. Forrest will see you now," he heard her say from the doorway.

David followed her trim, gray-clad figure into a suite of offices as old-fashioned looking as the waiting room. Dark oak doors, with polished brass knobs, lined the narrow corridor down which she led him. On the walls were framed prints of Manchester, the way it had looked when David was a lad and did no more. The prints were mounted on yellowing parchment, and had probably been there since those days, David thought as he passed one of Poets' Corner, where there had once been a secondhand bookshop in which he and Jim had browsed when they were boys. Though David had not had much time for browsing, he recalled wryly. With his afterschool job, and *Bar Mitzvah* classes, in addition to homework.

The mustiness assailing his nostrils continued to do so when he stepped inside Jim's office.

"Please forgive me for the delay, Mr. Sanderton," Jim said, shaking hands with him.

"If you keep your old pals waiting this long, I'm sorry for your mere acquaintances," David answered with a smile.

"And what's all this with the Mr. Sanderton? We used to be Jim and David."

Jim eyed him uncertainly for a moment. Then the grin David remembered from their schooldays creased his still-freckled face. "Good God! It's David Sandberg!"

"That was," David said dryly.

"The new name didn't help me to recognize you. Nor did the avoirdupois," Jim added with another grin and a glance at David's waistline. "Where's the lanky lad I used to know gone to?"

"Ask my missus," David laughed. "But you've hardly changed," he said, surveying the stocky man his old chum now was. The unruly hair the schoolboy-Jim had tried, unsuccessfully, to plaster down, looked as obstinate as ever. Only it was now gray, instead of straw-colored. "I'd have known you anywhere," David said, swallowing down the lump that had risen in his throat. Jim Forrest had been a very special friend.

"So take a seat already!" Jim smiled. "Remember how I used to mimic you?"

"From you, I didn't mind." Knowing Jim had taught David that all Gentiles were not anti-Semites. That friendship between Christian and Jew was possible. It had been the difference in their backgrounds socially and materially, not religion, that had cut David off from Jim. The poverty from which only hard grind could free David, while Jim continued along the golden path upon which the accident of birth had placed him.

David sat down in the client's chair and watched Jim move behind the desk to sit in his.

"I got into a spot of bother at Flanders," Jim said casually, apropos his stiff gait. "My grandchildren call me Long John Silver."

"I was in Flanders, too," David said, hiding his distress. "But I was one of the lucky ones. Not even scarred." He changed the subject. Commiseration with a man like Jim was not called for. "But I didn't make this appointment to talk about old times. You're a busy chap, Jim, and so am I." He told Jim the purpose of his visit.

"If you're sure that's what you want to do, David, I'll carry out your instructions," Jim said.

David watched him select a pipe from the rack beside his pen-tray and fill it with tobacco from an antique humidor.

The note of caution in Jim's voice had been plain, but he was not the kind to say more and for this David was grateful. Aaron would have been reading him the riot act by now.

"I've made up my mind, Jim."

"Very well."

Jim looked surprised when David insisted upon signing a simple last will and testament there and then.

"I have a heart condition, Jim," David revealed though Jim had not asked for an explanation. "When I've made my will, I can forget it. I'd like you to be my executor."

"Fine." Jim made no further comment and, after the will was signed and witnessed, walked with David to the lift. "It's good to see you again," he said simply while they waited for the ancient contraption to creak its way up from the ground floor.

"Same here," David answered gruffly. "Do you still live in Alderley Edge?"

"No. My wife prefers Prestbury."

David had noticed the photograph of a pretty silver-haired woman on the desk, the kind he would have expected a man from Jim's background to have married.

"Nigel, my son—he's in the practice with me—lives in Prestbury, too," Jim smiled. "So I see a lot of my grandchildren, which compensates for never having seen my daughter's kids. She married a New Zealander and went to live out there, after the war. My wife has been out to see them, but I've never managed to make the time."

"I know the feeling," David said. It had taken him nearly ten years to get around to visiting Miriam and Sammy. "Are your parents still living at 'Forrest Dene,' Jim?"

"Father died some time ago. Mother stayed on there for a while, then she had a stroke and my sister took her to live with her."

A scene from the distant past flashed before David's eyes and, for a split second, he was a gawky lad again, watching little Lucy Forrest play with a puppy on a sunlit lawn. "I remember your little sister," he smiled.

"She's a parson's wife now, in the depths of Devon. And not so little!"

But the way she was then, playing with the dog while a housemaid in a frilly apron retied the satin ribbon in her Alice-in-Wonderland hair, the gracious house and well-kept gardens, the whole ambience of that long-ago afternoon, had brought home to David the insurmountable difference between his life and Jim's.

The lift arrived and Jim drew back the heavy iron gate. "Perhaps you and your wife would come and dine with Clarissa and me one evening, David?"

David thought of the woman in the photograph. Whom Bessie would call "the pearls and twinset type." And what would Clarissa, whose name epitomized David's preimpression of her, call Bessie? With the best will in the world, the twain could not meet on any but the most strained and superficial ground.

David was probably wealthier than Jim, but had long since lost his youthful illusion that affluence was an equalizer. A compensator, yes. But when you had to compensate yourself for something, the original lack remained. Bessie would have nothing whatsoever in common with Clarissa Forrest. And what did David share with Jim, now? Only their schoolboy past.

"Why bring the women into it?" he said with a chuckle that belied his feelings. "You and I can meet for lunch sometime, Jim."

"Fine."

They shook hands and David stepped into the lift.

"I'm glad you've done so well, David," Jim said. But there was no condescension in his voice.

"I know you are, Jim."

The next time David saw his mother, he told her he had reencountered Jim Forrest.

"Him, I blame for everything," Sarah said.

David laughed. "Because the first time I broke the Sabbath laws was when I went by train on a *Shabbos* to his house?"

"That, you would have done sooner or later anyway. Like the rest of the *Shabbos*-breakers in this family! What I blame him for is giving you such big ideas."

"Bigger than I've yet achieved, Mother."

"And you won't be satisfied until you do, though getting there could put you in your grave, David."

Chapter Eighteen

In the spring of 1958, Sarah received an invitation to a *Bat Mitzvah*.

"What next!" she said, displaying the gilt-edged card at her tea party. "All of a sudden, Jewish girls are being confirmed—like the boys!" She paused only to snort. "And a whole lot at a time, no less! Paula Frankl's granddaughter is not even getting the service to herself."

Nathan defended the congregation of which he was a member. "At our *shul*, it's always done in groups."

"And an Orthodox *shul* doesn't do it at all," Sarah retorted, which he knew. "There, girls don't expect the same treatment as boys. What was good enough for their mothers is good enough for them."

"I think it's a lovely idea," Leona put in. "And it wouldn't surprise me if, sooner or later, Orthodox synagogues latch onto it—"

Sigmund put down his teacup. "That will be the day! When the Orthodox start taking a leaf out of the Reform book!" he declaimed sarcastically.

"I wish they'd begun doing it at our *shul* when I was thirteen," Leona responded. "Why shouldn't girls have a ceremony to confirm them into Jewish womanhood, as our boys have, to mark their entrance to manhood? The *Bat Mitzvah* ceremonies I've attended have been beautiful occasions. The girls wore pretty white dresses and carried prayerbooks—"

"Like Catholic girls at their first communion!" Sigmund cut in scathingly.

The conversation had taken a turn Sarah did not like. "Christian or Jew, everyone has the same God," she glared at Sigmund, who was inclined to forget it.

"But Christians have Jesus and Mary and the Holy Ghost, too," little Margaret Klein said.

Sarah patted the child's silky black hair. Like Marianne, Margaret closely resembled Sarah and there was something incongruous about hearing such a Jewish-looking child speak that way.

The other children were looking shocked.

"Jews aren't supposed to say those names," Margaret's cousin Howard chided her.

Matthew sprang to his sister's defence. "But Margaret and I aren't Jewish." He glanced at his mother, who was quietly sipping her tea. "We aren't anything."

Howard looked uncomfortable. "I keep forgetting."

"And what you just told Margaret isn't correct," Hannah Moritz informed him.

Howard looked uncomfortable. "I keep forgetting."

"Since when were you an expert on the subject?" Sigmund flashed to his daughter-in-law. Hannah's agnosticism had always been a bone of contention between them.

"I bet if we searched the *Torah* from end to end, we wouldn't find a word about it," Hannah replied. "It's one of those customs people assume is the Law."

Sigmund did not deny it. "If you had your way, there wouldn't even be any Jewish customs," he said, venting his ruffled feelings upon Hannah. "You probably wouldn't have had my twin grandsons *Bar Mitzvah,* if you'd had your way."

"You're wrong about that," Hannah said coolly. "Because I happen to enjoy and approve of Jewish tradition. It's the glue that's held our people together."

"That I won't argue with," Sigmund conceded. "But without the religion, there'd be no tradition."

Sarah cut the debate short. "Be like me and leave well enough alone," she advised Sigmund. "Be thankful that even the glue Hannah mentioned has held fast!" She glanced around at the several vacant chairs, her disapproval graphic in her expression.

"People do occasionally have other things to do on Saturday afternoons, Mother," Nathan responded to her silent censure.

Bessie and Rebecca had gone to Liverpool, to wave farewell to a friend who was emigrating. Helga, whose long-standing courtship with Moishe Lipkin continued as ever, had accompanied him on a visit to his mother in the Home for the Aged. Harry's wife, Ann, had dumped her children at Sarah's and gone to have her hair set. And Shirley and Peter had taken theirs with them on a weekend jaunt to Paris. Esther had not yet arrived.

"Once, nobody would have dared to miss one of my tea parties," Sarah muttered.

David, who had so far kept out of the discussion, smiled dryly. "Mother's right."

"When wasn't she, so far as you're concerned?" Nathan said testily. For him, these weekly gatherings were more of a strain than a pleasure. Yet he could not bring himself to stay away.

"What is so special about your tea parties?" Sigmund exclaimed to Sarah.

Sarah gasped. How could Sigmund ask such a question?

The moment the words left his lips, he had regretted them. But, like Sarah, he was aware that the old-established Jewish values were changing and did not take kindly to her rubbing it in. Sarah was eyeing him rebukingly. "I'm sorry," he said grudgingly.

"You should be. Now why don't we all have another cup of tea?"

Sarah busied herself with her teapot, but her mind was even busier. And she had still not recovered from hearing Sigmund say what he had, which was like an open invitation to the family to start going their own way. As had already begun happening in some Jewish families—those in which there was no family custom, like Sarah's weekly gatherings, to hold them together.

"Kate and Margaret can pass around the teacups, like their Grandma Esther did on *Shabbos* afternoons, when she was a little girl," she smiled. Margaret might not be Jewish, but she was part of the clan.

"And when we grow up and get married, our little girls will do it," Kate said to Margaret.

"And I'll drive my children to the *Shabbos* tea party in my Rolls Royce," young Howard promised, to the adults' amusement.

Sarah had made her point and would not have minded had the whole brood arrived together in a double-decker bus. That they rode on the Sabbath had ceased to upset her.

The significance of his mother's charade with the children had not escaped David. He could read her like a book. But she had never been above connivance in a good cause.

Sarah had long since schooled herself to accept that her family did not live by the letter of the Jewish Law, that expediency had watered down their devoutness. But so long as Sarah lived, they would know where to find their own on *Shabbos* afternoons. Stray they might—who knew what the future may bring? she thought, glancing at the youngest generation. But nothing would have changed when they returned to the fold.

PART TWO

Chapter One

On a bleak January morning in 1960, Sarah sat in her kitchen polishing the brass and taking stock of the decade she had just put behind her. Which, unlike the three preceding it, had not been a bad one for Jews, she thought gratefully. The state of Israel, which gave Jewish people everywhere a feeling of security unknown to them before its birth, was now in its twelfth year. As was Sarah's widowhood; Abraham Sandberg had died on the day Israel was born.

When the last decade began, Sarah had not expected to be alive when it ended, to see yet another monarch ascend the throne. She had watched Elizabeth's coronation, on TV, in 1953 and had remembered the smiling little girl the new queen had been when her father King George VI was crowned. How fast time had sped by since then! And now, Sarah was eighty years old—and still doing the same household chores she had done as a young woman. Her mind still, thankfully, sharp as ever—though the same could not be said for her memory, she thought with chagrin. Which, these days, functioned better for long-ago events than for where she had put something yesterday.

Sigmund Moritz, who was a few years her senior, had said she would get used to mislaying things. But Sigmund had been absentminded all his life. To Sarah, it was a new and irksome experience that impinged upon her efficient and methodical nature. Who would be efficient when they had to spend half their time searching for this, that, or the other?

But I mustn't grumble, she chided herself. She was still able to get around, albeit at a slower pace. And lucky not to have cataracts, like Mrs. Evans next door. Or to have to pore over books and newspapers with the aid of a magnifying glass, as Sigmund now did; having to wear spectacles to read was bad enough! But worst of all was the senility that had reduced Paula Frankl to a state of childlike acquiescence, Sarah thought

111

with a shudder. That senility might be her own final lot was her greatest fear.

Sarah brushed the dreadful prospect aside and gave her candlesticks an extra rub, before returning them to the mantelpiece with the mortar and pestle. At her age, a person had to take life day by day and not think of what might be in store for them. The future was in God's hands, as it had always been. Though Sarah had never hesitated to give Him a little help in arranging the future of her children and grandchildren.

With her great-grandchildren, she had had less contact, she reflected with regret, while scrubbing the metal polish from her hands. Popping in to see her whenever they felt like it wasn't part of their childhood, as it had been for their parents. How could it be, when they didn't live just around the corner?

Sarah had always been aware that her relationship with Leona lacked the closeness that existed between herself and her other grandchildren. But, unlike her cousins, Leona had grown up in Broughton Park. She had never lived in what Hannah Moritz called the extended-family environment. As the newest generation never had.

Sarah had remembered that phrase, because it summed up what she now thought of as the old days. When people had lived close by their kith-and-kin and hadn't needed to board a bus, or ride in a car, to take their troubles to those who cared about them. Or to share their small everyday joys, as well as the big ones that even casual acquaintances would make a song and dance about.

These days, Sarah's grandchildren used the telephone to maintain regular contact with her. A day never passed when she did receive a call from one or the other of them, inquiring after her health and passing on their bits of personal news. The only exceptions were Leona and Arnold, whom Sarah sometimes thought of as her two big failures.

When Leona was younger, all Sarah's attempts to help her come to terms with her parents' strife had met with a silence impenetrable as a stone wall. And now she was a young woman, Sarah found her even less approachable.

As for Arnold! Sarah thought going to stir the pan of milky potato soup she had put on the stove to simmer for her lunch. He was still exiled from the family.

Yet Sarah's two big failures were successes in their own

right. Arnold was now a member of Parliament. Leona had passed her examinations with flying colors and was practicing law. And Sarah was proud of them both.

The doorbell rang, prodding her from her thoughts.

"You'll never guess what's happened," Sigmund said when Sarah let him in.

"In that case, I won't try. Hurry up, it's cold standing in the lobby," Sarah said, watching him fumble to unbutton his overcoat. But she was apprehensive about what he might be going to tell her.

The first three weeks of the new decade had passed without incident, but Sarah had not expected this to last. In a big family, something was always happening. Once, her heart would have lurched at the sight of Sigmund on her doorstep in the middle of the day. She would have known he had not left his tailor's shop for no reason. But his deteriorating eyesight and arthritic fingers no longer allowed him to sew and sometimes, now, he dropped in just for a chat. Sarah hoped this was one of those occasions.

"You should let David install central heating here for you, like he wants to," Sigmund said, following Sarah down the icy lobby to the kitchen. His house was smaller and cozier.

"If I had here central heating, where would you warm your behind?" Sarah smiled watching him do so in front of the fire. "David has finally stopped nagging me about it," she added, "but only to start nagging me to go to live at his house."

Sigmund sat down in the rocking chair. "Me, I don't know how you can live alone."

Sarah stirred the soup. "For a woman, it's different."

"Tell me how?"

"Men, they think they're the strong ones. But, in reality, they don't know how to fend for themselves. In childhood they have a mother to take care of them, and later a wife takes over from her. If they lose the wife, there's a daughter or a daughter-in-law—in your case both! When did you so much as boil yourself an egg, Sigmund?"

"I've never had to."

"Exactly. You've eaten lunch, yet?"

"No," Sigmund replied ungraciously.

Sarah smiled. He had never taken kindly to being beaten in a debate, least of all by a woman. "So you'll share mine." She ladled some soup into a couple of the thick willow-patterned dishes she had had for twenty-odd years. "Living alone I've got used to. But I'll never get out of the habit of cooking for two."

Sigmund eyed the saucepan. "You mean two dozen!"

"Sometimes David, or Nathan, drops in for a snack with me." But neither had done so for a long while.

Sigmund came to sit at the table and Sarah watched him lower his bulk onto the chair her husband had once occupied. "You're too fat, that's why you're always short of breath," she informed him, noting that the effort had caused him to pant.

"And you, you're a bag of bones!" Sigmund retorted. "But you always were."

"Thank you!"

They maintained a stiff silence for a moment, then Sigmund reached out and clasped Sarah's hand.

"All right. I'll forgive you for insulting me," she said.

"Ditto. Can I start on my soup now?"

Sarah brought her own dish to the table and sat down opposite her old friend. What did it matter that they got each other's backs up? They always had, but the acrimony was only skin-deep. Beneath it, a bond of deep regard and respect existed between them.

"What did you come to tell me?" she asked without further ado. Had his aging daughter Helga agreed to marry Moishe Lipkin at last? But Sigmund's pensive expression denoted that what he was about to impart was not a matter for rejoicing.

Sigmund took off his pince-nez and polished them. "In the forties, I lost my eldest grandson. And in the fifties, my only son. The sixties are only a few weeks old and—"

"Who is dead?" Sarah demanded with her heart in her mouth.

"My second wife."

"To you, it's no loss."

"Would I try to deny it? A hypocrite I'm not."

"So what is all the fuss about?" The dreadful woman whom Sigmund had married and left years ago would not be mourned by those who loved him.

"On the contrary, what it is is a gain," Sigmund said dryly. "Today, you are eating lunch with a wealthy man, Sarah." He replaced his pince-nez on his nose and contemplated the pepper pot, an expression of irony on his chubby face. "Gertie had nobody to leave her money to, after her sister and brother-in-law died. I am her only living relative, the letter I received from her lawyers informed me this morning. The property she owned and everything she had in the bank—which isn't buttons—will go to me."

"*Mazeltov!*" Sarah beamed and got up to kiss his cheek. "So what are you going to do with it?"

"Give it away to charity, what else? I wouldn't soil my hands touching that woman's filthy lucre!" Sigmund declared hotly.

"A pity," Sarah said, returning to her chair and resuming her meal.

Sigmund glared at her. "That, from you, doesn't surprise me. Money-mad you always were!"

"But for myself, never."

With this, Sigmund could not argue. All Sarah's ambitions had been for her family.

"Eat your soup," Sarah said and waited until he began doing so. "There are things money can do," she reminded him, "which even you, who have always despised it, cannot deny. Your grandson Henry wants to study in Paris, but the last I heard, it wouldn't be possible because he can't afford it. And Frank, though he's a clever boy, will take years to work up to a partnership in that law firm he works for. If he had the wherewithal to pay his overheads, he could maybe branch out on his own instead of others profiting from him—"

"Stop, you seductress!" Sigmund dropped his spoon into his soup with an angry plop.

Sarah went on calmly eating hers and gave him a mischievous smile. "That, I never expected to be told I am."

"A serpent is what I really meant."

"So even Sigmund Moritz is capable of mixing up words occasionally," she replied sweetly. "But the things a person can get called for speaking the truth to an old friend!"

"Every man has his Achilles' heel and mine is my love for my grandsons—but you are making use of it to erode my high principles," Sigmund said accusingly.

"I never even heard of an Achilles' heel."

"You didn't?"

Sarah laughed and shook her head. "Me, I'm the homespun kind. Intellectual ideas and big words I leave to the clever ones like you . . ."

"Now she's *shmoozing* me!"

". . . whose minds are on such a high level, they don't see the simple truths," Sarah went on. "You intend to give Gertie's money away, you said."

"So?"

"Didn't those other armchair professors you used to mix with in Vienna tell you that charity begins at home?"

Chapter Two

Sarah's home truth had the effect upon Sigmund that she had hoped it would. The matter of his inheritance was not raised between them again, but Henry was enabled to study at the Sorbonne and to rent a small apartment on the Left Bank, which he said he intended to share with a friend.

Who the friend was, the family did not inquire. Henry's private life had been his own for years. During his student life at the London School of Economics they had, from time to time, quizzed him. But Henry had met the questions with his usual witty banter and had managed to reveal nothing. He had never brought any of his college friends home, nor did he talk about them on his infrequent visits to Manchester. Marianne, on whom he had occasionally dropped in in London, had arrived at the conclusion that Henry had no close friends.

Frank had elected to use the cash his grandfather give to him to set up a poorman's-law practice.

"So a rich man you'll never be yourself," Sarah shrugged to him from behind her teapots on the *Shabbos* afternoon when she learned of his intention.

Frank tossed a recalcitrant lock of his mousy hair away from his eyes. "There's more than one kind of riches, Bobbie."

His mother was eyeing him with pride, Sarah saw. And why not? To have brought up a son whose values were those Frank had just expressed was something to be proud of. Hannah Moritz's boys would never mistake brass for gold.

"My daughter is another *meshugenah!*" Rebecca exclaimed, crumpling her paper napkin.

"That depends upon one's point of view," Nathan told her coldly.

Leona, who was standing by the hearth, turned her back

on her warring parents. "I'm going into partnership with Frank," she informed the family.

"And what will the pair of you ever be?" Rebecca asked sarcastically. "*Shnorrers* can already get legal aid. There's no need for you two to sacrifice your all for them."

"About Frank, I agree," David said.

"You would!" Hannah told him scathingly. "But my sons don't happen to have your ideas. Or your priorities," she added glancing at the small diamond twinkling in the ring on David's little finger.

"How can they have, with you for a mother!" Bessie snapped in her husband's defense.

"Which has saved us from turning out like some others in this clan," Frank said, giving Hannah a warm smile. "Whose names I shan't bother to mention!"

It was the Whitsun weekend and Shirley and Peter were spending it in Bournemouth, for which Sarah was grateful. If Shirley had been present, she would have known Frank was referring to her and given him a tongue-lashing. It was unlike Frank to have made the cutting comment, but he had been edgy lately. Possibly because being in love with Leona, which he had stopped trying to hide, was getting him nowhere, Sarah reflected with a sigh.

Leona went to sit beside David. "You said you agree with my mother that the kind of law practice Frank and I have in mind is wrong for him. But not for me, Uncle?"

"You're a girl," David said dismissively.

Leona smiled. "A woman, actually." She was now twenty-four.

"And when you marry, you'll have someone to keep you in luxuries," David said. "It won't matter how little you earn—or if you don't earn at all."

"The kind of man who could keep me in luxuries wouldn't appeal to me," Leona declared.

David surveyed her expensive green silk blouse and well-cut skirt. Leona's taste in clothes was simple and discreet, an effect she would find difficult to achieve without money. He could not imagine her wearing imitation patent shoes, instead of the real thing, or carrying a plastic handbag. Settling for less than that to which she had always been accustomed.

"Grow up, love," David advised her. "Or you're likely to be brought down to earth with a bump."

Where has living in luxury got my mother? Leona wanted

to ask, turning her gaze from David's humoring smile to Rebecca's sour countenance. God, what false standards the older generation had! Despite her own experience, Leona's mother still upheld those standards, as if she had not learned that affluence didn't compensate for unhappiness.

Maybe, for some people, money could buy their love, Leona thought, watching her Uncle David put his arm around his wife, whom, according to family history, he had married for her dowry. But Leona's love was not for sale. Her father's either, though he had, in effect, allowed his person to be sold to her mother. And had regretted it ever after. Better a crust of bread shared with the right person. Which would probably be the lot of whoever married Henry, Leona reflected with pain.

"I might never marry," Leona said brusquely to David.

Frank got up from the sofa and went to stare through the window, which induced a moment of awkward silence.

Then Sarah restored the atmosphere to normal by spitting delicately, three times, to ward off the dreadful possibility Leona's words had conjured up. These days, she rarely reverted to the Yiddish folklore of her youth and seeing her do so amused her family. Even Leona had to laugh.

"Remember how Ma used to make us tie a red ribbon around our babies' arms when we wheeled them out in the pram, so nobody would put the evil eye on them?" Bessie reminisced to Esther.

"Keeping away the evil eye was my mother's speciality," Esther laughed.

"Perhaps because, when I was a girl in Russia, for Jews there were too many evil eyes around!" Sarah said to her caustically.

Then they heard the garden gate, which had not been oiled since Abraham Sandberg attended to it shortly before his death, creak loudly, heralding an arrival.

Hannah glanced through the window. "What's Henry doing in Manchester?" she exclaimed.

Bessie peered over her shoulder. "And who is that with him?"

Hannah exchanged a glance with Frank. "Go and let them in."

Henry's companion was a beautiful Asian girl.

Nathan saw Leona pale at the sight of her.

"Meet the family!" Henry said breezily, escorting her into

the parlor. "Those who are present today," he added observing the empty chairs.

"Usually it's standing room only in here on Saturday afternoons," Nathan laughed to ease the sudden stiffness he could feel in the atmosphere.

"So Henry has told me," the girl smiled. "My name is Julekha Razak," she added. "As Henry hasn't bothered to introduce me, I must do so myself," she joked.

"I call her Julie," Henry put in.

"He wishes to Anglicize me," she said amusedly.

"Welcome to my home," Sarah said as she did to everyone visiting her for the first time. "Sit down and I'll pour you some tea."

"Thank you. I'm happy to meet you, at last," Julekha answered. Her English was impeccable, with little trace of her origin. "I, too, have a very large family. But, unfortunately, mine is many miles away."

"Are you the only one who lives in England?" Bessie inquired.

"I now live in Paris," Julekha replied, accepting the cup of tea Sarah offered her.

With Henry, Leona thought resignedly. There was no doubt in her mind that Julekha was the person with whom Henry was sharing a flat.

That the rest of the family had drawn the same conclusion was evident from their shocked expressions.

A bohemian Henry always was and still is—and in the worst sense of the word, Sarah thought, wondering how her good-living, dead friend Rachel Moritz could possibly have been his grandmother. Or the upright and God-fearing Sigmund his grandfather. Maybe Sarah had been wrong to influence Sigmund to assist Henry financially? Which seemed to have resulted in helping him along the road to ruin!

How did a boy from a respectable Jewish family acquire such tendencies? Sarah asked herself. But hadn't Sarah's own granddaughter Marianne also lived in sin once, with the man who was now her husband? Sarah consoled herself with the thought that Marianne and Henry were the exceptions that proved the rule. Few young Jewish people would dream of doing what they had done.

"Your outfit is very nice," she said to Julekha, though it seemed somewhat showy for the afternoon. And it's as well your family are so far away and don't know how you are

living, Sarah added mentally. She had heard that Indian
moral standards were of the very highest.

Julekha explained that her garments were customary for
Moslem women. "We call the trousers *salwar* and the tunic a
kurta. And this is an *odhni*," she said, fingering the piece of
fabric draped loosely from her shoulder to cover her breasts.

"How interesting," Leona managed to say with a polite
smile.

Bessie cast a covetous glance at the embroidered mauve
silk from which the outfit was made. "That material would
make a gorgeous evening gown."

"I could write to my uncle who has a store in Bombay and
ask him to send you a length," Julekha said.

David interposed before his wife had time to open her
mouth and accept the offer. "We wouldn't dream of putting
you to the trouble," he answered pleasantly but firmly.

Leona exchanged a look with Frank. They knew how
David's mind worked! Julekha was neither white nor Jewish
and the self-styled head of the clan had no intention of
helping her ingratiate herself with Henry's relatives.

Henry, too, was aware of David's ploy and gave him a cold
glance, which David pretended not to notice.

Why did this have to happen to us? Sarah thought, busying
herself pouring more tea. Was there no end to the changes
she and her family must adapt to? She handed round some
cake and noted Sigmund's set expression. He had not spoken
a word since Julekha's arrival. And his fingers were clenched
on his watch-chain, as if he was trying to contain himself.
What was he thinking? The same as Sarah, no doubt. That,
possibly, they would soon have Moslems in the family, as well
as Christians.

What of it? Sarah's reason demanded. But it was fighting a
battle with her emotions, and the odious conversation she
had had with the gentleman in New York, years ago, returned
to her full force. How is it possible for a Jew to feel that way?
she had thought angrily, then. But now, the same tendencies
she despised in others appeared to be present in herself. Not
being that way in theory was easy, she had to admit. But
putting your principles into practice with respect to your own
family was not. She loved Henry like a grandson and the
thought of him possibly marrying Julekha—

Leona cut into Sarah's thoughts. "You must have met a lot
of interesting people, living in Paris," she said to Henry.

"One in particular," he replied enthusiastically.

Hannah smiled. "And he's a revolutionary, I suppose? Who wants you to help him change the world?" She knew her son and shared his burning idealism.

Henry nodded. "With the help of students everywhere, Mother. His name is Daniel Cohn-Bendit and if you haven't heard of him yet, you will," he told everyone.

"We can't wait!" Leona said sarcastically.

Henry ignored the interjection. "Danny's what the Americans call a ball of fire. Isn't he, Julie?"

"By any stretch of the imagination."

"He's a born leader," Henry declared to his relatives. "Students in France have begun questioning the society in which they have to live," he added.

Sigmund ended his uncharacteristic silence. "Which students in Vienna were already doing when I was young!" he snorted. "Though I myself didn't go to the university, some of my friends did—those whose parents were wealthy, or influential in the arts, who didn't have to be little Jewish tailors or cobblers, living in the ghetto."

Sigmund toyed with his watch-chain, a reminiscent expression on his face. "And a long way sitting up all night debating about society got those students! Sometimes, I was invited to their homes and I joined in the discussion. But, in essence, the world now is no better place than it was then."

"I have the feeling the students of the sixties will do more than just talk," Henry said. "And not just in France, if Danny the Red has his way."

"To mix with communists I made it possible for my grandson to study in Paris!" Sigmund exploded with a recriminating glance at Sarah.

Julekha brushed some strudel crumbs off her tunic. "Our circle in London, when we were students at the LSE, was extremely left-wing," she told Sigmund with a smile.

Leona stared down at a snag in her right stocking. So Henry's affair with Julekha was no flash-in-the-pan; it must have been going on for years. She was aware of her father and Frank observing her covertly. Daddy was concerned only for her. But Frank—what could be worse than having the girl you wanted turn you down because she loved your brother? She had not given that as the reason for declining his proposal, but Frank knew.

She saw him glance at Henry, not exactly with malevolence, but with something akin to it. Was she to be the cause of rift between the twins? Frank didn't deserve to be hurt. But nor did Henry. It wasn't his fault that Leona had fallen for him. That she loved and loathed him at one and the same time. And was now suffused with jealousy of the girl she had today discovered shared his life.

"The London School of Economics has always been a breeding ground for left-wing intellectuals," Hannah said to Sigmund. "And, as you know, Henry's been left-wing since he was a kid. I'd be surprised if he and Julie had friends who weren't, wherever they lived."

Hannah's tacit acceptance of her son and this girl as a couple shocked Sarah. What Hannah had just said amounted to welcoming Julekha into the family, which Sarah had not yet schooled herself to do. She glanced at Julekha, who was gazing down at a pearl ring on her finger, avoiding the eyes of those whom she must know were observing and assessing her. Henry had not said their attachment was serious, but, if it were not, he wouldn't have brought her to the *Shabbos* gathering, subjected her to an inspection.

Sarah noted that, briefly, Julekha had lost her confident poise. Her proud bearing was still that of a person from the upper echelons of their own society, but, suddenly, there was something forlorn about her. As though she felt like an outsider—which nobody, whatever their creed or color, should be made to feel by others, Sarah's heart and mind told her in unison.

She rose from her chair and went to sit on the sofa beside the girl whom God—or was it Allah? —had decreed would meet Henry Moritz and now be sitting in a Jewish parlor. Sarah Sandberg's parlor. And so be it, Sarah said to herself. God and Allah were one and the same and you couldn't argue with what was *bershert*. The conflict between Sarah's reason and emotions was over. And, in a curious way, both had won.

"Tell me about your family," she said, taking Julekha's hand and receiving a grateful smile from Henry and a glare from Sigmund.

"They're all—except for my merchant-uncle—doctors," Julekha revealed. "And I'm studying medicine, now, too."

"Now she tells me!" Nathan smiled.

David sighed resignedly. He had not expected even his mother's flexibility to stretch this far. But she was right. "My son is a doctor, as well as my brother," he told Julekha, casting his reservations aside. "He's away on holiday at the moment."

"You don't know what you're getting into, Julie," Nathan warned. "Us general practitioners have to work hard to earn a rest."

Julekha smiled. "My father and brothers are in general practice, so I know all about it. But I intend to be a geriatric consultant."

Sigmund was now surveying her with grudging respect. Only her association with Henry made it grudging; he had nothing against Asians. And this one must be a brilliant girl, to have studied economics at LSE and now be reading medicine at the Sorbonne. He had always admired a clever mind.

Julekha met his glance with her soft brown eyes, which a harder heart than Sigmund's would have found difficult to resist.

"A geriatrics specialist would come in handy around here!" he said to Sarah.

"Speak for yourself," she retorted.

That evening, Frank called to see Leona and found her alone in the house. Her parents were at a silver wedding party and Bridie visiting a friend.

"Your mum and dad must get fed up with going to so many *simchas*," Frank remarked, following Leona into the lounge. Last time he was here, Nathan and Rebecca had gone to a *Bar Mitzvah*. And the time before that, they had passed him in the drive, on their way to a wedding.

"If we were setting up an ordinary law practice, we'd get lots of invitations, too," Leona answered. "Everyone invites their doctor, lawyer and accountant, it seems."

"Thank goodness we're not! But we'd each be asked in our professional capacity, wouldn't we? Not as husband and wife."

Leona changed the subject, before it led to yet another proposal. Saying no to Frank was as painful for her as it must be for him. "Why didn't you ring up and say you were coming? I might have been out."

"I didn't intend coming. I went out for a walk and found my legs carrying me here," Frank said with a wry smile. He watched Leona take an orange from the fruit bowl and peel it. "But I'd have been surprised not to find you mooning at home, this evening. As I would if you'd accepted my mother's invitation to join us for supper."

"Say what you mean, Frank! You may as well."

"You know, without my saying it."

"Then why bother referring to it at all?" Leona split the orange and gave Frank half.

"Your hair used to be this color, when you were little," he said, popping a juicy segment into his mouth. "And my brother used to tease you about it."

Leona went to gaze through the window.

"Me, I wouldn't upset you for the world and never did," Frank persisted. "So why was it him you fell in love with?"

Leona turned to face him. "You're upsetting me now. And since when was falling in love explicable? I doubt if anyone could put into words why they fell for someone."

"I must be the exception," Frank said quietly. "I know exactly why I love you. Because you're everything I admire and need."

"What about what I need?" Leona asked after a silence. "And if you're not it, how could you be happy with me?"

"I'd take a chance on it. And I don't think you know what you need, Leona. Want, perhaps. At the moment. But that's something else."

Leona drew the curtains on the blustery April night and went to sit on the sofa beside him. "Did you know Henry had a girl?"

"Of course I didn't. You think because we're twins Henry tells me all his secrets? Me, I'm an open book by nature. Henry's the direct opposite—"

"There's no necessity to give me a character breakdown on Henry—"

"I think there is," Frank cut in. "You might think you understand him, but there's plenty you don't seem to have tumbled to about my brother. Think back, Leona and tell me if you can ever remember Henry making a real commitment. To anyone or anything."

"Why are you talking this way, Frank?" Leona asked uncomfortably. "Behind Henry's back?"

Frank shifted a lock of hair that had fallen forward onto her forehead. "No good purpose would be served by my saying it to his face, or I would. My twin will never see himself except through his own eyes. But it's time you realized what he is really like."

"You don't have to denigrate him, Frank. In some ways, I loathe him."

"I don't want you to loathe him, Leona; he can't help being the self-absorbed person he is. All I want is for you to accept that even if he returned your feelings, he isn't for you."

"I've never thought he was, Frank."

"Well, that's a relief."

"Is it?" Leona said miserably.

"All that fuss this afternoon!" Frank went on. "Like you, I could see our elders' minds machinating, because Julekha is Asian. Even Bobbie Sarah had a hard time coming to terms with the thought of having dark skin in the clan. But they could all have saved themselves the trouble. Henry won't marry Julekha. He'll never marry anyone."

"You seem very certain," Leona said. "But it doesn't look that way to me."

"Henry told me some time ago that he doesn't believe in marriage," Frank disclosed. "Nor does he want children."

"After the home life he's had, I'd have thought he'd see married life as the ideal state," Leona said.

Frank took out his handkerchief and wiped some orange juice off her chin and Leona was consumed by irritation, as she always was when he babied her. Then the feeling gave way to affection. His protectiveness was a manifestation of his caring. She should consider herself lucky to have him, not resent it.

Frank resumed discussing his brother. "Henry's attitude to marriage was, initially, a mystery to me, too. Then I began to see it as just another symptom of what ails him."

"And what have you decided does ail him?"

"Fear of responsibility. Plus chronic indecisiveness and a permanent hankering for the ha'penny and the bun."

"You've been wasting your breath on me, Frank."

Frank looked distressed.

"I'd already made that diagnosis, myself."

They shared a smile.

"One thing I do know about the state of love," Leona said wryly. "Respect doesn't necessarily enter into it."

"But with you, it would have to eventually. That's how I know what you feel for Henry won't last."

Leona gazed pensively into the fire. "I'm sorry for Julekha. If Henry has no intention of marrying her, why did he bring her home?"

"He needs the blessing of the family, however halfhearted."

"Henry's never cared a fig about that."

"I said you don't really know him. Henry puts on a great act and always has. But underneath, when it comes to the clan, he's no different from you and me. But it's taken him a long time to screw himself up to seek that blessing. If Julekha had been *kosher*, he'd probably have brought her home ages ago. He told me tonight that they'd lived together since their first year at LSE."

"I'm sorry for them both," Leona said with tears in her eyes.

Frank handed her his handkerchief. "Don't weep for Henry. He's got his woman and his freedom, too."

Leona was weeping for herself. For the end of the dream she had foolishly cherished: that Henry Moritz would miraculously change into the kind of man she could respect, and fall in love with her. But dreams, like promises, were made to be broken—especially by Henry's sort. Deep down, too, was the aching knowledge that, even now, if Henry wanted her she would throw caution to the winds. Sacrifice marriage and motherhood, even, as Julekha was doing, just to be with him.

"Your face is flushed," Frank told her.

Leona did not allow the observation to impinge upon her thoughts. Meeting Julekha had made her admit to herself that she cherished that dream.

"Is your head hurting?" Frank inquired, placing a cool hand on her brow.

"I'm hurting all over."

"Off to bed with you then! I'll bring you up some aspirins and a cup of tea."

"What a fusspot you are, Frank!" But he was a dear, too. And would probably fuss over her if he knew her face had colored with shame because she lusted after his brother.

"Off you go then," Frank instructed, helping her to rise from the sofa as if she were an invalid. He escorted her into the hall and gave her a gentle shove toward the stairs. "I'll go and put the kettle on."

This was what life with Frank would be like, Leona thought. Blessedly on an even keel. With Henry— Stop it! she ordered herself as she reached the upstairs landing and entered her bedroom. Lust and love are two entirely separate things, she told her reflection in the mirror above her dressing table.

The same dressing table at which she had sat studying her face after she began menstruating, when she was twelve, and her father had told her about sex. That it was a man and woman's way of expressing their love for each other. Liar! Leona answered him, all these years later. She had had to find out for herself that this wasn't necessarily so. Because she knew, now, that she didn't love Henry. There wasn't a shred of tenderness in her feelings for him. To put it crudely, they emanated from between her legs.

Leona undressed and got into bed.

When Frank entered with the aspirins and tea, she was lying staring at the ceiling.

"I'm all right," she assured him when he hovered over her anxiously. Plain, he certainly was, but he was a beautiful person, she thought seeing his face light up with relief.

Frank stood watching her sip the tea, his eyes glued to her blotchy countenance, which weeping had made that way. Most men would be staring at her unfettered breasts beneath her flimsy nightgown, hoping to turn the bedroom tête-à-tête to their carnal advantage, Leona thought dryly. But not Frank. It was the whole Leona Sandberg he wanted, not just her body.

"I'll have to go now, Leona," he said, glancing at his wristwatch. "Henry and Julie are leaving on the midnight train and I promised to see them off at the station."

Leona recalled the many occasions during their childhood and youth on which Henry had arranged to meet Frank and herself, but had failed to turn up. Once, they had waited on a streetcorner for an hour for him, with snow on the ground freezing their toes. And Henry's only apology, when they returned to the Moritz's and found him toasting his by the fire, was that they were fools for waiting. But to Frank, a promise was a promise. He would never let anyone down.

"Who knows when I'll see my brother again, after tonight? —the life he lives!" Frank said with a rueful grin. "Though, in a way, both of us are using the money Grandfather gave us for the same purpose—to change the world."

"Your way will do some immediate good for society's underdogs," Leona declared. "But Henry will probably fritter away most of his money sipping absinthe in Left Bank cafés, expounding theories that only a revolution could put into practice."

One twin was reliable as a rock, Leona reflected, and the

other the proverbial rolling stone. Yet each had a deep regard for the other, of that she had no doubt. Frank's knowledge of his brother's shortcomings would never erode his affection for Henry.

"Say good-bye to him for me, Frank," Leona said brusquely and it was as though she was finally closing the door on her shameful dream.

"I'll drop in tomorrow morning and we'll get down to planning our practice," Frank said. "If you're absolutely certain you want to join me?"

Leona gazed silently into his earnest dark eyes. Everything had to be absolutely certain in Frank's world. And it was one in which you'd never have the ground knocked from under your feet. "Sure I'm certain," she smiled.

Chapter Three

Sarah could not recall a period in the family when joyous occasions followed one upon another, with no sorrows to mar them, but so it had been from the summer of 1960, until spring 1961.

In July, her great-grandsons Mark Kohn and Howard Klein were both *Bar Mitzvah* on the same *Shabbos* and had shared a splendid reception the following evening. Leona and Frank became engaged in August and were married in December. In February, Ronald's wife, Diane, had given birth to a daughter.

It was now March and the family was seated in *shul*, awaiting Martin Dean's *Bar Mitzvah*. Sarah had no qualms about it taking place in a Reform Synagogue; God would hear Marianne's son read from the *Torah* even if he did so in a backyard. And how wonderful it was that Martin would have his father beside him when he read his Portion of the Law.

Two years ago, Ralph had decided to convert to Judaism. "I'm part of a Jewish clan, so I may as well put the seal on it," he had said. And Marianne's happiness when she watched her husband open the Holy Ark—and honor bestowed on the father of the *Bar Mitzvah*—had been plain to see.

The service had begun some time ago and Sarah glanced

along the front row of seats, which the family was occupying—the second row, too. They had traveled to London yesterday, in a coach hired by Ben Klein, and had stayed overnight in a hotel.

Sarah noted Martin's nervous expression, which she had seen on the faces of countless *Bar Mitzvah* boys during her long life. But she had never before seen one seated in *shul* between his parents. In Reform synagogues, families sat together. Males and females were not segregated as they were in Orthodox congregations, which felt strange, to Sarah. David was on her right and Nathan on her left and it seemed unreal to be sitting in *shul* flanked by two men.

The synagogue was full. Which Orthodox ones, regrettably, were not, on Sabbath mornings, Sarah reflected. Marianne had said it usually was. And Nathan had said that Jackson's Row Reform *Shul* in Manchester also had a sizable *Shabbos*-morning congregation. Was it because parents and children sitting together made going to *shul* a family occasion? Sarah pondered. To her, Reform Judaism was a religion of convenience, but she had to concede that, in some respects, it had worked wonders.

All around her, the congregation was reciting the English translation of a prayer and that, too, seemed strange. She kept her eyes on the Hebrew words in the *Siddur* she had been handed, which was different from the one to which she was accustomed. Nathan, to whom this form of service was familiar, was intoning the English words on the opposite page. David and Ben, Sarah noted, had their lips clamped shut and a look of disapproval on their faces.

There were no greater exponents of the Orthodox-versus-Reform argument than Sarah's eldest son and her son-in-law. Yet both broke the Orthodox laws without a second thought. So what did their attitude represent? Sarah mused. Only an empty allegiance to the ways of their forefathers and this Sarah could not respect. It was those who lived by those ways, which in the twentieth century was not easy, who commanded respect. Some of whom had cut themselves off from their less-observant brethren and led simple lives in closed communities. One such community was right around the corner from Nathan's home, in Salford. And there were several here in London.

Sarah had maintained her personal devoutness without cutting herself off from outside influences. Her husband, too.

But Abraham would not have approved of her being where she was today. Even for the *Bar Mitzvah* of a great-grandson, he would not have crossed these portals. For an otherwise easygoing man, in religious matters Abraham Sandberg had remained immovable. But Sarah thought flexibility preferable to the divisiveness a too-rigid attitude begat. Better for a tree to bend than break. And the branch today's *Bar Mitzvah* boy and his parents now were had come very near to breaking, Sarah reflected when Marianne turned her head to smile at her. If the family hadn't forgiven Marianne for marrying a *goy*, she too might now be lost to them, like her brother Arnold. Instead, the *goy* was now a Jew, Sarah thought with satisfaction, watching Ralph and Martin leave their seats to join the rabbi behind the lectern.

Marianne felt as she did at the opening night of one of her plays. Only this production had to stand or fall by a single performance. And the leading performer was her son. Martin's face was as white as his brand new *tallith*. Ralph looked scared stiff, too. It was his *mitzvah*, today, to hold aloft the heavy *Torah*, which had just been taken from its velvet and gold covering, before it was placed upon the lectern. And he seemed afraid he might drop it. Or was his anxiety on Martin's behalf?

"Don't worry, Marianne," her mother whispered from beside her. "Martin won't let us down."

"How can you be so sure?"

"I've never known a *Bar Mitzvah* boy who did."

Nor had Marianne. Scared though the lads invariably were; they stood firm and did what was expected of them. As their ancestors had since time immemorial, Marianne thought as she heard her son's voice resound through the hushed synagogue.

"Who rehearsed him?" her agent joked to her when the service was over and they were in the synagogue hall partaking of cakes and wine, after the rabbi had said the *Kiddush* prayer.

"Forget I'm a writer, Charlie," Marianne smiled. "Today, I'm a mother."

Charlie kissed her cheek. "Once in thirteen years, you're entitled to think of yourself that way."

Esther pushed her way through the congregants who were wishing Marianne and Ralph *Mazeltov*. "Who was that man I just saw kissing you?" she inquired suspiciously.

"You met Charlie on the first night of that play of mine they did at Manchester Library Theater—"

"With all the men who kissed you that night, how would I remember him? I never knew such a business as you're in, for paying each other compliments and kiss, kiss, kiss!"

"But Charlie's one of the ones who mean it."

"You haven't invited a whole crowd of bohemians back to your flat for the party, I hope!"

Marianne smiled. To Esther, and Sarah too, anyone who worked in the arts was a bohemian. "Just a few."

"Which few? The only one I've met who seems even half normal is that editor-lady from your publishers."

"Her name is Arabella."

"That's a name?"

"Be quiet, Mam! She's right behind you—"

"Congratulations, Marianne!" Arabella smiled, squeezing herself into position beside them. She straightened the unaccustomed headgear Marianne had instructed her to wear for *shul*. "How are you feeling, now the great day has dawned?"

"Knowing my daughter, she'd rather be writing a book," Esther said.

"And what did you think of her last one?" Arabella inquired.

Marianne left her mother, who of course had not read it, to tell her, and plunged into the crowd. She found Martin and his cousins clustered respectfully around the rabbi. Her husband and father were with them.

"You can be proud of your son. He did very well," the rabbi smiled at Marianne.

Sarah appeared at Marianne's elbow in time to accept the compliment. "Naturally he did well. He's a Sandberg."

"My grandson is a Klein," Ben corrected her.

"In actual fact, he's a Dean," Ralph corrected them both.

"What does it matter what I am?" Martin muttered, aware that the other boys in the group were trying not to laugh.

The rabbi wagged a playful finger at him. "Family pride is very important, my lad. And woe betide the *Bar Mitzvah*-boy who tries to deprive his relations of their *nachas!*"

Later, when Marianne and her husband and son were racing home in their car, to get there ahead of the luncheon guests, Martin seemed unusually thoughtful.

"Some Yiddish words don't have an English equivalent, do they?" he mused. "What exactly is *nachas*, for instance?"

"What your father and I are hoping we'll get from you, but

I'm not counting on it!" Marianne said, drumming her fingers impatiently on the steering wheel, when she had to halt at a traffic light. Ralph had imbibed more than his share of wine and sherry and she had refused to let him drive.

"And what's *yichus*?" Martin went on.

"The glory that will rub off on you and me, love, when Dad becomes a famous painter."

"That was a bit below the belt," Ralph said.

"It's the only place left to hit you, dear," Marianne answered lightly, though the subject of Ralph still having made no real attempt to pursue his art was a sore one. Instead, he had accepted promotion at the ad agency and was now the studio director, which Marianne considered a retrogressive step.

"The caterers will think we've got lost!" she exclaimed when another red light held them up.

"Why isn't my party being held in a hall?" Martin asked. "With a dinner and dance, like Mark's and Howard's was?"

"Dad and I don't think it's necessary to turn a family occasion into a full-blown social event," Marianne said.

"You're not like the rest of the family, are you?"

"Do you mind?" Ralph inquired.

"No. But I wonder why it's taken me thirteen years to find out?" Martin gazed thoughtfully through the window for a moment. "Perhaps it's because I've only just started making comparisons."

"Oh you have, have you!" Ralph joked.

"Most of our relations live in big, fancy houses. But we live in a little flat," his son said. "Yet we're not poor, are we?"

"We're not rich, either," Ralph answered.

"But how people live isn't just a question of what they can afford," Marianne told Martin. "It's also a reflection of the people themselves. To some, a house is a status symbol—"

"You mean like Uncle David, and Cousin Shirley?" Martin cut in.

"Speaking for myself," Marianne said, diplomatically evading the question, "where I live is simply my home." Her son had begun making judgments, as well as comparisons!

"I wish you luck to pack everyone into it, today!" Martin laughed as Marianne parked the car in the forecourt of the modest block of flats.

"Your pals will have had time to knock back a few drinks already, Marianne," Ralph said, noting Charlie's Mercedes and Arabella's Mini parked side by side.

"Yours, too, Dad," Martin added pointing to a gleaming Jaguar.

Ralph had invited his colleague Len Richards, whom Marianne did not like. Nor did she care for his wife, who was a vacuous, simpering blonde.

"I told the caterers not to open the bar until we got home," she said as they entered the flat. It looked so crowded, already, Marianne feared there might not be room for the family when they arrived.

Because Sarah and Sigmund who, these days, both walked at a snail's pace, did not ride on the Sabbath, the rest of the Manchester contingent was escorting them.

"Some bar!" Martin grinned following Marianne into his bedroom, which had been commandeered for the purpose.

"You can open up, now," Marianne instructed the little man standing behind a white-clothed trestle table.

"That won't do my football togs any good!" Martin exclaimed when Marianne unlocked a cupboard and the barman brought out two cartons of liquor that had been dumped on top of a sports bag.

"So next time you're *Bar Mitzvah*, you'll know not to leave that bag there," the man laughed.

"You tell him, Mr. Slivowitz!" Marianne said harassedly. "I'll just pop into the kitchen to see how your wife and daughter are getting on."

"Rather you than me!" he called after her.

Marianne had had that feeling the moment she set eyes on the two ladies and it was confirmed when she entered her kitchen. She had—against her mother's advice—made the catering arrangements by telephone and had not met the Slivowitzes until this morning.

"We're only a small firm, but we know our business," Mrs. Slivowitz told her. "And we make it a rule that the hostess leaves everything to us," she added, pursing her fat lips.

"I'll be delighted to," Marianne answered pleasantly.

"But maybe you don't think it's safe to?" Miss Slivowitz, who was as lean as her mother was obese, demanded.

Marianne had to stop herself from backing away.

"Even the liquor, this lady saw fit to lock up!" Mrs. Slivowitz exclaimed. "I only wish we had the millions for how many *big* houses and flats we've been trusted in."

"We didn't have to *shlep* here through the traffic, from the East End, to be insulted," her daughter declared.

Mrs. Slivowitz nodded her agreement so vehemently that Marianne thought her wig might fall off. "I see you wear a *sheitel*, Mrs. Slivowitz," she said to change the subject. But not for the better, she realized immediately.

"Personal remarks, she's making now!" Miss Slivowitz flashed. "To my poor mother, who has unfortunately lost her hair."

Marianne, who had not paused to think that the wig could not be for religious purposes, or its wearer would not be working on *Shabbos*, apologized for her *faux pas* and made her escape.

The family had just arrived.

"Miles, we had to walk!" her Aunt Bessie was complaining. "My feet are killing me."

"And it isn't a sit-down do, Mam," Shirley said, peering into the living room, where Marianne's friends were standing drinking beside the buffet.

Her father went immediately to survey the spread. "Where's the smoked salmon, Marianne?"

"A person gets what they pay for," Mrs. Slivowitz said from behind him. "Mrs. Dean ordered our *B* menu."

"In that case, I wouldn't like to see your *C* menu," Ben said.

Mrs. Slivowitz, who had just brought in a platter of *gefilte* fish, plonked it on the table.

"Everything looks perfectly lovely," Marianne told her hastily—which was the truth.

"What there is of it," her mother said.

Sarah, who was not surprised that the Gentile guests were beginning to look uncomfortable, came to the rescue. "We should all be thankful that my granddaughter, who writes a lot better than she cooks, didn't do the catering herself!"

Marianne hugged her and led her to Ralph's wing chair, where she settled herself like a queen on a throne. Ready to cope with the next little crisis! Marianne thought with affection for her.

Of crises there was no shortage.

"How are we going to live through this?" Ralph whispered to Marianne later, as they passed each other carrying loaded trays. "What made us think that oil and water could possibly mix?"

The family was stationed at one end of the narrow room and Marianne's friends at the other. Charlie who, like Sarah, could be relied upon to make the best of a difficult situation, was ambling to and fro between. An actress, to whom Shirley had said she had never heard of her, had already left. Arabella had almost choked on a bone which ought not to have been present in *gefilte* fish. The whiskey had run out. And the Slivowitz ladies had dug themselves into the kitchen. Mrs. Dean had not requested the services of a waitress, they said. Their job was simply to prepare the food.

Marianne steeled herself for worse to come, when she heard her Aunt Bessie shriek, and had to will herself not to laugh hysterically when she turned her head in Bessie's direction.

Sigmund had dislodged a dash of trifle with his elbow and it had landed, upside down, on Bessie's feet. But it was that kind of afternoon!

When her friends left, in a flurry of kisses, she heaved a great sigh of relief.

Returning to the living room, after seeing them and the Len Richardses out, she was greeted by silence.

"Have you all lost your tongues?" she smiled. A moment ago, her relations had been shouting their loudest.

"They're upset. They think they've let you down," Ralph told her with a wink.

"I disgraced you, with the dish of trifle," Sigmund muttered contritely.

"It was very clumsy of you and you've ruined my snakeskin shoes," Bessie chided him. "But I shouldn't have made such a fuss about it," she added to Marianne.

"And I'm sorry I said the wrong thing to that lady," Shirley put in. "But how was I to know she'd be so touchy? I never met an actress before."

"Also, Dad and I should have known better than to criticize the catering in front of your friends," Esther said.

Marianne was taken aback. What was the matter with them all? Apologizing wasn't their style.

"So we've made her ashamed of her family," her father shrugged sheepishly.

"I'll never be ashamed of my family," Marianne declared with feeling.

"That's what I thought she'd say," David told the others with satisfaction.

"Me too," Nathan endorsed.

"Now can we get on with celebrating my *Bar Mitzvah?*" Martin inquired, restoring the atmosphere to normal.

Marianne saw her father sigh and lower himself into a chair. Why hadn't she noticed how exhausted he looked? Or the sadness in his eyes—for which Arnold's absence was responsible. Every family *simchah* was, for Marianne's parents, what her grandmother called the almonds and raisins of life. The bitter along with the sweet, because one of their two sons was never present.

The children went to sit together in a corner where Martin had just opened a box of chocolates, which was his idea of celebrating.

"Don't offer my Laura any of those, Martin," Shirley said to him. "She's fat enough."

Laura shot her a look of hatred and rushed out of the room.

"That wasn't very tactful of you, Shirley," Marianne said.

"If you had Laura to deal with, you wouldn't be very tactful, either!" Shirley got up and helped herself to a chocolate. "As you haven't got a daughter, Marianne, you don't know what girls of fifteen are like!"

Marianne recalled herself at that age. And Shirley, too. In essence, they had both been younger versions of what they were now—two very different women, on the wrong side of thirty-five. Young girls, like their elders, couldn't be pigeonholed together, as Shirley seemed to think. They were individuals each with her own hopes and dreams, Marianne thought, remembering her own.

"My granddaughter, bless her, has always been difficult," David sighed.

"That's why we've decided to send her away to school," Shirley informed the gathering.

Peter, who had been staring out of the window as if to dissociate himself from the discussion about his daughter, turned to rivet Shirley with a cold glance. "Why do you say *we*? When it was you who made the decision?"

Shirley played with the rope of pearls around her neck. "Somebody has to make them," she replied pointedly.

"Now, now, you two!" Bessie interceded, "we don't want to spoil Marianne and Ralph's *simchah*."

"You could've fooled me!" Ronald snorted. "If my wife had been here this afternoon, she'd have a lot more to say than she already does about us *Ashkenazis*."

Ronald's little boy had chicken pox and Diane had stayed at home with him. Leona and Frank were also absent. Leona was expecting a baby and had not felt well enough to travel.

"Without a cross word or two, it wouldn't be like a family *simchah*," Hannah said with a smile.

Marianne slipped out of the room before the next round got under way; David had just begun tackling Shirley about packing Laura off to boarding school. Only Hannah had noticed Marianne leave, and probably knew she was going to have a private chat with Laura. As she herself had done with Marianne, under similar circumstances, many years ago.

Would I have become what I am, if that chat hadn't taken place? Marianne wondered entering her bedroom, where Laura was dripping tears onto the pile of minks on the bed. Probably not. She had a lot to thank Hannah for.

"Go away!" Laura sobbed.

"A fine thing to tell a lady in her own bedroom!"

"Do you think it's right for them to send me away, Cousin Marianne?"

"We'll get around to that in a minute. Why don't you drop the 'Cousin' and just call me Marianne?"

Laura eyed her uncertainly. "Wouldn't it be disrespectful?"

Marianne smiled. "I'm not that old, love! And you're not a little girl anymore."

"Tell that to my mother!"

"I wouldn't dream of it."

"Because she wouldn't listen to you," Laura declared, wiping her eyes on the cuff of her party dress. "At least, she never listens to me."

"That isn't uncommon between mothers and daughters."

"But not all mothers insist on choosing their daughters' clothes," Laura sniffed. "I mean—well, look at me!" She gazed down with disgust at her dress. "I look horrid in yellow, and frills make me look fat."

Marianne agreed with Laura's opinion of her appearance. A simple style of dress, in a more flattering shade, would have disguised Laura's puppy-fat and enhanced her pale cheeks and fiery curls.

"My mother wants me to stay a little girl forever!" Laura burst forth. "Maybe she thinks I don't know why, but I do. It's so she won't seem so old."

"I'm sure that isn't true," Marianne answered. Endorsing Laura's perceptive assessment of her mother would not help matters. "Can I trust you with a secret, Laura?"

Laura nodded solemnly.

"I didn't get on too well with my mother, when I was your age."

"But I bet I would, if you were my mum."

Marianne ruffled her curls and smiled. "If I were, you'd probably wish someone else was. It isn't easy for any young person to achieve a real understanding with their parents."

"I get on quite well with my daddy," Laura said. "He tries to stick up for me—so does my brother—but they don't stand a chance against Mum."

"I'm sure she does what she thinks is best for you," Marianne said carefully. Shirley's ears must be burning!

"But it's never what I think is best for myself. I'm not a child, Marianne."

Marianne remembered the feeling well.

"I'm nearly sixteen. And I want to be a photographer."

"That's an interesting ambition."

"But my mother won't hear of it. Whoever heard of a lady-photographer? she says! I think girls should be able to be anything boys can be."

"I quite agree."

"If I wanted to be chimney sweep, I'd bloody be one!" Laura flared. "You don't mind me swearing, do you?"

"Go right ahead, if it makes you feel better."

"I didn't think you would," Laura said with a smile.

My black sheep reputation is obviously no secret with the kids, Marianne thought ruefully. Ten-to-one Laura knew Marianne had left home, against her parents' wishes, and come to live in London to make her own life.

"Why do I need to go to finishing school, if I'm going to be a photographer?" Laura demanded.

"Is that the kind of school your mother has in mind?" Marianne said with astonishment.

Laura nodded miserably.

Shirley's delusions of grandeur knew no bounds!

"I don't want to be banished to Switzerland," Laura said.

"Siberia would be worse," Marianne answered to cheer her up. "And think of all the lovely pictures you'll be able to take of the Alps, and the lakes."

"Yes, I will, won't I?" Laura said resignedly. "Mum's taking me there on my sixteenth birthday—some present!"

"You won't be there forever, love."

"And when I come back, I'll start being what I want to be!"

Marianne patted her head approvingly.

"Thank you for listening to me, Marianne. I've never had a chat like this with an adult before."

"Well you can have one with me any time you feel like it, love."

"I'll remember that."

Marianne left Laura repairing her tear-stained appearance and returned to the party.

"We haven't toasted the *Bar Mitzvah*-boy yet," David said to her.

"Such formalities aren't necessary, Uncle," she smiled. "Martin knows that all his family wish him well."

"And I don't want to be toasted," Martin said.

"He'd rather be grilled," his cousin Howard quipped.

"Your Howard has the same sense of humor Arnold had at his age," Marianne reminisced to Harry. Then she saw her father's sallow complexion turn chalk-white and wished she had not said it.

"Why did you have to remind your dad that, in order to hurt him and me, Arnold isn't here?" her mother accused her.

Lyn, who had been subdued all day, tried to smooth things over. "My husband's absence probably hurts him most of all."

Margaret fled from the room, with Kate at her heels. From the day Lyn brought her children to claim their place in the family, the two little girls had been bosom friends.

Matthew stood biting his lip, beside Ben.

"I didn't meant to distress you and the children, Lyn," Esther said. "I love the three of you dearly, as you must know by now."

Lyn tried to smile. "It's all right, Ma."

"It isn't all right!" Ben thundered, as he had never been heard to do before. "How can it be?" he demanded of Esther. "When our own son doesn't want to know us? So it's our fault, that I admit. But why must he go on punishing us? Why can't he make the peace, now?"

"Because my brother is a stubborn devil!" Harry said hotly. "And I hope he feels proud of himself, sitting there in the House of Commons with the other MP's, instead of coming to his sister's *simchah*. Our Howard's *Bar Mitzvah* was spoiled for me because our Arnold wasn't there."

"Does the House of Commons sit on Saturdays?" Ralph asked irrelevantly.

"Don't change the subject!" Ben yelled.

Which Marianne knew her husband had been trying to do. She could see a vein throbbing in her father's temple. "Calm down, Dad," she pleaded.

"Would you be calm, if your son acted this way with you?"

The situation couldn't arise, she wanted to say, but remained silent. There was nothing Martin could do which would cause her to show him the door, whether it concerned religion or anything else.

"Oi," Ben groaned eloquently.

"Get Dad a drop of brandy, Ralph," Marianne instructed.

"Don't bother," Ben said. "Will it mend my broken heart? Only one thing can cure what ails me." A terrible sob wracked his bony frame. "But I'll go to my grave without it happening."

"Is Grandpa ill?" Marianne heard her nephew Howard whisper to Harry. Simultaneously, she became aware of a suddenly glassy expression in her father's eyes. A cold shiver rippled through her, but she could not make her feet move, or her lips speak.

"Catch him, somebody, before he falls!" she heard her grandmother, whom distress had rendered silent throughout the harrowing interlude, call. But it was too late. Dad had sagged forward in the chair and tumbled to the floor.

Her mother's scream shocked Marianne out of her momentary paralysis and she sank to her knees beside her father's inert body. Thank God Uncle Nat was here and Ronald, too. But an ominous feeling now had Marianne in its grip and a small voice inside her head was saying that even an army of doctors couldn't help her father.

"Take Esther out of here," Nathan instructed David. "All the kids, too."

For the first time ever, his eldest brother did not argue with him, but did as he was bid. Esther, now with a dazed expression on her face, allowed herself to be led away to Marianne's bedroom.

Mrs. Slivowitz chose that moment to enter and tell Marianne she had cleared up the kitchen and was ready to leave. Marianne did not raise her eyes from what Nathan and Ronald were doing.

"No manners the lady has, either!" Mrs. Slivowitz exclaimed and stalked to the door with Ralph behind her, as though she had not been surprised to see one of the guests stretched out on the floor.

This is a like a tragicomedy, Marianne thought in a remote part of her mind.

"The bill you'll get next week," Mrs. Slivowitz flung at her from the doorway. "And if you've got a daughter, don't bother asking me to cater for her wedding!"

But only an onlooker would see the funny side. A frightening stillness had descended upon the room. Marianne held her breath. Was her father dead? He couldn't be, or Uncle Nat and Ronald wouldn't still be examining him. She noted a froth of spittle on his lapel. And that his left hand was clenched. But his eyes were shut.

"Ben's had a stroke," Nathan said as David returned to the living room.

"I knew our *mazel* couldn't last," Sarah sighed. "In *shul*, this morning, I was thinking that for too long we've had no *tsorus* in the family. How bad is it?" she asked Nathan.

"Not good," he answered, exchanging a glance with Ronald and avoiding her eye.

"Esther isn't here and me you can tell," Sarah said. "Marianne is also strong enough to hear bad news."

Marianne raised her head and became aware that she and Sarah were now the only women present. The others were probably trying to comfort her mother. Ralph returned from seeing out the caterers and came to put his arm around her. Why didn't Uncle Nat and Ronald do something useful, instead of just standing there like a couple of lemons! She wanted to ask them, but was unable to make herself do so. It seemed like an hour since her father slumped to the floor, but she knew it could not be more than a few minutes.

Nathan cleared his throat. "Ring up for an ambulance, Ronald."

"We must have Ben taken to a good nursing home," David said.

Ronald exchanged a glance with his uncle, which his father did not fail to note.

"Have I said something wrong?" David inquired.

"Let's just say it was in character," Nathan replied.

"What you mean, Uncle Nat, is it was bloody typical!" Ronald put in disgustedly. "Only the best" was his father's motto whatever the circumstances.

"Ben is unlikely to regain consciousness," Nathan told David. "I regret to say it will make no difference to him where he's taken to."

"But if he has to die, let it be in the comfort he strove for all his life," David insisted. "Not in a public hospital ward, like his poor immigrant parents ended their days in, when he was still a kid. Ring up the London Clinic," he ordered Ronald.

Even in a matter like this, there has to be a family altercation, Marianne thought. But again she was unable to make herself speak.

"It's for Harry to decide, not you, David," her Uncle Nat said.

Harry was seated with his head in his hands and had, so far, not uttered a word. He looked up at Nathan, his homely features crumpled with distress. "What does it matter? I'll leave it to you."

After Ronald had gone to the kitchen to use the telephone, Sigmund heaved himself up from his fireside chair. "You can't even bother to help an octogenarian up?" he snapped to Peter Kohn, who was standing silently beside him.

Peter, who was the essence of politeness, looked surprised. The younger members of the clan knew better than to offer such assistance to Sigmund Moritz, whose independence as a rule came second only to his ego.

Sigmund shuffled to the window and gazed down at the Saturday evening traffic. Hansom cabs had been the means of transport when he was a boy and how very long ago that seemed. He turned to cast a sorrowful glance at Ben.

"I know what you're thinking, Sigmund," Sarah said. "Why couldn't it have been you or me?"

"God has let us live for more than long enough already," Sigmund sighed.

"But who can argue with Him?" Sarah answered.

Marianne was gazing absently at the messy table. The caterers had done nothing more than remove the dishes and platters which were their property. She had planned to stay up all night, returning the room to rights. But instead—I'm having a nightmare, she told herself. This isn't really happening. Then she glanced at the twisted grimace on her father's face. He was still lying on the carpet—her Uncle Nat had decided not to move him—and looked as if the lopsided grin that had always been his most endearing feature had gone permanently awry. A nightmare this wasn't.

But the sense of unreality remained with Marianne, and later she found herself going mechanically through the motions of what was required of her. Comforting her mother, when her father was carried from the flat on a stretcher. Arranging with Shirley and Ann to take Martin to stay at their hotel if she and Ralph had not returned from the hospital by bedtime. Making everyone another cup of tea. And, finally, attending to an exotic houseplant, which would wilt if it did not have its nightly drink of water.

"To darn her husband's socks, my daughter can't remember!" Esther vented her feelings upon her. "But at a time like this, she remembers to water plants!"

"Our Marianne was always a 'funniosity,'" Harry declared as they left the flat.

Marianne had not heard that Lancashire expression for years. Hearing it now was so evocative of her childhood and youth, she had to swallow down the lump that rose in her throat. But not until she was getting into the car, to go to the hospital, did she emerge from the once-removed haze through which she had watched herself do this and that.

Harry settled Esther in the back of the car and got in beside her. "If our Arnold was here, I'd bloody shoot him!" he exclaimed.

Oh, the ifs of life! Marianne thought poignantly. Her father would not have had a stroke, had Arnold been there. "If you had a gun," she said to Harry.

Lyn Klein and her children were staying at the small apartment in Westminster which Arnold had rented when he was elected to Parliament.

"Oh, you're in, are you?" she said to him savagely the moment she entered the living room.

Arnold raised his eyes from the papers he was studying and watched her remove her coat and hat. "You put me through it enough before you left for *shul* this morning, Lyn," he said in a clipped voice. "Kindly don't start again. Had I known what was in store for me, I'd have gone home this weekend and held my usual constituency-surgery, instead of staying in London to see you."

"I wish you had," Lyn retorted, "because, at the moment, I have no desire to see you!"

Arnold became aware of his children standing together in the doorway. Margaret's lower lip was trembling. And Matthew was eyeing him with something akin to—what? It looked like contempt. "What's the matter with you two kids?" he barked to them.

Margaret turned tail and fled to the kitchen.

"Your father's had a stroke, Arnold," Lyn said and watched him pale.

"And you're the cause of it, Dad!" Matthew accused him before stalking out to join his sister.

The papers on Arnold's lap slid to the floor. Lyn retrieved them and tossed them onto the sofa, where they landed in an untidy heap. She waited for her husband to reproach her for dealing so carelessly with his notes, which normally he would have done. But these circumstances were not normal. Nor was his nonrelationship with his family, Lyn thought grimly, which, in its turn, had eroded the life Arnold shared with his wife and children. Each of them individually had been damaged by his foolish pride. And not least Arnold himself, Lyn reflected, surveying the pompous politician he now was. Where had the breezy naval officer she'd married gone to?

She went to gaze through the window at the lights glimmering distantly on the Embankment. Transients would soon be settling themselves down on the benches for the night, with the chill breeze from the Thames rustling the old newspapers that served them as blankets. People who would give anything to have what Arnold had eschewed. The love and heritage that bound father to son, from generation to generation.

"They've taken your dad to the Royal Free Hospital," Lyn told her husband, who was staring into the flickering blue-red glow of the gasfire, beside which he was seated in a leather armchair. "And if you ever want to see him again, you'd better run there."

Lyn turned her head and saw Matthew standing in the doorway.

"Though it's probably too late to do Grandpa any good," he said brusquely.

Matthew will soon be a man, Lyn thought with a maternal pang, watching him walk into the room and place himself strategically between herself and Arnold. He was tall and handsome, as she had been told his great-grandpa Abraham Sandberg had been in his youth. But the cynical expression Matthew was presently wearing ought not to be on the face of a lad of sixteen.

Matthew ran a hand through his wavy red hair. "You said that when I'm an adult, I can choose which religion I want to be," he reminded his parents. "I thought you might like to know I've already made my decision—"

"This isn't the time to announce it," Lyn interrupted.

"Personally, I can't think of a better time," her son replied with the clear and confident enunciation that had made him a leading light in his school dramatic society. "What has brought my father, and all of us, to this unthinkable situation, if it isn't religion? Which isn't to say I don't blame Dad for allowing his well-known pigheadedness to pile on the agony," Matthew added, piercing Arnold with a rebuking stare. "But religion was the first link in the chain of events that's led up to all this. And I've decided to live my life without espousing any branch of it. In my considered opinion, religion does more harm than good!"

Margaret had just entered the room. "I hope God didn't hear you say that, Matthew."

For a child without a religion, Margaret was uncommonly obsessed by thoughts of God, Lyn reflected, watching her daughter fiddle pensively with the sash of her blue velvet dress. But Matthew had veered in the opposite direction.

Margaret went to squat miserably at Arnold's feet. "Maybe I'll be a Catholic when I grow up and live in a nunnery, where nobody can upset me," she said eyeing her father's pensive face.

Arnold patted her knee absently, but she brushed his hand away.

And well she might! Lyn thought. She studied her daughter's aquiline profile in the lamplight, then glanced at Matthew. Everyone said that Marianne and Arnold were replicas of Sarah and Abraham, but Lyn, the *shiksah* of the family, had produced this generation's likenesses of the Jewish matriarch and patriarch.

Jewish or Christian, why did it have to matter? Lyn said to herself wearily brushing a stray lock of hair away from her forehead. There were times, and this was one of them, when Lyn agreed with every word her son had just said on the subject of religion.

What was Arnold thinking? He had not removed his gaze from the gasfire, but his expression denoted an inner conflict. Lyn had never doubted that he cared deeply for his father and, for a moment, she pitied him. What could be worse than being torn, as Arnold had been for years, between an all-consuming pride and filial love?

Matthew too was surveying Arnold, and showed him no pity at all. "If Dad doesn't go to the hospital and end his ridiculous vendetta, I shall be the next one who never speaks to his father again."

Arnold shuddered. Then he went to embrace Matthew, which he had not done since his son was a small boy.

Matthew broke away from him. "Are you going, or aren't you?"

Arnold nodded wordlessly. Matthew's threat had brought home to him, full force, the pain he had inflicted upon his own father.

When Arnold entered the small side-ward in which Ben was the sole patient, Esther and Marianne were seated beside the bed. Arnold had telephoned his Uncle Joe Klein, which nobody else had thought to do, though Joe lived in London, and they had come to the hospital together.

"I only got back from a foreign assignment this evening, or I'd have come to Martin's *Bar Mitzvah*," Joe said to Marianne.

Esther gave him a cold glance. "I'm glad you didn't, or your poor brother might have had the stroke earlier in the day and not heard his grandson read his Portion in *shul*."

"Please, Mam—" Marianne protested quietly.

"If I can't speak my mind now, when can I?" Esther demanded. She had not allowed her eyes to linger upon Arnold, though the effect his arrival had upon her was evident from the two patches of scarlet staining her pale cheeks.

Nor did she now address her remarks to him. Instead, she spoke to Marianne, as if Arnold was not there. "What your father has been through, because of his brother and his younger son, I don't have to tell you, Marianne."

The reference to Joe harked back to his years of estrangement from Ben, after marrying out of the faith. The breach had later been healed superficially, but neither Esther nor Ben had met Joe's wife and son.

"So what did you need, the two of you, moral support?" Esther asked sarcastically. "That you've turned up at my husband's deathbed together?" She rose from her chair and went to the washbasin in the corner of the room, turned on a tap, then turned it off again, as if she must busy herself, however uselessly. She gave Arnold a baleful glance. "A lot of good it will do your father, you being here now!"

Arnold was at the bedside, gazing down at Ben's face, his own working with emotion.

Joe had glanced at his brother once and turned away, as though he could not bear what he saw. "I'm going home," he said gruffly. There was nothing he could do here.

Marianne got up and kissed him, aware of her mother eyeing her rebukingly for doing so. What did Mam hope to gain by forever raking up the past?

"Keep in touch, chick," Joe said to her affectionately.

"I will." Over the years, Marianne had grown very close to her journalist uncle.

"I may as well go, too," Arnold said after Joe had left. The air was thick with his mother's animosity.

"Members of Parliament must have more important things to do than sit with their dying fathers!" Esther flashed.

Arnold moved to the door and paused to look at her, but she did not meet his glance. "You don't want me here, do you, Mother?" he said quietly. "And where I'm not wanted, I don't want to be."

Marianne left the room with him. She wanted to be there if he encountered Harry on the corridor. Harry didn't have a gun, but he had big fists.

Kids, Esther thought poignantly after they had gone. "We certainly had our share from those two, didn't we?" she said to Ben and was beset by a feeling of utter desolation because he could not answer her. "But in the end, our Marianne, despite her funny ideas, turned out to be a good daughter," she continued her monologue. Then a long sigh escaped her. If only Arnold had turned out to be half as good a son.

"Don't be too hard on the lad," she knew Ben would say if he were conscious.

"A peace-loving man you always were," she told him. "And so soft with our children, I had no option but to be strict with them," she added reminiscently.

"Except for Harry, where did it get you?" Ben's voice whispered in her mind's ear.

This was something he had said to her many times. But there was plenty he had not said. She, not he, had shown

Arnold the door on that wartime afternoon when he told
them he was going to marry a *shiksah*. But Ben had never
once rubbed salt into the wound by reminding her of it.

Ben Klein wasn't the kind to hurt anybody, Esther reflected
and a great gust of anger swept through her. Because nothing, now, could prevent him from going to his grave without
the heart's-ease of a reconciliation with his younger son. And
for this she could not forgive Arnold. Let him stay an
outsider! His reappearance in their midst had come too late.

She heard someone enter and thought it was Marianne
returning, then raised her eyes and saw her mother standing
beside her. How old Sarah looked tonight. She too had had
her share of *tsorus* from her children, one way and another.
From her grandchildren also. But usually a person forgot
Sarah was now in her eighties; she had the kind of personality
that was ageless and a zest for life still shone in her eyes.
Now, there was a weary look about her, as if this long day,
that had begun with joy and ended in tragedy, had taken its
toll of her fading strength. Nevertheless, her wrinkled face
was wearing what the family called her Queen Victoria expression, Esther noted. Which meant she was about to
deliver a lecture.

"You're a silly girl," Sarah said without preamble, as though
her daughter were a five-year-old. There was no need for her
to say to what she was referring. "When will you learn,
Esther?"

Esther regarded her impassively. A row with her mother
right now, she didn't intend to have.

But Sarah was determined to say what must be said. "All
kinds of fools there are in this world," she went on briskly,
"but the ones who don't want to learn are the worst." She cast
a sad glance at Ben. "For everything the Almighty does, He
has a reason, Esther. Though it isn't always easy for us to
fathom out."

Sarah sat down and took Esther's plump hands in her own
small ones. "I've been asking myself, over and over again,
why would God do this to Ben? Then Marianne came to tell
me Arnold had been here."

"You and your ill winds!" Esther knew how her mother's
mind worked.

"And isn't it the truth?"

Esther withdrew her hands and Sarah played with her
brooch, pensively, for a moment, then brushed a speck of fluff

off the skirt of her gray wool dress. It was warm in the hospital and she had taken off her coat and left it in the waiting room.

"But you, you won't let the good blow on you," Sarah accused her daughter. "You won't let the sweetness of reconciliation that's there waiting for you to taste, along with the bitterness of losing Ben, touch your stubborn lips!"

"I haven't lost Ben yet," Esther whispered, though both of them knew that, in effect, she had. "And you're too cunning by far, Mother." In every family crisis, Sarah dipped into her store of old wives' proverbs and homespun wisdom. And the ill wind and the bittersweet had always been her two favorites, Esther recalled.

They fell silent and Sarah reached out and stroked Esther's hair, as she had when her daughter was a little girl. Only now it felt stiff, from the lacquer with which it had been liberally sprayed that morning. To keep her smart hairset in place for the *simchah*, Sarah thought with a pang. It was a blessing that a person never knew in advance how any day would end.

"All right. I'm a crafty old woman, but I want you to humor me, Esther," Sarah said managing to smile. "Grasp what God has offered you. Accept that losing your husband can be the means of regaining your son. The chance to make *sholom* with Arnold might not come again."

Chapter Four

The day before Laura was due to leave for Switzerland, she called at the factory to say farewell to her grandfather.

"I'm going to miss you," David said. He had pleaded with Shirley not to send Laura away, but it had fallen on deaf ears.

"And I'll miss you," Laura said, giving him a hug.

"I suppose your mother is up to her ears in clothes, packing for you?" Shirley had taken the afternoon off.

"And for herself," Laura answered. "She and Daddy are only going to stay for a few days, until I settle in—which I never will! But the amount of stuff Mummy's taking, you'd think she was going for a year."

Laura plonked herself on a corner of the desk and David

pinched her cheek affectionately. "By the time you come back, I expect you'll be fashion-conscious, too."

"That's why Mum's sending me, isn't it?" Laura said derisively. "To turn me into a lady!"

"Ladies are born, love. Not made."

"You mean a sow's ear can't be turned into a silk purse, don't you?"

"That's right." David got up and went to gaze through the window. "But I'm not saying it can't be turned into an artificial-silk purse."

"I'm not sure what you're getting at, Grandpa."

David turned to look at Laura. Why had he said that to her? Because he was against what Shirley was trying to do. Turn her into a replica of herself, with the same false values. Remove the rare streak of individuality David had always known was in the girl, which Shirley saw as rough edges that required smoothing. But it wasn't just that, David thought. If Laura had been gifted academically, Shirley would have been content to let her enter a profession, along with the new breed of bright Jewish girls who, these days, pursued a higher education along with the boys. The time when a female child was automatically relegated to domesticity, with no other future options open to her, were long gone. But if their daughters were not clever, women like Shirley set about grooming them for the marriage stakes—though few went to the lengths to which Shirley was going! David thought with feeling.

"Don't let your mother change you," he said to Laura. "You're fine the way you are."

"You haven't got a very good opinion of Mummy, have you?" she answered stiffly. Nor had she, but that was different.

David noted his granddaughter's sudden defensiveness and knew he must tread carefully. "I have certain reservations about her ideas, love. That's all," he said with a smile. One of which was trying to turn her daughter into the Jewish equivalent of a debutante. David had been climbing up the ladder of achievement all his life, but a social climber he had never been. In that respect, he had kept his feet firmly on the ground, never lost sight of his humble beginnings.

"Did you know I was once so poor I had to walk around with holes in my boots?" he said to Laura.

"You're kidding, Grandpa."

"Why would I do that?"

"To take me down a peg or two, in case I become a snob because I'm going to finishing school," Laura smiled.

This was exactly what David feared might happen. Once she became entrenched in that upper-crust ethos, at her impressionable age it was inevitable. "I wasn't kidding, Laura. The Sandbergs fled to England from the Russian pogroms without a penny in their pockets."

"I've heard Bobbie Sarah say that, lots of times. But I always thought it was an exaggeration. What's a pogrom, by the way?" Laura asked.

"Are you saying you don't know?" David found this difficult to believe.

"Only vaguely. It's Daddy's family history, not Mummy's, that gets talked about in our house. The way he lived in a beautiful apartment in Vienna and had to leave all the family heirlooms behind and come to England, when the Nazis took his parents and grandfather away. My mother told Mark and me all about it."

Shirley would have done that, David thought. She would prefer her children to associate themselves with that kind of background, rather than the one from which she herself had come.

"I know what the word 'holocaust' means," Laura added.

For the young Jews and Jewesses of the postwar generation, the most recent evil chapter of their people's history had blocked out the one prior to it, which was written in blood before they were born. "Look up the word 'pogrom' in your dictionary," David instructed Laura. "And ask your great-grandma to give you her firsthand version. I was only a little boy when we left Russia. She'll remember the details better than me."

"I once asked Mum to show me the house you used to live in, in Strangeways," Laura said. "But she couldn't be bothered."

Couldn't be bothered my eye! David thought. Not for anything would Shirley want her daughter to see the back-street house where the Sandbergs had put down roots in England.

"Come on, I'll show it to you now," he said to Laura.

"I expect there are Pakistanis or West Indians living in it now," Laura smiled. "Strangeways is that kind of district."

David stiffened. "What kind of district?"

"You know, Grandpa." Laura glanced through a glass partition into the workroom, where some dark-skinned women and girls were visible among the machinists.

"No, I don't know, Laura," David said.

"I mean where immigrants live." Laura noted his tight-lipped expression. "What the matter?"

"It ought to be me, asking what's the matter with you! Who the hell do you think you are? Talking about immigrants that way!"

"What did I say?"

"It was the way you said it."

"I don't think I want to go and see that house," Laura said sulkily.

"All the more reason why you should!" Finishing school would put the tin lid on it, David thought. Shirley had done plenty of damage already. He took Laura's arm and propelled her out of the office.

"Where are you going? In case I need to contact you," his secretary inquired as they passed through her adjoining sanctum, which was the most direct route to the stairs.

"On a pilgrimage to our ancestral home," David said.

"Immigrants are people," he informed Laura after he had bundled her into his car. "With the same hopes and dreams as anyone else."

"Did I say they weren't, Grandpa?"

David started the engine and headed for Strangeways. "I doubt if you've ever given it a thought."

"Why should I?"

"Because that's what Jews once were."

"I'm not entirely ignorant!"

"Just forgetful," David said for want of a better way of putting it. "Not that I would want or expect you to walk around with it in the forefront of your mind."

"You could've fooled me, Grandpa! I mean from the way you've been going on about it."

"All I expect from you, Laura, is not to be condescending about, or toward, those who are just starting out along the road that your own family had to travel to reach where they are now. From the top drawer you're not and don't you forget it."

"You've made me feel ashamed, Grandpa," Laura said after a silence.

"I'm delighted to hear it, love." David pointed to a shop

displaying a multifarious assortment of clothing. "That used to be Mr. Radinsky's greengrocery store, when I was a lad. He paid me in fruit and vegetables to clean the place up every night, when I got home from school."

"It's a sort of warehouse now, isn't it?" Laura said as they drove past it.

The new ethnic communities had injected their presence into the city's commerce, as the Jews had before them, David reflected. And the same repetition of that pattern was happening countrywide. Good luck to you! he smiled, mentally taking his hat off to a white-turbaned gentleman staggering with a heavy stack of boxes from a warehouse to his car. Those who weren't afraid of work—and in that respect, the Asian immigrants reminded David of his own brethren—were entitled to their reward.

David turned the car into a mean little street and pulled up outside a grimy terraced house. In which the respected Dr. Nathan Sandberg was born, he thought wryly. And the forebears of a girl about to go to finishing school had their beginnings. More than half a century later, it was difficult for David to believe, and how much more so it must be for Laura, he thought, glancing at her.

"Hm," she muttered playing with the strap of her expensive cowhide shoulder bag. "I'm not surprised my mother wouldn't show it to me."

"Personally, I'm rather proud of it," David said.

"Well, that's the difference between you and Mum, isn't it?"

"And which of us are you going to be like, Laura? Your no-nonsense granddad, or your mother the artificial-silk purse?"

"Need you ask?" Laura said with feeling. "And this does it! I'm not going to that school."

"There no need to go to those lengths," David said. "Just don't lose track of who and what you are, when you get there."

"I said I'm not going. And I mean it. But don't worry, Grandpa, I shan't bring you into it," Laura said, noting David's dismayed expression.

"I'll take you back to the factory with me," David said, "and you can get a lift home with your father."

"When I get there, I'll have to tell my mother a few home truths," Laura said as David started the car.

David did not reply. Bringing his granddaughter down to

earth was one thing. Inciting her to mutiny was quite another. Shirley's wrath, if she found out he was responsible, would fall upon his head. What had he done!

Laura did not speak throughout the short journey back to Sanderstyle, but David sensed her inner excitement, that she was privately plotting and planning.

"If Mummy insists upon taking me to Switzerland tomorrow, I'll run away the moment she and Daddy have gone home," she said as David parked the car on the factory forecourt.

"You'll do no such thing!"

Laura regarded him silently for a moment. "I thought you were my ally," she said stiffly, "because of the things you said to me. But apparently you're not. Nor have you the courage of your convictions."

David was conscious of a familiar telltale tightening in his chest. He took a deep breath and then another, which he had learned helped him relax, and the tension slackened.

"You're not feeling ill, are you?" Laura asked, eyeing him anxiously and remembering he had once had a heart attack.

"If I am, who could be surprised?" David got out of the car, locked his door and waited for Laura to get out, so he could lock her side.

"I'm sorry," she said contritely.

David ignored the apology. "Now I know my granddaughter's opinion of me, I can go back to work," he said striding away from her, without pausing to defend himself against her unjust accusation. Not got the courage of his convictions indeed! If that were so, would he have stuck his neck out by taking her to see the house? Giving her the talking-to he had? He was prepared to uphold all the sentiments he had expressed to Laura, even if it led to a confrontation with Shirley. But he hadn't expected Laura to use them as a weapon against her mother, a reason for defying her.

Laura remained beside the car, watching her grandfather walk away. She hadn't meant to upset him. But she had momentarily forgotten he was an old gentleman who couldn't be expected to encourage a schoolgirl to run away.

Run away to where? she thought dejectedly. Grandpa's reaction had made her plan seem stupid and impractical. She didn't know anyone in Switzerland. But there was no one she could turn to here, either. She rested her back against her grandfather's Bentley, then glanced at her father's car and at the space which her mother's usually occupied.

Money's no object in our family, she said to herself bitterly. But that doesn't stop this member from feeling like a lost soul. Destined for a Swiss purgatory! If Mummy's car were parked here now, her darling daughter would lift one of the white-painted boulders that bordered the forecourt and hurl it through the windscreen!

Laura thrust her hands mutinously into the pockets of the tweed tent-coat her mother said camouflaged her pudginess, though it made Laura feel ten times her size. "As you're no brainbox, we must make the most of your female charms," Mummy had pronounced the first time that damned school was mentioned. And had added that Laura could be quite attractive if she lost weight. Diet and exercise had featured in the school's prospectus, Laura recalled, gazing up at some scudding clouds in the autumnal sky. And it struck her that she was the proverbial ugly duckling, being sent away to be streamlined into an elegant swan, to equip her for the kind of life she had no intention of living.

This thought returned her full circle to the one that had initiated her bout of despair. There was nobody to whom she could turn for support. If she were in some other kind of trouble, the whole clan would be putting their heads together to try to help her. But none of them would do so in her present plight. Even those who sympathized with her would consider it best to keep out of it—as Grandpa obviously did.

It seemed that having the courage of your convictions wasn't a common adult quality, Laura reflected. Then a pinprick of hope appeared like a light in the tunnel of gloom surrounding her. There was someone to turn to! Why hadn't it occurred to her sooner? Someone to whom she was sure her assessment of adults in general did not apply.

David assumed that instead of coming into the factory to wait for a lift home with her father, Laura had gone off to sulk somewhere. He felt obliged to tell Peter why.

"The poor kid has all my sympathy," Peter said.

"Then why don't you put your foot down with Shirley, for once in your life?"

Peter looked down at a stock-list he had been studying

when David entered his office. "Do you really want to know?" he asked brusquely, raising his eyes to meet David's gaze.

"You've never struck me as being a weakling in any other way," David said.

"Thank you. Nor am I weak in this way. Indeed, some might say it takes strength to maintain the *status quo* with a woman like your daughter."

With this, David could not argue.

"I had to make a decision in that respect a long time ago," Peter revealed. "Which, to be precise, was a choice between two alternatives. To stay with Shirley or to leave her."

David took a cigarette from the box on Peter's desk—his resolution to give up smoking entirely was long gone and he allowed himself a few a day, the number varying according to the need to calm his nerves. Right now, he needed one badly! "I think that's a decision a lot of men have to make, at some time or other in their marriage," he said carefully. Though, despite the traumas he had experienced in his early years with Bessie, it had never once occurred to him to walk out on her. "Marriage is supposed to be for better or worse," he reminded his son-in-law.

"And mine has been mostly the latter," Peter answered evenly. "But I'm not complaining. To stay was my considered decision."

"What would you have done if you'd decided not to stay?" David inquired, though he was not sure why. Nor could he account for the once-removed feeling he had, as if it were not his daughter whom they were discussing.

A faraway expression entered Peter's eyes, reminding David of the occasional dreaminess he had displayed as a boy, which in his manhood had not been evident. Perhaps because Peter no longer had anything to dream about.

"You'd have gone to live in Israel, I suppose," David answered his own question. And enjoyed an interesting life with your old friends from Vienna who settled there, he thought. Why had it never struck him before that Peter was like a fish out of water in the big-spender circle in which he and Shirley mixed? That coming to live in David's home and marrying his daughter had diverted Peter from the intellectual path he would doubtless otherwise have trodden?

"Except that Israel was still Palestine when I decided I must remain with my wife," Peter nodded.

Must? David thought. Remain with? The words had a chilling ring. He had not deluded himself that Shirley and Peter were blissfully happy, but had not realized things were that bad. Or that the rot had set in so long ago.

"I stayed for our children's sake," Peter said.

"That's the usual reason."

"But not just because I couldn't bear to leave them or hurt them," Peter declared. "I didn't want them to be raised by Shirley alone. Though how much impression having me around has made on their characters remains to be seen."

More than you think, David thought gratefully. But he said nothing.

"I hope this conversation hasn't upset you," Peter said. "I didn't intend giving you something else to worry about."

David managed to smile and returned to his own office. Sometimes he thought there wasn't space for one more anxiety to be lodged in his head.

The events of the afternoon had left David drained and weary, but a telephone call from Shirley put an end to the quiet evening he had promised himself.

"We're at Bobbie Sarah's," she said without bothering to greet him when he lifted the receiver. "Laura's disappeared. Peter and I weren't going to tell you—not that you deserve such consideration; it's your fault she has. But Bobbie said we must let you know."

The receiver clicked down at the other end before David had recovered from his shock. How was he to tell Bessie? Somehow he managed to and had to spend ten minutes calming her before they left the house.

When they arrived at his mother's house, he was not surprised to find that the clan had gathered. In an emergency, they always did. As it was a weeknight, and Sarah only used her parlor weekends, they were in the kitchen.

"Shirley has rung up all Laura's friends and nobody has even heard from her," Sarah told David and Bessie. "How are we going to find her?"

"If my father were in Manchester, he'd tell us what to do," Matthew, who was there with his mother, declared. "Shall I put through a call to him at the House of Commons? Mum spoke to him this afternoon and he said they'd be sitting late tonight."

"There's no necessity for us to disrupt the workings of government," Hannah Moritz said, tongue-in-cheek. "It would be more useful to telephone the police."

"But not very suitable," David countered.

"A fine thing it would be if this got into the Jewish newspapers!" Bessie moaned.

"Exactly," David said brusquely. His innards were churning with anxiety and guilt, in equal quantities.

"I agree," Rebecca said. She was sucking a peppermint and rolled it contemplatively around her tongue. "If this gets around, Laura's reputation will be ruined."

Shirley glared at David. "My dad wasn't thinking of her reputation when he talked her out of going to Switzerland!"

"I had to tell Shirley about your chat with Laura," Peter apologized to David.

"After you'd let me drive myself crackers for an hour!" Shirley flung at him. "Wondering if something I'd done was to blame."

"Blameless you're not, my darling."

"Pack it in, you two," Ronald intervened.

"We haven't come here to listen to you bickering," Nathan told them.

"Which you and Mummy never do, of course," Leona said to him sarcastically. "I'm not surprised that Laura's hopped it! I thought of doing so many times, when I was her age."

Frank put a hand on her shoulder. "Hush, love. You'll waken Carla," he said glancing down at their baby daughter, who was asleep on his wife's lap.

During the day, while Leona was at the office, the baby was left in Bridie's care. The Frank Moritzes could not afford to employ an au pair and baby-sitters had to be engaged in advance, which was why Carla was with them tonight.

"A baby can sleep through everything," Leona answered. "Little children, too, in a manner of speaking." Since learning that Laura had run away, she had been reliving her own traumatic youth. "Unfortunately, the sublime ignorance of one's early years doesn't last."

"This was intended to be a family conference and we're not doing much conferring," Frank said in his down-to-earth way. "How do you propose to find Laura without calling in the police?" he asked David.

"There are private detective agencies."

"Come off it, Uncle! Finding a missing person can be a large-scale operation."

"Oh God—my daughter is a missing person—" Shirley whispered as if Laura's absence had not yet struck her in those terms.

She had paled visibly. Bessie too. Sarah fetched a bottle of brandy from the dresser cupboard and poured a drop for each of them.

"I don't want it," Shirley said. "Give it to Dad. He probably needs it after what he's been the cause of. What will the police do, if we notify them? Drag the Irwell to find Laura's body?" she asked Frank with a shudder.

"Not unless you've made her so miserable she decided to drown herself," Leona said brutally.

Shirley leaped up from her chair to pace the room, but was foiled by the absence of space. "Why am I being blamed for this?" she shrilled, then tripped over her son's feet.

Mark was squatting on the hearthrug beside his cousin, Howard Klein, a tense expression on his darkly handsome face. "It's time you stopped thinking of yourself, Mum," he said tersely. "And started thinking of Laura."

Shirley had regained her balance and stationed herself against the brass-topped fireguard. "What did I ever think about, but you and your sister, Mark?" she demanded. "Since the minute you were born, all I've ever wanted was what's best for you."

"What you think is best for us," her son replied, standing up to her for the first time in his life.

"For a lad of fifteen, you're much too big for your boots!" she responded.

"Don't let it get you down, Shirley. Harry and I get the same from our Howard," Ann Klein commiserated.

But Shirley had turned her attention to David and riveted him with an icy stare. "It's you who is the guilty party, not me."

"All I did was tell Laura some things it ought not to have been necessary for me to say. You brought her up to think she's something she isn't. I thought it wise to disillusion her, before going to a finishing school put an irremovable coat of varnish on it."

"You always did take too much upon yourself," Nathan told him witheringly.

"Is that so?"

"Raking up old coals will get us nowhere," Sarah intervened.

"But when did this family ever lose an opportunity to do so?" Sigmund put in. "In a minute, everyone present will be at each other's throats—like always happens when we have a crisis. And it will take another hour to remember what we are here for!"

"I'm beginning to wonder what we *are* here for," Ann said to Harry, who was gloomily puffing a cigar. "We don't seem to be doing much good."

"Your family, the Smolenskys, don't rush to each other's side when there's trouble?" Esther said to her caustically.

"Of course they do."

"Rushing to each other's sides is a Jewish quality," Sarah declaimed.

"Nevertheless, I agree with Ann," Hannah said in a voice which commanded attention.

She was wearing a black suit with a white blouse, which lent severity to her aging appearance, reminding the others that she was not just a retired headmistress. After a lifetime of dedicated work with deprived children, Hannah Moritz was now a justice of the peace.

"I came here in case I could be of some practical use," she declared. "But it's obvious that even a person to whom delinquent juveniles are, unfortunately, no novelty, is wasting her time offering advice to this family."

"Are you calling my daughter a delinquent?" Shirley flashed.

"I'm suggesting it's possible she could become one, if you don't heed the warning she's given you," Hannah replied evenly. "Perhaps you're not aware of it, Shirley, but a new phenomenon has entered our society—the youngster who goes off the rails despite having everything. As opposed to those who do so ostensibly because they have nothing. Your daughter has carried out what amounts to an act of desperation and I advise you to bear that in mind."

"When she's found," David said after a silence.

Sarah poked the fire to hide her anxiety, which had increased tenfold after what Hannah had said. "So let it get into the newspapers, who cares?" she exclaimed. "One day they'll also print Laura's engagement announcement. All that matters now is for her to be safe. Go and ring up the police, Peter."

* * *

Marianne was contemplating the blank paper in her typewriter, when the doorbell rang. "I'm not in! No matter who it is," she called to Ralph as he went to open the door. "If I don't get this chapter started before bedtime, I won't sleep."

"Good God!" she heard him exclaim from the hall.

That their son had arrived home on crutches was Marianne's first thought. Martin was spending the night with a schoolfriend whose home had a basement playroom—and had probably fallen down the railless stone staircase, her mind raced on. Stop being a Jewish mother! she chided herself. Invariably, she met trouble halfway and steeled herself for the worst, in relation to her one ewe lamb.

When she went into the hall, the sight that met her eyes was another kind of shock. Shirley's daughter arriving here unannounced, late at night? And dirty and disheveled?

"You said I was welcome to come and talk to you anytime," Laura reminded her.

"And I meant it, love. But how on earth did you get into that filthy state?"

"I hitchhiked to London."

"Good God!" Ralph said again. He removed a bit of muck from Laura's tangled hair.

"My last lift was in a potato truck and I had to squat in the back with the spuds," Laura explained. "The driver already had another hitchhiker in the front with him."

Marianne was trying to take it in. Laura Kohn thumbing rides? But daughters had been known to survive their mothers' influence and become their own person, she reflected wryly. Marianne's own lifestyle was poles apart from the teachings of Esther Klein. "Why didn't you phone to tell us you were coming?" she asked Laura.

"I was going to, then I decided against it. If you'd known in advance, Mummy'd think you'd encouraged me to run away. Or even that you'd put me up to it," Laura replied sagely.

Undoubtedly, Marianne thought. "So you've run away, have you?" she said.

Laura nodded. "You and Mum have never liked each other, have you?" she added.

Marianne evaded the question. "Come into the kitchen, Laura."

"While I go and fill the bath for you," Ralph grinned. "You look as if you need one!"

"One thinks of authors shut away in a book-lined study,"

Laura remarked, glancing at Marianne's typewriter and notes on the kitchen table.

"But this one hasn't got one. Now tell me all about it, Laura," Marianne requested. "Tomorrow's your birthday, isn't it?" she added irrelevantly. "I sent you a card."

"But it would have seemed more like my death-day, if I'd had to go to finishing school!" Laura said with feeling. "So I thought: to hell with it; I'm not going! And came here, instead. But I didn't have enough money with me for the train fare—I wasn't at home when I made the decision, or I could have opened my piggy bank. I just had the bus fare to Knutsford, where the long-distance lorries pass by, heading south."

"Weren't you scared of what might happen to you, Laura? Accepting lifts with strange men?"

"Of course. But when there's no alternative, a person does what they have to do."

Guts, this kid certainly had! But Marianne had realized when they'd had the chat at Martin's *Bar Mitzvah* that there was a good deal more to Laura than met the eye.

Ralph appeared in the kitchen doorway. "Your bath is drawn, milady!" he told their unexpected guest, with a mock bow.

Laura gave him a warm smile. "This afternoon, I felt like a drowning person without even a straw to clutch," she revealed. "And all the while, there was a strong, comforting bough within my reach—you two," she said, kissing them both before departing to the bathroom.

"We've been called some things in our time!" Ralph grinned, sitting down on the chair Laura had vacated. The others were occupied by some sheets and towels Marianne had laundered and forgotten to put away.

"Fill me in on the details of our young relative's escapade," Ralph requested. "I'd have let her fill her own bath, needless to say, but I thought it best for her to have a few minutes alone with you."

Marianne smiled. "It won't take her long to learn nobody gets waited on in this *ménage!*" The Kohns had a Spanish housekeeper who treated Laura like a princess, Marianne had heard.

"Now hold on, sweetheart!" Ralph said. "What exactly did you mean by that?"

"That Laura is likely to be under our roof for some time."

"Hm," Ralph said doubtfully. He took his tobacco pouch from his cardigan pocket and filled his pipe. "I remember her once kicking my shins when she was a nipper," he said irrelevantly.

"So do I," Marianne laughed. "I also remember you saying at the time that you wouldn't like to have to cope with her, when she grew up."

"Which will teach me to tempt Fate! But, joking apart, how exactly will we cope with this situation? What we ought to do is the sensible thing—pack her into the car and drive her home to her mother."

Marianne made a pot of tea. "When were you and I ever sensible—in the way you mean? And the sensible thing isn't necessarily the right one."

"Dependent upon one's point of view."

"Let's end the sparring match, Ralph! Do you agree we should be Laura's port-in-a-storm?"

"Reluctantly, yes. And what kind of cliché is that for a writer to mouth?"

"A very succinct one, love."

"We'd better let Shirley know Laura's here. She's probably having hysterics right now—"

"It won't do her any harm," Marianne said unkindly. "We'll call her when we've had a cup of tea. It may even do some good to let her stew."

"It isn't like you to be so cruel."

"Well this whole bloody mess is her fault, isn't it?" Marianne flared. "For trying to mold her daughter in her own image. That way lies disaster for any parent, as my mother could tell her."

She simmered down and dunked a digestive biscuit into her tea. "As Laura's come to us, we must work out a plan to help her."

"Oh yes?" Ralph said warily. His wife's expression now was the one she wore when at her most devious. "And what do you have in mind?" He had no doubt at all that whatever it was would rebound upon him. "Apart from having another teenager living here, to double what I already have to put up with from my son?" he said ruefully.

"You could find Laura a job at the agency."

"What! Have her around my neck at work, as well as at home?"

"She wouldn't be around your neck. She'd be in the

darkroom. She wants to be a photographer and that'd be a good way for her to begin, wouldn't it?"

Ralph had to laugh. "When it comes to conniving, you come second only to your grandmother!"

"But, like her, I usually do it for a good reason. And what you call conniving, I call planning." Marianne put down her teacup and smiled at her husband. "Now everything's settled, we can call Manchester. And present my cousin with a *fait accompli*."

"Call your conniving what you like, sweetheart. You're a past master at it," Ralph grinned.

"A writer has to be—on paper. I spend my days arranging my characters' lives, don't I? And sometimes the art comes in useful in real life."

"But, in real life, Shirley is unlikely to allow you to tell her what to do about her daughter," Ralph countered. "You don't seem to have taken that into account."

"You should know me better than to think that, dear. I intend to phone Bobbie Sarah, not Shirley. And tell her the whole thing. Only my grandma could put Shirley in her place and get away with it."

After receiving Marianne's telephone call, during which she made no comment, other than a final, "Leave it to me," Sarah put down the receiver and disclosed Laura's whereabouts to the rest of the clan.

Shirley's relief expressed itself as a great gust of anger. "When I get my hands on my daughter, I'll—"

Sarah allowed her to say no more. "Come with me, Shirley. I want to talk to you," she said, marching out of the room.

Nobody was surprised to see Shirley meekly follow her. When Sarah Sandberg addressed you in that tone, you were impelled to do as she said.

When, ten minutes later, they returned, it was Sarah who did the talking.

"But how did you get Mum to agree to it?" Mark asked when his great-grandmother announced that Laura was to remain at Marianne's, instead of going to finishing school.

"Your mother is a sensible woman," was all Sarah said. That she had given Shirley the kind of dressing-down she had never before received from anyone, was nobody's business. Sarah had followed it with a reminder of Hannah's warning that these days even well-to-do youngsters were going astray. Plus a chunk of her own wisdom—learned the hard way—that the way to avoid a dangerous rebellion was to remove the cause. Especially when the cause in this case was, in Sarah's view, not worth making an issue about.

Peter lit a cigarette and surveyed his unusually subdued wife.

"I wish Bobbie Sarah would come and live at our house," Mark smiled, voicing his father's approximate thoughts.

"For my part, you can go and live somewhere else," his mother snapped, stepping back into character. "Like your sister has," she added sourly. That Laura had gone to Marianne was the most bitter pill.

"If a war ever breaks out between Israel and the Arabs, you'll get rid of me for a while," Mark replied.

Shirley broke the silence his words had caused. "I beg your pardon?"

"If it happens, I'll go there and do my bit."

"We no sooner recover from one worry than we're presented with another," Shirley groaned.

"You should be proud of what your son just said," David told her.

"Haven't you caused enough trouble, championing your grandchildren, Dad?"

Sarah intervened. "Meanwhile, Mark is still a schoolboy. And what is all this talk of war?"

"Sooner or later, it won't just be talk," Sigmund, who was known as the family doom-merchant, pronounced, gazing into the fire.

"Regrettably, I have to agree," Hannah endorsed. "Because there hasn't been a major confrontation since Suez, the volcanic Middle East situation has moved out of the forefront of the news."

"Not for active Zionists," David declared.

"Like me," Mark put in.

"Going to live on a kibbutz, when you grow up?" Nathan smiled to him.

"Don't put such ideas into his head, Uncle," Shirley said. "Nobody could be more Zionist than I've been all my life, but we don't all have to end up in Israel. There wouldn't be room!"

"For once, I agree with my mother," Mark said. "I'll be working at Sanderstyle, after I've taken a business course at

college. England's my home and I don't want to live anywhere else. But if Israel ever needs me, I'll be there."

Shirley's depression was written on her face. Mark got up
and went to kiss her.

Kids! she thought emotionally. They could have you up in
the clouds, or down at rock bottom, just by a word or an
action. Or melt your heart with a single glance, she reflected,
gazing up into her son's soft dark eyes. The power they
wielded was formidable. But she had never believed in
letting hers know it.

"All right, Mum?" Mark asked her.

"Sure I'm all right," she lied, thinking again of her daughter's attachment to Marianne. How would she ever recover
from such a blow to her pride?

Shirley's ruffled feathers were eventually smoothed by Laura's first small success in the field of free-lance photography,
Marianne learned-via the family grapevine.

"I find it absolutely sickening that my cousin has to have
something to boast about regarding Laura being here, in
order to reconcile herself to it!" Marianne fumed to Ralph
one night.

Lyn had rung up that evening and had mentioned that
Shirley now referred proudly to Laura as "my photographer-
daughter."

Laura had been in London for almost six months. Five
days a week, she worked in the ad agency darkroom. On
weekends, and in the evenings, she roamed around with her
camera photographing street scenes, one of which had recently
been accepted by a weekly newspaper.

She had sent a copy of the paper home, after which
Marianne received her first telephone call from Shirley since
Laura's arrival. It had been Peter who brought his daughter's
clothes to London and he, too, who kept in close touch with
Marianne and Ralph.

"There's nothing like *nachas* and *yichus* to help the Shirleys
of this world come to terms with things," Marianne told her
husband with asperity.

They were preparing for bed and she was seated at her
dressing table, eyeing her reflection. "I'm beginning to look
my age," she said critically. But it was hard to believe she was
now thirty-eight.

Ralph surveyed her diminutive figure in the high-necked cotton nightshirt that made her look like a child, and went to kiss her tenderly. "To me, you're no different from the day we met, sweetheart."

He brushed her fringe aside and fingered the horizontal lines on her forehead, which she called her concentration grooves, then touched the tiny ones around her eyes and mouth. "Your face just looks more lived-in. Now come to bed!"

People said a married couple's appetite for each other diminished with the years, but with us it's been the very opposite, Marianne reflected as they lay together in the warm darkness after they had made love. Ralph, at forty-three, was now middle-aged—and herself not far from it. But the outward changes in their appearances were immaterial to their relationship. Neither felt any necessity to try to slow down nature's aging process, or to take pains to hide its effects from the other. And Marianne pitied those for whom this was necessary in order to hold on to their marriage partner. Or to attract the admiration of other people's, to compensate for what their personal life lacked, she thought with regard to Shirley.

"In some ways, I'm sorry for Shirley," she said against Ralph's stubbly cheek. If he ever took to shaving at night, it would be like sleeping with a stranger!

"But in a certain respect, you're exactly like her," he answered.

Marianne was sufficiently affronted to remove herself from his embrace.

"You're not above claiming your own portion of *nachas* and *yichus*, are you, sweetheart? And in advance! Last time we went up north, you were boasting to the family that Martin's school consider him a cert for Oxford."

"That's just the Yiddishe mamma coming out in me."

"Then why don't you look at Shirley's boasting about Laura in that light? Let me answer the question for you, love. Your dislike of your snobby cousin colors everything she says and does."

"It always has," Marianne admitted.

"So much so, that I was astonished to hear you say you're sorry for her. I had the impression it was quite the opposite, sweetheart. That there was an element of triumph in how you feel about her daughter turning to you."

"It was time Shirley got her comeuppance!"

"But, now she has, it's time you showed her a little compassion, Marianne. Before I ever met her, I'd got a picture of her from you," Ralph said. "The girl who's got everything summed it up, and meeting Shirley confirmed that preconception. But now, I'd call her an all-time loser. Her marriage is a mess—"

"That's the count on which I am sorry for her," Marianne cut in. "Though she's got what she deserves there, too."

"Losers are often people who've asked for it, sweetheart. But that's something else. And Shirley's a loser on all counts. Her dream of selling out Sanderstyle for a fortune has been scotched by her father. Then, to cap the lot, she was flatly rejected by Laura."

"And I'm a bitch because I'm enjoying her plight," Marianne said, with a surge of contrition she could not have envisaged ever being evoked by Shirley. "And what would you like me to do now I've admitted it, Ralph?"

"Send Laura home for the weekend, occasionally. And try to help her acquire a little tolerance toward her mother."

Marianne gazed contemplatively at a moonbeam that had filtered through a gap in the curtains. Ralph was right. But his last suggestion was something Marianne could not contrive.

"That's something life will eventually do," she told him. "As I learned in relation to my own mother. As your mum and dad died when you were a kid, Ralph, you'll just have to take my word for it that those of us who are blessed—or is it cursed? —with minds of our own don't begin to understand or sympathize with our parents until we're parents ourselves."

The blare of pop-music was issuing through the wall from their son's bedroom, as it did every night.

"In that case, I look forward to the time when Martin becomes one," Ralph grunted.

Chapter Five

In the spring of 1967, Leona discovered that her mother was an alcoholic. How could Mummy have become one without me knowing? she asked herself, averting her shocked gaze from the bottles of vodka which a moment ago had been hidden by a pile of sweaters in Rebecca's wardrobe.

The assortment of knitwear was now lying in an untidy heap on the carpet, catapulted there when Leona had tugged a chunky cardigan from the center of the pile.

She slipped it around her shoulders and shivered, but not just because the day had turned cold. If it hadn't, she would not have made this shattering discovery, she thought, retrieving the other woolens to fold and replace them. Oh, the commonplace things that affect people's lives, she reflected while doing so. Had Leona not, unwisely, gone to the office this morning wearing only a lightweight dress, she would still be in blissful ignorance of the major problem now staring her in the face.

Literally staring her in the face and she did not want to see it. Or even to think about it. She plonked the sweaters onto their shelf, to screen the telltale liquor from view.

"Carla's finished her boiled egg, Leona," she heard Bridie call from the foot of the stairs. "Will Oi be givin' me wee darlin' sum sago puddin'? Or is she t' have sum stewed fruit?"

"I'll have a bit of both," Carla's voice piped. "But I want my mummy to give it to me."

Leona shut the wardrobe door and hurried downstairs to supervise the rest of her daughter's tea. She was not always here to do so. Often, work kept her chained to her desk until long past teatime, and usually Bridie collected Carla from school, as she had today.

Bridie is more of a grannie to Carla than my mother is, Leona thought, surveying the child's neat and clean appearance. Carla didn't look like that when she emerged from the school playground. Anything but. The dear, devoted Irishwoman had even tied a big bow of white ribbon in Carla's unruly, red hair.

"I don't know where my grandma gets to in the afternoons," the precocious six-year-old declared, wiping her fingers on her pinafore. "She's never here, waiting to see me, when I come here after school."

Leona watched her dig into the dish of dessert Bridie had just put before her. "Where is my mother today?" she asked Bridie casually.

"Off wi' yere Auntie Bessie at wun o' them Zionist ladies meetings, Oi expec'," Bridie answered. "Israel'll be needin'

more money, Oi reckon, wi' wun ting an' anuther," she added
in the partisan manner with which she always spoke of the
Jewish State.

Leona smiled, momentarily detaching her thoughts from
the bottle of vodka. Bridie's loyalty to Israel was not surprising; she'd been what amounted to one of a Jewish family for
most of her life. And right now there wasn't a Jewish family in
the land not deeply concerned about the endless bombardment
of Israeli settlements below the Golan Heights, which had
begun last year and was still going on. Or that General
Nasser was encouraging and supporting the Fedayeen perpetrating the attacks. Jews everywhere feared that Israel was on
the brink of a war of survival, and were alarmed by the Soviet
Union's current vocal intervention on the Arabs' behalf. Not
that this was any surprise, Leona reflected. It was no secret
that Russia had begun arming Egypt before Suez; as long ago
as 1955.

Bridie returned Leona's thought to the mundane.

"Whin Carla's eaten up all her tea, she can have a sweet,"
she promised the child, who had wolfed down the fruit, but
was dawdling over the sago pudding.

"May I have one of grandma's peppermints?" Carla asked.
"As a special treat? She keeps some in the dresser drawer."

Peppermints, Leona thought. Her mother was rarely without one in her mouth. To hide the liquor fumes on her
breath. Mummy had been sucking peppermints for years. By
now, her tippling must be well established.

She vented her troubled feelings upon her daughter. "No,
you can't have a peppermint! They're bad for your teeth."

"Why aren't they bad for Grandma's teeth?"

"Be quiet!"

Leona had encountered alcoholics in the neighborhood law
practice she and Frank had set up in a working-class district,
usually when acting for some poor woman whose married life
was being made unbearable by a drunken husband. Apparently,
Rebecca had not added that aspect to her marital strife.
Instead, she had carefully concealed her mode of escape from
unhappiness. To spare her husband? Leona wondered briefly.
Not at all! Her parents were not in the habit of sparing each
other. Mummy's secrecy was entirely self-protective. Drunk-
en women were even less socially acceptable than their male
counterparts. And for a Jewish woman to be a *shikkerteh* was
unheard-of, Leona summed up with her clear, lawyer's mind.

"Did my aunt pick my mother up in her car?" she asked Bridie. Rebecca did not drive and Leona was now thankful she did not.

"No, peteen. Herself said she felt like a bus ride."

To a pub, probably. Leona's disquiet deepened. Had her mother descended to that level? Going, unescorted, into a bar? On the other side of town, where she would not be seen entering by anyone who knew her? And where would she go when the pub closed? Possibly, she had joined a club where out-of-hours drinking was permitted. And went there whenever she could think up a valid excuse to present to Auntie Bessie, instead of accompanying her to the respectable, tea-and-biscuit gatherings of Manchester and Salford's Zionist ladies.

"Grandpa's here!" Leona heard her daughter cry out delightedly, and saw her father pulling funny faces at Carla through the kitchen window.

Was it possible he didn't know what had happened to his wife?

Nathan entered through the back door and received a rapturous welcome from his granddaughter.

"I love-love-love you, Grandpa!" the little girl said, clinging to his neck when he lifted her from her chair.

"The feeling is mutual, my doll," Nathan answered, whirling her around.

"Will ye luk at himself, now!" Bridie exclaimed. "'Tis makin' the wee wun sick an' dizzy, he'll be after doin'!"

"But as Grandpa's a doctor, he'll be able to make me better," Carla countered.

Nathan sat down with the child on his lap and fondled her dimpled cheek. She aroused in him the same tenderness Leona had as a child. But, as others had told him before he became a grandparent, there was an extra dimension to the love a person had for their children's children.

"I bet you came home because you guessed I'd be here today," Carla said while Nathan was drinking the tea Bridie made for him.

"Correct," he smiled.

"This is my second home, isn't it, Grandpa?" Carla said sharing his chocolate biscuit.

She enjoys being here, Leona thought with a pang. What a shock the kid was in for, when the rosy mist with which little children's eyes are blessed drifted away and she saw her grandparents' home for the empty place it was. And Leona had a feeling that when that day came, Carla's sympathy would be all for Nathan.

"Come into the lounge, Dad, I want a word with you," she said. She had allowed her thoughts to stray from the dreadful discovery she'd made, but could do so no longer.

"Is it important, Leona? I mustn't be late for evening surgery," Nathan replied. Why was she eyeing him that way? As if she was—what? Assessing him?

"It's very important," Leona said, leaving the room.

Nathan had no option but to follow her.

"Sit down," she said brusquely when he entered the lounge.

Her distressed expression compelled Nathan to do so.

"You knew, didn't you?" Leona accused him, when he remained silent after she had told him her mother had taken to drink.

Nathan nodded. "But I was hoping to keep it from you."

A surge of anger swept through Leona. "I know you don't care about Mummy, but in a matter of this kind I would have expected your professional scruples to have taken precedence over your personal feelings toward her."

Nathan gazed through the window at a flowering cherry tree by the garden gate and did not reply.

"What kind of person are you?" his daughter demanded. "To have watched my mother become an alcoholic and do nothing about it?"

"When it first began, I tried."

"And how long ago was that, exactly?"

After I made love to her and she was disgusted with herself for responding, Nathan thought. That was the first occasion on which he had seen Rebecca go to the wine cabinet and pour herself a drink. After that night, she had done so regularly.

"Answer my question, Daddy!"

"I can't remember exactly when I warned her it was becoming a habit," Nathan said. Which was true.

"You should have stopped her!" Leona said with feeling. "I'd noticed that Mummy enjoyed a sherry, or a cocktail, at family *simchas* in recent years—but this! What sort of doctor are you, that you've let such a thing happen to your own wife?"

"Lou is your mother's doctor."

"I shall have a word or two to say to him, too!"

"Lou's done his best, Leona. With drink, nobody can help a person who doesn't want to be helped."

"My poor mother," Leona whispered.

"How about your poor father?" Nathan could not prevent himself from saying.

"But you haven't come to grief like Mummy has. Liquor is her escape."

And mine is women, Nathan thought. Which Rebecca knew. Since his briefly rekindled hope of marital happiness was snuffed out, he had sought consolation elsewhere, which until then he had not done. His few earlier amorous encounters had been opportune and a secret from his wife, but he no longer resorted to subterfuge. He was as entitled to his compensation for their mutual misery as Rebecca to hers, he thought bitterly.

"We can't just leave things the way they are," his daughter said. "And you were wrong not to tell me."

Nathan lost his temper. "If you spent a little more time with your mother, you wouldn't have needed telling!"

That evening, Leona called to see her grandmother.

"What a nice surprise!" Sarah said when she opened the door.

Leona followed her into the kitchen. "You might not think so when you hear why I've come."

Sarah had known there must be a reason. Leona had never dropped in on her before. And her composure seemed a little forced. "You've had a row with Frank? I hope not," she inquired.

Leona smiled. "Who can row with Frank?"

Sarah returned the smile. Theirs was a good marriage, she thought gratefully. The kind that would never go wrong.

"I want your advice about something," Leona said.

"That's what grandmothers are for." Mothers, too, Sarah reflected. But Leona's mother had enough problems of her own.

Sarah managed to hide her horror when she learned from Leona what Rebecca's latest problem was. And things which had been previously insignificant assumed meaning now. The peppermints. Rebecca regularly requesting a drop of brandy to ease indigestion. And her habit of leaving early, to go home and watch television in bed. With a bottle for company, Sarah thought sorrowfully.

"I spoke to Uncle Lou Benjamin, on the phone," Leona said. "He told me what Daddy did. That you can't help an alcoholic who doesn't want to be helped. And on a personal level, my father seems to have resigned himself to it," Leona added with distress. "That's why I came to see you."

"Your father has had a terrible life," Sarah sighed, casting her mind back to the harrowing months after Leona's birth, when Rebecca had refused to so much as look at her baby. "You don't know the half of it, Leona." And thank God she didn't.

"I know enough to be aware that Mummy's life hasn't been all roses, either."

"That is also true."

"But Daddy had his work. My mother has nothing to occupy her mind except herself." Leona felt awkward, talking about her parents to her grandmother. But Sarah Sandberg was a wise woman and she made herself continue. "Mummy is the kind of woman to whom marriage is their be-all and end-all."

"You mean marriage and motherhood," Sarah corrected her. "Your mother has a granddaughter, too."

"But Carla and I can't help her personal loneliness, can we, Bobbie? And there's no doubt in my mind that that is what drove her to drink."

Sarah stopped poking the fire. "If there were no other remedy for what you are talking about, every woman who is widowed would take to the bottle for comfort. Including me. But I'm part of my children's lives. If you want to give your mother a reason to stop drinking, you must make her part of yours, Leona."

Sarah spooned some tea into her ever ready teapot and filled it with water from the kettle that lived on her hob.

Her grandmother's homily had stung Leona. Her father, too, had implied that she neglected her mother. "Mummy could see Carla and me every afternoon, if she wanted to. But she's never there when Bridie brings Carla from school," she told Sarah defensively.

Sarah stirred the tea carefully. "For that there can only be one reason, Leona. She knows you don't care whether she is there or not. That you only come for your own convenience."

It's true, Leona had to admit. She hadn't expected this talk

with her grandmother to turn into a chastisement of herself—
but she deserved it.

Sarah poured the tea into her everyday willow-patterned
cups, from which Leona had not sipped before, because she
only came here on *Shabbos*. She eyed her youngest granddaughter's conscience-stricken expression and sighed. Though
Sarah's other grandchildren had, for one reason or another,
clashed with their parents in later years, they were able to
look back on a happy childhood.

"Well?" Sarah asked Leona eloquently.

"I intend to take your advice."

"Good. It will help your mother."

"You hope!" Leona said gloomily.

Sarah smiled. "Hope has kept me going all my life." She
steered the conversation to more inconsequential matters;
she did not believe in laboring the point, once she had made
it.

"Next time you see you mother, tell her you love her," she
said later, when she was seeing Leona out.

"She'll think I've gone crackers!"

Sarah glanced down at her pregnant cat, which had just
loped into the front porch. The bond between mother and
child was natural to all God's creatures, but from the beginning something had gone terribly wrong between Rebecca
and her daughter.

"People of my age don't usually say things like that to their
mothers," Leona informed her.

"Usually, it doesn't need to be said."

Chapter Six

The luxurious *kosher* hotels in Bournemouth had long been a
holiday venue for British Jews, but Sarah did not visit the
resort until Whitsuntide 1967, when David and Bessie persuaded her to accompany them and find out what she had
been missing.

"Such a long journey," she complained as they headed
south in David's car on Friday afternoon.

"It will soon be over, Ma," Bessie placated her. "Look,

we've reached the New Forest already," she added glancing through the window at the tall trees now lining their route. "And when you arrive, you'll think the traveling was worth it. At those hotels every night is like a wedding, with dancing and everything."

Sarah snorted. "For someone to ask me to dance, I can't wait! But my ball gown, I forgot to bring. All I'm concerned with is will we get there before *Shabbos* begins?"

"Of course," David assured her. "And you'll find *Shabbos* candles on our table this evening, for you and Bessie to light. They provide them for all the women."

"Which is no different from the boarding house I stay at in Southport," Sarah rejoined. "To where it doesn't take me all day to get."

"But until you've been to Bournemouth, you haven't lived," Bessie informed her.

Sarah rested her elbows on the two hatboxes Bessie had brought, for which there was not space in the crammed boot, and allowed the rustic beauty of the surroundings to briefly soothe her. "Be careful, David!" she exclaimed nervously as a couple of wild ponies wandered into the road. "Dead animals I wouldn't want my expensive holiday to be responsible for."

Bessie exchanged a long-suffering glance with her husband. "First it was the length of the journey! Now, it's the expense! Why did we talk Ma into coming? She's decided in advance she won't enjoy it."

"Who, me?" Sarah said innocently. But there was more than a grain of truth in Bessie's accusation. "If I'd known when you asked me to go with you that you'd be staying for ten days, I wouldn't have let you talk me into it," she added. "And David had already paid a deposit on the rooms, before I found out."

"To spend just a few days there, it's too far to go," Bessie declared. "We'd hardly have time to unpack before it was time to leave again."

"Speak for yourself," Sarah retorted. "The luggage you've got with you, it will take you the whole holiday to unpack anyway. When you'll wear all those clothes at the seaside, I can't imagine, Bessie. Unless you intend sitting on the sands in a suit, with one of your fur stoles around your shoulders and a model hat on your head."

David laughed. "Holidaying at the Bournemouth Jewish hotels is like watching a nonstop fashion parade, Mother, as you'll discover. And we don't sit on the sands, we sit by the swimming pool."

Sarah gave him a withering glance through the driver's mirror. "To watch fashion parades and not sit by the sea they're *shlepping* me all this way! And I'll also miss two *Shabbos* tea parties."

"That's what's really eating Ma," Bessie said to David with a smile. "That she won't be at home tomorrow, or next Saturday, to queen it behind her teapots and find out what everyone's been up to."

"Is that all you think my *Shabbos* gatherings mean to me?" Sarah demanded.

"Bessie's joking," David intervened. "But you do make a big thing about them, don't you, Mother," he added.

"After sixty-odd years, who wouldn't? And those who haven't gone away for the holiday wouldn't agree to have tea at my house without me there—like when I went to New York," she added sadly.

"What does it matter where the family get together, so long as they do?" David said.

Sarah remained silent. But David was right, she thought, simmering down. In her absence, the tea parties would be held at Esther's, which was preferable to the custom not being maintained at all. And Sarah wanted to think it would still be maintained when she had gone forever. She was now eight-seven and the family unity she had woven over the years was the inheritance she would leave to her descendants, as her husband had left them the shining example of a devout Jew. Upon which none of them had modeled themselves, came the painful addendum.

Abraham's religious principles had been eschewed by his children and grandchildren in his lifetime, Sarah reflected, gazing down at the little garnet ring he had bought for her the day before he died. But what Sarah represented was the homely traditions that were still the core of Jewish life and she clung to the hope that they would live on.

Bessie patted her blue-rinsed coiffure and glanced at her diamond wristwatch. "Shirley and Peter will be in Cannes by now."

And Rebecca will be in Wales, with Leona and Frank and Carla, Sarah thought with satisfaction. The rest of the family had been astonished to hear that Rebecca, the essence of sophistication, had agreed to spend the weekend in a tiny

Welsh village. But Sarah knew it was a step toward her daughter-in-law's recovery.

Leona had heeded Sarah's advice, as she had promised to do. It was now Rebecca, not Bridie, who fetched Carla from school and she had begun knitting for her grandchild, though she had never knitted before. When Leona and Frank went to concerts, which was their favorite relaxation, they took her with them. Rebecca still sucked peppermints, but not all the time. And Sarah doubted that she had bothered taking any to Wales. Where would she manage to conceal a bottle in the young Moritzes' small caravan?

Sarah had not deluded herself that Rebecca would ever give up drink entirely. The emptiness of her marriage was always before her eyes. Nathan often went to meetings in the evenings, Bridie had said, and did not return until late. Meetings with whom? Sarah sometimes wondered. Her youngest son was not a committeeman like his elder brother, and medical conferences didn't go on into the early hours. A man was only human. But a doctor must be discreet.

Sarah pushed these worries to the back of her mind and returned her thoughts to Rebecca. No doubt she still comforted herself with a *schnapps* when she had a bad day. But now, she also had good days and that was something for Sarah to be thankful for.

"What are you looking so pleased about, Ma?" Bessie inquired.

"Not long ago, you were complaining because I wasn't pleased. With you, a person can't win."

"Straighten your hat," Bessie instructed while powdering her nose.

"We're nearly there, Mother," David said.

"That I can tell from what your wife is doing!" Sarah gave her summer straw, which was black like her winter felt, a cursory twitch and gazed through the window at the lush shrubbery and tall pines that lent splendor to Bournemouth's East Cliff.

"It's very nice here," she conceded, eyeing some gracious old houses. Familiar like Southport, it wasn't. But she had to admit that Bournemouth, too, had an unmistakably respectable charm.

Familiarity greeted her in a warm wave when they entered their hotel, which seemed to Sarah palatial, but like a home from home, nevertheless. With the special atmosphere, noisy and feverish, friendly and inquisitive, present wherever Jews get together.

Little girls, with big bows of ribbon in their hair, stood clutching their dolls. And one was being chased around the foyer by a host of small boys, Sarah noted tolerantly as her crustiness dissipated in the perfumed air.

She noticed too that here you couldn't smell the Friday night dinner simmering in the oven, as you could the moment you crossed the threshold of the Southport boarding house on Sabbath Eve. But in other ways, everything was the same—on a bigger scale.

"What line are you in?" she heard a stout gentleman ask David in the melee waiting to register at the reception desk.

"Garments. My son is a doctor, though," David replied.

"One of mine is a barrister."

"And you?"

"I only own a string of outfitting shops," the man laughed.

David laughed too. "But who's counting?"

Jews are counting, Sarah thought sitting down on an ornate chair just vacated by another old lady. Always trying to prove our worth. But haven't we always had to? she said to herself. And boasting about our children is part of it, though there was another aspect to that, too. Sarah had never met one of her brethren who minded standing in his son's shadow. That the children should have the glory was a timeworn Jewish tradition. It was sufficient for the elders to have some of it rub off on them.

She watched an enormous lady waddling toward her. "Here comes your old pal, Ma," Bessie smiled.

"What? I don't know her, Bessie."

"Put your glasses on and then you will! You really ought to wear them all the time."

Sarah was fumbling for her spectacle case when the lady halted in front of her. "Malka Berkowitz!" she exclaimed.

"So how is my *landsleit*?" Sarah's old friend beamed. "Your ma-in-law seems surprised to see me here," she chuckled to Bessie. "Leeds people can also afford Bournemouth prices," she told Sarah. "And also, my name is no longer Berkowitz."

"Ma's a bit forgetful these days, Mrs. Hymanson," Bessie apologized on Sarah's behalf.

"Me too," Malka sighed.

Sarah exchanged a warm smile with her and noticed that she had acquired the hint of a fourth chin since they last met, at Leona's wedding. Her second had already been there when the Sandbergs arrived on her doorstep from Russia and were given shelter in her home, Sarah recalled. Malka had been a plump young beauty in those days. She was now an obese old woman, but still radiated the joy of life as she had then.

"You'll have to excuse me, Malka," Sarah said. "It slipped my mind that you remarried after poor Chaim died."

Malka glanced over her shoulder at her stringy second husband, who was talking with a group near the hotel entrance. "Another Chaim there'll never be, Sarah. But Lazer is very good to me." She shrugged philosophically. "Me, I'm not like you are. I could never live alone."

"Don't be surprised if you get a proposal while you're here, Ma," Bessie said after Malka had gone to join her husband.

"Are you out of your mind, Bessie? Malka was only seventy-five when she married Lazer. Whoever heard of an octogenarian lady receiving a proposal of marriage!"

But before that weekend ended, Sarah had received two and had to take pains to avoid the elderly gentlemen who had popped the question to her. The first, a resident of Golders Green, had done so after sitting beside her in the hotel garden for only half an hour. The second, whom David said was obviously a slowcoach, did not pluck up courage to ask her to share his home in Liverpool until he had dogged her footsteps for a whole day.

"What do they see in me?" she asked David at the dinner table one evening.

Bessie had gone to the powder room between courses.

Sarah was toying with a fruit knife and David surveyed her critically. She looked a good ten years younger than her age. The last time he had really studied her had been on the plane to New York, in 1956. Eleven years ago. But time had dealt kindly with her, and when you gazed into her eyes, you didn't notice the crinkled skin around them, David thought as Sarah turned to look at him. Nor the lines around her mouth when she warmed you with a smile.

"So?" Sarah prodded him. "Answer my question. And don't tell me those suitors of mine are after my money. I made sure they knew I haven't got any."

"But they know I own Sanderstyle—and you're my mother," David said teasingly. "Maybe they want me to keep them in comfort, as well as you!"

"The comfort I allow you to keep me in, nobody could call luxury," Sarah retorted. "Like some mothers of wealthy sons, I'm not."

"I wish you were. Then I could move you out of that drafty house in Cheetham Hill."

"Which I'll never allow you or anyone to do," Sarah flashed. "Bessie says all those men want is a companion for their old age and anyone will do," she added.

"And you can't bear to think that's the truth?"

"Could you? Old I am. But pride I've still got."

David smiled. "My wife has never been renowned for her tact. Though in this case, I think there's something in what she says."

"Thank you!"

"But when it's you an old gentleman proposes to, Mother, I think he sees more in you than just that."

"Tell me what?" Sarah fished. "Right now I could use a little flattery!"

David hid his amusement and wished he could record this conversation for the family. Inside the Sandberg matriarch there was still the heart and vanity of a young girl! "A person doesn't have to talk to you for long to know you're an intelligent woman, Mother. An understanding and sympathetic one, too."

"That's all?" Sarah said disappointedly. "I thought maybe you were going to say I'm not a bad-looking old lady," she smiled.

David eyed her silver hair, which in recent years she had taken to wearing piled high on her head. Despite her age there was only a slight stoop to her shoulders and back. She had on a black crepe dress, with a touch of white at the throat and, as always, pinned to it was the little gold brooch she had brought from Russia. Regal was the word for her, David thought, leaning over to kiss her cheek.

"What was that for?"

"Because I'm proud of you, Mother. And a bad-looking old lady you're not!"

"I just heard some upsetting news," Bessie imparted when she returned to the table. "From some people who've just arrived. I've met them here before, so I went to have a word with them while they were registering. They said there's been an announcement on Cairo Radio that Egypt is ready to plunge into total war that will be the end of Israel."

"I wish them luck!" David exclaimed, putting down the glass of lemon tea he had just picked up. "They'll find out that the Jews in the rest of the world will stand by her."

It did not take long for the news to spread. By the time the guests were served with their late night snack in the hotel lounge, it was the sole topic of conversation. Anxiety about the Jewish State had blighted the relaxed holiday atmosphere. Some people wore resigned expressions on their suntanned faces; Egypt's intention was no surprise. But most were suffused with anger and gave vent to it volubly.

"If I were young enough, I'd go and fight the Arabs," said Sarah's Liverpudlian suitor, who had seated himself beside her.

"Don't worry, Pa, there'll be no shortage of volunteers," his portly son-in-law declared while consuming a chocolate éclair.

And my grandson will be one of them, David thought, recalling Mark's youthful vow that he would be there if Israel needed him. That had been five years ago, the night Laura ran away. But the fine young man Mark now was would remember his vow and honor it.

Bessie helped herself to a pastry, then replaced it in the dish. "It seems wrong for us to be enjoying ourselves on holiday right now," she said watching the portly man swallowing down the rest of his. "We should be at home, holding meetings to plan how we're going to help Israel," she added, fiddling thoughtfully with her pearls.

"My daughter-in-law is on a lady-Zionist committee," Sarah informed everyone within hearing.

"Whose daughter-in-law isn't?" the woman seated on the sofa beside her said.

"If there's a war, Israel will need blankets and medical supplies—all sorts of things will have to be sent there," Bessie put in. "I think I'll go and ring up my vice-chairman," she said to David. "What's the betting they've started organizing things already?"

"God bless the ladies," the portly man said, biting into a chunk of cheesecake as Bessie left the room, to telephone.

"If you had family living on a kibbutz, like I have, you wouldn't be sitting stuffing yourself with cakes!" a woman seated opposite him snapped edgily.

"For me to stop eating won't win the war."

"Maybe it won't come to war," Sarah said hopefully.

But everyone feared that it would and anxiety built up as the week wore on.

On Thursday June 1, the Egyptian and Syrian forces massed, and King Hussein decided to join Nasser. London and Washington expressed sympathy for Israel, but were not prepared to take any action. General de Gaulle declared that under no circumstances must Israel make the first move; if the Arabs attacked, France would step in to save the situation, he promised.

"By which time it'll be too late!" David exploded angrily to the fellow-guests with whom he was discussing this in the hotel lounge. "Israel is alone, like the Jews have always been. Nobody cares a damn if she gets wiped out."

"You think the Israelis don't know that?" said the portly son-in-law of Sarah's number-two suitor, dunking a piece of cake into his cup of tea. "They've got brains as well as brawn in their army. They won't need telling that he who strikes the first blow has the advantage."

That evening, a man who had been trying all week to put through a call to his doctor-brother in Tel Aviv, succeeded in reaching him. A crowd of guests, including David, waited for him to emerge from the foyer telephone booth.

"What's happening there?" David asked him.

"Plenty. Eskol's ordered mobilization. Makeshift air raid shelters are being prepared. My brother's cellar's been taken over for the purpose. And this—it made me go cold—they're consecrating all the parks for possible use as cemeteries."

"God forbid!" someone shouted.

A terrible silence fell as the grim realities of a major Arab-Israeli war hit home. The population of the Jewish State was only two and a half million, every one of whom would be prepared to fight to the death for their hard-won homeland. And many would without doubt be called upon to give their lives.

"I feel like jumping on a plane and going there to help them," a tousle-haired teenage boy declared emotionally.

"If this wasn't your A-level exam year, I'd let you," his father, who was beside him, said.

David thought of Mark again and shuddered with foreboding. Then he had to smile at the man's reply. To a Jewish father, nothing came before his son's education! But wasn't it Jewish philosophy that even in the face of death and destruction, you kept your eye on the future? Perhaps it was this above all that had helped the Jews to survive.

"I want to go straight to *Habonim* House," Bessie told David when they returned to Manchester and had taken Sarah home.

The local headquarters of the *Habonim* Youth Movement had been transformed into an emergency receiving station. Commodities of every kind had been pouring in all week, to be sent to Israel, one of Bessie's committee colleagues had told her on the telephone.

It was "all hands on deck," she had added and the Sandertons were thus prepared for what they were about to see. But not for the extent, or the feverishness of the activity.

Upper Park Road, where the big old house was situated, was jammed with vehicles unloading blankets from household linen chests and camp beds from family storerooms and attics. Inside the improvised depot, Zionist committee ladies were working nonstop to deal with the assortment of goods received. Blankets and beds were just the major items. People were also queuing to offer anything they thought might be useful.

"Here, have my electric kettle," a plump young matron in a crimson trouser suit said, dumping it in the arms of one of the harassed helpers, who was simultaneously receiving some enamel mugs from another donor.

"I doubt if they have sockets for English electrical goods in Israel," the helper said.

"Take the kettle all the same. I can't give you my spare sheets, they're at the laundry."

Bessie took off her coat and rolled up her sleeves. "You'd better go home," she told David. "I'll probably be here all night."

Returning to where he had parked his car, David passed a group of young children who had set up an improvised grocery stall beside a garden gate. On it were some choice items from their mothers' larders. Jars of olives and pickled walnuts. Crystallized ginger in a fancy pot. A rich fruitcake and a carton of cream. Several apples and a bunch of grapes.

"Buy something for Israel, Mister," a little girl called after him.

David turned to look at her. "So that's what you're doing. I thought you were playing shop."

"We're raising money to buy guns with," a small boy said, adjusting his *yamulke* which had fallen askew on his fair curls.

A cold shiver raised the gooseflesh on David's arms. Oh, what it was to be Jewish! And how unreal it seemed that these kids were standing on an English pavement on this sunny June day, thinking about ways and means to help preserve the Jewish State.

When David was their age, a scared little lad living in fear of the *pogromschiks* in Russia, who would have thought there would ever be an Israel? "Next year in Jerusalem" had, until 1948, been just a ritual phrase recited each year at the Passover *Seder* table. An impossible dream. But it had come true. And even little children, like these, had no intention of allowing Israel to be wiped out. They and their small efforts were a microcosm of what World Jewry was doing and would continue to do, to support their brethren in the homeland, uphold the Jewish nation. Because without it, no Jew anywhere could feel truly free and safe.

"I'll take everything you have to sell," David told the children gruffly, fumbling in his wallet and handing them a bundle of pound notes.

The little girl ran into the house and returned with a carrier bag, into which another child packed David's purchases.

He strode away with the bag. He had been tempted to give them the money and take nothing, but felt that would have been wrong. Those kids wanted to do their bit, even if it was only selling groceries, and who was he to deprive them of the sense of satisfaction he wouldn't mind having himself? As it was, David felt restless and frustrated. He was an elderly gentleman, though still young in heart, capable of doing nothing more to fight those who sought Israel's eradication than ladle out cash.

He was soon to be called upon to ladle out a good deal more. The war began the following day and triggered off the most intensive spate of fund-raising British Jewry had ever known. David put through a call to New York to wish Sammy a happy birthday, as he did each year, and learned from Miriam that cash was being frenziedly raised by American Jews, also. But he would not have expected otherwise.

"Sammy's out," Miriam said. "And I'm just back from

helping at our local receiving station. With sore hands from folding blankets! I guess Sammy hasn't had time to know it's his birthday, David. Harold Bronley has co-opted him onto an emergency committee and they're driving around Long Island, collecting checks from millionaires!"

"I've just been to a meeting where everyone made cash promises," David told her. "I'm making a really big donation. So is everyone else who can."

"Apart from the war, how are things?" Miriam asked.

"I've got a problem, Miriam."

"Oh?"

"My grandson Mark wants to volunteer. And Kate Klein, Harry's daughter, too. Everyone in the family but me is against it."

"I see."

"Mark and Kate have asked me if I'll pay their fares to Israel," David disclosed. But why was he telling Miriam this? Because she was family, though removed from the scene? No; because he felt he could talk to her, share the problem. After their showdown by his hospital bed, the easy relationship they'd shared in their youth had sprung to life again.

"You're thinking of doing it, aren't you, David?" she said.

How warm and vibrant her voice was. For a moment, David could feel her presence beside him in his living room. See her regarding him thoughtfully, her long, black lashes shadowing the green of her eyes to charcoal. Miriam was his brother's wife, but had been his own first love. Correction. His one and only love. Bessie was part of his life; he had respect and affection for her, but there were depths to him she was incapable of fathoming, aspects of his character she would never understand.

"You're thinking of making it possible for those two youngsters to do what they feel they must. I know it," Miriam said softly.

"Because you're the only person who's ever really known me." David lit a cigarette and watched the smoke disperse into nothingness, as some of his own youthful hopes had. "If a person doesn't do what they're burning to do when they're young, before they get caught in the trap, bogged down with responsibility for others, they never will, Miriam. Also, I admire Kate and Mark for wanting to do more than just state their allegiance," David added.

"And I admire you," Miriam said.

She hung up without saying good-bye and David was sure there had been the tremor of tears in her voice. Did she too sometimes think briefly of their shared past? Then shove the memories aside and immerse herself in the present, as he did? They had lived their lives apart, neither of them truly happy. But David had learned long ago that happiness was a fragile, fleeting thing. You grasped it while and when you could and spent the bulk of your days on earth making do and getting by. Accumulating as few regrets as anyone could reasonably expect to by the time they had lived for sixty-nine years, David thought, catching sight of his old-gentleman's face in the mirror above the mantlepiece.

But he didn't intend to add not helping Mark and Kate to his collection of regrets, he said to himself resolutely. He would not only pay their fare to Israel, but drive them to London in his car, tomorrow. And, if necessary, connive with them in order to do so without their parents' knowledge.

Was he being rash and reckless? No. It was a considered decision. As his interference in Laura's destiny had been. His granddaughter was now a self-reliant young woman making a name for herself as a photographer. What would she have been had he not interfered, set her on the path to finding herself? A discontented replica of her mother.

David sat down beside the telephone and waited for it to ring. He had told Mark and Kate to call him tonight and he would tell them yes, or no. Well, it was yes and the wrath of the entire family would doubtless descend upon him because of it. But David did not care. And how incongruous it seemed that Laura had once told him he did not have the courage to his convictions.

Putting his grandson and great-niece on a plane to Israel was not the simple exercise David had envisaged. First, he learned from Mark and Kate, volunteers must be interviewed at Rex House, the Jewish Agency office in Regent Street, which, on their arrival, they found besieged by young people. And not just Britishers; volunteers from all over the world, some of them non-Jews, had flocked to lend support to the Jewish State.

Later, seated in the midst of a mixed group at the airport, David heard some boys expressing disappointment that they would not be involved in the fighting. Volunteers were to be absorbed into industry, or work in hospitals, and on kibbutzim, replacing Israelis now engaged in active service.

But all of them will be at risk, nevertheless, David thought, surveying the motley of resolute young faces. Not just resolute, but something else too, for which David could not find a word. It was as if a great fire had been lit, inflaming the consciences of freedom-loving youth, impelling them to support the fight for survival being waged against tremendous odds. And if picking apples and emptying bedpans would help Israel to survive, they would undertake such tasks willingly. May God keep them all safe, David thought emotionally.

"This isn't good for you, Grandpa," Mark said, eyeing David's wan and weary appearance.

David had insisted on remaining with Mark and Kate until their flight left and had been seated for several hours on an uncomfortable chair. It was now late at night and Marianne and Laura, whom Mark had telephoned, had joined them at the airport.

"Our granddad is made of stronger stuff than you think," Laura said to her brother. She smoothed her wrinkled blue jeans and poised her ever-ready camera to photograph David.

"Do me a favor, Laura!" David protested.

"I'm doing myself one. This picture will go into a folio I'm preparing of faces that tell a story."

"You should see the one she took of me, when I let the dinner burn to cinders. Laura happened to be there at the time," Marianne smiled. But smiling did not come easily to her, right now. Her son had already flown to Israel, via Rome, with the Oxford college-mates with whom he had been visiting Florence. Marianne had not slept a wink since Martin phoned to tell her he was going. "I wonder if Kate and Mark will run into Martin, when they get there," she said.

Kate adjusted the crimson scarf she had tied peasantwise around her long black hair. "Any message if we do?" she asked Marianne in the soft voice that matched her gentle nature.

"Only that I'll kill him if he doesn't come back safe!" Marianne answered irrationally. But her feelings had never been rational where Martin was concerned, she reflected. He was the darling of her heart. Dearer to her even than his father. And, when he'd called her from Rome, she'd thought of her Aunt Miriam whose only child had been taken from her, and had shed tears for her as she had not done then.

Marianne looked at Kate, small and neat in her navy skirt and white blouse. And Mark, seated on a borrowed rucksack, dressed in the tailored flannels and sports jacket that made him look like a young businessman off duty. Mark was still at college, but a businessman was what he was destined to be and suited for. A future managing director of Sanderstyle. As sweet little Kate was the material good and docile housewives were made of. Yet here they were, on the brink of hazardous adventure, for no other reason than an inborn allegiance to their heritage.

Marianne suspected that thirst for experience, for the adventure itself, had played some part in Martin's having gone to Israel, along with the fierce Jewish partisanship she knew was in him. But with Mark and Kate, it was the latter alone; they were unequipped by nature to do what they were doing.

"Take a picture of Mark and Kate for me, Laura," Marianne requested. "I want it for posterity!"

"Me too," Laura said clicking her camera. "Or, when they're fat and forty, nobody will believe they did it."

Kate kissed David's stubbly cheek. "If it weren't for you, we couldn't have."

"Too true," Mark said. "And heaven help him when he gets home!"

"If the family are too rough on him, he can come back to London and bunk at my place," Laura declared.

"Or mine," Marianne said.

"I'll bear those offers in mind," David chuckled exchanging a conspiratorial glance with the four of them. The mantle of patriarchy he had worn for most of his life had, it seemed, slipped briefly aside, allowing them to see him as a person in his own right. And, just for a moment, he felt young again.

A few weeks later, David felt he had aged ten years. The Six-Day War had left Israel victorious and Jerusalem no longer a divided city. Though a permanent peace was unlikely to be the outcome, World Jewry was still rejoicing. But the family's jubilation was laced with personal sorrow. Mark was now dead and buried in the Holy Land.

"I still can't believe it," Bessie said at a *Shabbos* gathering.

Then she burst into tears, as she had been doing ever since Shirley and Peter learned, by cable, that their son had been fatally injured in a tractor accident. "Why did Mark have to stay on there when the war ended?" she sobbed piteously.

Shirley went to comfort her. "He didn't have to, Mam. He wanted to. There's a lot of clearing up to be done. That's why Kate and Martin aren't home yet. Why plenty of kids are still going there, now the schools and colleges have closed for the summer holidays."

David watched his daughter take a handkerchief from her cuff and dry her mother's eyes. That Shirley would find the inner strength to behave as she was doing, after losing her only son, he could not have imagined. Nor had she uttered a word of recrimination to David about the part he had played in sending Mark to his untimely death. Possibly, she thought it punishment enough that he would never forgive himself.

Outwardly, Peter had taken it harder than Shirley had, David thought, surveying him. There was a shrunken look about him, and a carelessness about his usually immaculate appearance.

Shirley was as well groomed and chic as ever. She had lost weight and was smoking more, but otherwise it was as though she had made up her mind that what could not be changed must be accepted. Which had always been Sarah Sandberg's philosophy. David had not thought there was anything of his mother in his daughter, but revised his opinion now.

He emerged from his brooding and found that Ronald's son, Alan, had come to perch on the arm of his chair.

"All right, Grandpa?" young Alan asked, reminding David that he still had a grandson.

David patted the boy's hand and experienced a pang of guilt because Mark had always been the apple of his eye. "I'm trying to be all right, Alan," he answered with a wan smile.

"You've still got me, haven't you?" Alan declared comfortingly. "And, if you like, I'll come and spend a few days at your house, during my school holidays."

What a kind lad Alan was, David noted for the first time, and it struck him that he had not taken the trouble to get to know him. "Your grandma and I would be delighted to have you, Alan."

"We'll fix it up, Dad," Ronald said.

Harry Klein had just arrived with Howard, after their day's work. "We've been run off our feet, today," he told his wife.

"So get some more staff," Ann replied unsympathetically. "When your father was alive, you were always telling him the stores were understaffed," she recalled.

"And now, our Howard is saying it to me," Harry sighed to David. "He thinks like I did at his age. That a few more assistants can lighten the boss's load."

"In my experience, the bigger your staff, the bigger your worries," David replied.

"Exactly," Harry endorsed.

"Because you and my father aren't clued up about productivity," Howard declared.

"He wants me to send him to America, to learn their methods," Harry informed David. "So he can come back with a few more ideas like the ones he already has," he added witheringly.

"In the States, they're miles ahead of us, businesswise," Howard opined. "What they're doing today, we don't even find out about until tomorrow."

"My son is a short-cut merchant!" Harry expostulated. "He'd like to turn our stores into another Harrods, overnight!"

"What's wrong with that?" Howard demanded. "Though it isn't quite what I have in mind. What I'm after is the kind of business that caters for the young. I don't suppose anyone here has ever seen Carnaby Street, in London. If they did, they wouldn't need yelling that way-out clothes are the thing of the future."

"I've been there," Shirley said, "and I didn't like what I saw."

"Because you're yesterday's generation," Howard said. "And it's beginning to show in the garments you design."

"That's enough, Howard!" Ann intervened. "How dare you upset Shirley? Hasn't she had enough?"

"I'm sorry," Howard muttered.

A heavy silence followed and he went to stare through the window at the weeds in his great-grandmother's garden, which he and Mark had planned to tackle together. He had not only lost a cousin, but his dearest friend.

Sarah studied Howard's tense profile. He was burly, as his maternal great-grandfather, Yankel Cohen, had been. But with red hair, inherited from Abraham Sandberg. And the selfishness of his mother, Ann. With only one person had Howard not been selfish—Mark, to whom he had been protective all their lives.

"If I'd gone to Israel, I could have kept an eye on him," Howard said gruffly, turning to look at the family. "He never was very good at watching out for himself."

"Why didn't you go?" young Alan asked.

"I'm the kind who leaves things to others, I suppose," Howard answered self-deprecatingly. "And I keep thinking that if I'd been with Mark, it might not have happened."

"What good are you doing talking this way?" Harry asked him.

"Let him get it off his chest," Nathan advised.

"People in our family are always getting things off their chests," little Carla declared from Rebecca's lap. She wriggled to her feet and gazed around the room, restlessly. "I wish I had somebody to play with."

"Well, don't expect *me* to play with you," Alan said. "I'm long past the age of playing."

"And even if you weren't, I wouldn't play with you!"

Alan was now eleven and Carla six. She went to smile down at the child who should have been her playmate in the family, but was lying in an armchair, oblivious to her surroundings.

"Isn't Sharon beautiful?" Carla said, kneeling to stroke the little girl's silky, auburn hair. "It's a pity she can't walk or talk, isn't it?" she said to Alan, whose sister Sharon was.

"Yes," he replied shortly. "And she'll never be able to."

Ronald exchanged an agonized glance with Diane. Their daughter had been born brain-damaged.

"I think we should stop bringing her, Diane," Ronald said.

"In that case, you'll come without me."

Diane's reply did not surprise Sarah. Ronald had wanted to place the child in a Home where she would receive expert care, but his wife would not hear of it. Instead, she was allowing this child, who was no more than a living doll, to dominate and disrupt their once-happy homelife.

The doorbell cut into Sarah's ruminations. A moment later, Kate was in the room, being kissed and hugged by everyone.

Kate removed the rucksack from her slim shoulders and helped herself to a slice of cake.

"I'll make you a big supper tonight," her mother promised her. "You need feeding up after what you've been through."

"I haven't been through anything, Mum. Working on a kibbutz isn't an ordeal. I enjoyed it. Mark did, too," she added quietly to Shirley and Peter, then went to sit on the sofa between her parents. "I've come home to tell you something," she said to them. "I want to live in Israel."

"No!" Ann said emphatically.

"Your place is here with us," Harry declaimed.

Kate gave them each a wry glance. "If the parents of those who went there as *chalutzim*, years ago, had said that, there wouldn't have been an Israel."

"It's true," Sarah said.

"Keep out of it, Bobbie!" Harry glared at her.

"It won't do any good to shout, Dad," Kate told him softly. "I've made up my mind. And if you refuse me your permission now, I'll wait until I'm of age. You see, I've met a boy," she added shyly.

Her elders exchanged glances. This was something else.

"Who is he?" Harry demanded, noting that his daughter's face suddenly looked radiant.

"His name is Zvi Levi. He's a *sabra*."

"What's a *sabra*?" Carla piped.

"Someone who was born in Israel," Kate explained.

"And what does this young man do for a living?" Sarah inquired. A young couple could not live on love alone.

"He's in the army at present," Kate replied. "I was introduced to him by an Israeli girl, when the war was over."

Her mother gave her a withering glance. "After knowing him for ten minutes, she's ready to leave her family and settle in Israel!"

"Ten days, actually," Kate said.

"If David hadn't gone against the family's wishes, my granddaughter wouldn't have met this boy," Esther said. Since Mark's death, she had lived in fear that something would also befall Kate and had not taken her grateful eyes off the girl since she entered the room. "And Mark would still be alive."

The accusation nobody had until now put into words caused David's sallow complexion to tinge with gray.

Sarah cast a compassionate glance at him. "A person lives out the years the Almighty allots them, Esther," she sighed. "And they live them out wherever he intended," she added with conviction. "Nobody can blame David. He did what he thought was right and it was God's hand that guided him. As for not knowing after ten days that you love someone," she said to Ann, "the moment I laid eyes on Kate's great-grandfather I knew he was for me."

Kate gave Sarah a warm smile. "But I'd decided to settle in Israel before I met Zvi."

"Why?" Nathan asked, studying her. Outwardly, she was the same Kate. A pleasant, conventional girl. The kind one saw pushing a pram in a select suburb, while her young husband's dinner simmered in the oven. Nathan would have bet his life that Kate would always do what her parents expected of her.

"Yes, why? You weren't even an active Zionist, like Mark was," Howard said.

Kate gazed down at her hands, aware that the whole family awaited her answer. But how could she possibly describe what had brought her to that decision? Her experiences of the past few weeks. The way she had begun to relate personally to what was going on around her and had become not just a Diaspora-Jewess lending a hand, but part of everything. As if she had come home, though Israel wasn't her home. There, there was a special sense of belonging she had never felt in England; a feeling of sameness with the people, young and old. Not until she experienced it had she known such a feeling existed. Or become aware that she'd always been instinctively careful not to do or say anything to upset Gentiles, as though she were in some way beholden to them.

"That's an instinct bred in Jews from centuries of wandering," Mark had said when they discussed it. "A kind of eternal gratitude for being allowed to exist," he had added wryly. "And Israel is the only place where we don't have to feel that way," Kate remembered replying. Until then, she had viewed the Jewish State as a haven for her brethren whom oppression had ejected from the countries of their birth, and had been unable to comprehend why some uprooted themselves voluntarily in order to live there.

Would Mark have decided to do so, as she had? The conversation Kate had just recalled took place on the night before he met his death, she reflected poignantly. And the memory of him as he had looked then—the last time she saw him—caused her eyes to sting with tears.

They had been seated side by side on some sandbags, with the stars, brighter than they ever were in an English night sky, shining down upon the sleeping kibbutz.

No, Mark would have returned to England, Kate reflected. For him the experience had been a temporary diversion from the path he had already mapped out for himself. He had spoken about Sanderstyle as if it were a dynasty and himself part of its continuance. Mark had had no doubts about where he belonged.

And nor had Kate, now. It was as though, without being aware of it, she had lived a negative life. "I want to settle in Israel because, after being there, I couldn't live anywhere else," she declared, in a positive tone nobody present could recall her ever adopting before.

"Your young man has already proposed to you?" Sarah quizzed her.

Kate blushed and nodded.

"*Mazeltov!*" Sarah congratulated her. "Tell us a bit more about him."

"He's tall and blond—a lot of *sabras* have light coloring," Kate supplied. "He's very kind and thoughtful," she added.

"But penniless of course," her mother surmised with a sigh.

"On a kibbutz, you don't need money," Sigmund informed her.

"I'm glad Auntie Hannah and Leona and Frank aren't here today," Ann exclaimed. "Or they would be interfering, too!"

"Will you give me your permission to marry, or not?" Kate asked Harry.

"I'm thinking about it."

"You're behaving like Mr. Barrett of Wimpole Street, Dad," Howard said. "Not that I'm surprised."

"Elizabeth Barrett wasn't a girl of eighteen."

Kate gave her great-grandmother an appealing glance. She had no doubt that Sarah was on her side.

"What are you bringing Kate's age into this for?" Sarah asked Harry. "Like Mr. Barrett—I remember how he made poor Norma Shearer suffer, in the film—you just don't want to lose your little girl. Kate is two years older than I was when I got married. She knows what she wants and what she wants is no bad thing. Let her get on with it."

Harry exchanged an emotional glance with his wife, who was now dabbing her eyes. "All Ann and I want is for Kate to be happy."

"I shall be."

Harry cleared his throat. "All right then."

"We are all going to miss you," Sarah told Kate fondly.

"But can you stop a tree from growing new branches?" she asked the others.

"I was waiting for Mother to come out with something like that!" Esther exclaimed.

"But it's true," Sarah insisted. "And now we'll have a branch of the family in Israel," she declared with satisfaction.

Chapter Seven

The year 1968 was no less traumatic for the clan than the year preceding it. But now it was the Moritzes upon whom God and Fate were concentrating, Sarah reflected while she waited for her telephone to ring, one May evening.

In recent months, Sigmund's memory had begun to fail. Not only in the small, irritating ways in which her own had been letting her down for years—the inability to recall where they had put something, or what they had eaten for dinner yesterday, was something Sarah and Sigmund shared. But what was happening to Sigmund now was much more serious. And frightening, Sarah thought with a shudder. What was the word Nathan had used to describe it? Disorientation. Sigmund would go out for a walk, or to buy something, then lose his way. Not just his way, but his bearings, and end up in total confusion about his whereabouts, weeping like a child.

"Anyone could get lost around here, these days," Sarah told her cat with an upsurge of anger. What were they thinking of at the Town Hall? Demolishing whole streets. Turning folk out of the cozy homes they'd lived in all their lives, to erect blocks of flats in their place? Hightown would soon be unrecognizable and it was rumored that sooner or later the same would happen to Cheetham Hill. Some of the local street names had already been changed, which was enough to confuse any old person, Sarah thought in defense of Sigmund. Whom, at times, she was called upon to defend to the family, when they lost patience with him.

Nathan had advised him to stay at home, and this, too had angered Sarah. Why should Sigmund have to spend what was left of his life confined to his own four walls? But she knew Nat was deeply concerned about Sigmund's safety and welfare, as all the family were. About Helga, too, who had reached the stage where she was afraid to let her father out of her sight.

The telephone shrilled, jolting Sarah from her anxious thoughts.

"We've found him, Mother," David's relieved voice came through when Sarah lifted the receiver.

Sigmund had slipped out of the house early that morning, while Helga was upstairs making the beds. He had not returned for lunch and by mid-afternoon the whole clan had been out looking for him.

"Fortunately, it's Sunday," David said. "Last time, he did it on a weekday and none of us got any work done because of it!"

"Sigmund is more important than getting work done!" Sarah flashed.

"If I didn't think so, I wouldn't keep leaving my office to scour the town for him. Nat missed his afternoon surgery to go hunting for him, last week—"

"He's Sigmund's godson," Sarah interrupted.

"For heaven's sake, Mother! Stop supplying reasons why we shouldn't complain. Something has to be done about him. For his sake, not ours. He's going from bad to worse."

"I know," Sarah said sadly. "So where did you find him?"

"At Father's old *shul*. He was sitting there, staring at the *bimah* we endowed in Father's memory."

"What made you look there for him?"

"I'd run out of other places! And we once found him beside Father's grave, didn't we? Though he had no idea how he'd got there. It was the same today—only worse. He kept saying he wanted to see Rabbi Lensky." The old *Hassidic* rabbi had been dead for years and Sigmund had attended his funeral. "He's beginning to live totally in the past," David said after a silence.

Sarah thought of the other trouble presently facing the Moritzes. Henry was in jail, in Paris, after participating in a student revolt there. The family had seen pictures of the rioting on TV, and Leona had said Henry was probably in the midst of it. She was now in Paris with Frank, trying to get her brother-in-law released.

None of this was a secret from Sigmund. His daughter-in-law Hannah lived in his house, and was proud of her son's political activities. Sigmund was not.

"Maybe old people bury themselves in the past because they can't bear the present," Sarah told David before she rang off.

"Thanks for coming," Henry said to Leona and Frank after they had secured his release from jail. "And now you're here, why not spend a few days in Paris, with Julekha and me?"

"We have responsibilities at home," Leona answered curtly.

Henry grinned. "You and Frank and your responsibilities!"

They were seated at a pavement café on the Champs Elysées and Leona plonked her coffee cup down on the saucer. "That's the kind of remark one expects from someone who's never known the meaning of the word."

"You're beginning to sound middle-aged, Leona," Henry retorted.

"Pack it in, you two," Frank said.

"My God, that takes me back!" Henry laughed. "You were always saying that to us when we were kids."

"And you haven't changed since then," Leona informed him caustically. "Children usually grow up, but not you, Henry."

"If growing up means becoming like you and my brother, I never will."

How could I have thought I was in love with Henry? Leona thought, eyeing him with contempt. He had not yet inquired after his mother and grandfather, or Sarah. For Henry Moritz the sun rose and set only for himself! Yet the lovely Asian girl who was still his companion was gazing at him adoringly.

Henry noted Leona studying Julekha. "Wondering how she puts up with me?" he smiled.

"Yes, as a matter-of-fact."

Julekha smoothed a fold of her green chiffon *odhni*. "I sometimes wonder how Henry puts up with me."

How self-effacing can you get? Leona thought. But perhaps for a woman to be that way was part of the ethnic culture to which Julekha had been conditioned. Jewish women, too, had once been subservient to their men, and the marital equality Leona had with Frank, which included the right to pursue a career, was only now becoming accepted. But Asian women, even those who lived in the West, would probably take longer to assert themselves as personalities in their own right, Leona reckoned. To *want* to assert themselves; Julekha

seemed content to play second fiddle to her lover. And Henry
was the kind to take advantage of it!

"We're worried stiff about your grandfather," Leona told
him. Frank was having sleepless nights about how best to
deal with Sigmund. Why should Henry get off scot-free?

"Is he ill?" Henry asked.

Frank filled in the details.

"I hope I don't live to be old," Henry said with a shudder.

Leona riveted him with an icy stare. "If the day ever comes
when you stop relating everything to yourself, I'll eat my hat,
Henry."

The retort Leona had anticipated did not come. Instead,
Henry's handsome face crimsoned. Was it possible that he
was ashamed of himself?

"How's my little niece?" Henry inquired.

As if his grandfather's welfare was not his concern! Leona
thought. She listened to Frank extolling their daughter's
virtues, which, under other circumstances, she would have
found amusing. But she was presently gripped by anger. And
another emotion, to which she could not put a name.

She gave her attention to the leisurely passing parade.
Dark-suited men escorting elegant Parisian ladies. Tourists,
with cameras marking them out for what they were, slung
from their shoulders. Black faces and white. Yellow, too.
Long-haired boys and girls, in tatty jeans and T-shirts, who
would have looked more at home on the Left Bank. A
gendarme, picking his way through the motley crowd.

Leona noticed two young men holding hands at the next
table. Across the street, some prostitutes were soliciting
trade outside the Lido Nightclub, teetering precariously on
their stiltlike heels. Beside them, a priest, whose garb reminded
Leona of an Utrillo print she had at home, was conversing
with a pink-haired old lady.

"You're very quiet, love," Frank said to her.

"I was thinking that Paris has an ambience all its own."
There was a heady quality in the air, that was more than just
the mixed fragrance of coffee, perfume and petrol fumes
assailing Leona's nostrils. Here, you could feel life throbbing
all about you and, by comparison, the one you lived in your
own little corner of the earth seemed dull and insignificant.

"When you live here, you take it all for granted," Henry
smiled.

Probably, Leona thought. And her nameless emotion was envy. Of Henry, who had eschewed his family responsibilities in order to partake of all this.

Leona and Frank had reserved seats on a night-flight to London. That evening, Julekha cooked a farewell supper for them, at the apartment in Montparnasse her allowance from her father, and Henry's from Sigmund, enabled them to rent.

The flat was redolent of Indian spices and sandalwood, but otherwise bore no trace of Julekha's ethnic tastes, Leona noticed. On the contrary, the living room was reminiscent of the Moritzes' in Cheetham Hill; lined from floor to ceiling with books, and with an air of shabby comfort.

Leona and Frank had not been here before. Henry had never invited them to visit him—though he could have accommodated them, Leona thought eyeing the studio couch.

Julekha had gone into the kitchen to put the finishing touches to the side dishes she was serving with the curried chicken, and Leona stood by the window gazing down upon another slice of Parisian life—an eton-cropped woman was cuddling a young girl outside a club Henry had mentioned was a lesbian rendezvous.

Leona listened to him enthuse to Frank about the student uprising, and how "Danny the Red" would spread his message further afield. Did Henry really believe that the rioting that had taken place in Paris would ever be emulated by English students, or in the United States, where young people went to college for no other purpose than equipping themselves to enter a profession and earn their living? The London School of Economics was known to be a political hotbed, but even there students went so far and no further—which didn't include disturbing the peace.

Leona turned from the window to tell Henry it was time he grew up, but her attention was arrested by a collection of framed photographs on a side table. What was Henry doing with a family gallery in his flat? Pictures of everyone in the clan. Even Leona and Frank's wedding photograph was there. And there was one of Rachel Moritz, the grandmother Henry had never known.

It took a moment or two for Leona to recover from her surprise. It was hard to relate Henry to the sentiment and family feeling the portrait gallery implied.

Frank cut into her thoughts. "So that's where the family heirloom disappeared to, Leona!" he exclaimed, pointing to a brass mortar and pestle on a shelf beside the rusty-looking wood stove. "Mother and Auntie Helga refused point-blank to say where it had gone to," he told Henry.

Henry grinned. "They didn't want me to take them, in case you found out and considered it favoritism."

"But you didn't let that bother you," Leona said.

Henry flicked a recalcitrant lock of his straw-colored hair away from his eyes. "Frank will inherit our Viennese grandmother's candlesticks one day, for you to light *Shabbos* candles in, Leona. Me, I'll never need them."

"Why not? Julekha could light joss sticks in them," Leona answered unkindly.

"That isn't a Moslem custom," Henry said stiffly. "And I consider your remark uncalled-for."

"I'm sorry." Leona could have bitten off her tongue the moment she made the crack. Why had she made it? To rattle Henry.

He gave her one of his brilliant smiles. Which, once, had set her aquiver. Now, all he aroused in her was contempt.

"That's the first apology you've ever made to me in our life, Leona. Isn't it, Frank?" Henry said.

Our life? Leona thought. Henry's was a far cry from the conventional background he had shared with herself and Frank. Yet he still seemed to think of himself as part of it. Which was as incongruous as his treasuring the family photographs and wanting his dead grandmother's mortar and pestle, that was a little bit of home. But hadn't Henry always wanted the ha'penny and the bun? And it was beginning to seep through to Leona that despite having, in effect, cut his ties with the family, he harbored an inner need to belong.

The day Leona and Frank returned to Manchester, Sigmund eluded Helga's watchful eye yet again. The news that Henry was no longer in prison had cheered him and increased his determination not to be made a prisoner himself.

He plodded laboriously up Heywood Street, heading for the shops on Cheetham Village, but found himself sitting, instead, on a park bench. What was he doing here, when he had intended going to the delicatessen to treat his daughter and daughter-in-law to some smoked salmon for supper tonight? But that was how it was with him nowadays. He rarely reached the place for which he had set out, and sometimes could not remember which place that was. He turned his head and saw that a young black man, with whom he was sharing the bench, was eyeing him.

"What's wrong?" the man asked him.

"Plenty!" Sometimes, it was easier to talk to a stranger. "But why do you ask?"

"I heard you sighing."

"Sighing is one of the pleasures of old age. And believe me, there aren't many."

The young man's face creased into a reminiscent grin. "That's what my grampa used to say, back in Bridgetown."

"Where is Bridgetown?" Sigmund inquired. He enjoyed nothing more than conversation. Once, he recalled, Bellott Street Park had been full of elderly gentlemen like himself, casual acquaintances with whom he used to sit and chat. But one by one they had passed on. The park felt lonely without them.

His young companion had a faraway look in his eyes. "Bridgetown is in Barbados," he smiled. "The most beautiful island in the Caribbean."

"My next-door neighbors told me Jamaica was," Sigmund said. "But everyone has a special place in their heart for where they were born. For me, there'll never be anywhere like Vienna. Though I love England and have lived here for most of my life. What is your name, young man? I like to know who I am talking to."

"It's Winston Churchill Smith."

"A nice English name."

"But it doesn't match my skin."

Sigmund noted Winston's bitter tone. "Your skin you can't change," he said philosophically.

"Did I say I wanted to?"

"Who could blame you if you did? My name is Moritz, by the way. And we Jews also encountered prejudice when we first settled here. How long have you been in England, Winston?"

"Seven years."

"And you're not too happy here, I gather?"

Winston stared down at his big, workman's hands. "Happy, no. Better off, yes."

Sigmund knew the feeling. Hadn't his own people experienced it? To be where you weren't welcome was not pleasant. What England's new ethnic communities were experiencing now was like history repeating itself. Like the Jews, they had come here hoping for tolerance and had found themselves surrounded by the same old prejudice. Which, deep down, still existed toward Jews. But we've learned how to surmount it, Sigmund thought. Found a place in English society, though we'll always be regarded as different.

"It takes time," he told Winston. "But sooner or later your people will be accepted here like mine now are. First, you have to prove your worth, which strangers in a community are always called upon to do. And hold up your head."

"You're tellin' me to be patient, aren't you, Mr. Moritz?" Winston answered. "But did you ever share a house that has only one bathroom with three other families, as well as your wife and kids?" He eyed Sigmund's Homburg hat and pin-striped suit, which Helga made sure always looked immaculate, and his gold watchchain, with which he was thoughtfully toying. "What you're sayin' is all fine to say from where you're sittin'—with respect, sir."

"Oi," Sigmund sighed taking off his pince-nez to polish them. "Who even knew from bathrooms in the Strangeways ghetto? A cold-water tap was all we had—in the scullery. And the lavatory was outside in the backyard." He replaced his spectacles on his nose. "Believe me, young man, I wasn't always what I am now. A respected gentleman, to whom my non-Jewish neighbors raise their hats. Unfortunately for people like you and me, Winston, such respect is something for which we have to work extra hard."

The discussion was terminated by a shout from across the street.

"Winston Churchill! Your fried chicken is frizzlin' in the pan!"

"I eat dinner in the middle of the afternoon," Winston told Sigmund rising from the bench. "I'm on night shift."

Sigmund shook hands with him and watched him walk away and enter the doorway from which his wife had summoned him. The same doorway from which Bessie had no doubt called to David to come in from the park, years and years ago. And there seemed something historically significant in Winston living in David's old house.

Which David will appreciate when I tell him, Sigmund thought. A few minutes later, he had forgotten that Winston Churchill Smith existed. All he could remember was his intention to buy some smoked salmon.

* * *

At eight o'clock, when Sigmund had not returned home and nobody had succeeded in locating him, David called a family conference at the Moritzes' and everyone who was able to do so turned up.

"Father's never been lost for this long before," Helga wept to the family.

Because she was not one to weep, her distress was all the more pitiful to behold.

"Short of putting him on a leash, there's nothing more you can do to keep him at home than you've been doing," David comforted her.

"How dare you talk about Sigmund that way!" Sarah exploded.

"So I didn't put it nicely," David answered his mother. "But, in effect, that's what he needs."

"And if you live to be ninety-three, you will maybe need the same!" Sarah retorted. "Meanwhile, where is he? is what I am thinking about. Not about how he is a big problem to us all. Like everyone else is thinking, here."

"That isn't fair, Bobbie," Leona protested. "Nor is it so."

"It isn't? Then why did you say, 'Oh God, not again,' in the kind of voice you did, when I phoned your office to tell you he was missing?"

"Because we were up to our ears in work. And dead beat after getting back from Paris at six this morning," Frank replied for his wife. "We have other responsibilities, apart from Zaidie Sigmund."

"Don't let him ever hear you call him a responsibility," Sarah flashed. "And heaven help anyone who ever dares to call me one," she warned.

"Unless everyone calms down and talks practically, I'm going home," Nathan declared, though nothing could have persuaded him to leave until he knew the difficult old gentleman, who had carried him to the *mohel* at his *Brith*, had come to no harm.

"The police are looking for him now, and I hope they find him safe and sound," David said. "Why I called everyone together is to talk about the future. What are we going to do with Sigmund?"

"I'll take him to live at my house," Sarah said. "And never let him out of my sight, except when he's in bed asleep."

"If that's a rebuke to me, I suppose I deserve it," Helga said tearfully. "But he wouldn't agree to live at our house. And even if he would, I wouldn't allow anyone else to take care of my father."

Hannah cast a compassionate glance at her sister-in-law. Helga had spent most of her life caring for others and had seemed to thrive on it. She had never looked her age, but suddenly looked older. "Haven't you had enough, Helga?" she said gently.

"I wish Moishe were here," Helga whispered irrelevantly. Her faithful suitor, whom she had never married because she had put family obligations before personal happiness, had passed away a few months ago, leaving a gap in her life which, when he had hovered at her side, she had not realized he occupied.

"In my view, Helga's had more than enough, but that isn't the point," Nathan said briskly. "Her father requires expert care and supervision, which she is unable to provide. There's only one solution—"

The doorbell interrupted Nathan in mid-sentence. Frank made a hasty exit to the lobby.

"Zaidie's here!" he announced unnecessarily. The others had crowded behind him and could see Sigmund's stocky silhouette through the frosted glass pane in the front door. Behind it, a policeman's helmet was visible.

"You're giving a party, Helga?" Sigmund inquired when he saw everyone. He fumbled in his pocket and brought out a squashed package. "It's a good thing I bought some smoked salmon."

Helga burst into a fresh flood of tears. "Oh, Father—"

"You nearly 'ad summat to really cry about," the police constable told her. "Your dad nearly got 'imself flattened by a lorry."

"That does it!" Nathan exclaimed to David.

"I agree."

Sarah knew what they had in mind and was filled with dismay. Nathan had been about to put it to the family when the doorbell rang.

"All the traffic were 'eld up, because of it, near Bury Market," the policeman told the family.

"My father-in-law couldn't have walked that far," Hannah said. Bury was some miles away.

"But a bus I'm still capable of getting on!" Sigmund flared. "I got on a thirty-five, to come home. Was it my fault it was going the wrong way?"

The constable put a kindly hand on his shoulder. "That sort of thing 'appens to a lot of elderly folk, dad. It's nowt to be ashamed of."

A sob engulfed Sigmund. "But getting lost is a terrible feeling," he said piteously.

"Take your grandfather upstairs," Sarah said to Frank. "He needs to take a nap." Rest, Sigmund certainly needed. And Sarah wanted him out of the room, for his sake and her own. She could not bear to see what this strong-willed man, whose intellect she had on first acquaintance found formidable, had been reduced to. A burden to those whose most respected adviser he had once been, deprived of his dignity, and an object of pity.

Sigmund allowed his grandson to escort him to bed and it hurt Sarah too to see him so docile, as though he had finally given in.

"You'd best keep your eye on 'im," the policeman advised before departing. "The old chap 'ad a narrow shave, this evenin'. It were a good job that lorry 'ad good brakes. An' it weren't 'til 'alf an hour ago 'e pulled 'imself together to tell us where 'e lived."

"There's nothing for it but to ask the Old Home if they'll take him," David said heavily when Frank returned to the room.

No! Sarah wanted to cry out. But what was the alternative? she asked herself. Locking her old friend up in a room in his own house, to keep him safe? In the Jewish Home for the Aged he would have company, and the expert care and supervision Nathan had, rightly, said he required. Sarah could no longer fool herself he did not.

"We must do what's best for Father," she heard Helga say, and knew that this most selfless of daughters was thinking only of Sigmund's welfare. But what a way to end your days. Without your family around you.

"Take me home," Sarah said to David. Not until she was alone would she allow herself to weep.

Chapter Eight

"Damn!" Marianne exclaimed, perusing her morning mail. "I won't be able to attend Martin's Degree Day ceremony," she told Ralph. "It coincides with rehearsals for my new radio play."

It was Saturday and they were eating a leisurely breakfast. Ralph glanced at the rehearsal schedule Marianne had tossed on the table, but made no comment.

"Go on, say it! I'm a lousy mother."

Ralph helped himself to some marmalade and remained silent.

"You're thinking the author's presence isn't essential, aren't you?" Marianne persisted. "All right, it's only a courtesy invitation and some writers don't bother turning up, but most do. Like me, they prefer to do any necessary on-the-spot revisions themselves. Even though the BBC radio producers have the greatest respect for a writer's work—"

"Why are you defending yourself?" Ralph cut in. "I haven't accused you of anything."

But the air is thick with your disapproval, Marianne thought, pouring the coffee. Ralph gave his attention to *The Times* and Marianne was assailed by a strange loneliness. A feeling that they were together, yet not together.

"You'll just have to go to Oxford without me, Ralph," she said. Tell me you understand, she wanted to add. To which he would reply that of course he did. But he only understood from his own viewpoint. Never from hers. Which was why she was always finding herself delivering defensive monologues.

After Ralph had gone to synagogue—his conversion to Judaism had resulted in him becoming a more observant member of the faith than Marianne had ever been—she sat for a moment absently playing with the tie-belt of her comfortable old cotton housecoat. Last time her mother had stayed with them, she had threatened to buy Marianne a new one for her forty-fifth birthday. Which, knowing Esther Klein, would probably be made of expensive lace, or satin, Marianne reflected humorously, with half her mind. Humor was conspicuously absent from the other half, which was still concentrated upon her marital relationship, from which something was irrevocably missing. Why irrevocably? Because, though they still loved each other, the perfect accord she and Ralph had once known had gone and would never come back.

Marianne rose from the table and began stacking the dishes in the dishwasher Ralph had insisted on buying for her. It made life easier, as did the washing machine he had also bought. She could now set her machines going and get down to a day's writing stint, instead of having to trek to the launderette, as she once had, and tackle a sinkful of pots every evening. Her husband had finally organized her and she had to admit that she enjoyed the benefit. But sometimes she missed the topsy-turvy, easygoing ménage of old. And there were times when the transposition from that to this assumed the quality of a dream, she thought, surveying the gleaming pine units in the streamlined kitchen of her new home.

One evening, Ralph had returned from work and told her he was leaving the agency, and her heart had surged with joy. She had assumed he had at last decided to devote himself to painting, let his steady income go hang. But it was the very opposite that Ralph had had in mind. He had gone on to say he was opening his own ad agency, in partnership with Len Richards.

It was then that Marianne had finally accepted that her husband would never be a painter. And not just because he lacked the ruthlessness which putting your art before all else required. Ralph lacked something else, also, without which no amount of talent could get you where you wanted to be. A sense of purpose.

With that quality, on a materialistic level, Len Richards was well endowed. The first time Marianne met him—and she cared for him no more now than she had then—she had known he was determined to succeed. In that way, he reminded her of her Uncle David.

The new agency was now five years old and had a string of lucrative clients. The Deans' income had burgeoned accordingly and Marianne had not argued when Ralph said it was time they moved to a more spacious flat. Living the way they now did was part of the life her husband had finally settled for.

Marianne wiped a sticky patch off the marmalade jar, put the jar away in a cupboard and went to gaze through the window at the garden they had acquired with their Hampstead apartment. How fragile the May blossom looked, as if the gentle breeze ruffling it would whisk it away. Was the sadness in her heart evoked by the fleeting beauty upon which she was feasting her eyes? Or for Ralph? Who had lacked what it took to take a chance on his own talent. And now never would.

Martin emerged from the New College cloisters into the May sunlight, a downcast expression on his lean face.

"You look as if you've lost a quid and found twopence," said his friend Bill Dryden, who was leaning against a pillar, eyeing him.

"You couldn't have put my feelings more succinctly, Bill."

"Come and have a jar, then. Before the pomp and circumstance begins," Bill said with a grin that made him look like the snub-nosed youth he had been when he and Martin first met. "Nothing like a pint of ale to cheer a chap up."

But it would take more than that to raise Martin from the depression that had dogged him since he awoke that morning. He had returned to Oxford for the Degree Day ceremony, the official recognition of his achievement. The college precincts were awash with his peers and their relatives. Men in their best suits, and ladies decked out for the occasion in summer dresses and smart hats, were standing around with proud smiles on their faces. In anticipation of the glory to come, Martin thought. But when his portion of it was bestowed upon him his mother would not be there.

"You know how proud I am of you. Seeing you presented with a rolled-up parchment isn't important. It's just a formality," she had said when she told him she couldn't come. At the time, Martin had agreed; Bill's joking reference to pomp and circumstance was his own view of Degree Day. But now the day was here, he wanted his mother to be part of it. Though that didn't mean he did not understand that rehearsals for her play must come first.

His father was not here, either, but only because he'd suddenly gone down with tonsillitis. Not for anything would Dad have voluntarily missed this day. And he was probably lying in bed right now with a flask of soup and a packet of sandwiches at his elbow, put there by Mum before she rushed off to Broadcasting House. Marianne Dean's family would have to be at death's door before she'd put them before her work—and even then Martin was not sure that she would!

"Your face has gone red," Bill observed while they strode along a path beside the great expanse of lawn that lent an added charm to the ancient college buildings.

"Has it?" Martin answered gruffly. What the hell was the matter with him? He had never felt resentful toward his mother, though her work had come first all his life. So why now? Because he also felt letdown. By the person who mattered more to him than anyone in the world, who was not just his mother, but also his friend. "I must be sickening for something," he joked to Bill who was still eyeing him.

"You're too old! And, by the way, have you decided yet what you're going to do with your life?" Bill inquired as they passed the porter's lodge and dodged some bicycles, to cross the lane. In Oxford, jaywalkers were more likely to be knocked down by a bike than a car.

They made their way to the High Street and Martin gazed upon the familiar scene. Nostalgia, evoked by the sight of the old book-shops, the pubs and tea shops, and the cycling students, was a new emotion to him. And, momentarily, his soul hungered for the period in his life he would never experience again.

"The answer to your question is no," he told Bill. "I still haven't decided what I'm going to do."

Their college days had ended last year and Martin was filling in time working as a copywriter in his father's agency, for which he was well paid, and had shown a natural aptitude. Both his father and Len Richards had tried to persuade him to make a career of it, but Martin had declined. Dreaming up ways to persuade people to buy what they didn't really need—and probably couldn't afford—was not his idea of the way to spend one's life.

"Made up your mind what you're going to do, Bill?" he asked as they entered a pub they had frequented in their undergraduate years, the Lamb and Flag.

"Yes, as a matter-of-fact."

Martin eyed his friend's thoughtful expression and cast aside his own preoccupation. Bill came from a wealthy family and since leaving college had not been called upon to earn.

Instead, he had used his allowance to travel the world.

"By the way, my rovings included Israel, Martin," he said, stirring in both of them memories of their joint adventures during the Six-Day War.

Bill had been one of the party of students touring the art galleries in Italy when the war began, and had surprised Martin by going with him to support the Jewish cause. Until then they had not been especially close and Martin had occasionally wondered what Bill really thought about Jews. He came from the depths of Cornwall and had said he had not met any until he came to Oxford.

"Before we went to Israel together, I thought you were a bit of a dilettante," Martin grinned.

"A nice thing to think about a chap from a farming family!" Bill exclaimed.

But they're gentlemen-farmers, Martin thought, whose sons have gone to public school for generations. There was no hint of a Cornish burr in Bill's cultured voice, nor of the farmer in his well-kept hands. And it had seemed strange to see him with a hoe in them, on the kibbutz where he and Martin had spent the summer toiling in the fields.

"So you've decided on your future, have you?" Martin smiled to him after they had fought their way through the lunchtime crush at the bar and stood leaning against a wall, with their foaming tankards.

"Only I can't do it alone."

"It isn't back to the land for you, then? I thought it might be."

"The estate will pass to my brother, Martin. To the eldest son, as it always has. Which isn't to say I haven't inherited a love for the country."

Bill set his beer down on an adjacent table and brought a freshly laundered handkerchief from his pocket. Martin recalled him having a seemingly inexhaustible supply of them when they were students. And his slicked-back, sandy hair had never once looked awry—not even in Israel, despite the heat and scramble they had encountered. But his immaculate appearance went with his unflappable nature, and for someone of Martin's moody temperament, Bill was a good guy to have around.

"You'd like to spend your days amid the cowslips, then?" Martin said to Bill, apropos his last remark.

Bill nodded. "If the others agree."

"Which others?"

"I want to get some people together and start a commune, Martin."

"You're having me on!"

Bill wiped some foam from his upper lip. "Why do you think that?"

"Because you're not the commune kind."

"What exactly is the commune kind?"

"Oh, come off it, Bill! I just don't see you in that setting. You're not even a socialist. And you're too much of an individual to live a communal life."

Bill swallowed some of his beer. "If I may, I'll reply to the points you've raised one by one," he said in the tone Martin remembered him employing during the late night chats, which were more like debates, that had been a cornerstone of their undergraduate life. "Why are you looking amused?" Bill allowed himself to briefly digress.

"I just had a vision of you and me and our erstwhile mates at New College, fugging up the air with pipe smoke in someone or other's room, expressing our youthful opinions into the small hours." Nostalgia for that, too, had with the remembrance assailed Martin.

"We're not exactly old men, now," Bill reminded him.

"But we'll never again be the way we were then."

"To return to the subject," Bill said, "and the comment you just made isn't irrelevant—I'll come back to it later—if what you meant by socialism, when you said I'm not a socialist, is what the word has come to mean, you're right. The depersonalization of society, in all its aspects, is the last thing I want to see. Your two other points are interlinked, Martin. In the kind of commune I envisage, every member would be highly individual, so I'd fit into the setting admirably. You, in company with most people, have a stereotyped idea of what a commune has to be."

Martin grinned. "You mean a lot of tents, in the middle of nowhere? With everyone wearing flowers in their hair and going to bed together."

"Exactly! And God forbid that anyone who knows me could see me in that setting."

"But, speaking seriously, what you have in mind is a place where everyone works for the common good, I presume, Bill?"

"But not in the way you mean," Bill countered. "Lest if

you're now visualizing me seated with my fellows before a handloom, weaving linen for the garments in our communal wardrobe!"

Martin glanced at Bill's gray flannel suit, which looked as if it had been tailored in Savile Row. "That, I could never visualize. You, dipping into a communal wardrobe, I mean."

Bill took his pipe from his pocket and contemplated it thoughtfully, before putting it in his mouth. "Details aside, what I have in mind is living with a group of people who each value their individuality as much as I do mine."

Martin stared into his beer. "Why would such people choose to live communally?"

"Because they'd get something unique out of it."

"And what might that be?" Martin asked skeptically.

"Your recollection of our nocturnal talk-sessions at college, and the special camaraderie we shared with the rest of our set, should answer your question, Martin. That's why I said it was relevant. The companionship and stimulation that was there for us if and when we wanted it. We could take it or leave it, and get on with doing our own thing. Remember?" Bill filled his pipe from a leather pouch that looked brand-new, though it was the same one he had used as a student. "We'll never again be the way we were then, you said, Martin. Of course not. Because time doesn't stand still and youth lingers but fleetingly. I've aged at least five years in the past twelve months."

"I feel that way, too."

"But I see no reason to abandon the essence of what we had when we were students. Why not make it the basis of a way of life? With a group of like-minded people?"

"Doing what, exactly?"

"Whatever each of us would have done had we not lived under the same roof."

Martin's skepticism increased. "You might just as well rent yourself a flat, Bill, in a block that's full of eggheads. Preferably one that has a restaurant, so you can all eat your meals together!" Martin drank some of his beer. "If you could find such a block tucked away in the country!"

"What I have in mind can be done," Bill insisted. "My travels included California—"

"That's real hippy-land!" Martin interrupted.

"Indeed. But the commune I spent some time in was my kind, Martin. I met an interesting girl, there, actually."

"And meeting her seems to have affected your head."

Bill ignored Martin's facetiousness. "To give it to you briefly, a couple I met on a Greyhound bus to San Francisco invited me home for supper. Home turned out to be a commune. I enjoyed being there so much I accepted the invitation to stay awhile. The experience impelled me to try to set up a similar commune in England. I'd like you to be one of those with whom I do."

"Thank you for the invitation, Bill. But it's bad enough having to share a bathroom with my parents."

"But you'd find that the advantages outweigh the disadvantages, Martin. As I did."

"In your case, I gather one of them was female."

"Let's just say she was an added advantage," Bill laughed. "But think about it, will you, Martin? And get in touch if you're interested."

Martin went to the bar to refill their tankards. When he returned, Bill was talking to a girl.

"Allow me to introduce my friend Martin Dean," Bill said to her with the formality he always displayed when making an introduction. "Meet the Honorable Moira Danbury, Martin."

Martin had not met a titled person before and was briefly tongue-tied. "How do you do?" he smiled.

"Are you in Oxford for the ceremony?" she asked him after they had shaken hands.

"Isn't everybody?" The pub was full of chaps who had graduated last year and their guests.

"I'm not," Moira said. "I'm here on business."

Bill looked surprised. "Moira was at Cambridge, by the way," he told Martin.

"And I'm now endeavoring to convince my people I can be independent," she informed him with a dry smile. "I'm doing some subediting for a couple of publishers and I'm in Oxford to try to add a third to the list." She smoothed down her long dark hair. "But I wish I hadn't worn a suit for the interview, on such a warm day."

Martin hadn't noticed her suit. His gaze had been glued to her heart-shaped face and smoky gray eyes.

"My new independence includes a *pied-à-terre* in town," she was telling Bill. "You must come and see it."

"I'd drive you there, later, and you could ask me in for a drink but I've arranged to have a meal in Oxford with my entourage," Bill said. "Moira and I have known each other all our lives," he told Martin. "Our families used to have town houses side by side, in Kensington and they allowed us to run wild together—with our nannies of course! —in the square gardens," he added with a reminiscent laugh.

"I'd invite myself for a drink, too. If I had a car to drive you home in," Martin said to Moira.

She exchanged a smile with him. "Why don't I offer you a ride back to town in mine?"

"I say, you're a fast worker, Martin," Bill said after Moira had gone off to her interview. "Why did I never notice it before?"

"You were probably too busy being one yourself."

Martin recalled the brief encounters he had had as a student. Brief because the excitement had quickly palled. Perhaps, this time, it would be different, he thought as a lingering trace of Moira Danbury's musky scent mingled with the beer fumes.

Marianne hurried out of Broadcasting House and stood tapping her foot impatiently at the corner of Portland Place. Why was there never a cab handy when you needed one?

Eventually, three arrived together, but that was usually the case too! she thought edgily, on the way to her husband's agency.

Ten minutes later, she was in Len Richards's office. "I need to borrow a car, Len. I came into town by tube, today, and I have to get to Oxford *toute de suite*."

"Calm down," Len said to her.

Marianne stopped drumming her fingers on his desk.

Len glanced at his wristwatch. "The Degree Day ceremony will be over before you get there."

"I know!" Marianne snapped, "and I ought to have been there for it."

"When did you come to that conclusion?"

"During the final run-through of my play—I haven't time to sit here explaining to you, Len!"

Len fiddled with his moustache and sighed. "For an intelligent woman, you don't have much common sense, do you, Marianne? I could have told you that not going to your son's big day was a mistake. So could Ralph. And he would have done, if he were a different kind of man."

"Like you, you mean?" Marianne flashed.

"Call it what you like."

"If Ralph had been your kind of man, I'd never have got where I am career-wise, Len."

"We wouldn't have stayed married, if I'd been your husband," Len said.

"Will you lend me your car, or not? I'll drop it at your house, this evening, on my way home." The Richardses lived only five minutes' walk from the Deans. "As I've missed Martin's ceremony, the least I can do is go to Oxford and drive him back."

Len fished in his pocket for his car keys. "I never met a woman like you, Marianne! You can't even ask a favor graciously."

"Perhaps because I'm not in the habit of asking favors."

Len tossed the keys onto the desk. "And I'm not in the habit of refusing them. Especially when it helps someone to do what I think is right. How was Ralph, when you last saw him?"

"Does every single word you say have to be an implied rebuke? My husband isn't going to die of tonsillitis!"

"But a little wifely comforting would do him a world of good."

Marianne snatched up the car keys and ran. How dare that oily little man lecture her? She clattered down three flights of stairs—the lift was out of order—her cheeks aflame with wrath. Or was it shame? There was more than a grain of truth in some of the things Len had said.

She did not simmer down until she had left London behind and was speeding along the A40 in Len's white Jaguar. It was as well she wouldn't reach Oxford in time for the ceremony, she thought, glancing down at her faded denims and check shirt. All the other mums would be done up to the nines for the occasion.

Would Martin forgive her for letting him down? She had not seen it in that light until today. During a break in rehearsals the young actor playing the leading role, whom Marianne knew well, had told her bluntly that he wouldn't forgive her if he were Martin. And had likened her absence to his mother skipping the opening night of a stage play in which he had a part.

Only then had Marianne seen things from her son's point of view. When he'd said good-bye to her this morning, his voice had seemed a little strained, but she hadn't paused to wonder why. Well, now she knew. He was hurt by his mother's apparent indifference.

But I'll make it up to him, Marianne resolved. She switched

on the car radio and listened to "Woman's Hour." A cheerful voice was sharing the secrets of good pastry-making with housewives up and down the country, who were sitting in their kitchens with pencils poised to write down the recipe. But not Marianne Dean, who had opted for a different kind of life, with its accompanying traumas, she thought wryly.

By the time the program ended, she had reached Milton Common. Oxford was only ten miles away.

The Degree Day ceremony had just ended when she arrived at the Sheldonian Theater. She watched the graduates and their relatives spilling forth into the afternoon sunshine and tried to spot her son's burly figure among the capped and gowned young men.

"How nice to see you, Mrs. Dean!" a sandy-haired lad called, detaching himself from a group of straw-hatted ladies and striding to Marianne's side. "Martin said you couldn't make it."

"I found I could," Marianne smiled. "Though a little late, I regret. I thought I'd drive down and take Martin to the Randolph for a celebration meal, Bill." Marianne had not at first recognized him, but they had only met once before.

"Oh dear," Bill said. "I'm afraid you've missed him."

"Then I'll try to catch him at the railway station."

"You won't find Martin there, Mrs. Dean. He's meeting someone for tea—at that café on the High where he introduced me to you. He shot off a few minutes ago."

"I'll nip along there, then," Marianne said.

But Bill insisted that she must meet his parents and his three aunts, who, he said, were all fans of hers.

"You're better-looking than that picture of you on your book jackets," Bill's father smiled.

"I must apologize for my husband's personal remark," Mrs. Dryden said. "But we must put it down to him not having met an author before."

"That kind of personal remark is very welcome!"

"Do tell the BBC how much we enjoy 'Afternoon Theater,'" one of the aunts said.

Marianne promised to do so and took her leave of the Dryden family fan club, to go in search of her son. But the few words she had exchanged with the Drydens cheered her, as the letters she received from readers lent power to her elbow. Knowing your work was appreciated made the lonely hours you spent creating it seem worthwhile.

Martin leaped to his feet when she entered the café. She had not expected to find him tête-à-tête with a girl and observed Moira's casual elegance; her fine tweed suit had a Bond Street look about it, and the single strand of pearls around her slender neck were the real thing, Marianne saw when she joined the pair at their corner table.

"What brings you here?" Martin asked her with a grin.

And without reproach, Marianne noted thankfully. Nor the slightest hint of the sarcasm her unexpected arrival deserved. "Better late than never," she smiled, standing on tiptoe to kiss his cheek.

"Won't you join us for tea, Mrs. Dean?" Moira invited after Martin had introduced them.

Marianne was longing for a cup of tea, but felt distinctly *de trop*—a feeling induced by her son's gaze being riveted to Moira's face. She shifted her own to her wristwatch. "I mustn't linger too long. My husband isn't too well," she said, using Ralph as an excuse to make her escape. "He's been alone all day."

"A writer's family gets used to being neglected," Martin informed Moira with mock chagrin. "But you needn't hang around waiting for me, Mum. Moira's giving me a lift home."

"If you'd prefer to go with your mother, I quite understand," Moira said.

"I wouldn't," Martin answered.

"In that case, *I* quite understand," Marianne smiled.

"That's one of the advantages of having you for a mother," Martin told her.

Marianne bade them farewell, and turned around to wave to them when she reached the door, but they were exchanging a long glance, as if they had forgotten she existed.

Well, it's my turn to be hurt! she said to herself ruefully. She had made the trip to Oxford for nothing. And it served her damn well right.

A picture of Martin and Moira gazing into each other's eyes remained with her while she made her way to the car park. "See you again, Mrs. Dean," Moira had said casually before Marianne took her leave. And there was nothing more certain, Marianne thought. Something told her that her son had met his Waterloo.

Edging the car through the rush hour traffic, she envisaged Martin introducing the Honorable Moira Danbury to the family in Manchester and had to smile.

"Who would have thought it?" his great-grandmother would say—though not in Moira's presence.

And it was certainly difficult to imagine Sarah Sandberg, who had arrived in England on a herring boat, ending up with aristocratic *mishpocha*.

Chapter Nine

Matthew Klein had known since childhood what he was going to be. Since his parents took him to see *Macbeth* on his tenth birthday, he reflected while waiting in a restaurant near the Old Bailey for his father to join him for lunch. And Arnold Klein had probably never stopped regretting giving his son that treat, Matthew thought wryly, comparing his patched jeans and scuffed leather jacket with the somber sartorial style of the barristers and lawyers seated all around him. Or that the Royal Shakespeare Company had brought that rousing production to Manchester, in the fifties.

Like the rest of the clan, in retrospect Dad attached special significance to certain events; saw them as turning points and catalysts. But Arnold Klein invariably attached blame to them, too. Maybe he needed to, in order to come to terms with things, Matthew ruminated, fishing in his pocket for his Gauloises and lighting one. Like his only son being an actor. And both his children deciding not to convert to Judaism.

Matthew exhaled a cloud of pungent smoke and watched it form a blue haze above the table, recalling his father's expression when Matthew told him he was a confirmed atheist. "That's the easy way out," Arnold had informed him. Out of the dilemma you created for me and my sister, by raising us in a vacuum, Matthew thought now.

Margaret's recent revelation that she was contemplating becoming a Catholic had left Arnold stunned. As if it were surprising that a girl who had always felt God's presence was, in Margaret's circumstances, seeking Him in a creed not espoused by either of her parents.

It was no surprise to Matthew. But to hell with religion! Why was he sitting here thinking about it, when he had made up his mind not to let it affect his life? Because it already had done, in a multitude of ways, which was why he had finally rejected it.

But his father blamed the traumatic scene that had been enacted in his Westminster flat, years ago, while his own father lay dying, for his children's decision not to become Jews. Though he had allowed them a free choice, he had apparently hoped they would opt for his religion.

Dad wears blinkers in many respects, Matthew thought, stubbing out his cigarette in a pristine ashtray. The kind that allowed you to see only part of the picture, because seeing the whole of it might attach some responsibility to yourself. Arnold Klein, who was a stronger character by far than his wife, should have had the guts to raise his son and daughter as Protestants, which technically they were. He should have set our feet on a secure path, as his parents did for him, Matthew thought. Instead, he had left Matthew and Margaret floundering, rather than accept irrevocably that they were *goyim*.

As he had not yet accepted that Matthew would never abandon the theater. Each time they met, he suggested his son should come down from the clouds and study law. Only once in his life had Dad ever departed from convention, Matthew reflected: when he defied the family and married Mum. But he had never once stepped out of character again.

Arnold had just entered the restaurant and was receiving a deferential greeting from the manager. Had that pompous-looking gentleman, who epitomized staid and stolid respectability, really once been a daring young naval officer, sailing the treacherous wartime seas in a minesweeper? Matthew recollected his parents' wedding picture, with both of them in uniform. There was now no trace of the carefree wren his mother had been, either. What happened to people? It wasn't just their appearance that changed with age, but—if Mum and Dad were any example—everything about them.

His father gave him a cursory wave, then paused to speak to a group of men. He left Matthew cooling his heels for another five minutes before joining him.

"Well, Matthew. You're looking very thoughtful," Arnold said.

As if he were surprised that a member of the theatrical profession could! "I was musing about the way people change," Matthew answered cynically.

"I look forward to the time when that will apply to yourself."

Matthew managed to smile and toyed with his fork while his father studied the menu, to which he had just transferred his gaze from his son's disreputable attire. Subtle rebuke was Arnold Klein's usual opening gambit. The overt kind came later.

"Fancy a Dover sole?" Arnold asked.

"I'd prefer a steak, if you wouldn't mind."

"As you wish, Matthew. I suppose the odd meals you have with me are the only time you get one."

"You suppose right, Dad. I'm hardly in the Dover sole bracket, either. I'd like the steak medium-rare, please."

"I don't know how you can eat it that way."

Or how a son of yours can eat nonkosher meat at all, Matthew thought, while his father gave the waiter their order. Arnold was a living paradox! Though he'd married out of the faith, he never broke the Jewish dietary laws and it offended him to see his children do so.

"When are you going to see sense and do something worthwhile with your life?" Arnold said, averting his eyes from the blood on Matthew's plate, when their meal arrived.

Matthew had expected him to say something of the kind. Their luncheons *à deux* always followed the same pattern. Innuendo before the food was ordered and served, then pull-no-punches talk while you were eating it. As a schoolboy, Matthew had once lunched at the House of Commons with his father and a Labour MP with whom he was serving on a select-committee. Arnold had employed the same conversational tactics on that occasion.

"What one sees as sense is dependent upon one's personal vision," Matthew replied. "And the word worthwhile varies accordingly."

Arnold ate a mouthful of sole *meunière* and dabbed his lips with his table napkin. "In that case, it's time you adjusted your vision."

"And viewed life through your eyes, you mean?" Matthew said sardonically. "As I'm a very different person from you, that isn't possible. And you must accept that I shall live my life in my own way."

"You think you know it all, don't you?"

"I certainly know what I want for myself. Didn't you, at my age?"

"Get on with your meal! You look half-starved!" Arnold snapped, surveying his son's hollow cheeks and the shadows beneath his eyes. His red hair was the only thing about him that didn't look drab and lifeless—and here he was talking glibly about life! As if the way to live it was to wear yourself out, to no purpose, as fast as you could; live for yourself alone. What a cockeyed generation Matthew's was. Their vision stretched no further than today, saw nothing beyond the live-now shop fronts of Carnaby Street and its counter-parts. But one morning they would wake up and find tomor-row had arrived. A tomorrow for which they were ill-equipped and unprepared, Arnold thought.

"At your age, I was a married man, with responsibilities," he said with feeling. "Before which I'd had a maturing experience."

Matthew finished chewing the chipped potatoes he had just forked into his mouth. "You're referring to the navy, I suppose?"

Arnold nodded. "I joined up a boy and came back a man."

Matthew watched him spread butter on a sliver of crisp melba toast and manage to do so without breaking it. But Arnold Klein did everything carefully and efficiently. "I doubt if you were ever the same kind of person as me, Dad." They looked alike, but the resemblance ended there.

Arnold ate some of the toast. "I always had my feet on the ground, if that's what you mean."

"What I really mean is you'd have ended up the kind of man you are no matter what you experienced."

"Is that intended to be an insult?"

"No, Dad. Just a simple statement of fact. There are some people who allow experience to wash over them, whom nothing can influence. I think you're one of them."

"Oh yes?"

"Your kind of person expects others to conform to their own standards of behavior," Matthew went on.

Arnold put down his knife and fork. "I'm not the kind who thinks everything his children do is wonderful. If that's what you mean!"

"I wouldn't want you to be. But, speaking for myself as Margaret isn't here, because I don't fit in with your preconceived ideas of what your son should be I don't stand a chance."

"All right, so I'd like you to enter the legal profession," Arnold said, managing to keep his tone even. "And with your dramatic training, if you read for the Bar you'd be a knock-out. You might even finish up a QC."

All he wants is to be proud of me, Matthew thought, and

was momentarily sorry for his father. Then the fact that pride was more important to Arnold than his son enjoying a life of his own choosing evoked a surge of anger. "I'd rather finish up a second Olivier," he said curtly. "Not that I'm likely to."

"So long as you're happy," his father replied, surprising him.

They fell silent while the waiter served Matthew a large helping of treacle pudding and Arnold a small one of Stilton cheese. Arnold Klein had reached the age and stage where he felt it necessary to watch his waistline, and always limited his meal to two courses. Matthew would have liked some soup, but had not bothered to order any.

"Did you mean what you just said, Dad?" he asked, watching Arnold spoon some of the ripe cheese onto a cracker.

"What then?" Arnold shrugged.

The phrase and gesture were so Jewish that Matthew had to smile. Over the years, his father had acquired the accentless speech of an English gentleman. Arnold had long ago left his Cheetham Hill origins behind him, but occasionally a trace of them slipped out and it was at those times that Matthew felt a real affection for him.

"The way to prove you want me to be happy is to let me get on with doing my own thing, Dad."

"I don't think that phrase—or what it has come to mean—existed before the sixties," Arnold answered.

"Probably because young people are just wising-up."

"'Oi,' your grandmother and mine would say to that."

"No doubt. But the fact remains. Your lot didn't feel entitled to do as they pleased with their lives. Mine do. The following in father's footsteps concept, pleasing your family and all that jazz, has gone forever, Dad. Life is too short."

"A philosophy for which I blame the bomb," Arnold declared.

It did not surprise Matthew. He had expected his father to blame something.

"And ten years from now, where will your lot be?" Arnold demanded after washing down the Stilton with a small glass of port. "All right. Do your own thing and eventually you'll see," he added brusquely. "Now tell me why you wanted to see me today." Their meetings were usually initiated by him, not his son. "And you'd better look sharp. I'm due at the House shortly."

"I wanted to offer you a stake in a new theatrical venture,"

Matthew said, though it choked him to do so. This was tantamount to asking his father for money, which for himself he would never do. Since leaving the Royal Academy of Dramatic Art, Matthew had spent as much time eking out a meager living by doing this job or that, as he had acting. What he did between parts didn't matter to him, but his way of life sickened his father, who had once suffered the ignominy of entering a Westminster pub with a cabinet minister and seeing his son collecting empty glasses from the tables, Matthew recalled.

"What will it cost me?" Arnold inquired. "If a little cash will help you turn yourself into a star—"

"In my view, the star system stinks," Matthew cut in. But reaching the household-name heights was what it would take for Arnold Klein to take pride in his actor son! "And this isn't a commercial venture, Dad."

"What other kind is there? It takes money to put on a play—or you wouldn't be asking me to stake some of mine. And people who put something in expect to take something out, as in any other venture."

"There are still a few folk around who view the arts altruistically. I was hoping you might bend your nature and try to be one of them."

Arnold bit back a sharp retort. "I see."

"A group of us have decided to emulate the struggling young actors and writers in New York," Matthew told him. "You've heard of the off-Broadway theaters, I suppose?"

Arnold snorted. "A colleague of mine went to one last time he was in the States and nearly fell down a flight of rickety stairs, climbing to the top floor of the filthy old warehouse it was in."

"Did he think it was worth it?"

"On the contrary. He said they had no right to call what he saw a play. It was just two chaps talking about sex. And my colleague was sure they were pansies."

"Don't use that word!" Matthew flashed.

"I suppose some of your best friends are, in your profession," his father answered.

"Are you interested in helping the venture, or not?" Matthew asked him shortly. "We already have a venue, but it needs doing up."

"Where is it?"

"Near Billingsgate fish market."

"My God! Who do you suppose will consider a trip there a night out at the theater?"

"The off-Broadway theaters have created a new kind of audience, Dad. For a new kind of play."

"So my colleague gave me to understand. He said there were pansies in the audience, too. And if the sort of rubbish he sat through is what you're asking me to put money into, Matthew, forget it!"

Matthew gave his father an icy glance. "I ought to have known better than to waste my time discussing it with you. But we can manage without assistance from a narrow-minded devil like you."

"I beg your pardon, Matthew?"

"And so you should. I happen to be what you call a pansy myself."

Arnold paled. "You're joking, I hope?"

Matthew held his gaze. "To me and my kind, it isn't a joking matter." Beads of perspiration had broken out on his father's brow. Why had he told him? Because it was bad enough hearing others deride what you were and could not help being, and unbearable when your own parent did so.

"I don't feel well," Arnold said taking out a monogrammed handkerchief and mopping his face. "And I blame your mother for what you've just told me. When you were a baby, she used to dress you in little lace frocks."

Matthew, who was not in the least effeminate, felt like laughing hysterically. He lit a cigarette and inhaled deeply. His father fanned away the fumes and paid the bill.

They did not exchange another word until they had left the restaurant. It had begun to rain, but Arnold seemed unaware of it and made no attempt to put up his umbrella. Matthew unhooked it from his arm and did it for him.

"I'll get you a taxi. And ride with you as far as the House."

Arnold paused on the pavement and eyed him as if he had never seen him before. "Don't bother, Matthew. You go your way and I'll go mine." He turned away abruptly, unable to hide the repugnance in his expression.

So be it, Matthew thought, watching his father stride off along the street. His friend Pete would have the kettle on, ready to make tea when Matthew got back to their bed-sitter. And the other theatricals who lived in the building would probably be squatting beside the gasfire, waiting to cheer him up after the ordeal they knew lunching with his father was. In Matthew's profession, there was no shortage of sympathetic companionship. Why, then, the feeling of utter desolation that had suddenly enveloped him? As though a door had been slammed in his face and would never be opened to him again.

"You're getting absolutely soaked, darling!" a bubbly voice exclaimed.

An actress he knew had halted beside him. "Hi, Linda."

"If you're thinking of going home, you're welcome to share my brolly. But you'll have to hold it, you're so much taller than me."

"Who isn't?" Matthew managed to joke, taking the umbrella from her and linking her arm. Linda James lived in Islington, as he did, and was what his heterosexual chums called a half-pint-dish.

"I've been for an audition," she told him as they made their way to the Underground. "It was only for a one-night showcase production, but you should've seen the queue to read for the lead, Matthew! I was there all morning."

"Well, the TV casting scouts usually turn up to see those productions, don't they?"

"And also, every young actress wants to play Joan of Arc. Not that I think I'll get the part."

Nor did Matthew. Anyone less suited to that classic role he could not imagine, he thought dispassionately, eyeing the short, curvaceous figure beside him. The mischievous March wind was endeavoring to raise the hem of her tartan miniskirt still higher, and her thighs, encased in black fishnet tights, gleamed fetchingly above red patent boots.

Linda was a natural for the sexy au pair girl, or naughty French-maid parts she occasionally got in West End comedies, Matthew reflected. And knew it. But unlike Matthew, who had stopped hoping he would one day play Hamlet at Stratford, she still clung to her drama school dreams.

"What's news with you, Matt?" she inquired on the train.

Matthew told her about the experimental-theater group he and Pete and some others were trying to set up.

"It sounds exciting, darling. But where is it going to get you?" Linda said doubtfully.

"Who knows? We're breaking new ground."

"You and a few other people," Linda reminded him. A handful of companies of the kind Matthew envisaged had already been started. "And from what I've heard, it includes living on bread and jam."

"Since when was that anything new?"

"But none of us wants to starve forever, do we, Matt? And you're not going to get rich and famous doing what you have in mind."

"I'd rather help to give the English theater a shot in the arm. My aunt—she's Marianne Dean, by the way—agrees with me that it bloodywell needs one."

"Why didn't I know you were related to her?"

Matthew grinned. "I don't usually tell people. If I landed a part in one of her plays, it'd seem like nepotism. In her opinion, there hasn't been a play that says anything significant about our society since *Look Back in Anger*."

"So why doesn't she write one that does?"

"She told me she once did, but no producer would take a chance on it. That if you want your work staged, you have to write the sure thing—plays guaranteed to be big box office. She's offered to write a one-act for us, when we get set up. I said we'd certainly consider it."

Linda giggled. "You're no nepotist yourself, are you, darling?"

"It's the kind of play that today's struggling young dramatists are writing that we're after," Matthew said with the engaging smile his friends found immensely endearing.

Linda removed the sunglasses she wore for effect in all weathers and surveyed him. "If only you were straight, Matt—or swung both ways, even—I could really go for you. But don't tell Pete, will you?" she added with an impish grin.

"I wouldn't dare!" Matthew said, hoping his accompanying laugh did not sound as hollow as it felt. What was the matter with him? Linda wasn't the first girl who'd said that kind of thing to him. But hearing it today was a painful reminder of the world inhabited by his family, in which there was no place for people like him. Only Aunt Marianne, who in character was not of that world, accepted what he was.

"We're there, darling," Linda said, prodding him with her umbrella as the train pulled into their station.

"So we are," Matthew managed to grin. A picture of Arnold Klein striding away from him along a rainy street had just risen before his eyes; it remained with him while he strode the few blocks to the peeling old terraced house in which he and Pete had their top-floor pad.

"Pete's been going on like a mother-hen about you probably getting pneumonia from being out in the rain," someone joked as Matthew picked his way between the visitors squatting on the rug, to warm his hands at the gasfire.

"Well I just nursed him through flu, didn't I?" Pete said.

"And he wants me fit and well, so we can forge ahead with the new project," Matthew added, exchanging a smile with Pete, across the room which had looked like a barn when they moved into it, but together they had made it into a home.

Pete had on a fuzzy yellow sweater an aunt had knitted for him, which made him look like a teddy bear, Matthew thought with affection, watching him tug it down around his thick middle. They had been together for five years, but the tales that abounded about homosexuality didn't include a committed and loving relationship between two human beings.

Matthew lit a cigarette and tossed the packet to a pair of outstretched hands. The young sculptor who lived next door was demolishing the last of the bread and cheese intended for tonight's supper, and a couple of actresses, dedicated to the new theater group, were crunching the celery that went with it. By the window, a would-be director was in earnest conversation with a writer. There were a few people present whom Matthew did not know—one of whom was occupying his armchair. But this was the easy-come, easy-go world of the arts. His world. Where you didn't have to pretend.

Chapter Ten

Marianne was putting the finishing touches to a cold buffet on her patio table when her son arrived home.

"I hope the weather won't choose tonight to break," she said to him absently. The English summer of 1969 had been too good to be true; the sun had begun shining in May and was still doing so on this late July evening.

"Serve you right if it did!" Martin grinned. "You haven't said hello to me."

Marianne stood on tiptoe to kiss him, which was necessary despite the high-heeled sandals she was wearing. "You know how distracted I get when I'm giving a party, love."

Martin glanced through the window into the chaotic kitchen. "Fortunately, you don't do it too often! You look very nice, by the way, Mum," he added eyeing the black silk caftan Marianne had on. "Not like your usual self, at all."

"You and your dubious flattery!" Marianne laughed, surveying the table. She hadn't expected Martin to be home this evening, and with his appetite, the poached salmon probably wouldn't go round! "Why isn't Moira with you?" she inquired.

Marianne's premonition, when she first met Moira, had been right. Since then she had seen a good deal of her. Martin and Moira were by now inseparable and, in Marianne's opinion, her son couldn't have found himself a nicer girl.

"She's gone home for the weekend," Martin replied.

"Home" was a Queen Anne mansion in Kent, with magnificent gardens and acres of land, Marianne had learned.

"It's her father's sixtieth birthday today and there's a big celebration," Martin went on, stealing a slice of orange garnish from the avocado salad.

"To which you weren't invited?"

"That's right."

Marianne shifted a sprig of parsley from one side of a dish of potato salad to the other. So her son wasn't good enough for the landed gentry!

"You've spoiled the pretty pattern," Martin said, returning the parsley to its original position between a couple of tomato-tulips. "And I know what you're thinking, Mum."

Marianne had busied her hands to try to hide her anger, but had not succeeded. "You're damn right I'm thinking it!"

"But you're wrong."

"Am I?"

Martin changed the subject. "Who are you entertaining tonight? Your crowd or Dad's? Where is Dad, by the way? I didn't see his car in the drive."

"He's at the wine store buying the ingredients for champagne cocktails. Does that answer your question about who's coming to the party?" Marianne said with a stiff smile. Her friends were happy to drink plonk.

"It sure does." Martin no longer worked at the ad agency, but had been there long enough to know that his father's clients had champagne tastes. And that Ralph's social life was, these days, planned with an eye to business. "How did my father get into this trap?" he asked helping himself to a stuffed egg.

"Of his own free will," Marianne replied shortly.

"Don't take it out on me because you have to entertain people you don't care for," Martin said. "And I fail to see why you should have to."

Marianne threw a muslin cloth over the buffet, to protect the food from the flies and her son. "For the same reason Dad puts up with my pals. He must be bored stiff with them talking about books and plays, and staying till all hours when they come, so he can't get to bed. But you do things for each other's sake when you're married, Martin."

She sat down in a lounging chair and wriggled her feet out of her sandals, to cool them on the flagstones. For once, everything she had cooked had turned out well. Even the Sachertorte she had baked for dessert, because Ralph had said a new client whom he had invited had Viennese ancestry, like herself. Marianne had never made one of the rich chocolate confections before and had had to phone Manchester, to ask Aunt Helga for the recipe.

"What are you smiling about?" Martin inquired, admiring the full-blown tea roses which looked about to spill their petals on the lawn.

"The things we do for love," Marianne replied wryly. It was for Ralph she had risen at seven and slaved all day. Not his clients and cronies.

"Hm," Martin said thoughtfully. He ate some nuts from the bar. "If Dad isn't back soon, he won't get his cocktails cold enough."

Marianne shrugged indifferently. Why did she have this leaden feeling? Because Ralph had changed and she had not. Friendships, for her, had never been fostered with an eye to the main chance and she did not enjoy doing what she must to support Ralph along that materialistic path.

"What's that pendant you're wearing?" Martin asked her. "I haven't seen it before."

Marianne fingered the translucent jade oval, which Ralph had had set in diamonds for her. "It's an anniversary present from your father, Martin. Do you like it?"

"No, diamonds aren't your style. And your anniversary isn't until next week."

"Dad gave it to me in advance. He wanted me to wear it tonight."

"So his clients will know how well he's doing, I suppose," Martin said sardonically.

"That is quite enough of that, Martin!" Marianne rebuked him, though she had had the same thought herself. She watched a squirrel dart through the bushes at the end of the garden—Hampstead was full of them. And the relationship between a man and a woman was as fragile as those roses, she thought, breathing in their sweet scent. These days, she and Ralph were just two people living side by side, briefly coming together in bed.

Had her parents' marriage followed the same pattern as her own? she wondered fleetingly. No. She was sure it had not. Her grandparents' either. Mam and Bobbie Sarah had had no extra-marital interests, nor had they wanted them. Esther had worked as a saleswoman, but in her husband's store, helping to support her family. Because home and family were the length and breadth of her horizon. Perhaps it was the modern woman's refusal to subjugate herself to domesticity that changed the quality of her marriage? Marianne ruminated. And you couldn't have it both ways.

"If you met Moira's folks, you'd probably like them," Martin cut into her thoughts.

Marianne shifted them to him. "As I haven't, I must take your word for it, Martin."

"They're very pleasant people, Mum. But they'll never let Moira marry me."

Let? Marianne thought. In this day and age? And the word did not tally with what she knew of Moira. "They've probably got a duke lined up for her," she said tartly.

"Don't be daft, Mum! And, for your information, Moira's mother was once a chorus girl. Moira's inherited her gorgeous legs—"

"Keep to the point," Marianne interrupted.

"The point I'm trying to make is that me not being upper-class isn't what they object to. Her ladyship was working-class—which I'm not—until Lord Kyverdale saw her dancing at the Windmill Theater during the war and married her. Lady Kyverdale's father was a docker."

"Possibly. But blue bloods marrying showgirls is traditional."

"Unfortunately, Catholics marrying out of their faith, isn't," Martin said gloomily.

"I see."

"And it's certainly never happened in Moira's family," Martin went on. "Her great-great-uncle was a cardinal, by the way."

And one of your forebears was a *Hassidic* rabbi, Marianne reflected with irony. This was history repeating itself, only the other way round: Moira's dilemma was exactly what Marianne's had been. Almost a quarter of a century ago, but religion was still rearing its head like an ancient dragon, spitting fire and brimstone at those who defied it. And only pregnancy had impelled Marianne to do so, she thought eyeing the living evidence who had just helped himself to a handful of canapés from a tray on the bar.

"If you go on eating everything within sight, we'll have to take the guests to a restaurant," she said.

"And if I turned Catholic, everything would be fine."

Marianne held her breath.

"I shan't, of course."

"I'm glad to hear it."

"And Moira hasn't asked me to."

For which Marianne respected her. She had never asked Ralph to convert to Judaism. He had eventually done so of his own accord, but that was something else.

"Moira and I will just have to live together," Martin said.

"Oh no," Marianne answered firmly.

Martin shot her a surprised glance. His friends had always envied him his broad-minded mother. She knew Laura slept around, and that Matthew and Pete, who often dropped in to see her, were homosexuals. But maybe she wasn't so broad-minded about her immediate family?

Marianne dispelled his doubt. "If all there was between you and Moira was sex, I'd tell you to get on with it."

"We have been doing."

"But living together for always, embarking on a life partnership without marriage, won't do, Martin. Sooner or later you'll want children."

"We just won't be able to have any."

"And how will you resolve the problem if Moira conceives?"

"We'll cross that bridge if and when we come to it, Mum."

"It's a hard bridge to cross, Martin." Marianne held his gaze silently for a moment. "And you're hearing it from someone who knows."

"What are you telling me?"

Marianne felt her cheeks flush. This wasn't easy! She got up from her chair and took Martin's hand, then led him to a bench under a laburnum tree where, on fine days, she sometimes sat scribbling.

"Why have you brought me to sit here?"

"To get you away from the food, before you demolish the lot!" She could not say that when you told your child the story of how he came to be born, you wanted to be close to him.

After she had done so, Martin plucked a long blade of grass that had escaped Ralph's mower and chewed it thoughtfully.

Marianne sat listening to the traffic noise drifting from Haverstock Hill, waiting for him to speak.

"I must say it's a bit of a shock to hear something like that about someone of your generation, Mum," he muttered.

"I was before my time in many respects," Marianne replied with a reminiscent smile.

And stepping out of line in those days must have taken guts, Martin thought surveying her. And an unquenchable thirst for life, which Mum still had. Her glossy black hair had begun to display a touch of silver here and there, but she was the kind who would never age within herself. That was probably why she got on so well with young people.

"And you're still one on your own, Mum," he said kissing her cheek. "I wouldn't swap you for the world."

Nor would he swap his father, he thought as Ralph's thickening figure appeared in the kitchen doorway. Except for the man he had once been. Was that self-doubting artist still there beneath the deliberately arty facade Dad had, since throwing in his lot with Len Richards, presented to the world, his family included? The glances Martin occasionally saw him casting at the small still life he had painted before he and Mum were married indicated so. But he had allowed circumstances to metamorphose him, which I'll never let happen to me, Martin vowed.

"Giving us the pleasure of your company, are you?" Ralph called to him. "You'd better put on something respectable, instead of looking as if you're on the bread line."

"But I am, aren't I, Dad?" Martin was presently drawing the dole. And writing a play. Nor did he live at home. Bill Dryden had found a corner for him in his flat.

"You can come back to work at the agency any time you like," his father answered.

"No thanks. Other reasons apart, I shan't be in London

much longer. I've decided to join the commune Bill is setting up."

"What!" Ralph thundered.

"Cool it, Dad. Didn't you have dreams of a different kind of life, once?"

"Too true I did, Martin. But I came down to earth, as you will eventually. And the longer you stay up in the clouds, the harder it is when you fall. Now come and help me unload my car, will you? We'll have to chill the champagne in the freezer, for speed, sweetheart," Ralph added to Marianne.

"What took you so long, Ralph?"

"A flat tire." Ralph turned around and went into the house. But not before Marianne had noted his distress.

"You've upset him," she rebuked Martin.

"He shouldn't have sold out to the fleshpots!" Martin said with feeling. He glanced around at the expensive patio furniture and at the silver platters and dishes on the buffet and bar. "Who needs all this? Dad seems to enjoy it, but you'll never convince me you wanted it, Mum."

Marianne did not try to, or point out that material success was no compensation for artistic failure, though Ralph was making a good job of pretending that it was.

"Dad should have kept his eye on the stars, like you did," Martin said.

"I wasn't the breadwinner."

"But you didn't ask him for cake, did you?"

This was true. But it was too easy to reduce what they were discussing to simple terms of black and white, Marianne thought, casting her mind back to something her Uncle Joe Klein had once said to her. Uncle Joe had been dead for some years, but Marianne often had cause to remember the wisdom of that cynical old journalist. His face had resembled a walnut, crinkled and browned by the sunny climes to which his foreign assignments had taken him, she recalled with affection. The truth is like an onion, many-layered, Joe had told her. And so it was. The Dean's latter-day affluence was just the outer covering on the many layers of Ralph's experience that had led to it.

"Nothing will ever make me sell out to mammon," Martin declaimed.

With the burning resolve of youth, Marianne noted, which time would teach him wasn't easy to sustain when youth had fled and a man had a family to support. And, once the decision to sell out had been painfully made, aiming for cake instead of just bread was a natural consequence. For most men, the trap was inescapable.

But on a commune, perhaps it wouldn't be? Marianne mused, glancing at Martin and trying to visualize him living a communal life. She had heard of several such experiments that had ended up as microcosms of society—and, human nature being what it was, how could they not? The strong would flourish and the weak fall by the way and require support in any ethos.

She eyed her son's profile, which bespoke the strength of character his father's identical one belied. Martin was like her, purposeful and with a talent for words. What he would do with this double inheritance remained to be seen.

Meanwhile, Marianne thought angrily, he must stop behaving this way toward his dad. Tonight was not the first time Martin had rubbed salt into Ralph's wound. Why did he do it? she pondered. Because Ralph was a disappointment to him, came the answer. And it struck her that children expected their parents to live up to their own image of them. That this didn't only happen the other way around.

But didn't expectations enter into every relationship? Marianne thought. And, sooner or later, erode it? Marriage most of all. "As your father has made his bed, it's unkind of you to say things that make it painful for him to lie in it," she lectured her son.

"Believe it or not, I'm sorry for him, Mum."

"He doesn't need your pity. He needs your understanding. As you may from your son, one day," Marianne said. "Which returns me to the matter of you and Moira. I see no reason why you shouldn't marry. It wouldn't necessitate Moira abandoning her religion."

"But our children would have to be raised as Catholics."

"Yes. And I imagine that if Moira's parents could be sure of that, they'd agree to the marriage."

"Our kids would be your grandchildren, too, Mum," Martin said quietly. "How would you feel about them being Catholics?"

Marianne had not paused to examine her own feelings and allowed herself to do so now. The overriding one was regret. Martin's sons would not have a *Brith*, wear the yellowed-with-age gown Sarah Sandberg had brought from Russia, which male children born into the family had worn for their circumcision ceremonies since Uncle David's time. Nor would they be *Bar Mitzvah*. Or their sisters *Bat Mitzvah*.

Marianne would not have those proud, traditional occasions to look forward to. Or the simple pleasures that were a Jewish grandmother's. Seeing her grandchildren's eager faces when the *Chanukah* candles were lit, and their solemn awed ones when the *Shofar* was sounded in *shul*, on *Yom Kippur*. Sitting at the *Seder* table with them at Passover, while they tasted the bitter herbs that epitomized their people's history.

Martin's children would be born into a different heritage, but so be it, Marianne thought. What mattered was her son's happiness.

"I'd prefer my grandchildren to be Jews, Martin," she declared with honesty. "But I can live with them not being. And it won't stop me from welcoming them, when they arrive."

Chapter Eleven

Sarah sat in the stalls at Her Majesty's Theater, watching her long-ago past unfold before her misty eyes. She had not wanted to make the journey to London; in her ninetieth year, a person was content to sit by the fireside. But David had insisted upon bringing her to see *Fiddler On The Roof*.

"It's our story, set to music, Mother," he had told her. Sammy had written the same, after seeing it in New York. And so it was. Except that Sarah had never known or heard of a Russian-Jewish girl who married a *goy* and broke her parents' hearts, as Tevye the milkman's daughter, Chavah, had just done on the stage.

In all other respects, everything was as Sarah remembered it. The gentle, learned rabbi and the shrewd matchmaker. The *shul*, which was not just a house of worship, but a meeting place. The friendly market, where news was bandied back and forth. The poverty, laughter and tears. And hovering over everything, the ever-present fear and foreboding, as if a storm was brewing and you never knew when the lightning would strike.

David offered her a chocolate and observed her expression. "I bet it brings back memories," he whispered.

Sarah waved the chocolate box away. Bring back memories was right. Some of which were too painful to bear. The wedding scene, with Tzeitel, a plain girl as Sarah had been, looking suddenly radiant, had reminded Sarah of her own wedding day. When her dear parents were beside her and Abraham danced a joyful *kazatsky* with the male guests.

Seeing Tzeitel's dowry had moved Sarah, too; especially the feather-filled *perineh*, which Jewish parents had provided for their daughters' marriage beds. Sarah had brought hers to England and still slept beneath it, though it had, by now, been recovered countless times.

But most poignant of all was the way Tevye held conversations with God. Just like Sarah's husband and his *Hassidic* friends had always done.

After the show, while she and Bessie waited outside the theater for David to find a taxi, Sarah watched a party of Christian ladies—who probably thought what they had just seen was make-believe—board a coach that had brought them to the matinee. For *goyim, Fiddler On The Roof* was just entertainment, Sarah thought wryly. What you saw on the stage really happened, she wanted to call to the ladies. But they would eye the Persian lamb coat, which, despite her protests, David had bought for her, and her daughter-in-law's mink one, and would not believe it. Especially the poverty.

"We've come a long way since those days," Sarah sighed to Bessie, who was smoothing the wrinkles out of her expensive French kid gloves.

"I should hope so, Ma!"

But Sarah had not been referring to affluence. Tevye the milkman and his family had left their village to begin a new life in America in 1905, the same year the Sandbergs had come to England. And with the same hopes in their hearts, Sarah reflected. Looking back, she was filled with a mixture of pride and sadness. Jews were no longer the underdog, but could hold up their heads alongside their Gentile fellow citizens without being afraid because they were what they were. In little more than half a century, they had risen from the ghetto, never to return. But seeing *Fiddler On The Roof* had highlighted for Sarah that something irreplaceable had been lost forever in the process.

We've come a long way from the old days in plenty of respects, she said to herself grimly later, when they arrived at Laura's flat for dinner and a young man swathed in a bath towel opened the door. The elders of Sarah's girlhood would have dropped down dead if such a thing had happened.

Nowadays, we're only struck dumb, she thought observing David and Bessie's expressions, which matched her feelings. "We've come to the wrong address? I hope," she said, giving her great-granddaughter the benefit of the doubt.

David found his tongue. "Not unless Laura's moved since I spoke to her on the phone this morning."

The young man gave them a vague smile. "I guess you're her folks from Manchester?"

"That's right," David said curtly. "We're expected for a meal."

"She said something about it."

"I hope she's also done something about it. I'm hungry. Where is my granddaughter?"

"In her darkroom. I guess."

"Would you mind if we came in?" David asked, with a hint of sarcasm.

The young man moved out of the doorway and allowed them to enter. "You'll have to excuse me," he said with another of his vague smiles. "Good manners have never been my strong point."

Sarah averted her eyes from his hairy chest.

Bessie was watching the water dripping from beneath his towel onto the carpet her husband's money had bought.

Laura's entrance in a dressing gown did not improve matters.

"I wasn't expecting you so early," she said, as if there were nothing untoward about her attire, or her guest's lack of it.

"Obviously," David answered, casting a glance at the young man.

Laura surveyed her family's censorious expressions and smiled. "Oh dear!"

"So who is he?" Sarah demanded when the young man had ambled back to the bathroom, before Laura had time to introduce him.

"A friend."

"Enemies, I wouldn't expect you to let take baths in your home. He's Jewish, probably not?"

Laura grinned and shook her head. "His name's Rod and he's staying here at the moment."

"What!" David exclaimed.

"Well, why else would he be taking a bath here, Grandpa? And that's all there is to it," she lied because the truth would be more than they could take. "Rod got thrown out of his own place because he couldn't pay the rent." That, at least, was true. "He's out of work."

This, Laura's relatives were prepared to believe. The young man's vague smile extended to his manner. Useless-looking was how David had summed him up. And probably a layabout.

"So I said he could bunk here," Laura went on. "In the circle I mix in, everyone's very casual," she added with a smile.

"In Chelsea, what else can you expect?" Bessie asked the air. She handed Laura a package. "I bought you a house-warming present, as we haven't visited you here before."

"And here is a little something from me," Sarah said handing her a smaller one.

Laura thanked them and went to get some glasses and a bottle of sherry. In the rented flatlet from which she had moved a month ago, there had not been a wall long enough to accommodate the pale, Scandinavian sideboard where she now stored her drinks and glassware. There, she hadn't been able to entertain the family in the style to which they were accustomed. But a casual remark to Grandpa had changed things.

"Why didn't you tell me before?" he had asked when Laura mentioned in passing that she had to develop and print her pictures in her bathroom. And in no time at all, she had found herself the owner of this apartment, a stone's throw from Sloane Square. Her parents had once offered to buy her a flat, but she had declined with thanks.

"Pour the sherry already!" David said to her.

Laura surveyed his bowed shoulders as she handed him his drink. She hadn't wanted to give her mother the satisfaction of setting her up in style. But could not deny her grandfather, who had never recovered from her brother's death, the pleasure of doing so.

"Open the presents!" Bessie instructed her.

Laura knew what her grandmother's would be before she did so and hid a smile. "How absolutely beautiful!" she said though she thought it was hideous.

"For me, there's nothing like a nice piece of cut glass," Bessie declared unnecessarily. "And when you get married, I'll buy you a bigger one," she promised watching Laura set the large bulbous vase on the sideboard. "But I hope it won't be to the young man who's staying with you," Bessie added. "Even with clothes on, and Jewish, I couldn't fancy him for my grandson-in-law."

"There's no danger," Laura assured her. "Rod isn't the marrying kind." She had to stop herself from adding that nor was she. The nearest thing she had ever met to an independent married woman was Marianne—who in order to remain her own person, do her own thing, had accumulated inner conflicts and hang-ups that Laura had no intention of getting lumbered with.

She removed the wrapping from Sarah's gift and almost burst into tears. Her great-grandmother had brought her the bunch of grapes from the bowl of wax fruit that had always lived on her dining room sideboard.

"Me, I like a present to mean something," Sarah, who always gave *Shabbos* candlesticks for wedding gifts, said, observing Laura's expression. "The grapes will remind you of home." And would suffice until Laura qualified for the candlesticks, Sarah added mentally.

Your home, Laura thought, of which I need no reminding. It was to the big old house in Heywood Street, where family *Seders* were held at *Pesach*, and everyone gathered on *Shabbos* afternoons, that Laura's thoughts strayed when she occasionally felt homesick.

"You invited us for dinner, but I don't smell anything cooking," Sarah said, glancing through a narrow archway to where a corner of the kitchen was visible. "In winter you're going to give us a cold meal? I hope not."

"Oh Lord!" Laura exclaimed. "I meant to cook something. But don't worry, it won't take me long to knock it together."

"Meals that get knocked together, we can do without," Bessie told her. "Get dressed. Your grandfather will take us to Bloom's."

"Can Rod come, too?"

Rod chose that moment to enter, outrageously attired and reeking of perfume—or was it an overdose of aftershave? David wondered. "Why not?" he managed to smile to his granddaughter. "The more the merrier. But we'll eat here in Chelsea."

"You'll have to eat fish, then," Laura pointed out.

"So what's wrong with fish?" David had been looking forward to sampling Bloom's delicious salt-beef and potato *latkes*, but would not be seen dead in that respectable kosher restaurant with a chap in a pink velvet suit.

"Rod's a pop musician, by the way," Laura told her family.

"That's how Laura and I met," Rod supplied. "She took some promotion pictures of the Bouncing Beans. When I was still with them," he sighed, sinking into a red corduroy chair and draping one lanky leg over the arm.

Like a strawberry blancmange flopping onto a raspberry jelly, David thought. Anything less reminiscent of a bouncing bean, he had never met!

As Laura saw from his expression. "I'll go and get my dining-out togs on," she said hastily departing for her bedroom. "Entertain the folks," she instructed Rod before shutting the door.

Rod reached languidly for a guitar which was resting against a wall and proceeded to take Laura's instruction literally.

By the end of the evening, Laura's relatives had learned that hard rock was not, as they had always thought, just something that had to be broken up with a pickax. And that a gig was not a small horse-drawn carriage, but a "one-night-stand," in pop language.

"Hard rock is the coming thing," Rod assured them, over dessert.

"So what's with the Stones and the Who?" Sarah said with her head in a whirl, over coffee. "Before tonight, I thought there were only Beatles."

"You're learning, Bobbie," Laura chuckled.

Sarah certainly was. And not just about modern music. She felt as if she had been transported to another planet. All around her were young men wearing the same kind of unmanly outfits Rod had on, or—and Sarah could not decide which was worse—scruffy denims and shirts. As for the girls—Sarah wondered why some of them had bothered to put on skirts at all. Their knickers were showing! But, thankfully, not Laura's or Sarah would have refused to be seen with her. It was bad enough that she had done herself up in a flowing red robe and wound a band of flowers around her temple.

Directly above Sarah's head a loudspeaker was blaring a song. She tried to make out the words, but only succeeded in doing so with one line, which kept being repeated: "Give it to me!"

Which, for Sarah, summed up today's younger generation, Jewish and Christian alike. But what were they giving in return? Only aggravation to their families.

"You're a fab old lady," Rod said to her when they parted. But he did not bother to thank David for the meal.

"Give my love to Marianne," Laura said when she kissed them good-bye.

Marianne had insisted that they stay with her. The hall clock was striking twelve when they returned to her flat.

"Had a nice time?" she asked them.

None of them seemed able to reply.

"Out with it!" Marianne smiled. "I'm a big girl now, you can tell me anything." And she would not be surprised if her young cousin had done something to shock them.

The Deans' concern for Laura had not ended when she removed herself, years ago, from under their watchful eyes. Marianne was still her confidante. She noted that her uncle and aunt had a dazed look about them. And her grandmother was gazing thoughtfully up at the stained glass fanlight above the front door.

"Well?" Marianne prodded them.

"A nice time is not how I would describe it," Sarah said.

"You enjoyed the show, though, didn't you, Mother?" David put in.

"Enjoy is not the right word." Within Sarah, nostalgia for the old ways, which *Fiddler On The Roof* had evoked, mingled with the shock and bewilderment engendered by Laura's way of life. But there was no going back.

When Sarah returned to Manchester, she learned that her house had been included in a Compulsory Purchase Order. At first, she could not believe it. And when, finally, she had no option but to do so, she refused to accept it.

"You can't fight the planners," David told her.

"Like, ever since Father died, she's fought us about leaving here," Esther added. She and Nathan had joined David in his attempt to make Sarah see reason.

Sarah ignored Esther's addendum. "So what is the use of me having three lawyers in my family? One of whom is also an MP."

"Arnold isn't the member for your constituency," Nathan reminded her patiently. "And if he were, he could do nothing about this. It's a local government matter."

Sarah gave the fire an angry poke. "Are you saying I have to do what I'm told?"

Her children exchanged a glance. Leaving her home was a sorrowful prospect for her. Also, which accounted for her anger, Sarah Sandberg was not the kind to knuckle under.

"That's the way it is," David answered.

"But there's nothing wrong with my house," Sarah said as emotion overtook her. "Why should they pull it down?"

"I think the land is going to be part of a playing field," Nathan said.

Sarah's outrage returned. "Elizabeth Street park, round the corner, isn't enough for the local children to play in?"

Nathan shrugged wordlessly. Though he applauded the slum clearance programs, by which those who had been badly housed all their lives were being resited in better homes and environs, he too sometimes questioned the planners' reasoning in other respects, and what, slowly but surely, they were doing to the face and character of his native city.

"There'll be a lot of council flats in this district before long and that means many more children," David said in reply to Sarah's question.

"That's right," Nathan said. He had not thought of that aspect. And no doubt, on paper, the planners were doing the right thing. But the human element, the effects it would have upon people like his mother, had not been taken into account.

"So what can you do?" Sarah whispered as if the fight had suddenly gone out of her.

Her sons and daughters surveyed her bowed posture and knew that, momentarily, it had.

"We've been having a chat about you, Mother," David said gruffly.

Nathan cleared his throat. "About where you're going to live."

Esther dabbed her eyes with her handkerchief and shared a glance with her brothers. For forty-five years, this house had been the heart of the family. The solemn *Kaddish* prayer had been recited within its walls. *Yom Tavim* and *Brith* had been joyfully celebrated here, and matters of life and death debated and decided. For Sarah's children, this was an emotional moment on a personal level.

"You're welcome with any one of us," David told her, "as you must know."

"But if you prefer not to show favoritism," Nathan smiled, "you could live four months of the year with each of us."

How many years do they think I have left? Sarah thought. "I'm very grateful to you all," she said sincerely. "But it's out of the question. At my time of life, I can't start sharing a kitchen with another woman. Not even my daughter and daughters-in-law—"

"You wouldn't have to set foot in the kitchen, if you made your home with one of us," Esther cut in.

"But I'd want to. And nobody would want to let me. In no time I'd feel like a useless old woman, who's in the way. A lady I sometimes talk to when I visit Sigmund, told me that was why she's now in the Old Home."

"She must be infirm in some way, to be eligible for residency there," Nathan said.

"But she wasn't until she went to live with her daughter," Sarah countered. "That is the whole point of what I'm trying to say. The day you sit down in a rocking chair and let people wait on you, you're finished."

Her tone was so adamant, her sons and daughter felt unable to argue.

"Also, I want my own things around me," Sarah went on. "When I need looking after, I'll tell you. In the meantime, what I'd like is a little house, not too far from here. But it would have to have a parlor big enough for my *Shabbos* gatherings."

"And a dining room where we can hold the family *Seder*?" Nathan asked with a smile.

"Also a guest room, I suppose?" Esther said.

Sarah nodded. "What then?"

"All right, Mother," David said after exchanging a helpless glance with his sister and brother.

When Sarah Sandberg made up her mind, there was no arguing with her.

The next afternoon, Sarah went to see Sigmund and found him seated alone in a corner of the front lounge, with a copy of Proust's *Time Regained* on his lap.

"You were reading that on VE Day, when we sat together in my porch," she recalled. "You still haven't finished it?"

"She still doesn't know that my favorite books I read over and over again!"

"Where are all your friends, today?"

"They went to Blackpool, to see the illuminations."

"Why didn't you go?"

"Was I ever the kind for coach trips? Or getting excited about colored lights?"

Sarah smiled at Sigmund's irascible expression. He seemed more frail each time she saw him, but his spirit remained undiminished. He had settled down in the Home immediately, as if he had made up his mind to do so, and never complained to his many visitors. Sometimes, when Sarah came here, she found him holding forth on this or that to a cluster of other gentlemen, as she remembered him doing years ago in his tailor's shop. So long as he had people to talk to, Sigmund was content, and there was no shortage of companionship here.

"So?" he demanded. 'What brings you to see me on a Thursday? You usually come on Wednesdays and Sundays. See! I still know what day it is," he joked at his own expense, then stared morosely down at his hands.

Sarah patted them comfortingly. She had not deluded herself that he didn't have moments of self-pity and depression. Who, in his situation, wouldn't? The look that was in his eyes now, she had seen in those of his fellow-residents. Resignation was the word to describe it.

"I didn't come yesterday because I was worn out from my trip to London," she said. "But I have a lot to tell you." To whom but Sigmund, whom she had known since her first day in England, could she unburden herself? If he died before she did, Sarah would feel she had nobody left to talk to.

"Oi," Sigmund sighed when Sarah had talked, nonstop, for twenty minutes. First about losing her house and then about Laura.

"It was seeing *Fiddler On The Roof* on the same day I found out how Laura is living that brought everything home to me," Sarah summed up.

"And my grandson Henry is another example," Sigmund declared bitterly. "I was a fool to give him money. And it was you who told me to do it!"

"Money has nothing to do with this," Sarah replied, airing the view to which her distressed conjectures had brought her. "Nobody has put cash in the bank for Martin and Matthew to live their *meshugenah* lives," she added to illustrate her point. That these two great-grandsons had no interest in securing a stable future for themselves grieved Sarah. How would they ever support a family? But they seemed not to care. As Laura showed no signs of finding the right man and settling down.

"Once, such choices would not have been open to them," she declaimed. "Young people got married and brought up children. Respected the sanctity of the home, like their parents did."

"Plenty still do," Sigmund reminded her. "About my grandson Frank, I have no complaints."

"But he and Leona don't live the way we did, Sigmund. Which of our grandchildren does? Last time I went to Shirley's for Friday-night dinner, I had to remind her to light the *Shabbos* candles!" Sarah went on hotly. "So why should I be surprised that her daughter lets young men stay at her flat? Religion and morals go hand in hand, and nowadays most Jewish youngsters don't feel God looking over their shoulder."

Sigmund gazed pensively at the tea trolley a lady attendant was wheeling into the room. "If we didn't want things to change, we should have stayed where we were. In the ghetto. Everything has its price, Sarah."

"Don't I know it?" But Sarah had not expected integration to cost quite what it had. Over the years, she had schooled herself to accept her family's increasing laxity in matters of religious observance. But the way some of her young descendants were now thumbing their noses at hard-won middle-class respectability! Perhaps, if she had been firmer about the former, the latter would not have followed in its wake? She communicated this thought to Sigmund.

"The stable door she wishes she'd shut, after the horse has bolted!" he said derisively. "And if she had, it would have leaped over it, to where the new horizons were visible."

"Horses and stables he's bothering my head with!" Sarah exclaimed, venting her feelings upon him. But the analogy was all too clear to her. David's first glimpse of a new horizon had been during his high-school days. And, in effect, he had leaped over the stable door. Sarah's attempt to stop him from traveling to Alderley Edge by train, on *Shabbos*, to go to his Christian friend's birthday party, had not succeeded.

That was sixty years ago, she reflected, fingering her

brooch. And from such small and long-ago beginnings had sprung the great changes she and Sigmund found so painful today. But short of keeping their children chained to the ghetto, where no outside influences would touch or tempt them, there was no way that Jewish parents could have prevented it from happening.

"Freedom begets enlightenment. Which in its turn begets change," Sigmund declaimed as though he had read Sarah's thoughts.

The attendant had halted beside them to pour their tea. "Mr. Moritz is such a clever talker," she smiled to Sarah, laying a plate of sugary biscuits conveniently at Sigmund's elbow.

"Gifted in that way, he always was," Sarah agreed, noting that the biscuits looked homemade.

Sigmund acknowledged the compliments with a courtly inclination of his head and watched the tea trolley being trundled away. Then he gazed through the window at the buses passing by on Cheetham Hill Road, and the drab buildings silhouetted against a murky sky. "What I'm looking at now is, these days, the sum total of my own horizon," he declared with irony. "Literally speaking, of course. My incarceration hasn't brought on a sudden insularity of mind."

"You're not a prisoner here," Sarah reminded him. "And your relatives are tired of asking you to let them take you out. Even to my house you refuse to come—"

"Because I couldn't bear to be collected and delivered back here like a parcel!" he interrupted with an onrush of feeling. He sipped some tea to calm himself and replaced the cup in the saucer with a trembling hand. "But I don't want the family to know. You I can tell."

Oh, the indignities age inflicts upon people, Sarah thought. The lengths they had to go to, to maintain their self-respect. And Sarah, like Sigmund, would fight to her last breath to keep hers.

She surveyed his pale face, which looked as if a fine line had been etched upon it for every one of his ninety-five years. Last week, he had joked to her that at eight-nine she was still a spring chicken. And except for my joints, I don't feel very old, she thought now. But there was no guarantee that Sigmund's lot would not eventually be Sarah's.

"I wouldn't dream of telling anyone what you told me," she

assured him gently. He had always been a proud man and must be allowed to cope with his situation in his own way. As Sarah would have to do, if and when the time came.

Sigmund's gaze strayed to a splendid *menorah* someone had donated to the Home. "It will soon be *Chanukah*," he said heavily. "Another decade is drawing to a close." One in which Israel had been plunged into the Six-Day War—and the family bereft of Mark Kohn, he reflected with sorrow; in which Neo-Nazism had, in England, burgeoned into the National Front, and Russia had sunk her fangs into Czechoslovakia; in which President Kennedy and his brother were mown down by assassins' bullets, and the flower of American boyhood was sacrificed on the altar of political expediency, in Vietnam . . .

"Laura and her friends call this decade the swinging sixties," Sarah said, cutting into Sigmund's grim mental catalogue.

. . . And young people had gone suddenly haywire, he added to it. "Posterity might call it the decade when we finally had to stop fooling ourselves," he said.

"About what?" Sarah, who defied anyone to pull the wool over her eyes, inquired skeptically.

"That the golden prospect of peace we saw ahead, after the war, wasn't a mirage."

"He's here with his doom and gloom again!" Sarah told the air scathingly. "And since when did everything that glitters prove, in the end, to be gold?"

Something the youthful members of the clan who had rejected the tried-and-true way of life, to pursue a more exciting one, had yet to discover, Sarah thought, and her mind returned uneasily to Sigmund's graphic analogy. "How much further from the stable will the horse have galloped by the end of the next decade?" she wondered aloud.

Sigmund spread his hands for want of an answer, thankful that he would not be here to see it.

PART THREE

Chapter One

Sigmund was relieved of the burden of his years early in 1970. The manner of his going epitomized his life. He breathed his last with a book on his lap, listening to a symphony concert on the radio.

Though his presence had, in effect, gone from their midst when he entered the Home, to the family it was as though an ancient oak had been removed from their landscape, leaving an immense void where it had stood.

Some arrangements he had made in the late sixties did not come to light until after his death. Which amounted to causing trouble from the grave, Sarah reflected uneasily when she heard about them.

On the day he learned Henry's political activities had landed him in jail, Sigmund had gone secretly to a lawyer and had arranged for the money he inherited from his second wife, of which he had not spent a penny upon himself, to be held in trust for Frank.

"I'd rather he hadn't given a sou to either of my sons," Hannah Moritz, who had telephoned to tell Sarah, declared before ringing off. "Henry couldn't care less about money. But he's going to be exceedingly hurt when he finds out."

Who wouldn't be? Sarah thought. Henry had believed himself loved equally with his twin by their grandfather and was certain to see this as evidence to the contrary.

Which wasn't so, Sarah felt. Nor were Sigmund's motives in doing what he had a puzzle to her. To put the money into Frank's hands seemed sensible. The steady twin wouldn't fritter it away, but would not see his brother go short, was doubtless how Sigmund had reasoned. But the arrangement had created an unpleasant situation in the family, from which heaven-knew-what repercussions could ensue.

Sarah went to stir the soup she was cooking for her solitary lunch, before giving the cat some leftover fish.

"A brilliant man Sigmund Moritz was," she told her furry companion. "But a wise one? Never!" Unwittingly, Sigmund had given Frank the kind of power it was dangerous for one brother to have over another. With the irregular life Henry lived, there would always be times when he would have to come to his twin, cap in hand. As he had to his grandfather.

Paradoxically, two of Sarah's sons had received a joint legacy from Sigmund. He had left his library to David and Nathan. But Sammy, who was his son-in-law, would not mind, Sarah reflected with the special tenderness she had for her lame, middle son. Sammy wasn't interested in books, nor had he a resentful bone in his body.

Which was more than could be said for his brothers, Sarah thought regretfully, especially in matters relating to each other. And what an ever-festering sore fraternal resentment was, she mused, adding a knob of butter to the soup. The kind that, once there, nothing could heal. Sarah had always envied mothers whose sons escaped that pernicious affliction and was sorry for Hannah, now the makings of it had touched hers.

She reached absentmindedly for the salt jar, then realized it was not there and went to fetch it from a small table which stood against the opposite wall. She had been in her new home for some weeks, but had not yet accustomed herself to there being no handy, built-in dresser beside the cooker. Or to the layout of the rooms which led off the small front hall. And sometimes she would open a door to enter the parlor and find herself in the dining room, which gave her a confused feeling.

She sprinkled some salt into the pan of soup and glanced with distaste at the clinical white surface from which she had taken the jar. "That thing sticks out like a sore thumb with my old kitchen furniture, Tibby," she sighed to the cat.

The new table, bought for her by Esther to use as an additional work surface, was made of Formica, which Sarah thought sounded as unfriendly as it looked. Esther had said it was heat-resistant, but Sarah had not put this to the test. She had wanted a small scrub-top table, like her big deal one which stood in the center of the room. But her daughter had said the shops didn't stock them anymore; everyone wanted the kind that was easily wiped clean. And which removed the homeliness from a kitchen, Sarah thought, averting her eyes from the modern interloper that had found its way into hers.

Her family could not understand an old lady not wanting things that made her life easier. But how could Sarah tell them that she didn't want the ugliness around her that went with it. It would be like insulting their tastes. Esther had recently moved into an apartment in Whitefield, in which the entire kitchen was fitted from floor to ceiling with white Formica units. Sarah had told her it was very nice, but got the shivers every time she went into it.

But Sarah's family did not spare her feelings in the matter of where she now lived. She had refused to let them move her to what they called "a better district" and they had eventually found her this house, which was conveniently near to Cheetham Hill Road. She had friendly black neighbors on one side—their little boy ran errands for her—and a lodging house on the other.

Bessie in particular turned up her nose whenever she came here. And, last *Shabbos* afternoon, had summed up her feelings: "The rest of the family's going up in the world, but Ma's moved herself down."

Once, Sarah too would have seen it that way, she mused, ladling some soup into a bowl. But when you grew as old as she now was, "going up in the world" wasn't important to you. It belonged to the future you no longer had. For your family, you still hoped for good things, but you found yourself living more and more in the past, and cherishing everything that reminded you of it.

For Sarah, leaving her house in Heywood Street had felt like having a comforting blanket torn from her aged shoulders. A blanket of memories that had warmed her in her loneliness after Abraham died. She had only had to glance at his rocking chair by the hearth to feel his presence. The rocking chair was still there, but it was a different hearth.

Now, Sigmund too had gone and Sarah had never felt more alone in her life. It wasn't possible to feel his presence and Abraham's in a house they had never entered. But it was there in the familiar streets the three of them had strolled together, in the Cheetham Hill air that had a subtle tang of soot about it, that wasn't present in the cleaner atmosphere of the more affluent suburbs.

Sarah carried her soup to the table and sat down to eat it. "If I'd let them, my children would move me to near Heaton Park, Tibby," she informed the cat, watching it give itself an after-lunch wash with a gleaming pink tongue. "But what use is fresh air in your lungs, if the place where you breathe it in doesn't warm your heart?"

She cut a chunk of blackbread from the board at her elbow and dunked it into the soup, to soften the hard crust. Then her thoughts returned to the legacy David and Nathan had received from Sigmund. Had he specified how the books were to be shared? Sarah hoped so. If not, there would be trouble about which of them had which. The only thing the two of them had ever managed to see eye to eye about was the welfare of their widowed mother.

The brothers were at that moment together in David's office. It was a bleak January day and Nathan was gazing through the window at the rime of frost on some big Sanderstyle delivery vans, which were dwarfing the cars lined up nearby.

"I still can't believe Sigmund's gone," he said gruffly.

"Me neither," David answered. "It's like a bright light suddenly being switched off."

"You said something like that when Rachel died," Nathan recalled. He also recalled the circumstances under which David had said it. David had gone looking for Nathan at the university, to tell him Sigmund's wife was dead, and had eventually found him in a nearby park with his forbidden girl friend, Mary.

The moment returned to David's memory, too. Did Nat still hold the Mary-episode against him? Or had he, as people often did, lost track of how his long-standing acrimony toward David had begun?

"I probably did say the same about Rachel," David replied, remembering the gentle lady who, in his childhood and youth, had been one of the pillars of his life. "But what brings you here, Nat?" It was years since his brother had walked in on him at the office.

"I was out doing my house calls and suddenly found myself driving here," Nathan said wryly. "If it's inconvenient, I'll go."

"No. It's just a surprise. You can stay and share my lunch, if you like." David rose from his desk and went to fetch a bulky package from his overcoat pocket.

Nathan watched him sit down again and remove the greaseproof wrapping. "There's certainly enough there for two."

"Tell that to Bessie. I can't seem to impress it on her! But today I'm in luck. You're here to help me out."

Nathan eyed the mound of smoked salmon sandwiches, and the butter, which Bessie had applied so thickly that globules of it were visible on the outside of the fluffy white bread. "Did what you just said mean that if I weren't here, you'd scoff the lot, David?"

David laughed. "I'm the kind of wealthy man who can't forget he was once poor, Nat. I can't abide waste."

"Which your waistline confirms," Nathan said, glancing at David's paunch with disapproval. "As your doctor is my partner, I know you've been told all about animal fats producing a surfeit of cholesterol in the bloodstream."

"Lou did mention it."

"So what are you eating the wrong things for? Do you want your blood to clot? What you're asking for, David, is another coronary—"

"All right!" David cut in. "I'll tell Bessie and Lizzie to give me margarine in future."

"And less of that doughy bread," Nathan counseled.

David managed to smile. "Did you come here to remind me about my heart condition?" He pushed the sandwiches away and fumbled in his pocket for a cigarette.

"If you carry on as you are doing, you won't need reminding," Nathan said, watching him light it.

David blew some smoke rings, with more nonchalance than he felt. "It's nice to know you care, Nat," he said dryly.

"What made you think I didn't?"

"Well we've never exactly hit it off, have we?"

"But that's never led me to suppose that you don't care about me."

They fell silent.

A brother is a brother, David thought emotionally. No matter how he treated you, you still felt something for him.

How is it possible to go on caring about someone who has caused me so much misery? Nathan was asking himself. Yet a combination of love and hate was the only way to describe his feelings for David. The hatred sprang from the long-ago past, when David's misguided sense of duty and domineering character had bulldozed Nathan onto the path which had led him to his desolate present. Yet he loved David, too.

Why? he pondered, surreptitiously studying his brother's arrogant profile, and the tiny diamond twinkling in the ring on his little finger. The ring had aroused distaste in Nathan the first time David wore it and still did. I loathe and detest everything about him, Nathan thought. But this didn't erase the brotherly emotion presently making itself felt within him.

"Something must have triggered off this visit," David said putting out his cigarette. "There's no such thing as suddenly finding yourself driving somewhere."

"It was probably Sigmund's letter. I read it again, just before leaving the surgery."

Sigmund had not made a will. Instead, he had disposed of his few personal possessions, including his library, informally. The lawyer who had arranged the trust fund for Frank had, too, held a number of letters to be delivered after Sigmund's death.

"I found it touching that he'd left his watch-chain to my granddaughter," Nathan said. "But what did he imagine a little girl would do with it?"

"Wear it as a necklace when she's a young lady," David answered with a smile. "But I don't suppose you can imagine Carla grown up."

Carla was now nine, but to Nathan it seemed like yesterday that he had dangled her on his knee. "I couldn't imagine Leona grown up. And when I look at her now—God, I feel old!"

"When we look at our grown-up children, who doesn't?"

They shared a brief moment of rapport, then David glanced down at some papers on his desk.

He isn't comfortable with me, Nathan thought, nor I with him. It had been so long since they had a friendly chat, neither of them knew how to handle it.

David broke the awkward silence. "About Sigmund's books—"

"Some of which are more valuable than others?" Nathan said brusquely. David translated everything into monetary terms. And was now eyeing him coldly, he noted. They were back on familiar ground!

David tried to ignore the tightening in his chest. What Nat had just implied was unforgivable.

"I know how your mind works, David," Nathan declared. "To me, the library is a cherished legacy from my godfather, who bought me the first book I ever owned—"

"Me too," David cut in icily.

"I'm not suggesting that you intend selling your half."

"That's very big of you."

"But, sentimentality aside, I don't doubt you'll want the library to be valued. And divided between us in a way that ensures you'll get your full money's-worth."

"What a bad-minded devil you are, Nat." David felt like punching him on the nose and was glad the desk was between them.

"If I am," Nathan said coolly, "you've helped to make me that way. Regarding yourself especially. But if I misjudged your intention *re* the books, all you need do is say so," he added crisply.

"Are you asking me to apologize for a thought that never entered my head?"

"It was foolish of me to think perhaps we could sort out this matter between ourselves," Nathan said. "It will have to be done through a third party. Hannah, for instance?"

"For me that won't be necessary," David answered. "I intend leaving my share of the library where it is. In the Moritzes' house, on the shelves Sigmund built for it with his own hands. Emptying them would leave a constant reminder to Helga that her father has gone. And how the books are apportioned between us doesn't matter to me. You can take your pick."

"I'd decided the same," Nathan said.

"Then there's nothing more for us to discuss and I'd be obliged if you'd get out of my office."

Nathan turned on his heel and left, his innards churning not just with anger, but also with regret. For once, their two minds had harbored the same thought, and their hearts the same sentiment. The acrimonious climax to Nathan's visit—which now felt like an anticlimax—could have been avoided. If we'd been two other people, Nathan thought resignedly as he made his way out of the factory, past the huge workroom from which the noise of the sewing machines was reverberating along the corridor.

When he reached the car park, some bales of shiny black stuff—which he supposed was for what his daughter, who owned one, called wet-look coats—were being lugged into the loading bay. Fashion-rainwear was very big business these days, Nathan reflected. And David had helped it become so. He not only saw everything in terms of hard cash, but had a gift for making it, too.

David's whole life has been cash-orientated, Nathan thought, turning up his collar against the cold north wind and pausing beside his brother's Rolls to survey the Sanderstyle building. David was not a well man and ought to have retired years ago, but was still sitting up there in his ivory tower, guarding his empire. It had been built with his own hard labors— Nathan granted him that—but was founded upon the *shekels* he had received for contracting a loveless marriage.

Would the day come when David would realize it hadn't been worth it? That he'd missed out on the best things of life, which, as the old song said, were free. Only then will he know what he did to me, Nathan said to himself with an onrush of bitterness. Then David appeared at his office window and stared down at him, enigmatically.

Nathan got into his frost-dewed Rover saloon and slammed the door on David's expression, but could not wipe it from his mind's eye. What was the self-appointed head of the clan thinking? he wondered as he started the engine and drove away. Probably that "our Nat"—whom he still treated like an obstreperous schoolboy!—ought to show more respect for the brother whom duty had impelled to put through medical school.

David is a very astute man, but he still has some things to learn, Nathan ruminated, leaving the rainwear district behind and heading for his surgery. Not least of which was that respect, unlike gratitude, could not be bought, but had to be earned.

"If my brother ever arrives to see me unexpectedly again, tell him I'm out," David was instructing his secretary.

Rita had just entered with the tea she made for him when he lunched at the factory and paused before setting the cup and saucer down. "Certainly, Mr. Sanderton. But I shouldn't think he's likely to, judging by the way he stormed out."

"You don't miss a thing, do you?"

"No," she replied, removing the packet of cigarettes David had left lying on his desk—as she had been doing since he had the heart attack in 1956.

Fourteen years ago, David thought wryly. During which time he had lived—for a man with his condition—as if there was no tomorrow. It must be willpower that had kept him going. Or maybe he had a charmed life!

Rita brandished the cigarettes. "I'm running out of hiding places," she rebuked him. "There'll soon be nowhere left to

put these except my knicker pocket!" She eyed the uneaten
sandwiches. "And you haven't touched your lunch. You don't
just need a secretary, Mr. Sanderton, you need a keeper!"

"I got one, the day you came to work for me."

"My fifteenth birthday he's harking back to. But who's
counting?"

David surveyed the middle-aged woman perched on a
corner of his desk, in order to harangue him at close quarters.
He had watched her ripen from a willowy teenager into
voluptuous maturity, but hadn't noticed her turning into the
matronly figure she now was.

"Eat!" she ordered him, thrusting a sandwich into his
hand.

If Rita were aware of the latter-day medical ideas on the
part dairy products played in coronary heart disease, she
would personally scrape the butter off my bread, David
thought. Lou Benjamin had left it to David to convey this
information to Bessie, which he had carefully refrained from
doing. Nor had he mentioned it to Rita. The trouble they
gave him about smoking and overworking was enough for one
man to bear! he reflected while biting into the tasty death-
potion his wife had unwittingly provided.

What was bread without butter? A graphic example of the
lackluster existence his condition would, if he let it, reduce
him to. And, for David, a life without work would not be
worth living—which had been his father's sentiment though
David had paid no heed to him at the time. Not for David the
choice his old acquaintance Hugo Frankl had made, he
thought vehemently while reaching for another sandwich.
Hugo, too, had been struck down as David had, around the
same time, and was still sitting in an armchair, waiting to die.

"I'm sorry to have to tell you a friend of yours has passed
away," Rita said as though she had divined David's thoughts.

Or did she just want to give him an object lesson? Was it
Hugo? David wondered with the sinking feeling that invariably assailed him when he learned that yet another of his
contemporaries had passed on. "Who is it this time, Rita?"

Rita usually read the *Guardian* personal column during her
lunch break, which David avoided doing. A dose of depression every Friday evening, when he perused the Jewish
weeklies, was enough, without supplementing it with a daily
one.

"So tell me already," he demanded, noting her eyeing him

hesitantly. Even if the deceased was someone he had not seen for years, he must go to the funeral. Attending funerals was a traditional Jewish duty, one of the few that was still respected, David reflected while awaiting Rita's answer.

"I let you have your lunch before I broke it to you, Mr. Sanderton. Because you're going to be very upset. It's Mr. Forrest."

David's teacup clattered onto the saucer.

"I knew you would be," Rita said, surveying his stricken expression. "You went to school with him, didn't you? I remember you telling me, after you went to see him at his office. I got the impression you thought a lot of him."

David swallowed hard. "I did."

"It says in the announcement he died in his sleep, which isn't a bad way to go," Rita said to comfort him.

It's the going that's bad, David thought bitterly, when you still hadn't done all the things you'd intended to do. Fulfilled your promises to yourself. Jim had promised himself a trip to New Zealand to visit his daughter and the grandchildren he had never seen, but kept putting it off, he had told David when they last lunched together, a few weeks ago. A fortnight's holiday a year was all he allowed himself from his law practice. New Zealand must wait until he retired, he had said with a wistful smile.

And I'm no different, David said to himself after Rita had left him alone with his thoughts. So I take more breaks than Jim did. But I'm already seventy-three, and could kick the bucket without my lifelong promise to myself being realized. Without moving to a house in Alderley Edge.

Not that there was anything unusual, or special, nowadays, about a Jew living in Cheshire. But when David had resolved that one day he would do so, he and most of his Manchester brethren had still been poverty-stricken immigrants in the Strangeways ghetto.

What an eye-opener my visit to Jim's home was, David recalled poignantly. Like discovering there was another world, peopled by a different breed from yourself and the folk you lived among. Whose life-style and appearance went with the lush ambience of tall trees, velvety lawns and elegant houses.

An ambience that wouldn't take my breath away anymore, David thought wryly. Viewed in retrospect, some of the homes in Alderley Edge were no more imposing than the one he now owned in Whitefield, which his mother referred to as "David and Bessie's palace"!

He picked up his pen to write a letter of condolence to Jim's wife, but could not find the right words. What did you say to a gracious, English-rose-type lady, who had just been bereft of her husband? A lady whom you had never met. A letter from David would mean nothing to Clarissa Forrest. He would send flowers for Jim's grave, instead.

David put down the pen and leaned back in his chair, feeling as if he had lived through the last few hours in the midst of death. Sigmund's ghost had stalked the room during the traumatic encounter with Nat. The butter and cigarettes had triggered off reflections in the same genre, and learning Jim had gone had put the seal on it.

But Jim's death, by making David more aware of his own mortality, that time was speeding by, had also shocked him back to life—on the personal level he had subjugated to family and business. He could no longer afford to put off doing what he wanted to do, for indeed there may be no tomorrow.

David flicked the intercom switch on his desk, decisively. "Ring up some estate agents, will you, Rita? And ask them to send me lists of houses for sale in Alderley Edge. Big ones."

"So you're finally going to do it, are you, Mr. Sanderton. Good for you!"

"But don't tell my wife."

Chapter Two

Carla arrived home on a rainy spring afternoon and found her mother busy in the kitchen. "Does this mean I'm no longer a latchkey child?" she inquired taking off her damp King David School blazer.

Leona watched her hang it over the back of a chair to dry off, and remove her beret which she wore at a rakish angle. "You're certainly a precocious one."

Carla was studying her reflection in a small mirror Leona kept propped up above the sink.

"A vain one, too!" Leona added with a smile.

"I've seen you looking at yourself, Mum, when you stand here peeling potatoes."

"That's the only time I can spare to look at myself! And for your information, I only keep a mirror there so I can tidy myself up quickly, without going upstairs, before I dash out to the shops."

"Instead of giving me a talking-to, why don't we have a conversation?" Carla said.

"About what?"

Carla sighed. "With my mum, it always has to be about something. Other mothers and daughters just chat." She helped herself to a slice of the green pepper her mother was chopping. "But I suppose a person can't have everything."

Too true! Leona thought. And one thing she didn't have was spare time to chat with her daughter. "Was that a complaint, by the way?" she asked.

Carla finished eating the slice of pepper, dipped into a jar of raisins, and popped some into her mouth. "Well, I do sometimes feel deprived, because you're not—as a rule—here when I get home from school, like my friends' mothers are," she said, fetching a platter of cheese from the refrigerator and adding a cube of Danish blue to the assorted contents of her stomach.

Oh, the digestion of the young! Leona thought wryly, recalling her own culinary forays when she was Carla's age. And it struck her that being a career woman had deprived her of something, too. Of moments like this; enjoying her daughter's childhood.

Carla was now munching a slab of the big currant cake which Bridie made for them each week. Leona did not have time to bake and her mother, too, made sure there was no lack of homemade goodies in the Moritzes' larder. But the heavy currant cake, made from a traditional Irish recipe which entailed boiling the fruit, was Carla's favorite.

Carla spooned some strawberry jam onto the bit of it that remained in her sticky hand and contemplated it thoughtfully. "But a person has to balance one thing against another, don't they, Mum?"

Leona had begun cubing beef for the casserole and gave her an absent smile.

"Like I've had to," Carla went on, "with what we were just talking about."

"Feeling deprived, you mean?"

Carla nodded and went to rinse her fingers at the sink. "If you were the kind of mum who stayed at home cooking, etcetera—well, you wouldn't be you, would you?"

This sounded to Leona like one of the dubious compliments Marianne had once said she received periodically from Martin. Which, probably, every married woman who chose to work—and chose was the operative word—got from her kids from time to time, Leona reflected. The children had to find a way of coming to terms with it, and had no idea of the inner conflicts a mother suffered because she had made that choice.

"You wouldn't be such an interesting person, if you didn't have your career and meet lots of people," her daughter declared. "All you'd be able to talk about would be the latest fashions, and the price of fish."

Leona stopped cubing the meat and hugged her.

"I didn't used to see it that way, but now I do, Mum. When we went to that charity luncheon at Cousin Shirley's, and all the other women sat gossiping together, but you were talking about your work to the men, I was very proud of you."

"That's nice to know, Carla."

"But to what do I owe the pleasure of your company at this time of day?"

"Uncle Henry's coming for dinner tonight," Leona replied noting that her daughter's face had lit up at the mention of his name. "He rang Daddy at the office, this morning."

"Where from?" Carla asked excitedly.

"Heathrow. He'd just flown in from New York."

"Has he been visiting my great-aunt and uncle who live there?" Carla had not met Miriam and Sammy.

"I understand he stayed with them for a day or two," Leona said, severing the beef with heavier strokes of the knife than were necessary.

"You don't like Uncle Henry, do you?" Carla said.

"No."

"Why not?"

Leona transferred the meat to the casserole and did not reply.

"I think he's fascinating," her daughter declared.

"Who doesn't?" But integrity and loyalty counted, too. Qualities notably lacking in Leona's brother-in-law! When Frank telephoned Paris to tell Henry their grandfather was dead, he had been too busy to come to the funeral. He had just become the editor of an underground newspaper, he had said. And had added that attending funerals was pointless; that showing respect for someone was meaningless after they had gone.

"Why did Uncle Henry go to the States?" Carla inquired putting on the kettle, to make a pot of tea.

"To lend his support to the anti-Vietnam-war demonstrations, he told your father," Leona answered with a cynical edge to her voice.

"What's wrong with that?" Carla demanded.

"Nothing. I'd join the protest movement myself, if I lived in America."

"But you don't seem to approve of Uncle Henry fighting for causes."

"Because with him, fighting for causes has become an end in itself. If he really wants to help rid the world of injustice and inequality, there are more useful ways of doing it than being a professional left-wing demonstrator."

"Do you mean he gets paid for it?"

"If he did, he probably wouldn't do it," Leona said cuttingly. "Contempt for money is your uncle's speciality, Carla. Which isn't to say he doesn't spend any. What I meant by professional was full-time."

"I think what Uncle Henry does is very self-sacrificing," Carla declared staunchly.

Leona gave the casserole a whisper of garlic and allowed Carla to keep her childish illusions. There was plenty of time for her to find out that her idol had feet of clay.

"Is he bringing his Indian lady with him?" Carla asked.

Leona put the casserole into the oven. "No."

"Hm," Carla said thoughtfully. "If she were his wife, she wouldn't let him keep going away without her, would she?"

Which was part of why Henry had not married her, Leona wanted to say. Henry Moritz self-sacrificing? He was totally self-orientated and had arranged his life accordingly. "You'd better go and do your homework, Carla, or you won't get it finished before the family knight-errant arrives," she said.

"Is that what you think Uncle Henry is, Mum?"

"For want of a better way of describing him."

"And how would you describe Daddy? I mean they're nothing like each other, are they? Even though they're twins."

"Your father is the salt of the earth," Leona answered

unhesitatingly. "And you're very lucky to be his daughter, as I am to be his wife," she added as she heard Frank's key in the lock. Then the man who was so very dear to her entered the room.

"You've closed the office early," she said to him when Carla had gone to do her homework.

Frank sat down on the kitchen stool and removed his spectacles to polish them, and Leona thought how much he resembled his father, whose name—with the addition of the letter *a*—was perpetuated in the family by their daughter.

"I didn't get the chance to be alone with you before you left, and I want to talk to you before Henry gets here," Frank said.

"About what?"

"My grandfather's money."

Leona knew what her husband had decided without him having to tell her and her reaction was written on her face. "You bloody fool!" she exclaimed putting it into words.

"My brother is entitled to half of it," Frank declared.

"I don't agree. Where was he when Zaidie Sigmund needed the care and support of his family? When you and I had to leave our work, day in, day out, and go looking for him, out of our minds with anxiety until we knew he was safe? How often did Henry drop him a line? A line that wasn't a hard-luck story, that is! Which he knew would result in him getting a check by return post—"

"That has nothing to do with Henry's entitlement," Frank interrupted.

"I happen to think it has."

"And if I didn't know you as well as I do, I'd think your Sandberg blood had risen to the surface," Frank retorted. "But you care no more for affluence than I do, Leona."

"That doesn't mean I'm not practical where money is concerned. Which is more than can be said about the Moritzes."

"Touché," Frank answered crisply.

Carla popped her head around the door. "Why are you insulting each other's family?"

"You shouldn't be eavesdropping," Leona said closing it to shut her out.

"Eavesdropping!" Carla called from the other side of the door. "I'm trying to do my sums in the living room which is right next door to the kitchen. And I can't hear myself think because you two are shouting."

"Go away!" Leona and Frank yelled in unison.

"I'm glad you don't come home early every day, if this is how you'd always carry on!"

"Carla isn't used to hearing us quarrel," Frank said stiffly after a moment of silence.

"She will be, if you give half of the money to Henry," Leona replied in the same tone.

"What I do with it isn't your business, Leona. I'm telling you, not asking you."

An icy feeling gripped Leona. Had Frank really said that to her? Until now they had shared everything, decisions included. Counseled and heeded each other through ten years of marriage. Worked side by side in the neighborhood law center that had sprung from their joint desire to provide caring legal aid to the underprivileged. And had rarely exchanged a cross word. Now, Henry's hovering shadow had stepped between them to destroy the comfortable peace for which Leona had settled in lieu of passion.

"You might be fooling yourself about why you're so hard on my brother, but you're not fooling me," Frank said with a bitter smile.

"What is that supposed to mean?"

"Come off it, Leona!"

"Are you harking back to my foolish youth? When I thought I was in love with Henry?"

Frank held Leona's gaze. "Thought nothing! You were mad about him."

Leona turned away and opened the oven to hide her confusion. Was her hatred for her brother-in-law really rooted in the unsatisfied desire she had once allowed to overwhelm her? And been ashamed of, because she could not respect him, she thought as her cheeks flamed with remembrance.

"What I felt for Henry wasn't love," she said with conviction. "Love is what I feel for you, Frank."

Frank ignored the addendum. "Call it what you like, Leona. It's still there."

"If that's what you want to think, fine!" Leona flared. "But I could kill your bloody brother. He doesn't even have to be here to cause trouble." She lifted the casserole out of the oven, forgetting, in her fury, to use her oven gloves.

"You can't blame that on Henry," Frank said eyeing the mess of meat, vegetables and smashed earthenware swimming in sauce on the floor.

"Get me that stuff Daddy gave us for burns," Leona winced, blowing on her singed fingers.

"What are you doing now? Throwing things at each other?" Carla demanded from outside the door.

"No. We're wading in gravy," Frank answered, slithering to the other side of the kitchen to get a tube of acriflavine ointment from a drawer.

"Can I do anything to help, Dad?"

"Yes, keep out."

"Our guest will have to be satisfied with a snack," Leona said malevolently, while Frank applied the soothing salve to her painful hands.

Would she ever get his twin out of her system? he wondered, noting her flushed face and heaving bosom. Sometimes, when he made love to her and she lay passively in his arms, he could feel Henry's presence in the room with them.

It was a three-cornered situation that had existed all their lives, Frank reflected, replacing the cap on the ointment. And uncannily reminiscent of the one he'd heard that his Aunt Miriam had once shared with Leona's two uncles. It was family history that Miriam had been in love with David when she married Sammy.

The difference between that situation and this, Frank ruminated, is that one point of our triangle doesn't know it exists, and never has. Henry was a totally innocent party.

"Returning to the matter of my grandfather's money," he said calmly. "I hadn't yet mentioned that Henry's ended his affair with Julekha. When he returns to Paris, he'll have no place to live—"

"Stop it! You're making me feel sick!" Leona cut in with disgust.

"I'm just being practical—which you said the Moritzes never are, about money. Henry used to get an allowance from Zaidie, as you well know. Which must have stopped after Zaidie tied up all his assets in trust for me."

"But Julekha, who's a clever lady in every other way, made sure Henry didn't starve, no doubt! You don't have to paint me a picture, Frank."

"Would you like my brother to starve?" Frank inquired coldly.

Leona did not reply, but began shoveling the debris from the floor into the garbage bin.

"Let me do that, Leona."

"Why do so many otherwise intelligent people have blind spots where Henry Moritz is concerned?" she said, ignoring Frank's offer. "Your mother is afflicted that way, too; she thinks the sun shines out of him. But she takes you—and you're worth a million Henrys—entirely for granted."

"Thank you for those few kind words."

"I'm stating facts. And another is that your brother, though it doesn't seem to have occurred to you, could try earning his living," Leona said caustically. "Not that he'll ever have to. Henry is a taker, Frank. Also a charmer and he knows it. Put the two together and the easy answer, for him, is a woman with the wherewithal."

Frank was stung to a sharp reply; Henry had many shortcomings, but he would not have him classed as a gigolo. "The same could be said about one or two others in our clan. Your father, for instance."

Leona gave him a freezing glance. "It's no secret that Daddy married Mummy for material reasons, and you know as well as I do that he's had no joy from it, but that is another matter. He's worked hard all his life to support her in the style to which her background had accustomed her. Because marriage is a contract and my father honors his commitments."

She slammed the lid shut on the garbage bin and went to fetch a mop and bucket. "It was you, Frank, who told me, years ago, that your brother is incapable of making any kind of commitment, that he wanted the best of both worlds—or words to that effect. And oh, how right you were. Is it necessary for me to remind you of why and when you said it?"

Frank had put the occasion conveniently from his mind. Perhaps, he thought now, because he had afterward been ashamed of having painted his brother black, to emphasize to Leona the difference between them. And in retrospect it seemed like a character assassination perpetrated for his own purpose because Henry had done nothing to deserve it.

"I wonder if Henry's met his next meal ticket yet?" Leona said sardonically, while filling the bucket with water.

Frank snatched it from the sink and dumped it on the floor for her, but his hands were shaking with anger and the water spilled over Leona's shoes.

"You can't face up to the truth, can you?" she taunted him. "Or was grabbing the bucket just one of your boringly helpful gestures? As clumsily performed as usual!"

"I know you find me dull, Leona. Clumsy, too." If she had struck him, Frank could not have looked more distressed. "But I never thought I'd hear you say so."

Leona plunged the mop into the bucket. "Blame your brother!" she said vehemently.

The one to blame is myself, Frank thought, for talking you into marrying me.

Leona cast an anxious glance at him. "You don't look well, Frank." His face had paled.

He eyed her strained expression. "You don't look too good yourself."

"What are we doing to each other?" she exclaimed, abandoning the mop and flinging her arms around his neck.

"That's what I've been wondering," their daughter said, bursting into the room and inserting herself between them. "You've decided to kiss and make up, I see—but I was scared you weren't going to. And if you don't behave yourselves, I'll run away," she warned them with her customary precocity. "Like Alan Sanderton told me my Cousin Laura did."

For some reason, Carla always referred to Ronald's son by his full name, and quoted him as if he were the oracle.

"Family life, like law, is full of precedents," Frank said to Leona.

"Why are you bringing law into this?" Carla asked putting two and two together and making five. "Were you hugging each other just to fool me? I don't want my mummy and daddy to get a divorce."

Her lower lip was trembling and Leona and Frank exchanged a contrite glance. Carla's vocabulary and perception were so advanced for her years they sometimes forgot she was only a child. The conversation Leona had had with her about Henry was an example of this and she had afterward regretted it.

Frank managed to laugh. "This kid watches too much TV, Leona!" He stroked Carla's hair, which was as strident as Leona's had been, before she began rinsing it with something that toned it down, he reflected. "A little tiff between husband and wife doesn't have to lead to divorce," he assured Carla.

Leona kissed the child's dimpled chin that was a small replica of Frank's, she thought, while remembering her own insecure childhood and the anxiety her parents' strife had caused her. Not for anything would she inflict that upon her daughter.

Carla noted the empty oven and greasy floor. "The special dinner came to a sticky end, did it? Poor Uncle Henry will have to take pot luck, like we usually do on a Monday."

Frank saw Leona's expression tighten. Then the telephone rang and he went to answer it.

"Henry isn't coming," he said when he returned.

"That doesn't surprise me," Leona replied.

"He just called Mother from Amsterdam."

"That's no surprise, either." Leona would not have raised an eyebrow if Henry, though he had telephoned from London this morning to say he was on the way to Manchester, had just announced his arrival in Timbuctoo. Unreliability was his middle name.

"Weren't your mother and Auntie Helga expecting him for tea?" Leona asked Frank.

"Yes. But something cropped up, he told Mother. He asked her to tell me."

"There's probably a big march, or something, going on in Amsterdam, that he's just heard about," Carla said with shining eyes.

"Very likely," Leona agreed. But her lips had curled. How often in their youth, when they were still a threesome, had Henry used that convenient phrase to herself and Frank? Something would always crop up that her brother-in-law saw as sufficient reason to let down his family.

"Well, that's that," Frank shrugged.

"Is it?" Leona said ominously. Then she saw her daughter, who had begun mopping the floor, eye her anxiously, and put a smile on her face for Carla's sake.

Frank watched her take some eggs from the refrigerator and prepare to whip up an omelet her rigid back belying the cheerful tune she was studiously humming. Their differences about Henry had crystallized into something which could not be shrugged off, nor could the hurtful words they had exchanged on his account be unsaid.

Chapter Three

Martin stood by the kitchen window, gazing at the peaceful Cotswold scene beyond the gray stone garden wall and counting his blessings. Being married to Moira was bliss and they were expecting their first child. Living on the commune was, give or take the occasional irritation, all they had hoped it would be. His contribution to the budget was easily earned; he did the bare minimum of ad copywriting for his father's agency, each week, which left plenty of time to work on the novel he had begun last year.

So what the hell is it with me? he asked himself. He ought to be on top of the world but instead had a feeling that something was missing from his.

"Taking it easy, Martin?" Bill's girl friend teased him through the open lattice.

A feeling emphasized by the cheerful contentment of his fellow communards, Martin thought. "Who could compete in the energy stakes with you, Sukie?" he smiled.

He watched her haul a pail of water from the well, which was closer to her workplace than the kitchen tap was. But she would probably have used the well had it been less conveniently situated.

Sukie Palmer was, as she described herself, a fun-person, who even got a kick out of coping with tasks others found irksome. When Bill finally persuaded her to leave the San Francisco commune where they had met and join him here, meeting her had been a shock, Martin recalled.

Bill's friends had expected him to return from the airport with the kind of female he had dated at Oxford—the classic bluestocking type. Not this gorgeous little blond, whose warm, bubbly personality had quickly endeared her to everyone, Martin thought, watching Sukie carry the water into the outhouse where she had installed her potter's wheel and kiln.

"Enjoying the view? Or indulging in some morning meditation?" Bill inquired from the doorway.

He joined Martin by the window as Sukie reemerged into

the sunlight to chat with Rhoda Frolich, who was busy at her easel beside the hen-coop. Rhoda illustrated children's books and had taken advantage of the mild spring weather to sketch out-of-doors, instead of in the chilly attic studio she shared with a sculptor.

"Sukie and Rhoda together make an arresting picture," Martin remarked.

Sukie's Afro hairstyle, with the sun behind her, was a halo of spun-gold and her complexion had the pale gleam of honey. A white caftan enhanced her ethereal appearance. Rhoda's smock was black, accentuating her somewhat saturnine features, which spiky raven hair made seem the more so.

"Someone should put them on canvas," Bill said.

"And call it 'The Angel and the Witch,'" Martin quipped.

Bill laughed and unhooked a mug from the colorful assortment hanging on the big pine dresser. "Captions are your stock in trade, Martin!"

"Thanks for the insult!" Martin replied.

Bill filled the mug with coffee from the outsize pot which those who worked at home kept ever simmering on the Aga stove. "It wasn't meant to be one."

"That doesn't alter the import of what you said."

Bill carried his coffee to the shabby chintz sofa, removed the toys which were occupying it—some of the communards had children—and sat down. "If I had a flair that enabled me to earn a quick buck, I'd consider myself fortunate, Martin."

"You're not in need of a quick buck, Bill."

"That isn't the point."

"What is the point?"

"I'm coming to it. Why are you so touchy about your sideline, Martin? Sukie isn't, about hers."

Sukie subsidized her art by making toby jugs for the Stratford-upon-Avon tourist trade.

"Maybe her real work is going better than mine is," Martin answered sourly. There was no maybe about it; some of Sukie's less commercial offerings were shortly to be exhibited in a London gallery. As for Martin's work, he was discovering that having time in which to write did not cause creativity to flow.

Moira was spending a couple of days with his parents and he had hoped to be able to tell her, when she returned, that he had completed a chapter that had been giving him trouble. But he hadn't yet put pen to paper this morning.

"I hadn't noticed before how much you resemble your old man," Bill remarked, surveying him.

Martin's brilliant hazel eyes which, like Ralph's were his most striking feature, darkened pensively. People often remarked on his resemblance to Dad. Was it possible that, in some respects, they were alike in character, too, that Martin was destined by his genes never to attain his goal?

"If I may express an opinion," Bill said, lighting his ancient briar and puffing it ruminatively. "It's occurred to me that possibly you don't yet know what your real work is."

"You mean whether I'm a novelist or a dramatist, I suppose?" Two plays, which Martin intended to rewrite when he finished his book, were presently gathering dust on his desk. "And that I ought to make up my mind, because being my mother's son doesn't mean I'm what she is—both?" he added.

Bill puffed his pipe in silence for a moment, then looked Martin squarely in the eye. "I hope what I'm about to say won't precipitate the end of our friendship. I think you're neither, Martin."

"I see." Martin felt as though he had been punched below the belt. Why had he let Bill read his work? "Being paid an advance by a publisher to write about your foreign travels doesn't make you an authority on contemporary English fiction, Bill," he said stiffly. "On drama either."

"I knew you'd be cut to the quick," Bill answered. "But you and I have always been honest with each other. And while I'm about it, it's time you stopped identifying with your mother, Martin."

Martin was momentarily rendered speechless. Was that what he had been doing? Because, no way, did he want to identify with his father? Was his desire to write motivated by nothing more than that?

"You'll tell me I've got an Oedipus complex next!" he said, summoning a laugh to hide his confusion and wondering if it sounded as forced to Bill as it did to him.

"According to Freud, that isn't uncommon," Bill informed him. "But most of us leave it behind with our childhood." He relit his pipe, an activity which always punctuated his conversation, and dropped a charred matchstick into one of Sukie's big pottery ashtrays. "I've known you since we were pimply youths, Martin and while it's never entered my head that you're in love with your mother—"

"I should bloodywell hope not!"

"—I could hardly be unaware of your inordinate admiration for her," Bill went on unperturbed. "Or of your wish to emulate her."

"My mother is an author worth emulating."

"Indubitably. But returning to the point, Martin, you are wasting your time trying to be one."

"In your opinion," Martin said dismissively.

"You're not even going to think about it?"

"Think about what? That my best friend considers me a literary hack?"

"On the contrary. Your prose is irreproachable and your dialogue spot-on—"

"Which hardly lends credence to your assertion," Martin interrupted.

"I was about to add that something is, nevertheless, lacking."

The discussion, and Bill's dispassionate tone, reminded Martin of the aspect of their college days that living here with their own kind had enabled them to recapture. All the male communards, except Rhoda Frolich's husband Andy who was a musician, were Oxford graduates, and when they got together in the evenings, or late at night when their wives and kids were in bed, it was like old times, a return to the intellectual plane whereon the writing of pillars of literature and philosophy were coolly analyzed. But it was difficult to maintain a cool approach when your own work was under the microscope, Martin thought.

"I'd be obliged if you'd tell me what the lack is," he said, trying to do so.

Bill applied another match to his pipe, while considering his reply. "The *je ne sais quoi* that breathes life into a work," he said eventually, "which no amount of technique can impose. You haven't the gift your mother was born with, Martin. If you had, even if your work was technically bad it would come shining through."

Martin fetched a mug and filled it, barely aware of what he was doing. The inexplicable feeling that all was not right with his world was, he realized now, rooted in self-doubt, which had just crystallized into sickening certainty. He had thought his mood was affecting his work, but it was the other way around.

"No hard feelings, I hope?" Bill asked, eyeing his expression.

Martin shook his head. "You've given me what I needed, Bill."

"Glad to have been of help," Bill said, and left the room to resume work on the traveler's notebook he was preparing for publication.

Help? Martin sat down on the sofa. The disillusion his friend had effected felt more like a bruising. But Bill was right. Martin's writing inspired no feeling whatsoever. It was stone cold dead, though he had not wanted to recognize this. As Bill had said, Marianne Dean's son had not inherited her gift. And his own talent was limited to a superficial flair for creating pithy punch lines, turning a phrase to dry and droll advantage. The advertising copywriter's stock in trade. Which accounted for his touchiness on the subject.

Martin sipped some coffee, allowing acceptance to flood over him like a torpid tide. He would have to tell Moira he had wasted two years of his life trying to be something that wasn't in him. And what he would now do with the rest of it, he had no idea.

"Let's go out and choose the baby's pram," Marianne suggested to her daughter-in-law. "Ralph and I would like to buy it for you."

"Thank you."

"Jewish grandparents consider it their privilege," Marianne added with a smile.

"So I've heard," Moira replied.

She had arrived last night, looking strained and exhausted and, though she had retired early, seemed no less so this morning, Marianne thought, surveying her lackluster appearance—Moira had not bothered to make up her face and her complexion had a pallid tinge which the lime-green blouse she was wearing did not enhance.

"Don't you feel up to going out?" Marianne inquired kindly.

Moira shook her head.

"Pregnancy is a trying time," Marianne recalled. "I haven't forgotten, though my baby is in his twenties now."

"Is that how you still think of him?"

"Of course not," Marianne laughed. "I was joking."

"Were you?" Moira toyed with the gold crucifix which,

apart from her wedding ring, was her sole adornment. "My pregnancy isn't responsible for the way I feel. Martin is."

They were seated on the leather Chesterfield in Marianne's study and she got up to remove a withered leaf from a begonia on the windowsill, busying herself to hide her alarm. "Would you like to talk about it?"

"That's why I'm here."

When Moira telephoned to ask could she come for a visit, Marianne had seen it as a sign that her daughter-in-law was at last lowering the barrier of reserve she had maintained between them, though she had been Martin's wife for two years. But she had come for a specific reason. The comfortable family affinity Marianne had hoped for was still not there.

After Moira had spoken at length, Marianne was overwhelmed by relief. She had imagined that something was terribly wrong, but it was just Martin's moodiness that was getting Moira down.

"He's always been that way," she said sympathetically. "And I'm afraid he takes after me. I don't know how his father has put up with my temperament all these years. You mustn't let it affect you, Moira."

"I didn't, before we were married, because I expected things to be different between us, once we were." Moira stared down at her hands, which were tightly clasped on her lap. "It isn't Martin's temperament that affects me. It's the way, when something is troubling him, he shuts me out." She pulled a loose thread from the hem of her Irish tweed maternity skirt and rolled it into a pellet. "A married man's closest friend should be his wife, not his mother."

She's jealous of my relationship with my son, Marianne registered with shock. And was reminded by Moira's sudden, imperious tilt of the chin that he had married an aristocrat.

"Martin hasn't been himself for some time and I don't doubt that he's told you all about whatever is the cause of it," Moira went on in a way that matched her posture. "Though he hasn't confided in me. But why should it be any different on this occasion? I've lost count of the number of times he's shot up to town to talk to you, about things he obviously thinks I wouldn't understand."

Is this really happening? Marianne asked herself in the silence that followed. The pleasant break from work she had expected Moira's visit to be had turned into a confrontation.

It felt like a scene in a domestic drama, with Marianne Dean miscast as the trouble-making mother-in-law.

Moira was recalling her father's cautionary words before her marriage. Lord Kyverdale was a merchant-banker and had many Jewish clients and associates, whom he respected and liked—but he had warned his daughter that Jews were a clannish people, to whom the blood tie mattered above all else.

Moira had told him confidently that Martin would always put her first. And, in everyday ways, he did, she thought now. She could not wish for a more devoted husband. But shadowing her happiness was the family feeling her father had mentioned, to which there was a dimension not present in her feeling for her family. A special, Jewish dimension. Rhoda Frolich had said that Andy, though he had never got on with his mother and disliked most of his relatives, was also imbued with it, and had once spent every penny they had in the bank on a flying-trip to Israel, to attend the funeral of an uncle he had never met.

Martin had, as yet, done nothing of that kind. Probably because a reason to do so hadn't cropped up, Moira reflected sourly. But, as if drawn there by a magnet, he went north for the gathering of the clan in his great-grandmother's house, when the Jewish festivals came around. Moira would have approved and understood had he been a religious Jew.

"Come with me, you're one of the family, now," he always said before leaving on one of these pilgrimages. But Moira did not feel one of the family. She had met them only once, when Martin introduced her to them *en masse*, at one of the legendary Sabbath tea parties he had said old Sarah Sandberg had been giving since 1905.

That afternoon had left Moira with a claustrophobic impression of a crowd of noisy people who had tried to make her feel at home among them, regaling her with family anecdotes which had only served to emphasize that she was an outsider.

Martin had told her that if they lived in Manchester, they would be expected to attend Sarah's gathering every week. Moira had been relieved that they did not, aware that her husband's obligations to his family would not end there. Doing what was expected of you was, she was learning, an aspect of the clannishness about which her father had warned.

"Ralph gave me this begonia for Passover, but it isn't doing too well," Marianne said moving the plant to a different position in the room. Did her voice sound as stilted as it felt? "I probably didn't give it enough water before we went up north for the *Seder.*"

Martin had tried hard to persuade Moira to go with them, but her Catholicism, which had strengthened since her marriage, had prohibited it. To sit at the ritual *Seder* table, as Jesus had before the betrayal that made it, for Him, the Last Supper was, to Moira, unthinkable. Nor could she bring herself to join her husband and his relatives for their New Year and other High Holy Days. She would not be expected to join them at synagogue, but partaking of the special meals afterward would be like celebrating a faith which was not hers.

Martin had no such scruples. He even helped her father dress the Christmas tree, which made his staunch allegiance to Jewish tradition all the more inexplicable. No, mysterious was the word for it, Moira thought, aware of Marianne surveying her with the opaque dark eyes which told you nothing of what she was thinking. As mysterious as the hold his mother had over him.

Marianne picked up the small copper watering-can she kept handily filled for her indoor plants and gave the begonia a drink. She could use one herself—and stronger than water! But it was too early in the day. How was she to set matters right with her daughter-in-law who suddenly looked as if the fight had gone out of her? There was now an expression of resignation on Moira's lovely face. What had the girl been thinking during her long silence?

"I did notice that Martin seemed a little depressed when he was here last week," Marianne said. "But I didn't ask what was wrong and he didn't tell me. Sometimes he does confide in me about this or that, as he always has. And I've always been glad that he feels he can," she added truthfully. "But if you'd rather he didn't, Moira, in future I'll tell him I haven't time to listen. That now he has a wife he must stop bothering me with his little ups and downs."

Moira gave her a surprised glance. "Would you really do that for me?"

"Yes," Marianne answered unhesitatingly. Better that her relationship with her son be damaged than Martin's with his wife. And my grandmother would agree, she thought wryly.

Sarah Sandberg would do the same, painful though it was to have to do it.

Moira was silently studying her.

"I'm not the stock character Jewish mother one sees in TV plays," Marianne assured her. "They make Christian viewers think there is only one kind—meddling in their family's lives when they're not making *gefilte* fish, or dancing at weddings, and *Bar Mitzvahs*. That kind of mother, give or take the details, exists in every religious persuasion. The kind who try to hold on to their adult children, too. But I'm not one of them."

You don't have to try, Moira thought. The child in her womb was stirring restlessly, impatient to be free. Soon, the umbilical cord binding it to her would be cut, but it was as if Martin were still bound to his mother by a metaphysical one, peculiar to Jewish males, which would remain unsevered until the day Marianne died. And perhaps it would not cease to bind him even then, but would reattach itself to her memory.

"You can rely on me to send Martin packing, *toute de suite*, next time he comes here to share his worries with me," Marianne promised.

"I'd rather you didn't," Moira replied. "But thank you for offering to. And you've helped me sort myself out."

"I got the impression it was me you were sorting out," Marianne said with a dry smile.

Moira managed to smile, too.

That she had undergone some sort of mental catharsis was plain and Marianne said no more. How many times in her own life had a confrontation had that effect upon her? There was nothing like getting things off your chest to purge you of bitterness and enable you to see things in perspective.

"I'll go and make us some ham sandwiches for lunch," she said to Moira.

Marianne's way of life is no more kosher than Martin's, Moira reflected when she was alone with her thoughts. No way was she like Rhoda Frolich's ma-in-law, who every Friday evening sent her chauffeur to the commune with a traditional Sabbath-eve dinner for Andy—lest he forget where he belonged.

As she had declared, Marianne Dean was not the archetypal Jewish mother. But, Moira thought, it's immaterial if she is or not. Martin was the archetypal Jewish son and if Moira wanted their marriage to work, she would have to accept it.

Chapter Four

Sarah was spending Sunday with David and Bessie and still unable to quite believe that her son owned this mansion in Alderley Edge, though he had lived here for three years.

Each time Sarah came here, which was not often, she marveled anew. Not about the house itself, which was not her idea of home, but about what it signified. That David had risen to the top.

"How does Lizzie manage to keep this place so spick-and-span?" she asked Bessie, who was dishing up potato *latkes* from a silver dish to go with the cold tongue they were having for lunch.

"You know Lizzie," Bessie said with a smile and a shrug. "But I don't let her cook anymore."

"That I can see from the *latkes*. Hers are always lighter than yours. I'm surprised you don't feel lonely, sitting in that great big parlor you have here," Sarah continued airing her views.

"It's a drawing room, Mother," David corrected her.

"An assembly hall would be a better description."

"Our lounge in Whitefield wasn't exactly small."

Sarah, who had never understood why the best room was called by a different name according to where the house was situated, allowed herself a mental snort. A parlor was a parlor.

"We don't use that room much, Ma," Bessie told her. "We usually sit in the breakfast room. We have all our meals in here, too."

The breakfast room was—comparatively—cozy.

"That's what you did in Whitefield," Sarah reminded them. "Me, I don't see the point in moving from bigger to bigger homes, when you don't really use them."

"Stop stirring things up, Mother," David said.

"All of a sudden I'm not allowed to speak my mind?"

"Not about this house, Ma," Bessie said glaring at David. "Nobody is."

When David bought "Forrest Dene," Bessie had made it plain to the family that he had not done so with her approval. But Sarah had assumed she had made the best of it. I ought to have known better, she thought. Bessie had always been one to harp.

"This house is all wrong for us," she declaimed. "I feel like a stranger here. It doesn't fit in with the way we live."

Sarah had to agree that *latkes*—even in a silver dish—did not sit comfortably in an English mansion.

"But my husband had a dream that it's taken him all his life to make come true!" Bessie went on with feeling. "And I have to suffer because of it. Which woman in her seventies wants to be uprooted, like David did to me? Forced to live miles away from town, in a place where you never see a Jewish face? And in a mausoleum like this!"

To David, "Forrest Dene" was a shrine. His decision to move to Alderley Edge had not been implemented immediately, though he had viewed a number of houses in and around the village, one of which Bessie had grudgingly said she liked. Not until his dead friend's boyhood home came on the market had he realized why none of them had appealed to him; that his dream was bound up with the house where it had arisen within him and no other would do.

"A mausoleum is a tomb," he informed his wife, who rarely used such words and, when she did, invariably used them wrongly.

This time she had not done so. "That's what it feels like to me."

"That big parlor is beautiful, the way you've furnished it, Bessie," Sarah said to placate her. "It reminds me of Buckingham Palace."

"How can it, when you've never been there!" Bessie, whose grandiose ideas had not included being the mistress of a house full of antique furniture, gave David a sour glance. "It's your son's taste, Ma, not mine. If I'd had my way, I'd have done it like this room," she said, glancing fondly at the bleached maple sideboard and cherry wall-to-wall carpet.

David eyed it and shuddered. His wife had added to this garish opulence a liberal assortment from her collection of cut glass. Every inch of surface on the sideboard, mantelpiece and window ledges was crammed with glistening bowls and vases and her *pièce de résistance*, an enormous goblet which she had filled with artificial roses—though the garden was bursting with the real thing—was a permanent centerpiece on the table.

"This is the only nice room in the house," Bessie declaimed.

David remained silent. He had made one concession to please her and this was it.

"I see you now use your silver tea service," Sarah remarked to distract them.

Bessie was putting slices of lemon into the tall glasses on the tray Lizzie had just brought in.

"What is there to preserve it for, Ma? My children already have silver tea services." She waited for Lizzie to leave the room. What she was about to say would upset her. "And my granddaughters? Poor Sharon even when she grows up will still be a baby. And I've given up hope that Laura will ever get married and need a silver tea service," she sighed.

For Sarah, "need" was not the right word. But her family had forgotten its true meaning, and the younger generation had never experienced it. She gazed pensively through the window at some colorful birds which were hopping around on the lawn—the kind you never saw in North Manchester—assailed by memories of the past, which, in some respects, was more real to her than the present.

It had taken seventy years for Sarah's family to achieve the status they now had, but when she looked back, there was a dreamlike quality about the time between then and now. How had the young Sarah Sandberg, who had stepped off the herring boat in England in 1905, turned into the matriarch of what a local newspaper had recently called a "distinguished Jewish family"?

Some of the things we are distinguished for, we could do without! Sarah thought with asperity. That Arnold was a politician of repute and Marianne a well-known author was something to be proud of. About what Martin and Matthew and Laura were famous for, she was not so sure.

"We're in for some more publicity," David said telepathically. He was glancing through the feature pages of yesterday's *Guardian*, while sipping his lemon tea.

Bessie put down her glass with a clatter. "It isn't Laura again, I hope?"

In addition to the reputation Laura had earned for photographing scenes of urban decay and violence, she was active in the Women's Movement, and had once been photographed by a male colleague, while removing and burning her bra outside the hotel where the "Miss World" contestants were staying. The picture had appeared in every tabloid in the country and Bessie's shame had prohibited her from leaving the house for a week.

"She hasn't done it again, has she, David?" Bessie asked apprehensively.

"How could she?" he answered crisply. "She no longer wears a brassiere." Of which his wife was well aware.

Their granddaughter's unfettered bosom embarrassed them whenever they saw her. But Laura had paid no heed to her female elders' pleas on that account—and had returned the dozen bras Bessie had had delivered to her from Harrods.

"I bet it's Martin who's in the news this time," Bessie guessed while sighing with relief. "Have he and his partner won the European Song Contest, David?"

"With the kind of songs they write?" David replied scathingly.

Martin's creativity had finally found its true métier in lyric-writing and he had teamed up with Andy Frolich, who had long been a struggling composer but was struggling no more. Their searingly satirical ballads had ensured their success on both sides of the Atlantic.

"How anyone can like songs about drugs and assassinations!" Sarah exclaimed. Martin had sent her his latest album, which her colored neighbors had played for her on their music-center. "My neighbors have asked me to get Martin's autograph for them," she conveyed. "I gave them the record to keep—but don't tell Martin. If he had been there when I heard it, I would afterward have broken it on his head."

"He sent me that one they wrote about the three-day week!" David said grimly. "As if I needed a souvenir of that nightmare I went through at the factory, last year. After what went on between Mr. Heath and the unions, I'm never going to vote for my nephew Arnold's party again."

"You think you'll be better off now there's a Labour government?" Sarah asked him skeptically. "Or that this country will?"

"Speaking for myself, a businessman can't win whoever's in power. These days, he's entirely in the hands of his workers," David sighed.

"Why are you two talking politics?" Bessie inquired. "I'm

waiting to hear which of the family is in the news. Did you see that picture of our Shirley sweeping the streets, that was in the paper a week or two ago, Ma?"

"I beg your pardon?"

"It's one of the things the Thirty-five Group do, Mother," David explained. "To draw attention to the way Russian Jews are being oppressed."

"In that case, they can give me a broom and I'll do it with them," Sarah said vehemently. She had rarely had occasion to feel proud of Shirley, but was proud of her now. "Every Jew who lives in freedom should do something to help the 'Refusniks,'" she declared.

"And many are doing," David assured her. "There are all kinds of committees dedicated to the cause. Sammy wrote me that there are in the States, too. People all over the world—and not just Jews—are raising their voices on the 'Refusniks' behalf. Trying to get visas for Jews who want to leave Russia and settle in Israel has become part of the wider movement to help Soviet dissidents."

"In my time, we were not prevented from leaving," Sarah reminisced. "Those of us who managed to survive the pogroms," she added grimly. "We were a big thorn in the tsar's side, because we refused to convert to Christianity, and he must have been glad to see the back of us."

"But now it's a different kind of oppression," David said. "And wanting to leave Russia amounts to an offense against the State—it's like standing up in public and declaring you don't approve of the regime, which no Russian is allowed to say. Or even to think. And in the prisons where dissidents are incarcerated, horrific methods are being employed to change the way they think—which in some cases has reduced intellectuals to vegetables."

Bessie stopped eating the strudel she was enjoying with her lemon tea. "You've ruined my appetite, David."

"You said something like that to me in the thirties," David reminded her, "when I mentioned what was happening in Germany. Hasn't it ever struck you, Bessie, that whether or not a Jew is oppressed is dependent upon where our ancestors put down roots? Or whether or not they left there and rerooted themselves at the right time?"

"There but for the grace of God go I," had haunted David throughout Hitler's persecution of his people and had returned to do so again when the new Russian one began. He had, too, experienced similar pangs of guilt during the two wars in Israel. Two years ago, when the *Yom Kippur* War, in which Kate had lost a brother-in-law, broke out, he had made a large donation, as he had in the Six-Day War. But the sense of security Israel's existence gave to Jews in the Diaspora could not be counted in money.

"Shirley told me that some Russian Jews have been given visas to leave," Bessie said defensively. Her husband was still eyeing her with rebuke in his expression.

"But many who want to leave are still there," David answered. "Being harassed, persecuted and deprived, for daring to apply for exit visas."

"So we'll adopt a 'Refusnik,' if it will help you to feel better, David. And make our phone bills bigger."

Those who adopted "Refusniks" maintained contact with them by telephone and letter, which lent moral support and eased the sense of isolation.

"I've already done so," David replied. "But I ring him up from my office."

What have the Jews done to deserve it? Sarah asked herself, as she had had cause to do too often during her long life. The Sandbergs had escaped from one kind of Russian tyranny and now, all these years later, her son and his daughter were aiding Jews being victimized by another kind. It was as though a wheel had turned full circle. The same one that had revolved through the centuries, returning always to the same place.

Bessie observed Sarah's expression. "A nice cheerful day you're giving your mother," she chided David. "And you still haven't told us who is in the news."

"I don't want to know," Sarah said.

"Of course you do, Ma. Give her the *Guardian*, David. Let her read it for herself."

"I didn't bring my magnifying glass with me," Sarah countered.

Bessie sighed. "You never do. We must get you a nice gold chain to attach it to, then you can wear it and you'll always have it handy."

"Don't bother!" Sarah said crossly. Who wanted a reminder that their eyesight was failing, dangling from their neck!

"That's what you said when I wanted to buy you a lovely stick, with an ivory handle," Bessie answered.

"My umbrella is good enough to lean on, thank you," Sarah

retorted. The signs of age were demoralizing enough, without drawing attention to them.

Bessie had picked up the *Guardian*. "This time it's double publicity," she told Sarah after scanning the column David had been reading. "Marianne has written a play for Matthew's company."

"I hope it's different from the last one I saw him in!" Sarah exclaimed.

"New Arena," the group founded by Matthew and his friends, had by the mid-seventies carved a place for itself in London's theatrical scene. A production in which Matthew had played the leading role had recently been televised.

Sarah had not enjoyed it. "How does a great-grandson of mine come to be such a revolutionary?" she wondered aloud.

The group's work was rabidly left-wing.

"I don't know how Arnold can hold up his head in the Conservative party," David said.

"But how did Matthew get that way?" Sarah ruminated. "Wanting to pull down everything his family has worked so hard to become?" She finished the last of her lemon tea. "Like his sister he isn't."

"I wouldn't call what Margaret is doing exactly the usual," Bessie put in.

"But at least she is helping the underprivileged in a practical way," Sarah defended her great-granddaughter who, after qualifying as a nursing sister, had gone to Haiti with a church medical team, to work among poverty-stricken children.

"And depriving her parents of the pleasure they'd have if she settled down and had kids of her own," Bessie declared.

Which there's no chance of them ever getting from Matthew, David thought. His great-nephew's homosexuality was no secret to the worldlier members of the clan, who viewed it as an unmentionable skeleton in the cupboard. How would Sarah react, if she knew? David cogitated.

He cast these troubling thoughts aside. "Shirley and Peter aren't getting that kind of pleasure from Laura, either," he reminded his wife. "Nor are we."

"But if Laura does get married, I hope the man will be Jewish," Sarah said wistfully.

David divined his mother's thoughts. Of her great-grandchildren, as yet only Martin and Kate had married. Kate and her Israeli husband now had two small daughters, but would never have a son; Kate, after two Caesarean deliveries, had been advised by her doctors that it would be unwise for her to become pregnant again. And how ironic it was, David reflected, that Sarah Sandberg's sole great-great-grandson was also the only grandchild of a Catholic peer. And incongruously named Abraham Patrick, after his two great-great-grandfathers. David eyed his mother with compassion. She was still hoping to see a full-blooded Jewish male descendant born into this generation.

"Me, I wouldn't mind if Laura married an Eskimo and lived in an igloo," Bessie said. "Let her just find a husband is all I ask."

Nowadays, Jewish families don't ask for too much! David thought wryly. Small mercies are enough to be thankful for. But why should we expect to be unaffected by the times? he had to ask himself. To be part of the wider community was what we wanted and nobody can have things both ways. In the seventies, young people did as they pleased and those from Jewish homes were no different from the rest.

Bessie cut into his cogitations. "You'll be able to see Matthew in Marianne's play," she told Sarah. "It says in the paper that they're going to tour the country with it and it's coming to Manchester."

Sarah quailed.

"I know just how you feel," Bessie said.

"Who wouldn't? On our own doorstep we are going to be disgraced! And what is Marianne thinking of," Sarah demanded hotly, "writing a play for those scruffy reds!"

"Calm down, Mother," David soothed her. "You don't know what the play is about yet." He scanned the article in the newspaper again. "It says here that Marianne wrote it after attending a National Front rally—"

"How could she breathe the same air as those Fascists?" Sarah shuddered.

"Writers have to rub shoulders with all kinds, Mother, or how would they know what was going on around them?" David answered. "But these days, a person can breathe the same air as Fascists without knowing it," he added. "The National Front is already strong enough to have had candidates in the General Election, last year—and plenty of people voted for them. And not just ignorant 'yobbos.' Middle-class folk are among their supporters, too. The Neo-Nazi movement that's risen again in Germany and France has its counterpart here and it's getting stronger, make no mistake—"

"But it's only the blacks they want to get rid of," Bessie interrupted.

David laughed sardonically. "That's a popular misconception, Bessie—especially among Jews."

"What did you mean about breathing the same air as them without knowing it?" Sarah inquired.

"That there are plenty of people around who agree with them about the kind of place England should be," David told her grimly. "Though they wouldn't say so in public. And we're probably rubbing shoulders with them every day. You could sit beside one of them on a bus and they'd probably be very nice to you, Mother."

"Don't be ridiculous, David! I never ride on a bus."

But Sarah's agitation was plain. Was she really living in a country where wolves in sheep's clothing lurked behind every hedge, as David had made it appear? "Do you think England could ever become a Fascist state?" she asked him uneasily.

"Germany did, didn't it? But it didn't happen overnight," David replied. "Fascism is a slow poison—as I remember Hannah Moritz saying when there was that outbreak of anti-Semitism here, during the lead-up to the birth of Israel."

Twenty-eight eventful years had passed since Jewish traders on Cheetham Hill Road had their shop windows smashed, after two British sergeants were hanged by the Irgun guerillas, in retaliation for the hanging of some of their own. But David had not forgotten the bitterness that anti-Semitic backlash had aroused in him. Or his shock that such a thing could happen in England—and only a year after the Nazi war criminals had been tried at Nuremberg.

"I don't remember Hannah saying anything about poison," said Bessie, whose predilection for harping included exactitude.

"So maybe she didn't say exactly that, but it was what she meant," David answered. "She also said that nobody is born hating Jews. I didn't agree with her at the time, but I do now. And the same goes for blacks. What the Fascists do is make use of existing tensions to achieve their own ends—like they're doing now with racial tension here. Trying to whip up antiblack feeling to explosive proportions."

Bessie finished her second glass of tea and dabbed her lips with a damask serviette. "Some people wish the blacks had never been let into this country, but I'm glad they were. It stops the Jews from being the scapegoat."

For the moment, David thought, but was too sickened by his wife's sentiments to reply.

"You should be ashamed of yourself, Bessie," Sarah told her.

Chapter Five

"Those two are not sharing a room here!" Arnold Klein told his wife vehemently.

He had just arrived home for the weekend, after a grueling week at Westminster and had not had time to give himself a whiskey before Lyn informed him that "New Arena" was due in Manchester that night, and that Pete would be staying at the Kleins' home.

"You'll be fast asleep when they arrive—they're not leaving Birmingham until after this evening's show," Lyn replied coolly. "And you'll have gone back to London long before bedtime tomorrow—"

"Kindly don't mention bedtime to me in relation to Matthew and his—friend," Arnold cut in.

"I was under the impression that was what we were discussing. And you didn't allow me to finish. I was merely pointing out that you won't be here when those of us who still are retire for the night. Unless you intend departing from your usual routine."

"Did I detect a sour note in that last bit?" Arnold asked, reaching for the decanter to fill the glass Lyn always had waiting beside it.

Lyn watched him add two squirts of soda to the inch of liquor he habitually allowed himself; even in moments of stress, Arnold rarely deviated from what she had come to think of as his pattern. "What have I to be sour about, darling?"

Was that another crack? Arnold was not sure. Lyn had been his wife for more than thirty years, but sometimes he felt that he didn't really know her.

"I've arranged for the party I'm giving the company to be on Monday night, so you'll have an excuse not to be here for it," Lyn said.

And that she didn't care a damn about him! Arnold set

down his glass with a thud. "So you're giving them a party, are you? And on the night the play opens in Manchester—which could mean a few pressmen will drift along to it. Matthew is sure to invite them, he loves publicity."

"Actors need it."

"And my son has had plenty at my expense! That last play they put on was a lampoon on the Tories—with Matthew in the part of Ted—and I'm still trying to live it down. I doubt if I could ever live down giving a shindig for a Red theater group—and in my own home!"

"You won't be here, remember? And this is Matthew's home, too."

"Some would say he's forfeited the right to it."

Lyn helped herself to some peanuts from a dish on the coffee table and crunched them. "I'd say he is as entitled to his political viewpoint as you are to yours." She watched Arnold swallow down his whiskey. "If I adopted your attitude, I wouldn't have either of you in my house. As you well know, I always vote Liberal."

Arnold took a handkerchief from his breast pocket and mopped his brow. It was a sultry afternoon, but the temperature was not responsible for the beads of sweat. "It wouldn't do me any good if that got into the newspapers, either."

Lyn left him alone with his apprehensions and went upstairs to make up the twin divans in Matthew's room.

Matthew had not asked her if Pete could stay here while the company was in town, but she had brushed aside her misgivings and invited him. The forbidden ground which for years had stood between Lyn and her son had to be trodden sooner or later, and she had taken this first step.

"Are you sure?" Matthew had asked when she told him on the telephone that Pete was welcome here.

"Certain," she had replied and would not forget the sound of his voice when he had thanked her. Only then had she felt his private pain, as well as her own, had a glimpse into the world he inhabited—where a man was rendered huskily speechless by gratitude for a gesture of understanding from his own mother.

Lyn smoothed down the plaid counterpanes and polished the brass compass Arnold had bought for his son, which Matthew had kept on his bed table since he was a small child. He had always kept his room neat and tidy, almost monastic.

Nothing but a brush and comb had ever sat atop his chest of drawers and, unlike other teenage boys, he had not pinned any posters to the walls. The room had looked no more lived-in when he occupied it than it did now, Lyn thought. And when he went away to drama school, he had left the compass behind him.

How different the flat Matthew shared with Pete was, Lyn reflected. She had been there only once, when Matthew was alone for an afternoon, and had seen his belongings strewn around as they had never been at home. It had struck her then that her son had not begun living until he met the man who had helped him discover what he was.

There was no doubt in Lyn's mind that Pete was Matthew's first and only lover. That before meeting him, Matthew had repressed his true self and, as an adolescent, had withdrawn behind a defensive screen of asceticism.

But there had been times when flashes of emotion had suddenly blazed from him—the time his Grandpa Ben had been dying in hospital and Arnold had at first refused to go there and end his long rift with the family, had been one of them. And even had there not been those signs, Lyn would have known there were passionate depths to her son—one had only to see his dramatic performances to know it.

Lyn glanced up and saw Arnold standing in the doorway.

"It seems I'm no longer the master in my own house," he said averting his eyes from the beds.

"Don't be a bloody fool," Lyn answered brusquely and saw his face redden with anger. Then her own anger simmered down into a dull acceptance. Arnold would never come to terms with this. In his eyes, his son had done him a terrible injury. But Lyn did not see it that way. The tears she had shed about it had been for Matthew, not for herself, and largely because he would never know the joys of parenthood, which compensated a thousandfold for the heartache it also brought.

Though Matthew and Margaret had flown the nest, their very existence continued to fill Lyn's life. Her days were spent working with the Women's Royal Voluntary Service— she had not allowed herself to become part of her husband's political scenery, in the way some MPs' wives did, or his ideology to replace her own. But her son and daughter remained her deepest concern, which Arnold, too, had once been, she thought dispassionately, glancing at him.

"I said I won't have Matthew and that man sharing a room here!" Arnold shouted in an upsurge of rage.

"Why not? When you know damn well they share not just a room, but a double bed, in London," Lyn reminded him cruelly.

"Oh God," Arnold whispered as if she had delivered him a body blow. Then his face crumpled piteously and he covered it with his hands.

It was not until a tear splashed onto his jacket that Lyn realized he was weeping.

"Why did my son have to be that way?" he sobbed.

Lyn took him by the elbow and led him along the landing into their room.

"I expect your late father also asked that question, when you fell in love with a *shiksah*," she said, sitting down on the bed beside him.

Arnold gave her an agonized glance and she surveyed the lines on his face, more than a man of fifty-two had any right to. Many of them had been put there by his children, Lyn reflected.

Margaret's departure to Haiti had grieved Arnold deeply and only his admiration for the work she was doing had reconciled him to it. But the blow Matthew had dealt him was of a different kind and Lyn had never known her husband come to terms with that for which he could find no redeeming feature.

"Are you saying this is retribution for the *tsorus* I gave my father?" he asked her bitterly.

For Lyn, her son's happiness had helped her to accept the situation. But Arnold had, as usual, related it only to himself, she thought, hardening her heart against him.

"I don't believe all that nonsense about retribution," she answered. "My reference to your father was just a way of pointing out to you that parenthood is a highly vulnerable state, and if your kids don't put you through the mill one way, they'll do it in another."

"My grandmother would die, if she knew about Matthew," Arnold said irrelevantly.

But Lyn knew the thought was not really irrelevant. Though he had once himself disgraced the family—in the days when marrying out of the faith was the most scandalous sin a Jew could commit—Arnold, like the rest of the clan, was anxious to preserve its good name.

"From what I know of your grandmother, she'd take this in her stride, as she has so many other things," Lyn declared. A matriarch Sarah indisputably was, but in many respects a good deal more flexible than some of her juniors. "She'd be shocked, of course. But I'm sure she wouldn't reject Matthew because he's homosexual. And, by the way, he isn't the only one of his kind in the family."

Arnold was momentarily struck dumb.

"I ought not to be telling you," Lyn went on, "but I'm doing so in the hope it will bring you to your senses."

"Who is it?" Arnold asked in a hushed voice. "Not my nephew Howard, I hope?"

Lyn shook her head. "But I understand from Marianne that his parents are in for a blow of another sort. Howard has fallen for a girl who isn't just a *shiksah*, she's a German one—"

"He can't possibly marry her!" Arnold interrupted in horror. "Her father was probably a Nazi."

"Your reaction doesn't surprise me," Lyn replied coolly. "And your brother's will be the same—that's why Howard hasn't yet told Harry and Ann. He knows his parents will say exactly what you did. It's no wonder the younger end of the family turn to your sister. Apart from me, Marianne is the only open-minded one of our generation in the whole bloody clan! It was she who told me about Laura."

Arnold was growing increasingly bemused. "Where does Laura fit into all this?"

"I understand that her permissiveness is no longer confined to men. As I was about to tell you before we digressed."

"I need a drink," Arnold said weakly.

Lyn followed him downstairs. "There'll be liquor fumes on your breath when we arrive at the *Shabbos* tea party," she warned.

"So the family will think I've become a *shikker*," Arnold answered. "Compared with the things you've just told me, boozing shrinks into insignificance," he added pouring himself two inches of whiskey, instead of his customary one.

His complexion had paled, Lyn noted. But he had needed shock treatment, she thought, watching him add the barest splash of soda to the glass. And shocked he certainly was, or he wouldn't be having a second prelunch drink at all. It was time Arnold woke up to the changing world around him, of which the younger generation's rejection of their elders' moralities was a part, Lyn thought. And not just in relation to sex.

To Arnold's generation of Jew, it would have seemed obscene to marry a member of the race at whose hands Jewry had suffered the Holocaust. But his nephew was contemplating bringing the German girl he had met at St. Moritz into the family, and Harry and Ann Klein would have to accept it if they didn't want to alienate their only son.

Lyn hoped the things her husband had just learned would help him see Matthew's diversion from the norm in perspective, and waited for him to speak after he had gulped down the liquor. She was due for a disappointment.

"If Uncle David ever finds out about Laura, it will kill him," Arnold said.

His rigidity hadn't given an inch since he made the same sort of melodramatic pronouncement about his grandmother; Lyn had wasted her breath!

"If old people dropped dead every time their children's children defied convention, in this day and age the streets would be littered with corpses," she told him cuttingly. "And the same goes for middle-aged parents like us—not excluding your fellow MP's. You're fighting a losing battle, Arnold. So why not give in gracefully? Learn to grin and bear it, along with the rest of us."

Arnold replaced the stopper in the decanter. "The way you put it, I seem to have no option."

Chapter Six

On her thirtieth birthday, Laura rose early and took a shower. Afterward, she wiped the steam off the bathroom mirror and surveyed her body, which she had begun to hate. Not its shape—the reflection she was eyeing was lithe and leggy, a far cry from the chubby teenage Laura Kohn—but what it had come to represent.

Not for nothing had the expression "turn me on" entered the English language, she mused cynically. In the sense in which it was used, there could be no more apt description for the mechanical process Laura's sex life was.

Like eating when you're hungry, she thought, putting on the burnt orange bathrobe that matched her pubic hair. And her transient affairs with women could be likened to a gourmand indulging in a change of diet, she said to herself dispassionately. Nothing more and nothing less.

That anyone could be bisexual if they allowed themselves to be had come as a shock to Laura. Not until the night she got stoned, and bedded, at an all-female party had she believed it possible. Or what certain of her feminist friends who were lesbian had told her. That for them, being so was cerebral, not instinctive; they had chosen to fulfil their sexual needs with women, rather than be what they had previously been—putty in the hands of men.

Laura had never been putty in anyone's hands, nor did she ever intend to be, she thought, padding barefooted into her kitchen to drink the lemon juice with which she started her day.

"In a good relationship, the other person is as much at your mercy as you are at theirs," Marianne had declared when Laura had aired that sentiment to her.

Don't you believe it, Laura had thought. Like every other married woman, Marianne was dependent for her happiness upon her husband—and, Laura had noted, though she and Ralph still seemed devoted to each other, did not seem as happy as she had once. You couldn't have a committed relationship without being emotionally prey to your partner which was why Laura had never entered into one—with a male or a female.

In Laura's view, the lesbian couples she visited in their homes were kidding themselves if they thought they had retained their independence. What they had in fact done was swap conventional dependency for an unconventional kind, she ruminated, plugging in her electric coffee percolator, and by doing so deprived themselves of a woman's natural right—motherhood—which some of them did not deny they regretted.

Laura heard the mail land on the doormat with a heavier thud than usual, but had no need to wonder why. Year in, year out, birthday cards arrived for her from everyone in the family. And nostalgia for home—which was how she still thought of Manchester—arose within her when she opened the envelopes and read all the fond messages.

How could they still think of her as one of them? she asked herself, reading the cards and propping them up on the breakfast bar. She only went home for *Rosh Hashanah*—and sometimes not even then if it coincided with a magazine assignment abroad. Yet every card was addressed, beneath its sentimental, or funny, verse to "our dear Laura." As if she was, to her aged and aging relatives, still the little girl who had been raised in their midst.

She poured herself some coffee and perched on a stool, gazing at these graphic reminders of her roots, and it was as if they had come from a different planet from the one Laura inhabited. One in which people meant what they said and, if they cared about you, did so for ever. Where life had a stability solid as rock, as opposed to Laura's life, which by comparison was built on shifting sand.

Was it because Marianne's flat had the stable feeling of home that Laura always felt secure there? Probably. But stability was the product of commitment—which Marianne, despite her career, had not shirked, but which Laura wanted no part of.

Her grandfather had enclosed with his card a check for thirty pounds, one for each of her years, he had scrawled in his customary green ink. As though Laura needed reminding that time was speeding by. In her teens and twenties, she hadn't noticed it doing so. But there was something about being thirty that made you stop short. And take stock. Workwise, she was a success, as the blowups of her magazine pictures above the breakfast bar illustrated. But on a personal level?

"My niece is the family fly-by-night," her Uncle Ronald had once joked to a friend in Laura's presence. And his words returned to her mind as she sat sipping her coffee.

Like a moth flits by, only skimming the surface of whatever it encounters, so it had been with Laura. The people she thought of as her friends were, in truth, no more than acquaintances. Because friendship, too, demanded commitment, and cluttered your life with other people's problems.

Laura's life had remained as uncluttered as her neat apartment, in which other human beings were briefly allowed to linger before being dispatched on their way—and on her thirtieth birthday her life seemed as coldly empty as the place she called home suddenly felt.

But her life could not be otherwise without sacrificing the total independence she had ruthlessly pursued and achieved, she reflected wryly. Without allowing the emotions that had occasionally threatened to entangle her to rise from the secret place where she kept them dormant. But only by doing so would she herself ever be a whole human being, she was thinking when the telephone rang.

"Happy birthday, Laura!" Marianne's voice breezed over the line. "How do you intend spending it?"

"I haven't a clue."

"On my thirtieth birthday, I was nursing Martin through chicken pox—and Ralph had flu," Marianne reminisced.

"Oh."

"You sound down in the dumps, Laura."

"Any suggestions to lift me out of 'em?"

"Yes, as a matter-of-fact. There's nothing like having someone else to worry about for making one forget one's personal blues."

Marianne must be telepathic! Laura thought. Or is it just that she knows me too well? "Why not just say I'm a self-centered bitch and have done with it?" she answered dryly.

"Well, aren't you?"

"Sure."

"But so long as you're happy, as Bobbie Sarah would say!"

"I'm not."

"Then do something about it—before it's too late."

"Too late for what, Marianne?"

"A woman's childbearing years don't last indefinitely."

"Are you out of your mind?" Laura exclaimed.

"You're as hetero as I am," Marianne said coolly, "and you know it. So you've had a few lesbian encounters, just for the hell of it. That's not so uncommon nowadays. It doesn't mean a thing."

"How true."

"Look—I hate to sound like your Grandma Bessie, love. But you've had your fling. It's time you found yourself a permanent man and had a child."

"I don't want a permanent man," Laura declared emphatically. Her birthday ruminations, bleak though they had been, had not changed her mind in that respect!

"So shoot me for suggesting it!" Marianne answered. "Drop in for coffee, later, if you've nothing better to do. You can bring the shotgun with you!"

When Laura arrived at Marianne's flat, she found little Abraham there.

"Martin and Moira are in New York," Marianne explained while building a Lego tower on the living room rug, for her grandson.

"They've gone to hear my daddy's songs at a big concert," Abraham added with pride.

"In Carnegie Hall," Marianne told Laura. She ruffled Abraham's ginger curls and marveled, as she often did, that her *Hassidic* grandfather's features and coloring had been passed down to Martin's Catholic son. Lord Kyverdale's grandson was the image of the late Abraham Sandberg.

"I could've stayed at home with my fwiends, but I pwefer to stay here when Mummy and Daddy go away," Abraham informed Laura.

"Give Laura a birthday kiss," Marianne instructed him.

"I don't like kissing ladies."

"But this one has no little boy or girl of her own to kiss her."

"You must come and stay with me sometime, Abraham," Laura smiled after he had obligingly pecked her cheek.

"I will if I can have baked beans for bweakfast," the child bargained. "Gwanma lets me. At home and at my other Gwanma's, I'm only allowed them for tea."

"You can have ice cream and chips for breakfast," Laura laughed and was rewarded with a hug.

She spent the rest of the day with Marianne and her grandson. Before she left, Abraham allowed her to bath him and tuck him up in bed.

"This has been a most cathartic birthday," she said pensively when Marianne walked with her to where she had parked her car.

It was a bleak February evening and Marianne wrapped the coat she had slipped on closer around herself, as she scanned Laura's face. "In what way?"

Laura unlocked the car door and slid behind the wheel. "What you said on the phone, this morning—about it being time I found a permanent man. It wouldn't work, Marianne."

"How do you know when you haven't tried it?"

"I have no desire to try it. That kind of setup isn't my style. One of us would end up being downtrodden. And it wouldn't be me."

"In that case, I wouldn't wish you on any man."

"Exactly," Laura answered smiling up at the forthright woman who, it had struck her today, was the only real friend

she had ever had. But even this had been a one-sided
relationship, Laura thought with a pang of shame. Since her
youth, Marianne had always been there for her, but Laura
had taken her for granted; done nothing for her in return.

"I don't suppose you'd wish me on a child, either," she
added.

"The two go together, don't they?"

"Not necessarily. One-parent families all all the rage, these
days."

Marianne leaned weakly against a garden wall. What sort of
shock was the clan in for now? She considered herself a
modern woman, but the traditional concept of family had
remained, for her, sacrosanct. If a girl became pregnant and,
for one reason or another, had to raise the child without a
father, so be it. But to put oneself and the baby in that
situation from choice? And for Laura to have strayed so far
from her Jewish conditioning, in which the sanctity of home
and family was the core, seemed to Marianne inconceivable.

"I've decided to have a child," Laura said confirming her
fears.

"Just like that?"

"Why not?" Laura started the car engine, her voice as
businesslike as the manner in which she placed her capable
hands on the steering wheel. "It shouldn't be too difficult to
find an obliging man."

Marianne watched her drive away and would not have put
it past her to pull up the car near Hampstead Heath, smile at
the first passing male and get what she proposed to do over
and done with, on the grass verge at the side of the road.

What is the world coming to? she asked herself, though
she had never thought she would. Her mother and aunts
were always mouthing that cliché with respect to the young
end of the family. But Marianne, the "with-it" granny, had
believed herself unshockable. "With-it" nothing! she thought
as she returned to the flat to prepare the evening meal. Laura
had just made her feel like Methuselah.

Chapter Seven

"We only have three evenings in New York and Martin wants us to spend one of them with his elderly relatives!" Moira complained to Rhoda Frolich while they waited for their husbands to claim the baggage from a carousel at Kennedy Airport.

She had been seething since Martin said on the plane that his great-uncle and aunt would no doubt invite them for dinner. "He doesn't even know them," she added to Rhoda. "They emigrated to the States before he was born."

"Fortunately for me, Andy's American relations live in California," Rhoda answered. "Or he'd think it his duty to spend all three evenings with them. Are Martin's coming to the concert?"

"The aunt is—my mother-in-law called to tell her we were coming. She said her husband doesn't go out at night anymore."

Rhoda waved to Andy, who was trying to locate them among the milling throng that had just disembarked from the Jumbo jet. "Maybe the old chap's scared of getting mugged," she said to Moira, airing their joint apprehension about visiting New York. "I'm expecting to see Kojak lurking around every corner!"

"Me too."

"Though from what I hear, the police can't cope with it," Rhoda said with an anticipatory shiver. "Our husbands will get plenty of material for their ballads from this trip."

When the bags were located and the two couples had assured the customs officers that the only vegetable matter they had brought to America was for tea for Martin's great-aunt, they made their way to the exit foyer. Miriam Sandberg was there, waiting for them. Moira was not surprised.

Miriam recognized Martin immediately, from snapshots Marianne had sent to her.

Those Martin had seen of her were not recent ones, but her face was still that of the beautiful young woman in the photograph on his great-grandmother's dining room sideboard, he thought when she introduced herself. But time had snowed her hair and etched in some lines.

"I thought it would be nice to welcome you to New York," she smiled. "Your mother mentioned that you were taking the British Airways midday flight."

Martin felt an immediate rapport with her, though he was not sure why. She had not kissed or embraced him, but he felt she would have like to do so and, without releasing the hand she had given him, he kissed her cheek.

"It was good of you to take the trouble to come," Moira said sincerely, though she was wishing Miriam had not bothered to do so.

Miriam gave her a warm smile. "For family, nothing is too much trouble."

This, Moira knew all too well. Her husband seemed mesmerized by his aunt—or was he just suffering from jet lag? She exchanged a glance with Rhoda and prodded Martin. "Hadn't we better get a cab?"

"I have one waiting," Miriam said. "It can drop you at your hotel and take me on to Washington Heights." She ushered them to where the vehicle was parked.

"Not so fast, there, baby!" the driver said, eyeing Andy's violin-case as he was about to get into the car.

Though Andy was no longer a working musician, he still took with him everywhere the valuable instrument his late father had bought for him.

"I gotta take a look in that case," the cabdriver said.

"What on earth for?" Moira demanded in her haughtiest voice.

The driver cackled. "What for, the lady wantsta know! Because this guy could be packin' a machine gun is what for."

"Does my husband look like a gangster?" Rhoda demanded.

"These days, lady, they come in all shapes'n' sizes," the man replied, surveying Andy's thin, stooping shoulders and habitually melancholy face. "So open up, baby," he instructed him. "Or we ain't goin' no place."

"I guess you'd better do as he says," Miriam advised Andy.

"He'll do nothing of the kind!" Rhoda intervened.

"I agree," Moira said. "Let's pay this gentleman off and get another taxi."

The cabdriver shifted his dead cigar from one side of his

mouth to the other. "Suit yourself, sweetheart. But you ain't gonna find no Noo York cabdriver who ain't watchin' out for hisself."

"That's correct," Miriam endorsed.

Martin grabbed the violin case and proved his partner's innocence.

"Now why didn'tya do that in the foist place?" The driver ushered them into his car.

In which, the two English couples noted, he was protected from possible assault by his passengers by a solid metal partition, relieved only by a small slot through which the fare could be paid.

"I already have the creeps, and I haven't set foot in the city yet," Andy voiced their feelings.

"You'll get used to it," Miriam told them. "On your next visit here, you won't even notice the half a dozen different security locks on your hotel room door." She smiled at their expressions. "I have them on my apartment door, too. Everyone has to."

"Thank goodness we live in England," Rhoda said to Andy, though violence was on the increase there, too.

Miriam smiled reminiscently. "The United States wasn't always like this. I've lived in New York since I was quite a young woman and I can remember when it was safe to ride the subway, and to take a walk at night. Which I regret isn't so anymore. But as you can see, I'm still here to tell the tale."

"Why not stop off at our hotel and have some coffee with us?" Andy invited her when they were speeding toward Manhattan.

"I wouldn't dream of it," she answered graciously. "You must all take a rest, so you'll be fresh to go out on the town tonight."

"I feel fresh as a daisy," Martin declared, though he looked anything but. "We'll drop the others off, Auntie Miriam, and I'll go on with you. I want to meet Uncle Sammy."

Miriam did not try to dissuade him. She was longing for news of the family, the intimate details which would bring them closer to her, which could not be told in letters. Or in the presence of strangers, she thought, glancing at Moira's set expression. There was something about Martin's wife that gave Miriam the feeling she was, in the family sense, a stranger—though nominally she had been one of them for several years—and that she had some kind of chip on her shoulder.

"I won't keep your husband too long, Moira," she promised when the taxi halted at the Waldorf-Astoria.

Moira alighted with Rhoda and Andy and managed to smile. Her decision not to let Martin's allegiance to the clan cause trouble between them had not proved easy to sustain and her patience was wearing thin.

"I hope all four of you will join my husband and me for *Shabbos* dinner, tomorrow evening," Miriam said.

"Rhoda and I would be delighted to," Andy replied.

"It's kind of you to ask us, Mrs. Sandberg," Rhoda echoed.

Moira said nothing and Miriam was left wondering why, as she and Martin were borne away.

"Is your wife always so quiet?" she asked Martin. "Or has meeting your elderly great-aunt overwhelmed her?" she added with a chuckle.

"Moira is very possessive," Martin answered. But why was he confiding to an old lady he had only just met something he would not have admitted to his mother?

"Then she must love you very much," Miriam said, casting her mind back to the way she had, in her youth, felt about David. And how long ago it seemed now! But the destructive emotion Martin had mentioned had never been part of Miriam's love for Sammy.

Martin exchanged a smile with her and they sat in contemplative silence until they reached the West Side.

"When your great-grandmother was here, in the fifties, she couldn't believe this was Broadway," Miriam said. "And it hadn't yet begun to deteriorate, then."

Martin gazed through the window at the huge plastic sacks spilling garbage on street corners and outside seedy-looking stores. There was a depressed look about most of the pedestrians, black and white alike, that went with the ambience and reminded Martin of certain districts in London and Manchester.

"I sometimes yearn for the clean and safe English city I left in forty-seven," Miriam said nostalgically.

Martin did not bother telling her that, though it had not reached New York proportions, urban decay and what went with it had made their mark in England, too. An old lady should be allowed the comfort of unblemished memories, he thought, studying Miriam's pensive profile.

When they reached and entered her apartment block, two middle-aged men, huddled in overcoats, were standing together by the lift.

"How is Romeo today, Mr. Perelman?" Miriam asked one of them who had an Alsatian dog, on a chain.

"If I gave him half a chance, he'd be out havin' himself a good time! My four-footed friend here is a real lady-killer," Mr. Perelman chuckled to Martin. "But better he should be a man-killer, eh, Lester?" he added grimly to his black companion.

"I guess so, Issie."

The ferocious-looking animal was growling and sniffing Martin's shoes.

"It's OK, Romeo," Miriam soothed it. "He's one of us."

She introduced Martin to her neighbors and told him they were members of the apartment block vigilante committee. "Your Uncle Sammy used to take his turn of duty, too. But that kind of thing isn't for him anymore."

"It shouldn't have to be for anyone," Mr. Perelman sighed. "But in this city, good people have to protect themselves and their property from the bad guys, or it would be God help us. Isn't that the truth, Lester?"

"It sure is."

"How can you live here?" Martin asked Miriam when they were alone in the creaking lift.

"Like I said in the cab, I guess a person gets used to it."

But the need for self-protection could brutalize decent people, Martin reflected, thinking of the vigilantes—and the bloodthirsty dog. To Martin, the menacing undertones he felt all around him were chilling. But for those who lived with them day-in, day-out, it had become the norm.

These observations were shaping in his mind as lyrics for a ballad when Miriam led him into her apartment. With an accompanying tingle, which he had never once experienced when he was trying to write books and plays.

He wished Andy were there to share his creative excitement. Or Moira, so that he could hug her and whirl her around and around—and had to stop himself from doing this to his great-aunt, who would think him a lunatic if he did!

"Look who's come to see you, Sammy!" Miriam said gaily as Martin followed her into the living room.

"It's a pity to waken him, Auntie Miriam."

The frail old gentleman in the wing chair by the window was fast asleep.

"He won't mind, Martin. We don't get a family visitor every day." Miriam gently shook her husband, then stepped back, sharply, as his head lolled forward onto his chest. "Oh dear God," she whispered.

Martin moved to his uncle and tried to find a pulse beat in his wrist, but none was there. He picked up the walking stick that had slid to the rug from its resting place beside the chair and gazed mutely at his aunt.

For a moment, neither of them spoke. Then the shriek of a police car siren outside in the street broke the heavy silence.

"The doctor warned me—but I didn't expect it to be so soon," Miriam said. She sat down on the sofa, holding herself together for Martin's sake. "I'm so sorry it happened while you are here, my dear," she told him. "And that you'll never know what a beautiful person my husband was," she added softly.

Martin went to sit beside her. "I'm glad to be here when you need someone."

"And I'm so grateful for you, Martin."

After the doctor and the rabbi had been and gone, Martin insisted that his aunt rest in her room. He had never before been in the presence of death, but was not affected by it in the way he would have supposed. Instead of shrinking from the sight of his dead uncle, he sat gazing at him with compassion.

It was no secret in the family that Miriam had married him after David jilted her. Or that Sammy Sandberg had never, in any respect, been treated to more than the crumbs of life. How had he reconciled himself to his lot? And remained the gentle, good-natured man everyone said he was?

Was it an innate weakness, or a special kind of strength that had characterized Sammy? Martin pondered. And what would Miriam do, now he was gone? Martin had asked her if she would like him to call up her close friends, but she had answered that there were none. Only the neighbors. And some ladies with whom she worked on a charity committee, whom the rabbi would let know.

To Martin, it seemed inconceivable that she had lived in New York for thirty years without having established any close relationships. Americans were warm and friendly people. But nobody could get close to you if you didn't allow it, he thought, gazing at the bedroom door behind which his aunt was secluded with her private grief.

When his uncle had been taken to a Jewish funeral parlor, Martin telephoned his wife.

"Would you like me to come?" Moira asked when he told her he could not think of leaving Miriam alone.

"Only if you want to," Martin replied.

To his surprise, half an hour later Moira arrived.

"I'm not as hardhearted as you apparently think," she said noting his expression.

Martin helped her off with her red fox coat, under which she was wearing a bottle-green dress that clung fetchingly to her shapely figure. "Hardhearted I've never thought you, darling," he said gathering her close. "Just a little fed up."

"With what?"

"Me and my relations."

Moira did not deny it.

Martin led her to the sofa. There was something that must be said and now was the time. "Except for the concert, I shan't leave Auntie Miriam's side, Moira. Uncle Sammy's sister and brothers are too old to fly here in wintertime, at a minute's notice. I told them on the phone not to think of doing so."

"Isn't his sister your grandma?" Moira asked.

Martin nodded. "But none of them are coming, as I'm here with my aunt."

"I'll stay here, too," Moira replied. "Under the circumstances, it's up to us to look after her."

Us? Martin thought, after he had recovered from his astonishment.

Miriam entered from her bedroom. "How nice of you to come, my dear," she said to Moira.

"It's the least I could do, Mrs. Sandberg."

"I do wish you'd call me Aunt Miriam."

Moira had been similarly invited by all Martin's aunts, but had not been able to bring herself to do as they asked. Would she now? Martin wondered. And could not believe it when she did.

"I'll scramble us all some eggs, if you don't mind, Aunt Miriam," Moira said. "It's long past dinnertime."

"I couldn't swallow a bite, Moira."

"But you must try. Sit down and talk to Martin and I'll get cracking in the kitchen."

Martin watched his wife pass through the narrow archway that led to the kitchen and dinette. The apartment was small, but well planned as he had heard American homes were.

Thank God for that, he said to himself, returning his thoughts to Moira. But how sad it was that it had taken Uncle Sammy's death to slot her into her place in the family.

For Miriam, devoid for so long of the comfort of family, it seemed unreal to have these two young relatives sustaining her with their presence. And indeed, she thought later when Andy and Rhoda arrived from the hotel with the Deans' suitcases and stayed awhile, to have young folk around her at all.

Moira brought in the Sachertorte Miriam had baked that morning and served it with coffee, and a distant memory of her mother-in-law's parlor on *Shabbos* afternoons returned to Miriam; of youthful faces and voices—Marianne and Shirley, Ronald, Harry and Arnold, her own dead boy and, playing on the rug because they were younger, Leona and the Moritz twins.

Miriam glanced at Martin, whose generation had taken over from those whom she had been remembering. But she had not witnessed it, and there were children in the clan whom she did not know. Oh, what she and Sammy had missed.

Sammy was laid to rest the following morning. Martin, representing the family, intoned the mourner's prayer.

If our son had lived, this solemn duty would have been his, Miriam thought poignantly. Her own dear Martin would have been beside her. But Fate—or was it God, in whom she had had no faith since her son was taken from her? —had arranged that his family namesake would deputize for him.

"We must talk about what you're going to do," Martin said to her in the car they shared riding from the cemetery.

"Do?" Miriam answered absently.

She looked strained and weary, her pallor accentuated by her mourning attire and Martin put a comforting arm around her, as though she were one of the old aunts he had known all his life and not someone he had met for the first time yesterday.

Miriam glanced up at him and straightened the *yamulke* on his unruly black hair. It was one her son had worn, which she had lent to Martin. Andy, who had attended the funeral, had produced his from his pocket, but Martin was not the kind of young Jew who carried one with him when he traveled, Miriam thought.

That his Hebrew was rusty had been evident from the way

he had stumbled over the words when reciting the *Kaddish*, but Miriam had not minded that. She had met unprincipled, regular *shul*-goers in her time and, conversely, less devout men who lived impeccable lives. Her husband had been one of the latter kind, she thought warmly as they reached Washington Heights and sped past Fort Tryon Park, where Sammy had liked to sit on summer afternoons.

"I called Mum this morning, while you were taking your bath," Martin said to her. "She told me I must persuade you to go home with me. And that everyone else agrees."

"I shan't need persuading," Miriam answered. She would spend her few remaining years in the place where she had been raised. And how good it would be to be back among her own.

Chapter Eight

On a sultry June evening in 1977, Nathan was about to leave his surgery when the telephone rang. He had had a heavy day and hoped the call would not necessitate his visiting a patient.

"Yes, Peggy?" he sighed to the secretary through whom all calls were filtered.

"A Miss Ann Barker wants to speak to you, Doctor. She says the call is personal."

The name rang a distant bell, then clicked into place in Nathan's mind. "Put her through."

"Do you remember me?" a brusque voice inquired.

"Of course I do." She had been Mary's friend when Nathan was a medical student. "How are you, Ann?"

"The same as ever," she answered enigmatically and Nathan recalled her life having been spoiled by a hopeless and endless love affair with a married man.

"Are you still in touch with Mary?" he asked.

"We share a house. And Mary is very ill."

"I'm sorry to hear that."

"She still has your photograph on her bed table, Nat. That's why I decided to call you. Need I say more?"

Nathan had not seen his boyhood sweetheart since they

reencountered each other on the wards of a military hospital, during the war. But no woman had ever engaged his emotions as she had. "Give me the address, Ann," he said gruffly. "I'll come tonight."

"Make it tomorrow. And afternoons are her best time."

The following day was Saturday.

"I shan't be coming with you to the *Shabbos* tea party today," Nathan told his wife when they arrived home from synagogue.

"Any particular reason?" Rebecca inquired pleasantly.

The bitterness she had once displayed to Nathan was no longer present. Once, we were like enemies under the same roof, he reflected. But now we're not even that. In recent years, his home life had been equable.

Rebecca took off her coat and handed it to him to hang up.

Equable, but none the less empty, Nathan thought, watching her fiddle with the floral arrangement on the hall table. It was as if his presence was of no consequence to her, but no longer a thorn in her side.

"How was yere sermon this mornin'?" Bridie called to them from the kitchen.

Since espousing Progressive Judaism, in the forties, Nathan's religion had come to mean more to him. And probably to Rebecca too, he thought, glancing at her composed expression as they went into the lounge. Though her regular attendance at synagogue was of fairly recent vintage. Had communion with God helped to make life more bearable for her? Nathan wondered. If not God, something else had.

Rebecca sat down on the sofa and crossed her shapely legs. The time when she would have rushed to the wine cabinet— or to her secret liquor store upstairs—was long gone.

She's still a beautiful woman, Nathan thought studying her. She was now sixty-three and the drinking in which she had indulged in her middle years had left its mark on her complexion, but nothing could detract from the perfection of her features. And her full-bosomed body was as firm and graceful as it had been when she was young.

Nathan averted his eyes from it and sipped his sherry.

Bridie brought Rebecca a glass of tomato juice.

"Would you mind if I asked you something, Rebecca?" he said when they were alone, in the polite way all their conversations were now conducted. "How did you get yourself off the bottle?"

"Not without a struggle," she replied in the same tone.

"That, I observed."

She had refused Nathan's offers of treatment and had initially suffered several lapses. Then he had noticed that an uncharacteristic calmness had replaced her fraught demeanor. And that she was not drinking anymore.

"It got a lot easier after I woke up one morning and realized how near I'd come to throwing my life away," Rebecca said. Then she gazed at Nathan silently for a moment, the expression in her tawny eyes as dispassionate as if she were examining a specimen in a glass case. "Or, to put it in a nutshell, that my daughter and grandchild needed me, and I them. That I still had a life to live and it didn't have to include you."

Nathan made no comment. There had been no accusatory element in his wife's voice. She had simply stated a fact, and he was not in the least affected by it. They had lost the desire—and the power—to hurt each other.

"I can't come to Mother's this afternoon because I'm going to see Mary. She's dying," he said. There seemed no reason not to tell Rebecca the truth.

"How sad," she answered sincerely. Her hatred for the Gentile woman whose existence had marred her marriage had, along with her love for Nathan, dissipated into nothingness years ago.

Throughout that summer, Nathan made regular trips to Glossop, where Mary and Ann had set up house after their retirement from nursing.

For Nathan, his visits were like pilgrimages back to his lost youth, though there was little of the Mary he remembered in the frail woman with whom he sat in the cottage garden, gazing at the Derbyshire hills. Only her cornflower-blue eyes and her way of calling him Nathan, which nobody else ever did, told him it was she.

They never talked of the present, only of their shared past. As if the time between then and now had been meaningless, Nathan reflected one August afternoon. But for him that was not so. He had fathered and raised a daughter and had a grandchild to comfort him in his old age. Compared with the empty vessel Mary's years had been, his own had brimmed full.

Rebecca's reply, when he asked her how she had cured her alcoholism, assumed a new significance for him, as he sat beneath a gnarled old crab apple tree with the woman he had wanted for his wife. He had fed on self-pity because he could not have her, grown sour as the fruit those heavy branches would soon bear. Lost sight of the blessings he had, in the mist of resentment engendered by what he had not—which was what Rebecca had come to realize about herself. And oh, what their joint foolishness had cost them.

"It's all like a dream, now, Nathan," Mary said pensively, drawing her cardigan closer around her thin shoulders. "The way we were when we were young."

But on it had been built her barren life and his empty marriage, Nathan thought.

"You won't forget me, will you?" she said before he left.

The following day, Ann telephoned the surgery to tell him Mary had not awakened that morning.

Nathan had felt yesterday that he would not see her again. What did he feel now she was gone? Regret that her days on earth had ended. And for himself? As if a door had finally closed on the past.

He rang up a florist and ordered some red roses to be sent to the cottage. The woman on whose grave they would lie was not his Mary, but the girl she once was had been the one true love of Nathan's life.

Chapter Nine

Peter and Shirley went together to David's office to tell him they had decided to end their marriage.

As if it were some kind of business matter they'd come to discuss, David thought, eyeing their unemotional expressions. "Why now? After you've lived together for so many years?" he asked them.

Peter was standing by the window. Shirley had placed herself on the opposite side of the room, in an armchair.

"Divorce isn't a scandal anymore, Dad," she said casually. "Not even among Jews. Ours must be one of the few families in which there's never been one. It's no disgrace."

"It seems that nothing is, nowadays," David said stiffly.

"Don't start on about Laura again," Shirley said sharply. "My daughter is a liberated woman."

"Is that what you call it?"

"It takes courage to decide to have a child when you're not married, Dad. Laura doesn't want a husband. And I don't blame her," Shirley added glancing at Peter. "Mine blames me for the way our daughter has turned out!"

"Me, I blame the pair of you," David declared withering them both with a glance. "You, Shirley, for raising her with your own false values—it's no wonder that an intelligent girl like Laura questioned those values—"

"With a little help from you," Shirley cut in.

David ignored the interruption. "It isn't surprising that she ran for her life the other way. Peter I blame for letting you raise her the way you did."

"We didn't come to your office to talk about Laura," Shirley said coldly. "We came to talk about us."

"So get a divorce. I should care!" David answered. "You always were fashionable."

"We also want out of the business," Shirley said.

"What?"

"It would hardly be suitable for us to continue working together, would it, Dad? But, in any case, Peter is going to live in Israel."

David eyed his son-in-law. "Why don't you, for once in your life, let Peter speak for himself?"

"What is there to say?" Peter asked quietly.

"That you want to marry someone else," Shirley put in coolly. "And I've decided to allow you to."

David was momentarily stupified. He had thought their incompatibility the sole reason for them wanting a divorce, that it had suddenly become more than either of them could take.

"Do you remember Hildegard?" Peter asked him.

For a minute, David could not attach the name to a face. Then a distant memory returned to him, of Peter as a boy, disembarking from the cross-channel ferryboat at Dover with a terrified young girl.

"She was a relative of the Frankls and lived with them in Manchester, until she went on *Aliyah*," Peter said.

"Yes. I remember her, now. So you kept in touch with her,

did you, Peter?" David surveyed him as if he had suddenly become a Jekyll and Hyde.

"No. I ran into her at the home of some mutual friends in Jerusalem, the last time I went there to visit Mark's grave."

As always when Mark's name was mentioned, David was assailed by a pain which had not lost its edge, though ten years had passed since his grandson's untimely death. If Mark had lived, he would now have been beside David in the business. There had been between them a special closeness which David, though he had tried, had not succeeded in establishing with his other grandson. Perhaps because Alan was Ronald's son, he reflected heavily, and Ronald had always been and still was closer to his Uncle Nat than to his father.

"You may as well tell me the rest of your sordid story!" he said, venting his feelings upon Peter.

"I assure you there is nothing sordid to tell," Peter replied.

"If you want the truth, Dad," Shirley put in, "I'm the one who's had an affaire. Not Peter."

David was thunderstruck.

"Don't look so shocked!" his daughter exclaimed. "I'm not the only woman in our crowd who's found consolation elsewhere."

"But there was no necessity to tell your father," Peter rebuked her.

"Better he should hear it from me, than on the grapevine."

"Are you going to marry this man, Shirley?" David inquired when he found his tongue.

"Good heavens, no!"

David surveyed the chic and shapely woman who was his daughter, but it was like looking at a stranger. "I see."

"You don't see at all, Dad," Shirley said sounding suddenly weary. "But believe me, middle-aged women who've always been respectable don't go off the rails for no reason."

Her eyes had brimmed with tears and David was briefly sorry for her. She had never recovered from the loss of her son; her husband no longer loved her; and her daughter, though Shirley had vigorously defended her, was the very opposite of what a young woman from a good family should be.

Shirley pulled herself together and lit a cigarette. "About me wanting out of the business," she said briskly.

David's sympathy for her dissipated in a flash. Peter's going was inevitable. But Shirley? Oh no!

Shirley read his expression. "It's useless arguing, Dad. I've made up my mind. I was ready to get out when we had that takeover bid. But you wouldn't hear of accepting it and I stood by you. Twenty years have gone by since then and running Sanderstyle—in addition to being the firm's designer—is a good deal more difficult now. And don't say I don't help you to run it, because you know damn well I do."

Sanderstyle had become a union shop, though David had hoped it never would, and the employees who had replaced those who had been with him all their working lives had brought with them a totally different attitude.

"I wish I still had Eli and Issie to depend on," he sighed.

Shirley flicked a speck of fluff off her shirt sleeve. "Don't be ridiculous! They should both have been pensioned off long before they were."

"You'd rather have what we have to contend with nowadays? Shop stewards? And everyone watching the clock?"

"Can we return to the subject?" Shirley said impatiently.

"Which subject?"

"You seem to be losing your powers of concentration, Dad."

"Is that so?"

"Which isn't surprising, at your age," Shirley went on. "On a nice day like this, you should be sitting in the garden. Not driving yourself *meshugah* with business problems, behind a desk."

"And what would become of Sanderstyle if I didn't sit behind this desk?"

"Ask yourself what will become of Sanderstyle when you're dead."

"Why must you be so brutal, Shirley?" Peter said.

"Somebody has to make my father face the facts."

"Leave me alone, both of you," David muttered.

After they had gone, he went to gaze through the window at the hive of activity the factory forecourt was at this time of day. Bales of cloth being carried into the loading bay. Sanderstyle delivery vans coming and going. Rails of sample garments being trundled across the tarmac to the showroom. All this, David had achieved with the sweat of his brow and the shrewdness of his brain. He had thought himself the founder of a business dynasty, but a cruel fate had deprived him of his heir.

A telephone call from Ronald cut into his thoughts.

"I have some good news for you, Dad. Alan has got his sociology degree."

"*Mazeltov*," David said dully. "I'm very pleased."

"You don't sound it."

"You'll have to forgive me, Ronald. It's one of those days."

"It always is, so far as I and my family are concerned. Uncle Nat was over the moon when I told him."

"Naturally," David said stiffly. "But he isn't Alan's grandfather."

"What is that supposed to mean?"

"What kind of future will the boy ever have, with that kind of qualification? All he can be is a do-gooder, of which, I read in the papers, this country has too many already. And what will he earn? Buttons?"

"With you, it always comes down to money, doesn't it, Dad?"

David bit back a sharp retort.

"As if it's the only thing that matters," Ronald added.

"I learned a long time ago that it isn't," David said brusquely.

"Then what is it with you?"

"At the moment what it is with me is I feel all I've achieved has been for nothing." David had never confided in Ronald before. Why did he have the urge to unburden himself to him now? Because they were father and son and, despite their differences, the blood bond was there.

But Ronald had enough *tsorus* of his own, David reflected with sadness. The ever-present heartache of a daughter with a baby's mind in a teenager's body.

"Give Alan my congratulations," David said. "I'll send him a nice check."

"There you go again!" Ronald answered. But without acrimony.

"Well, who is my money for, if not my children and grandchildren? At my age, I'm not saving up to buy myself any presents! I wish Alan had shown an interest in Sanderstyle. If he had, it would have ended up his."

"Are you saying you'd leave your business to my son, if he wanted it?" Ronald inquired uncertainly.

"Who else have I got?" David sensed that Ronald was too taken aback to reply. "You've never really understood your father, have you?" he said gruffly. "You've always considered me a money-grubber."

"Not exactly."

"But one way or another, to you I've spent my life just

coining it in. There's been more to it than that, Ronald. Pride in my achievements, in the way I clawed my way up from nothing and nowhere. To me, that's what Sanderstyle stands for. And I'd like it to stay in my family after I've gone."

Ronald's voice was gruff, too, when after a moment of silence he replied. "I'll have a word with Alan about it, Dad. But don't build up your hopes."

"I won't."

Sarah's parlor was more crowded than usual. Henry Moritz's unexpected arrival in Manchester, with a couple of friends accounted for it. And for the added noise at the Sabbath gathering.

Alan was aware of his grandfather surreptitiously surveying him—and with a hopeful expression in his eyes. "Let's clear out of here," he said quietly to Carla, who was sharing a chair with him.

"A good idea," she answered. The sight of her Uncle Henry seated like a king, with the young man and woman he had brought with him squatting respectfully at his feet, was beginning to get on her nerves. To them, Henry was obviously some kind of guru! Carla thought with contempt. But hadn't she too once hero-worshipped him? Not until she grew up had she seen him for the empty idealist he was; realized that every word her mother had said about him was right.

"If the world ever becomes a Utopia, Uncle Henry will have nothing to spout about and no reason to exist," she said to Alan when they had taken their tea and cakes into the dining room. "But my Grandma Hannah, who takes my dad for granted, still thinks the sun shines out of Uncle Henry!"

"You're very mature for your age, Carla," Alan remarked.

"Thank you! May I remind you that I'm seventeen? Only five years younger than you." Carla sat down on the window seat, spread her pleated midiskirt like a fan around her boots and bit into a slice of strudel.

"You have nice teeth," Alan observed. "And orange suits you," he added eyeing her blouse. "It matches your hair."

Carla tossed her fiery curls. "I might have known that if I ever got a compliment from you, you'd have to spoil it."

They shared a laugh. Alan's condescension toward Carla, and her spirited retaliation, when they were children, had long since been superseded by friendship.

"I'm glad you got your degree," Carla said. "Any ideas about what you're going to do now?"

"Yes." Alan glanced thoughtfully through the window to where some black children were racing precariously up and down the street on skateboards. "But my grandfather has put me over a barrel."

"You're not cut out to be a tycoon," Carla declared after he had told her the gist of his father's telephone conversation with David.

"I wish I were, so Grandpa could die happy."

"Meanwhile, he's still very much alive and kicking," Carla said comfortingly. "And laying down the law about the evils of Reform Judaism, like he does every *Shabbos* afternoon," she smiled, as David's voice boomed through the dividing wall.

"That's another thing I'm going to upset him about," Alan said. "I've applied to the Leo Baeck College, to study for the ministry."

Carla's teacup clinked into the saucer. "Are you having me on, Alan?"

Alan met her astonished gaze with his grave one. "I've never been more serious about anything, Carla. But I haven't told my parents yet." His darkly handsome features clouded. "They've had no joy from my poor sister and if the college doesn't accept me, I don't want them to be distressed on my behalf. They don't have to know anything about it. As for my grandfather—if I am accepted, say no more!"

There could be no greater ignominy for David than his only grandson being a Reform rabbi.

"You can't let that influence you," Carla said.

"I'm glad you agree."

"My agreement doesn't mean I understand why you want to be a rabbi."

Alan gazed absently at the family photographs his great-grandmother kept on the sideboard.

"Well?" Carla prodded him. "I'm waiting for you to tell me."

"I began asking myself questions, Carla, during my final year at college. Why I was consumed by restlessness, like all my fellow students. I could never bring myself to smoke pot, or get mindless on beer, as others did. To me, that's just a nonproductive and temporary alleviation of whatever it is that ails us. Like taking an aspirin to dull the pain of an organic disease. I kept pondering about what was the matter with us all. Most of my pals have no time for their parents—"

"That's the generation gap, isn't it?" Carla interrupted. "And I imagine there's always been one."

"Sure. But with our lot it's got out of hand. And bit by bit, it's breaking up family life."

"Now you're beginning to sound like a rabbi," Carla informed him. "Did you go to bed perfectly normal one night and wake up the next morning this way?" she added jokingly.

"If you mean did I suddenly get a call from God, no, I didn't. As I've already said, I asked myself some questions. And the answers I came up with set my mind on a new track. Cannabis, for instance, is an opiate, isn't it? So, in effect, is alcohol."

Rebecca's erstwhile drinking was no secret to Carla and she was a loyal granddaughter. "People have to have something to help them get by," she said defensively.

"That's always been the case," Alan answered. "And, as Karl Marx immortally observed when it still was, religion used to be the opium of the people. For opium, substitute the word comfort. Which, in biblical terms, means a staff to lean upon. That's what God used to be, Carla."

Alan gazed out of the window again, but unseeingly. "And without the pernicious effects of the things people turn to for comfort now," he added. "I think a return to religion—and with it would come a renaissance of family life in the true sense—is the only hope for the future." He turned to look at Carla. "That's why I want to be a rabbi—to help bring it about."

"Then your wanting to be one makes sense. And I'll always remember it was to me you delivered your first sermon," Carla smiled.

"Does what I've said make sense for you personally?" Alan asked her.

"I'm not sure," Carla brushed some cake crumbs off her lap. "This whole conversation has taken me by surprise."

"And would it surprise you if I also told you I love you?"

She glanced at him sharply, then averted her eyes. "I love you, too. We're cousins," she said lightly. But her heart had begun thudding in her breast.

"Second cousins, once removed," Alan corrected her. "And I meant exactly what I said."

"What became of that skinny blond you were dating at college?" Carla fenced.

"She was only a passing fancy. How about the rugby type I

saw you sharing a hamburger with, at The Great American Disaster?"

"Ditto."

"Good." Alan's gaze roved to the *Shabbos* candlesticks on the table, which for him had always epitomized the meaning of a Jewish home. Nowadays, his great-grandmother was unable to polish them herself, her fingers had been stricken by arthritis, but there were plenty of willing hands to ensure that the treasured brass she had brought from Russia still shone.

"Why don't you and I make it a hat trick?" he said to Carla.

"I beg your pardon, Alan?"

"There've been two Sandberg-Moritz marriages within our clan. First Uncle Sammy and Auntie Miriam and then your parents. One in each of the past two generations. It would be a pity to let that historic pattern lapse."

"This must be the oddest proposal any girl ever had," Carla said. "How long have you been in love with me?" she added.

"Always, probably. But I didn't know it until I saw you sharing that hamburger." Alan pulled her to her feet and gazed gravely into her eyes. "Being a minister's wife won't be easy. If I'm given the chance to be a rabbi."

"And if I say yes to your proposal."

"Let me help you to make up your mind. Well?" Alan asked softly after he had kissed her.

Carla smiled up at him. "Fortunately for me, Reform *Rebbetzens* don't wear *sheitels*."

They held each other close and, to Carla, it was as if their union had always been planned.

"Henry's broke again," Frank told Leona when they arrived home from the tea party.

So that's why he came to Manchester, Leona thought with contempt. Her brother-in-law had not honored the family with a visit for some time. "I'd rather not talk about it," she said.

Frank lit the gasfire. The day had been fine and warm, but their north-facing living room grew cool in the evenings. "We must, Leona."

"Why?" Leona had bitterly regretted quarreling with her husband about his brother and had no wish to do so again. She had accepted that Frank had given Henry half of his legacy from their grandfather and had succeeded in putting the matter from her mind.

"I don't feel I can ladle out more money to Henry unless you agree," Frank said. "Though I'd do it out of my share of Zaidie Sigmund's capital."

"Then there's no necessity to consult me."

"I'd invested it for our retirement, Leona."

"Our what!"

"A person has to plan ahead."

Stop being so bloody cautious, Leona wanted to say to him. Live dangerously for once and let the future go hang. But if he did, he wouldn't be Frank, and her married life would not have been so stable and secure.

"I don't know how Henry has the *chutzpah* to ask you for money!" she exclaimed, venting her feelings upon the absent villain. "But as I'm not yet ready for a Darby and Joan bungalow, and doubt that I ever shall be, do what you wish with your damned capital."

Frank smiled his relief. "Henry's dropping in to see me tonight."

"Shall I bake a cake? Or just put the red carpet out?"

In the event, Henry did not call at the house, but telephoned Frank for his answer.

"He treats you like a banker, not a brother," Leona said with disgust.

"But if I ever needed him, he'd be there."

Six months later, Henry's fraternal feeling was put to the test.

Frank fell ill on the eve of Carla and Alan's wedding. Viral pneumonia was diagnosed and the young couple wanted to postpone their marriage until he had recovered. Their elders would not hear of it. In Jewish law, a marriage ceremony takes precedence over all else.

"My father will have to deputize for you at the ceremony, Frank," Leona said.

"I'd like my brother to do it," he replied.

Leona and Carla were sitting beside his bed and Carla opened her mouth to protest. Leona kicked her foot.

"Whatever will make you happy, Daddy," Carla said.

For no other reason would Leona have agreed to her husband's request. "You can have the pleasure of hearing your uncle say it isn't convenient," she told Carla when they returned downstairs to telephone Henry. "If he said it to me, I wouldn't be responsible for my reply."

Henry was in San Francisco, and not available when Cárla called the apartment he was sharing with friends. She left a message for him to call back and eyed Leona thoughtfully, after replacing the telephone receiver. "They said he's at a Gay Liberation meeting, Mum."

"No love. Your uncle isn't homosexual," Leona said reading her thoughts. "All it means is that Gay Rights is his latest crusade. If Henry had the pounds for all the different causes he's espoused in his time, he wouldn't need to keep asking your father for handouts," she added cynically. "And if there were no such things as causes, Henry would have nothing to live for."

"I'd worked that out for myself, Mum."

Carla was admiring her wedding gifts, which were set out on the table. "And I can't help pitying him," she said fingering the volume of Jewish folktales Henry had sent to her because she was marrying a rabbinical student. It wouldn't occur to Henry Moritz to give a heartwarming domestic present. "I used to think Uncle Henry was special," she reminisced with regret.

"Me too," Leona answered wryly.

"I thought you'd always disliked him."

"Yes."

"Then what you just said doesn't make sense."

Leona's feelings for Henry never had. "When I was a girl it was him I wanted," she revealed.

Carla put down the crystal sugar sifter she had just absently picked up. "Tell me more," she demanded.

"There's nothing more to tell. I married your daddy, didn't I?"

Leona had said more than she had intended already. Nor did she want to dwell upon the secret locked inside her; that she had never succeeded in stamping out her youthful desire for Henry, but had gone on wanting him with that part of her that could not be dealt with by applying reason. And if he suddenly asked her to go away with him, it would take all Leona's strength to say no.

Henry did not telephone until the following afternoon, when Leona was helping Carla dress for her wedding.

Frank took the call in his sickroom. "Henry said he would have hopped on a plane immediately, if he'd known last

night," he wheezed to his wife and daughter, when they went
to let him admire Carla, before she went downstairs.

"I'm sure he would, love," Leona smiled. She did not have
the heart to disillusion Frank; it was disappointment enough
that he would not see Carla married.

"My dear uncle wouldn't have come anyway—but trust him
to lie about it!" Carla said as she and Leona trailed their skirts
along the landing. "You're lucky you didn't end up with the
wrong twin, Mum," she added with a laugh.

In the way that makes a woman come alive, Leona thought,
glancing at her daughter's radiant face, I did.

Chapter Ten

In 1979, the clan was bereft of three of its old ladies. Why
did the Almighty take Bessie and Hannah and Helga, and let
me live on? Sarah pondered. Who needs me anymore?

On the contrary, in her ninety-ninth year it was she who
was dependent upon others. A few months ago she had finally
had to admit her inability to cope alone and make her home
with Esther. Who was no chicken herself, Sarah thought as
her daughter entered with a breakfast tray.

Esther set the tray down on the bed and drew back the
curtains. "I think it's going to snow," she said, glancing up at
the heavy skies. "And there's another strike," she added
gloomily.

Sarah, who could remember the days when workers took a
pride in what they produced, and bosses were respected,
stared absently down at her tea and *chalah*. Today, it seemed
that everyone wanted bigger wages for working less hard. But
where did they think the money would come from to pay
them, if they kept on striking and factories were forced to
slow down?

"David did the right thing, selling his business," she
declared. "And who is on strike this time?"

"The grave-diggers," Esther informed her.

Sarah hoped God would spare her until this particular
strike was over. "What else is news?" she sighed.

"Ralph's firm has gone bankrupt."

Sarah put down her teacup. "But I thought he was doing well?"

"So did my daughter, who lives with her head in the clouds. Her husband could fly to the moon and back, while our Marianne's writing a book or a play, and she wouldn't notice he was missing, I just told her on the phone."

"Plenty of women take no interest in their husbands' business affairs," Sarah replied. "And with less reason."

"I'm proud of her, too," Esther retorted, noting the pride in her mother's voice. "But making a name for yourself, like Marianne's done, is no excuse for not being a good wife."

She took a cloth from her apron pocket and began dusting the room, which was cluttered with Sarah's favorite ornaments. "It looks like a jumble sale in here," she said.

"Without my things, I wouldn't have come."

"Why else would I have let you bring them?"

Sarah was propped up against the big feather pillows without which she had insisted she would be unable to sleep. Not for her the newfangled foam-filled ones Esther had on her bed! But the old *perineh* keeping her cozy had suddenly become fashionable, she thought with a smile. Only these days they called them duvets. In some respects, people were discovering that the old ways were the best.

"When I think of how beautiful my guest room was—and look at it now!" Esther complained.

With Sarah had come her big brass bedstead and most of her parlor furniture, with which she had refused to part. And on *Shabbos* afternoons, if she felt her legs would not carry her as far as the living room in Esther's penthouse flat, she held court in what the family had begun calling "Bobbie's bedsitter."

"The carving on this china cabinet of yours is a real dust-trap, Mother!"

Sarah paid no attention to her daughter's querulousness. Life had not treated Esther Klein too kindly—except in materials ways, Sarah thought with compassion for her. And the luxuries Esther now had could not compensate for losing the husband who had labored to give them to her. Or for the shock, from which she had not yet recovered, of her grandson Howard marrying a German girl.

The family, Esther too, tried to hide their reservations about Christina, and her origins were never discussed. But her father had been in the Hitler Youth Movement and it was difficult not to associate her with what that meant. Though he had told his Jewish son-in-law that he had seen the error of his ways.

According to Christina, the whole German race had repented. But in Germany there was, Sarah knew, a strong resurgence of the Nazi evil and it had spread elsewhere. Including England, where swastikas had recently been daubed on synagogue walls.

The unexpected arrival of Miriam and David interrupted Sarah's uneasy rumination. She had not heard the doorbell, or noticed Esther leave the room to let them in, but she could only concentrate on one thing at a time, nowadays.

"You're looking very well," David said to her.

"Isn't she just!" Miriam smiled.

In their fading years, they're a twosome again, Sarah thought surveying them. "To what do I owe this early morning visit?" she inquired.

"Early morning? It's eleven o'clock, Mother!" Esther departed to make coffee for her guests.

"What else do I have to do now, but visit my family?" David sighed. The removal of both his business and Bessie from his life had left an immense void. "Who wants to sit alone all day, in that great big house?" he added.

"If I were fifty years younger, I'd come and share it with you," Miriam chuckled.

"I wish you'd come anyway," he replied.

They shared a glance that made Sarah feel like an intruder, and an ancient Jewish law returned to her mind. An eligible man had first right to his dead brother's widow and she must not marry another without his permission. But what was David thinking of? Bessie had not yet been gone three months.

"We'd be company for each other," David said to Miriam.

Since returning to England, Miriam had lived with Hannah and Helga in the Moritzes' old family home and now lived there alone.

"And Lizzie is there to chaperone us," David added with a smile.

So he hadn't been proposing marriage, Sarah thought with relief—and smiled at the implication that a chaperone was necessary for a woman of seventy-eight and a man of eighty-one.

"If you two lived under the same roof, you'd fight like cat and dog," Sarah told them bluntly. "And in my opinion.

which you haven't asked for, but I'll give it to you anyway, God never intended you to live together, or he'd have arranged things differently when you were young."

"I agree with Ma and God," Miriam smiled.

"And who am I to argue?" David shrugged. He ought to be grateful for Miriam's companionship on any basis, he told himself. He visited her often and poured his disappointments and heartaches into her sympathetic ear. And how odd it was, he thought, glancing at her composed countenance, that she seemed to have none of her own to unload. It was as if all she had been through in her long life had left no mark upon her, as though she had schooled herself carefully to accept her lot.

"Why are you staring at me?" she asked him.

David noted that his mother had fallen asleep, which had lately become her habit. He got up and took the breakfast tray from the bed. "I was wondering how you turned into the person you now are, Miriam."

"How was I previously?"

David cast his mind back to the day he had first met her. She had been five years old and had thrown a tantrum. Her girlhood had remained true to that pattern and it had been there when she was a young woman, too. "Tempestuous," he decided was the description for how he remembered her. "And as if there was something inside you, that wouldn't let you be still."

"I guess I can't argue with that."

"I'd have said it was your nature and that a person's nature can't be changed."

"But it can be held in check, David."

"Evidently," he smiled.

"For years I let mine get the better of me. Then I reached an understanding with myself."

"To me, you seem to be at peace with yourself."

"I guess I am," Miriam replied.

David glanced out of the window at the sleet that had just begun to fall. "I should be so lucky."

"Why not start by realizing how lucky you've been?"

David turned to look at her. "How well I've done, you mean?"

Miriam paused to rivet him with her still brilliant green eyes. "You always did have an upside-down set of values, David. If you hadn't had, your life and mine would have been a different story. Now, here we are, all these years later, an old man and woman—and what might have been no longer matters. But I sometimes wonder if you think what you have now is worth it, David. All that striving and sacrificing—to end up alone in that house you set your heart on, which doesn't mean a thing to anyone but you."

To thine own self be true, David thought. And he had been. But, as things had turned out, for what? Bessie was gone and with her the comfort of sharing which, nagging or no nagging, her presence had brought him. His children and grandchildren had, in effect, gone too—their separate ways, with which his way did not converge. Without the hope of an heir, what Sanderstyle had symbolized had soured for him and selling it had caused him no pain, only an all-pervading numbness, as if his emotions had been anesthetized. Every word Miriam had just said was true.

His sister's arrival with the coffee saved David from the necessity of replying.

"Tell David and Miriam what's happened with Ralph, Esther," Sarah said, opening her eyes.

"I never thought it was wise, the way Ralph and his partner built their business around just a few big clients," David declared after hearing Esther's news. "They're not the first ad agency to go down from losing one or two of their handful of accounts. But the country's in such a mess right now, firms are going bust right, left and center and it's going to get worse. I wonder what poor Ralph will do now?"

"He'll find something. God is good," Sarah said and dropped off to sleep again.

Esther was pouring coffee, beset by a feeling that her world was crumbling around her. It had never been her mother's way to leave things entirely to God. Or David's to leave things to anyone—God included. Once, they would both have been already making plans for Ralph's survival, she thought, returning to the kitchen to fetch the sugar, which she had forgotten to put on the tray.

Miriam followed her. "Your son-in-law's trouble has hit you pretty hard, I guess, Esther."

Esther nodded. "But it isn't just that I'm upset about. Mother used to be like a rock to lean on, didn't she? And David—though it wasn't always appreciated—was once the family fixer. It struck me, just now, that there's nobody among the younger members of the clan to stand in Mother and David's place."

Miriam took the sugar bowl from her sister-in-law's trembling hands. "Since I came home, Esther, all I've heard is criticism of the kids—"

"Some of whom already have kids of their own and ought to know better!" Esther cut in hotly. "Talking of which, if Laura didn't finish Bessie off, I don't know who did."

"What on earth are you talking about? Bessie would still be here, if she hadn't fallen downstairs."

"After which she didn't have the spirit to recover. Who would, if their granddaughter got herself—anonymously pregnant? Nobody needs a broken leg to carry them off, if they're already dying of a broken heart."

"Once, it was I who got worked up about everything and you who calmed me down," Miriam reminded Esther.

"A lot has happened since then and you weren't here to witness it, Miriam. You didn't watch the kids grow up, or share everyone's hopes for them."

"Maybe that makes me a better judge of how they've turned out," Miriam replied, thinking of Martin's kindness to her in New York. Of the affectionate way she had been received by all her young relatives, on her return, though none had met her previously. And of the concern and respect every one of them showed for Sarah.

"Say what you like about them, their family feeling is there and that's what counts," she declared. "And, in my view, there's a streak of David in Laura. As there is of Ma, in Marianne. Family characteristics, like looks, get passed on, Esther. I'd bet my boots that this family will always have its fixer. And someone who has inherited your mother's qualities, too."

Chapter Eleven

Laura had organized her proposed motherhood as carefully and methodically as she had everything in her adult life. The announcement of her pregnancy to her stunned relatives was coupled with the information that she had arranged for the father to be a Jew. This they learned with mixed feelings, as they did her decision to name the baby after her newly departed grandmother.

Shirley alone seemed unaffected by the chapter her daughter had added to the family history and, to Laura's surprise, actively supported her. Laura had only to call and say she had a foreign assignment on her calendar and her mother would immediately drive to London to look after the child.

Sometimes, Shirley collected little Bessie and took her to Manchester. By the time Bessie was twelve months old, she had her own special corner in which to play at the Sabbath tea parties, and was regarded fondly as "our Bessie," instead of being thought of as "our Laura's fatherless child."

In London, Marianne's flat had become, for Bessie, a second home.

"I wish my mum would come and live in London," Laura said to Marianne when she called to pick up her daughter one wintry afternoon. "Then I wouldn't have to trouble you when the baby-minder lets me down on a working day."

"It's no trouble," Marianne smiled. "What I didn't get written this afternoon, I can do tonight. But I bet your mother would move to London if you suggest it." Marianne stroked the little one's plump cheek and cuddled her close. "She's nuts about this kid."

"But Bessie can't be her whole life, can she?" Laura said wisely. "Since the divorce, it's been a whole new scene for Mum and I wouldn't want to tie her down. She's in Russia at present."

"Do they have fashion shows there?" Marianne quipped.

"My mother isn't quite the empty-head you've always thought her," Laura said sharply.

"But you must admit she's always been clothes mad."

"She still is. But what has that got to do with anything? She's gone to Moscow to visit a 'Refusnik' family."

More and more Jews were now establishing and maintaining contact with their oppressed Russian brethren. Every synagogue had an active committee for the purpose. But Marianne could not imagine her cousin devoting herself to the dogged, unglamorous work it entailed, which was a far cry from the fund-raising Zionist social functions that had occupied Shirley in the past.

"You and my mother still think of each other the way you were when you were young," Laura told Marianne. "One only has to hear the comments you make about each other, to know it. But people change, Marianne. And you must be somewhat out of touch with the family in Manchester, these days, or you'd have known all about Mum's 'Refusnik' work with the Thirty-five Group."

"I've been very engrossed in my work," Marianne defended herself. "Which was why I didn't see Ralph's bankruptcy coming—and got hell from my mother for not doing."

Laura wiped her daughter's sticky fingers and removed a splodge of chewed-up rusk from Marianne's sweater. "You deserved it, Marianne. If I were someone's wife, I'd consider it necessary to take an interest in every aspect of him and his life. You've fallen down on your job, mate!"

"As you're not married, it's all fine for you to lecture me," Marianne retorted.

"And the responsibility you've neglected is part of why I'm not," Laura countered. "What are you doing to help Ralph sort himself out?"

"Nothing. He wouldn't let me. My husband is a very independent man." Marianne went to draw the curtains against the wintry twilight and smoothed them absently. "Needless to say, with my earnings we're not on the breadline. The problem is Ralph himself. What he'll do from now on."

"Where is he now?" Laura inquired.

"Can't you guess?"

"Out looking for a job."

"And at his age—and in the present economic climate— he's unlikely to find one," Marianne said. "Which go-ahead ad agency is going to take on a fifty-eight-year-old artist? Those that aren't cutting down on their staff are after young blood."

"I'll have a word with my grandfather about Ralph," Laura said. "Grandpa could certainly use something to give him an interest and Ralph could run it for him."

"Ralph is no businessman, Laura."

"I had in mind an art gallery, Marianne, where people like me could exhibit our work. And Ralph—it would give him an incentive to paint again—could also show his. I have a feeling my grandfather wouldn't mind being a patron of the arts," Laura said with a smile.

"You're making this sound a dead cert!" Marianne exclaimed, though she knew Laura had always had David eating out of her hand.

"You know me, Marianne," Laura said briskly.

Marianne surveyed little Bessie. "I should!" With Laura, things were no sooner said than done.

And arranging Ralph's future proved no exception. She called Marianne that evening to discuss it.

"I just called Grandpa."

"What took you so long?" Marianne joked. But her cousin's concern for Ralph had moved her deeply.

"Grandpa went for the idea immediately. I didn't have to persuade him, Marianne. I suggested it would be best if he left you and me out of it. That he should put it to Ralph as if it's his idea."

"That was very wise of you, Laura."

"Do you think Ralph will go for it?"

"Oh yes," Marianne said unhesitatingly. To her husband, the opportunity Laura had created for him would seem like a raft to a drowning man.

"There's just one little snag," Laura said. "Grandpa wants the gallery to be in Manchester."

"Is that what you call a *little* snag?" Marianne felt as if the ground had suddenly gone from under her feet.

"If you're not willing to move there, we'll have to forget the whole thing," Laura told her.

Was Marianne prepared to return to the midst of the family? Have her everyday life complicated by their nearness; by the interfering and backbiting and the obligatory demands from which she had fled more than thirty years ago? She loved them all dearly, but the shackles they had once represented to her now made themselves felt again. Then she thought of the other aspect of family, the caring and doing for each other which Laura and David were illustrating right now, and was bitterly ashamed. Uncle David was willing to expend his hard-earned money on Ralph's salvation—

"I wouldn't do it if I were you," Laura cut into her thoughts. "But I've always been a selfish bitch."

Me too, Marianne said to herself. What other kind of woman would think twice, when it came to securing her husband's future? Which included his well-being. Because she could do nothing practical to help Ralph, she had buried herself in her work in order to shut out his gloom. But now there was something she could do.

"Tell your grandpa to put the proposition to Ralph," she told Laura.

* * *

Three months later, The David Sanderton Art Gallery opened in Manchester and Marianne had a new home, in Knutsford.

"Mother will never forgive me for not living in Whitefield, around the corner from her," she said to Ralph over breakfast one morning. "She keeps saying I might as well still be in London, as she can't pop in to see me."

"Half a dozen times a day!"

"Exactly. And I'd never get any work done. How are you putting up with Uncle David breathing down your neck?" Marianne smiled.

Ralph poured some more milk on his muesli. "Oddly enough, sweetheart, I never feel that he is. Though when he was younger I was never very comfortable with him."

Marianne recalled her uncle's once-bombastic manner. "Who was?" She drank some coffee absently. "He's a bit pathetic now, isn't he?"

Ralph thought about it for a moment. "I don't think Uncle David will ever be that."

"Perhaps he's just mellowed with age," Marianne said.

"Not that either. He's still capable of tearing a strip off people when he thinks it's necessary," Ralph told her. "And with the rotten workmanship that's around these days, when we were fixing up the gallery it was."

"All the same, Uncle David has changed," Marianne declared. "He isn't the bossy-breeches he was once."

"I think it's simply that it's taken him until now to accept that the other person is entitled to a point of view," Ralph said. "That others are capable of doing things as well as he would do them himself. When we mounted our opening exhibition, I expected him to interfere with everything I did, though he knows nothing about art. But he just sat in a chair and let me get on with it, as if he had decided to trust me."

And knowing that someone of Uncle David's caliber has faith in you, has done you a power of good, Marianne thought, noting her husband's cheerful expression.

Since leaving London, Ralph had metamorphosed into the man he had once been. He would soon have a picture of his own to exhibit, Marianne reflected with satisfaction. On Sundays he painted at home and on weekdays in a studio at the rear of the gallery, to which local artists came to chat and show him their work.

At last, Ralph had come into his own, she thought gratefully and got up from her chair to kiss him.

"What's that for?" he grinned.

"Because I'm happy for you."

Ralph eyed her quizzically. Despite her age, there was still about her the "gamine" quality that had captivated him the day he met her, and the same youthful zest.

"Your life's changed pretty drastically, hasn't it, sweetheart?" he said guiltily.

"A writer can write anywhere."

"But you miss London. And your pals, there. Don't you?"

"So what?"

"You made a bloody great sacrifice for me, that's what. And don't think I don't appreciate it."

Marianne could not deny the obvious. "Not half as big as the one you made, years ago. Setting aside your personal hopes, to be the breadwinner for Martin and me."

Ralph rose to leave. "Isn't that what love is all about?"

For Ralph it always has been, Marianne thought, as she waved good-bye to him from the garden gate. But she had viewed his settling for commerce, instead of pursuing his art, as a weakness.

If lack of ruthlessness could be called weakness, then that had indeed entered into it, she mused, gathering up some beech leaves from the porch, before reentering the house. But Ralph's love for his wife and son, for whom he had undertaken to provide, had played the major part and Marianne had not given him credit for that. She had lived with him for thirty years without really appreciating his finest qualities. Until now.

She was about to begin her day's writing stint when her mother telephoned.

"You haven't forgotten it's your grandma's birthday on Sunday, Marianne?"

"No, Mam." This was Esther's third reminder!

"What are you wearing for her party?"

"Sky-blue-pink, with a yellow border," Marianne joked.

"I'd rather you did, than you should turn up in your old jeans. And it's just our luck that the National Front are having a march that day."

"Nobody will skip the celebration because of that, Mam."

"But some of the younger end will probably join the

protest demonstration—and turn up at the party with black eyes. Also, Shirley's in Russia again."

"Don't worry. She's due back tonight."

"Supposing her plane gets held up? And Kate's plane from Israel, and Margaret's too?"

"Martin and Matthew and our Arnold could all have tire blowouts on the M1, driving to Manchester from London," Marianne said. "But I doubt if they will. Why are you driving yourself daft with worry about hypothetical calamities that could keep everyone away from Bobbie's birthday party, Mam? You didn't used to meet trouble halfway."

"How do you know I didn't. Since 1940-odd you haven't lived up here."

"But I've seen plenty of you."

"A few *Yom Tov* weekends my daughter calls plenty. Maybe it was, for you. And the times I did see you, I didn't spoil it by telling you how I feel about this, that and the other, Marianne."

"You've made up for it since I came back! I have to ring off, Mam. I have a play to finish."

"Me, I've got enough drama in real life. It's very important for everyone to be there on Sunday. Your grandmother will be ninety-nine."

"And on her next birthday, she'll get a telegram from the queen."

"If she's here to receive it."

A chill settled in Marianne's stomach.

"Even Sarah Sandberg can't go on forever, Marianne. That's why Kate and Margaret are coming. It would be tempting Fate to leave it until next year."

After her mother had rung off, Marianne could not settle down to work. Mam would probably telephone again, soon—to tell her she had just broken a cup, or some such mundanity. Like it or not, Marianne was now firmly back in the extended-family setup, which living in London had made it possible for her to avoid. Though she was still separated from her relatives by sufficient miles to make dropping-in impossible, her presence in the north had reestablished her as part and parcel of their everyday lives.

Did she mind? It was not conducive to work, but she had to admit there was a comforting warmth to it that she had forgotten existed. It reminded her of her childhood, and that the threads which held the clan together, spun not just of family loyalty, but of Jewish traditions, had withstood the test of changing times.

Chapter Twelve

"At my age, they start keeping secrets from me!" Sarah exclaimed with mock severity when she entered her daughter's living room on her birthday morn and found awaiting her all those, from near and far, whom she loved.

Esther had arranged for everyone to arrive by eleven o'clock, before which Sarah never emerged from her own room. "What else was there left to give you, except a surprise party?" she laughed, watching her mother embrace Kate's young *sabra* daughters, whom she was meeting for the first time.

Sarah hid her emotion. Thanks to her family, there was nothing she needed.

Which did not stop them from showering her with gifts. The scarves, handkerchiefs and colognes she received would last the years she no longer had before her, she thought wryly. And what would she do with the two new handbags David and Nat had given her? They didn't look too pleased about having duplicated each other's gifts, she noticed.

Once, the unfriendly glances they gave each other would have distressed Sarah. But not anymore. Nor was she upset by the petty bickering going on here and there. Without it, this wouldn't be a real gathering of the clan.

And such an assorted clan, Sarah reflected without pain as young Abraham Patrick Dean came to watch his Israeli cousins pin two little silver filigree butterflies to her dress.

Sarah's mind sometimes returned to Sigmund Moritz's words about the horse and the stable, and did so now. Apart from Esther having, in the heat of the moment, cut off Arnold, in this clan the horse had never been locked out—and it would be, by now, a much depleted clan if that policy had been adopted, Sarah thought, glancing at those who had married "out" and their offspring. It was wiser by far to let the outsiders in. The alternative was for Jewry to lose its own.

Howard's beautiful blond wife presented her with a carved musical box.

"I bought it for you in Frankfurt," Christina smiled lifting the lid. "Listen, everybody. It plays a Jewish tune."

For Sarah, there was something incongruous about hearing *"Hava Nagila"* tinkling from a musical box made by German hands. But no more so than Christina's being one of us, she reflected. Or that the girl would soon be the mother of Howard Klein's child.

Howard and his wife stood holding hands, while Sarah listened to the tune. Better love than hate, Sarah thought, smiling up at them. There was no other way she could come to terms with it.

The present-giving was not yet over. Margaret fastened around Sarah's neck a link of amber beads she had brought from Haiti and Matthew added to her finery some jet ones he had selected from a stall in the Paris Flea Market. Then Laura draped a colorful Peruvian shawl, bought on her last foreign assignment, about Sarah's shoulders and Martin placed in her hand the silk fan he had brought from Japan.

Shirley knelt down and slipped Sarah's feet into a mink foot-muff.

"Only my sister could dream up a present like that!" Ronald exclaimed amid shrieks of laughter.

Lizzie and Bridie's offerings were, as always, made with their own hands.

"I haven't had to buy myself any woolen gloves or mufflers since you two came into the family," Sarah said when she thanked them, and saw their faces light up.

"It's nice ter know yer think of us like that," Lizzie replied for both of them.

"How could I not?" Sarah smiled.

Finally came Moira's gift. "This was given to an ancestor of mine by Queen Victoria and has been passed down to me. But I thought it would look right on you," she said, fixing a tortoiseshell comb, set with seed pearls, in Sarah's snowy hair.

"Now you've really received the accolade, Mother," David chuckled.

"But what have I done to deserve it?"

While the buffet meal was being served, Marianne went to sit beside her grandmother, to whom she had sent a basket of flowers, which Sarah had always preferred to gifts. "You're a proper lady now, Bobbie. From tip to toe!" she said, eyeing the comb and the mink foot-muff.

"Ladies are not made by adornments, Marianne. But that, I don't have to tell you." Sarah's eldest granddaughter, despite her vivid imagination, had always had her feet on the ground in the ways that mattered.

"What I love most about you, is you never change," Marianne said, exchanging a warm smile with her.

But oh, how my ideas have had to, Sarah reflected, glancing at the garnet ring her husband had given her and thinking of all she had lived through since then. Of the bending and stretching she had had to do, to hold the clan together. And in their midst, as she was today, who would say it hadn't been worth it?

Marianne noted her pensive expression. "What are you thinking about?"

"So many things. Including that once, a Jew was not allowed to hold up his head. But now, there's no holding us down."

Matthew was standing nearby, with Arnold, and overheard what Sarah had said. "But the Neo-Nazis are still trying, Bobbie."

"Not to mention what they're trying to do to the Asians and blacks," Frank, whose neighborhood law practice was in a predominantly immigrant district, added exchanging a glance with Leona.

"They won't succeed," Martin declared.

"Any more than the anti-Semites did with us, when we were immigrants," David put in.

"In those days, and even in recent history, the Jews stood alone," Alan reminded everyone. "But the world has changed in that respect. One only has to compare the hue and cry there's been about the Vietnamese boat people with the indifference shown to the boatloads of displaced Jews in the forties, to be aware of it. People don't live in isolation anymore; there isn't an outrage against human rights anywhere that doesn't set up a chain reaction of protest around the free world."

That boy is going to make a good preacher, Sarah thought, then her eyelids drooped and closed. But she could still see the burning conviction in Alan's expression. He was the only male in the room wearing a *yamulke* and, though Reform, more devout by far than the Orthodox relatives surrounding him. Why else would he spend five years studying, in order to devote his life to the Almighty's work.

Sarah felt the fork with which she had been eating her lunch being gently removed from her hand. The discussion was still raging around her—back and forth—but politics, as well as bickering, had always been part of a gathering of the clan.

"The difference between previous generations and ours is that we care," she heard Alan pronounce. "About mankind as a whole, not just ourselves. And because of it, one day this world will be a better place."

Listening—for she was not asleep—the hope Sarah had never abandoned strengthened in her soul. She had never viewed the way some of her children's children and theirs thumbed their noses at convention as an indication that they had gone, irrevocably, to the bad. And it seemed to her now that in spirit there was great goodness in today's young people and that, slowly but surely, they were dismantling the age-old barriers of class, color and creed responsible for so much human suffering; that their rejection of long-established standards of behavior was a symptom of their disgust with the mess their elders had, one way and another, made of the world.

The amber and jet necklaces felt heavy around her neck and she was conscious of the Peruvian shawl about her shoulders and of the Japanese fan, lying on her lap. How far the family now spreads its once-clipped wings, she mused. Looking back, it seemed like a miracle that those who had presented her with these exotic symbols of their freedom were able to take it for granted. And more so that they were descendants of the poor immigrants she and Abraham were when they arrived in England, hoping for no more than the right to live, she was thinking when sleep overtook her.

When Sarah awoke, Esther was lighting the candles on an enormous cake.

"Trust Mother to open her eyes at the right moment!" Nathan declared.

How long had she dozed? Sarah wondered. The others were eating dessert, but, she noted glancing at the small table in front of her, she had not yet finished her fish.

"Shall we bring the mountain to Mahomet?" Martin joked, eyeing the cake. "Or will you come to it?"

Sarah fixed her gaze on the rows and rows of flickering

little flames shimmering above the blue and white icing. Every one of which could tell a story, she thought poignantly. Had she really been on earth all those years?

"My family can blow out the candles. Me, I don't have that much puff left," she said with chagrin.

When the blowing was done, everyone queued to kiss her.

Marianne, who headed the line, smiled at her grandmother's newly acquired finery and gently fingered the dented-with-age gold brooch Sarah had brought from Russia, which she was wearing at her throat as she always had.

"Bobbie isn't Mahomet, Martin," she told her son. "She's an institution."

Sarah reckoned that to those who had flocked to be with her on the day she had entered her hundredth year, she probably was. But what she stood for had been there long before her time and would stand fast when she was gone.

Glossary

Certain words and phrases have no precise English equivalent and the nearest possible definition is given. The original language is indicated by *(H)* Hebrew, *(R)* Russian, *(Y)* Yiddish or *(G)* German.

Aliyah *(H)*   (lit. going up) coll. going from the Diaspora to settle on a kibbutz in Israel.

Ashkenazi *(H)*   Jew of Eastern European descent.

bagel *(Y)*   Hard, ring-shaped bread roll; adapted from the Russian "bublitchki."

Bar Mitzvah *(H)*   Confirmation ceremony of a Jewish thirteen-year-old boy; also the term applied to the boy himself.

Bat Mitzvah *(H)*   Optional confirmation ceremony of a Jewish girl.

bershert *(Y)*   Fated.

bimah *(H)*   Platform in synagogue, from which prayers are led by ministers. Usually of imposing appearance and enclosed by a low railing, or panels of polished wood.

borsht *(R)*   Beetroot soup.

Brith *(H)*   Circumcision ceremony.

Bubbah/Bobbie *(Y)*   Grandmother.

chalah *(H)*   Traditional Jewish loaf.

chalutzim *(H)*   Pioneers in the land of Israel.

Chanukah *(H)*   Described variously as "The Festival of Lights," "The Feast of Dedication" and "The Feast of the Maccabees." Celebrated for eight days (in December). Instituted by Judas Maccabeus and the elders of Israel in 165 B.C. to commemorate the rout of the invader Antiochus Ephinanes, and the purification of the Temple sanctuary.

Chavurah *(H)*   Group of young Zionists in the Habonim Movement.

chevrah *(H)*   A small congregation.

cholent *(Y)*   Butterbean stew.

chupah *(H)*   Marriage canopy; a canopy supported by four poles, beneath which the marriage is solemnized, representing the home the couple will share.

chutzpah *(H)*   Cheek; audacity; brazen nerve.

droshky *(R)*   Low, four-wheeled carriage.

feinkochen *(Y)*   Omelet.

frum *(Y)*   Religious.

ganef *(Y)*   Thief.

gefilte fish *(Y)*   Fishballs, fried or boiled.

goy(im) *(Y)*   Gentile(s).

Habonim *(H)*   (lit. The Builders) A Zionist youth movement.

Haggadah *(H)*   The book containing the Passover Seder Service. *(see* Seder)

Hassid(im) *(H)*   (lit. The Pious Ones) Mystic Jewish sect founded in the mid-eighteenth century by the Ukrainian Rabbi Israel Baal-Shem. Hassidim seek God in everyday life, believe sadness hinders devotion and cheerfulness aids prayer.

holeshkies *(Y)*   Rolled cabbage leaves, stuffed with minced beef and cooked in a sweet-and-sour sauce.

Horah *(H)*   Traditional Zionist song, and group dance performed in a circle.

Kaddish *(H)*   The Mourner's Prayer, recited by immediate male relatives of the deceased.

kapora *(Y)*   A foiklore curse invoked by the superstitious to ward off evil.

kazatsky *(R)*   A dance performed in a crouched position, stretching out and bending first one leg and then the other.

Kiddush *(H)*   The benediction recited over wine.

knedl *(Y)*   Dumpling, usually accompanying chicken soup.

kosher *(H)*   In accordance with the Jewish dietary laws.

kuchen *(Y)*   Yeast cake.

landsleit *(Y)*   Fellow-townsman.
latke *(Y)*   Potato pancake.
liebchen *(G)*   Darling.
lokshen *(Y)*   Egg noodles.

Mabruk (Arabic?) Congratulations; Sephardi-Jewish equivalent of "Mazeltov."
Maoz Tsur *(H)*   (lit. Rock of Ages) Chanukah hymn.
matzo(s) *(H)*   Unleavened bread, eaten at Passover.
Mazeltov *(H)*   Good luck; a congratulatory greeting.
megiyah *(H)*   Conversion to the Jewish faith.
menorah *(H)*   An eight-branched candelabrum used for the Chanukah Festival.
meshugah *(H)*   Crazy.
mezuzah *(H)*   Small, rectangular piece of parchment, inscribed with the passages Deut. vi. 4–9 and xi. 13–21, written in twenty-two lines. The parchment is rolled and inserted in a wooden or metal case and nailed in a slanting position to the right-hand doorposts of orthodox Jewish homes (interior and exterior) as a talisman against evil.
minyan *(H)*   Quorum of no less than ten males required to form a congregation for prayers.
mishpocha *(Y)*   Relatives; family connections.
mitzvah *(H)*   Fulfilling God's commandment; an honor; a good deed.
mohel *(H)*   The religious functionary who performs circumcisions according to Rabbinic rite and regulations.

nachas *(H)*   Pleasure, pride and joy combined.
nosh *(Y)*   Food; to enjoy food. Usually applies to sweetmeats and delicacies.

perineh *(Y)*   Feather-filled duvet in a white cover.
Pesach *(H)*   Passover. The Festival commemorating the Jews' liberation from their bondage in Egypt. Lasts seven days, during which only unleavened bread and specially prepared foods are eaten. (March/April)
pisha-paysha. A card game introduced by Jewish immigrants. Probably Russian.
pogromschik *(Y)*   (derived from pogrom) One of the mob perpetrating a pogrom.

Rebbetzen (Y) Rabbi's wife.

Refusnik (word coined by Western Jews) Jew refused an exit visa from Russia.

Rosh Hashanah (H) (lit. head of the year) The Jewish New Year. (autumn)

Seder (H) The religious service conducted around the dining table in Jewish homes, recounting the liberation from Egyptian bondage. Is celebrated amidst festivity on the first two nights of Passover. (Reform Jews observe only one night.)

Sefer Torah (H) (lit. Book of the Law) The Five Books of Moses, in which are written the Law.

Sephardi (H) Jew of Spanish or Portuguese descent.

Shabbos (Yiddish for the Hebrew word "Shabbat") Sabbath.

Shalom Aleichem (H) Peace be unto you. A traditional Jewish greeting.

shadchan (H) Matchmaker.

sheitel (Y) Wig worn by ultra-orthodox Jewish married women.

shekel (H) Ancient Jewish silver coin. Pl. Colloq.: money, riches.

shikker (Y) Drunkard.

shikkerteh (Y) Female drinker; drunkard.

shiksah (H) Non-Jewish female.

Shivah (H) The ritual Jewish mourning.

shlemiel (Y) Fool; inept person.

shlep (Y) Drag; make a tedious journey.

shluff (Y) Sleep; snooze.

shmaltz (Y) Chicken fat, usually refers to the rendered-down chicken fat.

shmearer (Y) One who spreads the varnish (glue) on seams and hems in a waterproof-garment factory.

shmerel (Y) *Dolt;* stupid person.

shmooze (Y) Cajole, flutter; sweet-talk.

shmuck (Y) Twirp.

shnitzel (G) Thin slice of veal, coated in breadcrumbs and fried.

shnorrer (Y) Beggar.

Shofar (H) Ram's horn blown during synagogue services on "Yom Kippur" and "Rosh Hashanah."

sholom (Y) derived from Shalom (H) peace.

shpeil (Y) Play.

shtetlach (Y) Back-of-beyond townlets.

shtum *(Y)* Dumb; silent.

shul *(Y)* Synagogue.

siddur *(H)* Prayer book.

simchah *(H)* Joyous occasion.

Simchas Torah *(H)* (lit. Rejoicing of the Law) The Festival celebrating the completion of the reading of the Law. (autumn)

streimel *(Y)* Large, fur-trimmed hat.

Succah *(H)* A booth, usually in the yard or garden, in which Jews are required to dwell for seven days during the Tabernacles Festival. Only the ultra-orthodox still observe this law, but all synagogue congregations erect, and adorn with fruit and flowers, a large, communal "Succah," in which to celebrate the Festival with sweetmeats and wine.

Succoth *(H)* The Festival of Tabernacles, commemorating the Jews' departure from Egypt when tents sheltered them in the Wilderness. (autumn)

tallith *(H)* Prayer-shawl.

tefillin *(H)* Phylacteries worn by Jewish men for weekday morning-prayers.

Torah *(H)* Law; doctrine.

trafe *(H)* Nonkosher (*see* kosher).

tsimmes *(Y)* Carrot stew.

tsorus *(H)* Sorrow; heartache; troubles.

yamulke (Polish origin) Skull cap.

yichus *(Y)* Prestige; glory; also aggrandizement.

Yidden *(G)* Jews.

Yom Kippur *(H)* Day of Atonement. The holiest day of the Jewish year. A solemn Fast Day.

Yom Tov *(H)* Festival.

Zaidie (Zaida) *(Y)* Grandfather.

ABOUT MAISIE MOSCO

Raised in Manchester, England, MAISIE MOSCO was moved to write the trilogy which includes *From the Bitter Land, Scattered Seed*, and *Glittering Harvest* because she felt that the British Jewish experience was not being reflected properly in either theater or literature.

"I wanted to remove all the myths and mysteries which surrounded the Jewish way of life and to show Jews as real people," she says. "I was angry with the tired old cliches about Jews. So my husband, listening to my complaints, said, 'Well, you're the writer in the family. Why don't you do something about it.' So I did." In *From the Bitter Land*, she began the story of "the English/Jewish experience told in novel form from the inside, which I don't think has ever been done before." The result was applauded in Great Britain by both fans and critics alike and was received with the same enthusiasm when it was published in the United States in early 1981.

Maisie Mosco was brought up in a traditional Jewish household and draws upon her own past to weave her fictional tales. Her grandparents were Russian and Viennese and they settled in Manchester around the turn of the century. Many of the events told in *From the Bitter Land* were related to her by her grandfather and other family members and friends.

Maisie Mosco began her career as a journalist, once serving as news editor for the *Manchester Jewish Gazette*. While raising her family, she wrote freelance advertising copy and then began working on radio, stage and screen plays. *From the Bitter Land* was her first novel.

Maisie Mosco feels that writing her trilogy has helped her to learn a great deal about her roots and hopes to share that education with her readers. "I think as far as Jewish readers are concerned, for older ones, there will be nostalgia, shared experience. For younger ones, like my children's generation, I think it's going to be a great revelation to know what their forebears went through. And for non-Jewish readers, of course, I think it is probably going to remove a lot of the myths and mysteries that surround the whole of the Jewish way of life, and perhaps explain why we are the kind of people we are."

Maisie Mosco is married to an accountant and has four children. She is presently at work on a new trilogy.

THE LATEST BOOKS IN THE BANTAM BESTSELLING TRADITION